MURDER ON RUSSIAN HILL

A PEYTON BROOKS' MYSTERY

Volume 3

ML Hamilton

Cover Art by Karri Klawiter

www.artbykarri.com

D1739356

MURDER ON RUSSIAN HILL

As always, I dedicate this novel to my editing team.
Thank you, Mom and Dad, for everything you do.
I also dedicate this novel to my work family, who so
generously embraced Peyton and her adventures.
Thank you, my fellow educators!

"The worst crime is faking it."

-- *Kurt Cobain*

CHAPTER 1

I was so nervous, I couldn't sit still. I straightened the pens on the blotter again, then turned the recorder so it lined up with the edge of the desk. I'm not OCD, but when I'm nervous I like my ducks and pens in a row.

Who wouldn't be nervous, meeting a famous rock star? I wiped my hands against my skirt. I didn't want my palms to be sweaty when we shook. The knock on the door was so quiet, I almost didn't hear it over the pounding of my heart.

I hurried across the living room, reaching up to smooth down my hair and straighten my blouse. My heels made a sharp tattoo on the wooden floor of the foyer as I crossed to the door. *Okay, slow down,* I told myself. *You don't want to scare him away with your excitement. Be professional.*

Without bothering to look through the peephole, I pulled the door open. He was turned, looking down the street, so my first view was of his profile and what a profile. He wore dark glasses, but he couldn't hide the high cheekbones or the way his hair cascaded over his shoulders and down his back. He turned and reached up, removing his sunglasses. He wore a dark brown leather jacket and a pair of black jeans. Beneath the jacket, his white shirt gaped at the throat and showed a bronze expanse of chest. A silver necklace with a bear on it lay between the lines of his pecs and an earring peeked out of the fall of his hair.

His eyes were large, like black velvet, heavily ringed with lashes. His lips were full, but entirely masculine and those cheekbones cut sharp angles in his face, dropping down to a smooth-shaved, strong chin. The man was beautiful. There was no denying it.

I forced a smile and thrust out my hand. "I'm so glad to meet you," I said. My voice sounded strained, pitched way too high.

He smiled, showing even white teeth, and took my hand. His grip was firm and I felt the press of a ring against my palm. I looked down and saw a silver band with etchings that looked like feathers encircling it on his middle finger.

"Jolene Grey?" he asked. He had a smoky, sexy voice that rumbled from deep inside his chest. It was a voice I had listened to in the quiet of my room as a teenager, dreaming fantasies that would never be.

"One and the same." I reluctantly released him and stepped back. "Please come in." As he passed me, I looked out at the street. A Jeep Cherokee was parked in front of my house, but he seemed to be alone. That surprised me. Didn't rock stars usually have a huge entourage following them at all times? "No assistant?"

He turned, sliding one of the ears on the sunglasses into the neck of his shirt. "No, no assistant. Just me."

I'm tall for a woman, five ten in heels, and standing in the foyer with him, I looked him directly in the eye. He wore a pair of beaten up brown boots, the heels rundown. I knew it was a fashion statement. A man like him could buy the finest pair of alligator boots if he wanted.

"Please, come in." I motioned into the living room. When I decided to become a writer, I'd turned it into an office. I liked the open space and I especially liked the view of the street the bay windows afforded me. I had to admit it. I was a voyeur. Other people's lives had fascinated me from the time I was a child.

He entered the room, looking around. I had to brush by him to get to my desk. He smelled clean, leather and musky, all male. I drew a deep breath and blinked, trying to gain control of my raging hormones.

"Please, have a seat," I said, motioning to the armchair before my desk. "Can I get you something to drink?"

He removed his jacket, placing it on the back of the chair. The tails of his white shirt were out, hanging around his hips. The sleeves were rolled up to his elbows, displaying well-muscled, bronze forearms, and a leather-band wrapped around each wrist, held by a metal buckle.

"Water, please," he said, sinking into the chair.

I hurried into the kitchen and pulled open the refrigerator, grabbing the decanter and reaching for a glass on the drain-board. "I'm so glad you found time to meet with me." I poured the water and replaced the decanter, carrying the glass back to him. I placed it on a coaster in front of him, resisting the impulse to straighten it.

He was staring at the recorder, but looked up when I sank into my own chair. For the first time, his expression looked tense. "I'm still not sure about this," he said.

I folded my arms on the blotter, wanting to appear unthreatening. "I'll only write what you want me to write. I'm not interested in representing you in a way you don't want. This isn't an unauthorized biography. I only want to write what you tell me, nothing more. If you say you don't want something in the book, it doesn't go."

He nodded, but he was chewing on his lower lip. I got a strong feeling he might bolt if I wasn't careful, so I kept my mouth shut and let him work through whatever he was feeling. "My therapist thinks this is a good idea, but…" His eyes lifted and he gave me the ghost of a smile. Damn, the man exuded a potent sexuality. "…I think she needs a shrink herself."

I laughed and I could see his shoulders lower a little. "Why don't I tell you what I plan and then we'll just talk?"

He looked at the recorder again. "I'm not sure about being taped."

I grabbed the recorder and shoved it in the desk drawer. "It's gone."

He gave me an amused smile. "If you're going to be that accommodating, I'm not sure how I'll refuse."

I picked up a pen and twirled it in my fingers, anything to control the nervous flutter in my belly. I wanted to be professional, not some giddy fan. He was used to giddy fans, I wanted him to see me as a confidant, as someone he could share his secrets with, someone he could trust.

"So I thought we'd write it from first person, as if you were telling the story yourself…"

"No."

I sat back, dropping the pen. The word was so forceful, so unyielding. His expression had gone hard. "I'm sorry?"

He looked down and shook his head a few times as if he was trying to control himself. He reached for the leather band on his left arm and twisted it. "If this is going to work, we have to keep it clinical. It has to be third person. I don't want it to be me telling it. I want it to be you."

I caught a glimpse of the wide, jagged scar beneath the band and eased forward in my chair. "As I said, we'll do this your way. However you want to do it."

He stopped twisting the band and canted a look up at me. "I'm sorry. I don't mean to go all dark on you. I want to do this, but it's…hard."

I rose and circled the desk, going to the credenza in front of the bay window. I pushed the on-button for the MP3 player and the low strains of classical music filtered into the air. Turning back around, I saw him relax against the back of the chair, his shoulders lowering a bit more. *Nothing like music to soothe*, I thought as I went back to my chair.

"We'll only go for as long as you want. We can stop at any time. I don't have a deadline, so I'm willing to take as long as we need for this." Besides, I couldn't complain about the view.

He reached for his water. His hand shook, but I pretended not to notice as he took a sip and replaced it. Running a finger through the condensation on the glass, he nodded. "Okay, let's do this. Where do you want to start?"

I picked up my pen again. "Let's start at the beginning. Tell me your very first memory, the very first one that is clear to you."

His look became introspective as he traced another drop of water. "My first memory is of the reservation and meeting my step-father for the first time," he said. "I was almost five."

*   *   *

The boy flattened himself on the round river rocks, feeling the shifting of them against his belly. He crossed his arms and rested his head on the back of his hand, peering at the praying mantis ambling along, headed for the manzanita and safety. The tiny creature tilted its head and peered out of enormous eyes, its forearms held before it as if it were praying like the white people did in their churches.

He wanted to pick it up and place it on the branch of the tree, but Marshall Youngblood said everyone had their own journey to make and it was wrong to interfere. He wasn't sure he completely understood what that meant, but he guessed it probably had something to do with the praying mantis needing to make the journey over the river rocks on his own.

"Joshua!" His mother's voice floated to him over the roar of the river pounding down through the canyon.

He ignored it for a moment, but then he remembered Marshall also said he needed to mind his mother better. He scrambled to his feet and ran toward her voice, stumbling on the rocks and dodging the manzanita branches reaching out to tug at his clothes. He already had a tear in the knee of his jeans. His mother would be upset when she saw it.

He rounded an oak and saw her, standing on the parking lot along the river, her hands cupped to her mouth. When she saw him, she lowered her hands and braced them on her hips. He slowed to a walk and climbed the short embankment to her, scrubbing a fist under his nose to chase away an annoying fly.

She gave him a stern look and released a sigh. "Tell me you weren't by the river."

He swatted at the fly again. "I wasn't by the river."

She tightened her lips against her teeth. He knew that look. "Are you lying?"

"You said to tell you I wasn't by the river, so I did."

"But you were?"

"I was."

"You tore your jeans." She pointed needlessly at the hole.

He looked down, pretending he didn't already know they were torn. "Sorry."

She hunkered down in front of him, the plain skirt of her dress belling around her. Placing her hands on his shoulders, she stared hard into his face. "You know it scares me when you wander off, don't you?"

He nodded, studying her face the way he'd studied the mantis. She had large, velvet eyes and a nice mouth, when it wasn't drawn into a frown. Her black hair lay thick and lush on her shoulders. She didn't wear makeup like the other women he saw, always looking freshly scrubbed and simple. He liked simple. He didn't like women who wore jewelry or curled hair that was meant to be straight.

She rubbed at his cheek. He took it because he felt bad, but usually he would shake it off. Marshall Youngblood said he had to take care of his mom, not the other way around, because he was the man of the house now.

"You're filthy, but we don't have time to go home and take a bath."

"Why?" Not that he wanted a bath.

"The doctors are here today, giving shots, and you need yours."

He backed away from her. "Shots?"

"Yes, you had them as a baby, but you're starting school this year. You need a booster."

"You said shots, not a booster."

She smiled, reaching out to take his hand. "Right. A booster is a shot."

Marshall Youngblood hadn't given him any advice about this.

"Don't be afraid. It isn't anything to worry about."

"Who's afraid?"

"Good," she said, rising to her feet. "Let's go." She tugged on his hand until he was forced up beside her. They walked to the road and crossed, then angled onto the trail that would take them to the meeting house.

He trotted along behind her, until they came to the end of the trail, where it left the oaks and dropped down into the parking lot of the meeting house. The parking lot was filled with beaten up pick-up trucks and Jeeps. People milled about, climbing out of the cars, or meeting up on the asphalt, dragging their kids along behind them.

Joshua saw a couple of the boys from his street. They usually played soccer in an empty field. Today their black hair was damp and slicked back, their clothing stiff with creases.

He glanced up at his mother. She sighed and shook her head, tsking about his own ruined clothes

April Youngblood stood in the doorway of the meeting house, holding it open for the people to pass through. She smiled at Joshua and his mother as they arrived. She was one of the women who insisted on curling her hair. She had a round face and deep set eyes, and she always gave Joshua chocolate chip cookies after his lessons at the meeting house with her husband.

Marshall Youngblood was Chairman of the tribe and he taught classes to all the young tribal members so that they would know the history of the Patwin people. Most of it meant nothing to his students, but sometimes he gave bits of advice that actually stuck. The promise of homemade cookies to his best students didn't hurt, although Joshua had to admit he didn't remember ever seeing anyone go without one.

"How are you, Mary?" said April brightly.

"Very well, and you."

"Splendid." She focused her attention on Joshua. "I'm happy to see you, young man. You'll be starting school this year."

He mumbled a *yes, ma'am*, but his attention was captured by the activity inside the building. There were many tables set up around the main meeting room with white people standing beside them. A long line snaked around the left side of the building and an elder stood at the front of it, pointing out tables that were empty. The next person in the line would walk over to the table, where the white person would talk to him, then write something on a clipboard. Eventually, they would motion for the person to roll up his sleeve. After that, Joshua wasn't sure what happened, but the person would walk away, rubbing his arm and the next person would take his place.

He tugged on his mother's hand. He didn't want to be in that room. He didn't want to go up to the white people at the tables.

Mary didn't release him; in fact, she placed her free hand in the small of his back and propelled him into the room, calling a goodbye to April over her shoulder. She forced Joshua into the line and curled her fingers around his shoulders. He couldn't get away if he tried.

He watched as a girl about his age was led to a table. The white person hunkered down before her and talked to her. Finally, she reached for a cotton ball as the mother rolled up the girl's sleeve. After rubbing the cotton on her shoulder, the white person reached for a long object with a pointed tip. She placed it against the girl's arm and the girl burst into tears. The tears grew into a wail.

Joshua bit his lip and fought against an overwhelming urge to run. He didn't want to be here. It was hot and stuffy in the meeting room and it smelled funny. A moment later, he was distracted by a boy a few people in front of them. The boy was younger than he was, peering out from between his father's legs. He looked back at Joshua and stuck out his tongue.

Joshua blinked in surprise and glanced up at his mother, but she wasn't paying any attention. Leaning to the left, Joshua studied the father. The man was facing forward, so Joshua couldn't see his face, but his black hair lay on his shoulders and a turquoise wristband encircled his wrist.

Holding onto his father's jeans, the boy leaned around him and stuck his tongue out again. Joshua's eyes widened. This boy was asking for a beating from his father.

The line moved forward. The father simply placed a large hand on the boy's head and propelled him forward as well.

When the boy popped around again, he had a huge smile on his face. The father reached down and grabbed him under the arms. Now he was going to get it.

But rather than smack him like he deserved, he picked him up and held him in his arms. The boy looked back over his father's shoulder and stuck his tongue out again, but Joshua simply looked away. Something about seeing the boy in the man's arms made his stomach ache.

When he looked back up again, they had reached the elder. He smiled at Joshua and patted his head. "How are you, little man?" he said, then pointed behind him to an open table.

Joshua's mother tightened her grip on his shoulder and pushed him toward the table. "Thank you," she said.

A white man in a white coat sat on a little stool by the table. He had yellow hair and almost pink skin. A smattering of freckles created a line over the bridge of his nose and across his cheekbones. He smiled at Joshua's mother, then lowered the smile to Joshua. His teeth were enormous, his features blunt.

Joshua pressed back against his mother's legs.

"I'm Doctor Connor," he said, holding out his hand to his mother.

She took it, her own hand disappearing inside the man's. Joshua pressed back harder. The man had the largest hands he'd ever seen, long fingers, huge palms, with a smattering of freckles across the back.

He released Joshua's mother and held out his hand to Joshua. There was no way Joshua was putting his own small fingers in that grip. That didn't deter the man. He reached for Joshua's hand and shook it a few times.

"Nice to meet you, young man. What's your name?"

Joshua wasn't about to answer. He rubbed his hand on his dirty jeans and looked down.

His mother passed a slip of paper to the man. "He's shy," she offered.

The man looked at the paper and smiled up at her, then reached for a clipboard on the table and clipped the paper to it. "I understand. I'm shy when I meet new people too, Joshua."

Joshua's eyes snapped to his face. "How do you know my name?"

He held up the clipboard. "It says so right here. I'm just here to give you a booster today, but…" He reached into the pocket on his coat and pulled out a card, passing it to his mother. "I'm opening a clinic here two days a week. If you need anything or you'd like a physical, you can make an appointment on the number there."

Physical? What was that? Joshua knew he didn't want anything called a physical. He wasn't sure he wanted a booster.

"Thank you," said his mother. "The people really need a good doctor. We really appreciate you doing this."

No, we don't, Joshua wanted to say, but he didn't. Marshall Youngblood said he had to respect adults, even white ones.

The doctor smiled. "I'm delighted to help." He focused his attention on Joshua. "Now, let's give you that booster." He reached for a glass canister with white cotton balls in it, knocking the metal top with his huge hand. It fell behind the table.

Joshua's mother released her grip on him as she moved to get it. At the same time, the doctor unfolded himself from the stool and rose, up, up, up, towering over the two of them. Joshua's eyes widened. He'd never seen a man this tall before. This white man was a giant, and Joshua knew about giants. His mother read him a book sometimes that had a giant in it and the giant wanted to eat small people.

Joshua's mother grabbed the metal cap and handed it to the doctor. The doctor gave her a goofy smile and took it. "Thank you," he said.

Joshua wanted to warn his mother about the giant, but she was smiling in a funny way too.

The man reached for something on the table and moved it to the edge. Joshua's eyes fixed on it. It was a long cylinder with a sharp needle on the end. He knew he didn't want this giant to give him a booster now. He still wasn't sure what it was, but he knew it wasn't good. When the white doctor reached for his arm, Joshua bolted.

The doctor grabbed for him, but he missed. His mother shouted at him, but he ignored her, running for the sunlight streaming through the meeting house doors. The elder at the front of the line tried to block him, but he darted around his groping hands and pelted for the door, sliding around Alice Youngblood where she manned the entry.

She gave a cry of surprise, but he was too quick for her and leaped down the stairs onto the sidewalk. His instinct told him to bolt across the parking lot and down the trail to the river, but he knew that was the first place his mother would look for him, so he dashed to the left and rounded the side of the meeting house.

He kept running until he came to the end of it, then raced around the corner and into the back parking lot. A few trucks were parked back here, most of them belonging to the tribal elders. He found a battered green truck and scampered over the tailgate into the bed. Scrambling to the cab, he pressed his back to it, brought his knees to his chest, and hugged them.

He could hear his mother calling him. He heard other people calling him as well, and he knew that this was probably going to get him in a lot of trouble, but he wasn't going back in that building and he wasn't getting no booster from the white doctor.

He huddled in the bed of the truck for a long time, pressing his face to his knees, and listening as the voices got farther and farther away. He was feeling pretty proud of himself for tricking them.

He didn't want to worry his mother, but he felt a little angry at the way she'd betrayed him. She hadn't bothered to ask him what he wanted, she'd just forced him into that place and then she'd smiled at the white doctor as if she wasn't afraid of him.

But, it was wrong to worry her. She'd be afraid he'd fallen into the river and drowned. She was always afraid he'd fall into the river and drown.

Just as he'd decided to go find her, he heard a crunch on the gravel. He flattened himself against the cab and closed his eyes. If it was the white giant, he didn't know how he'd escape. Best to keep quiet now and hope he passed by.

Joshua jumped when a man cleared his throat beside the truck. His eyes flashed open and he breathed a sigh of relief to see Marshall Youngblood standing there, his hand on the bed next to Joshua's face.

"You think you're pretty clever, don't you, cub?"

Marshall Youngblood called all his young charges cub.

"Did you see the giant?"

Marshall fought a smile. "Yes, but he's not a giant."

"He was fifty feet tall."

Marshall laughed. "Not by half."

"Why we need a white doctor here?"

"Because we need the white medicine or we'll get white diseases. He's a good man, who's here to help the people. You shouldn't be ungrateful."

16

Joshua gave him a scathing look. "Did you get a booster?"

"I've had many and I didn't act like a scared baby about it either."

"Who's scared?"

"You apparently. You bolted like a rabbit."

Joshua came up on his knees, gripping the edge of the truck next to Marshall. "Did you *see* the white giant? Giants eat people…and rabbits," he added for good measure.

Marshall gave him a stern look, but his eyes glimmered with amusement. "He's not a giant." He ruffled Joshua's dark hair. "We talked about this, cub. We talked about how you're the man of the house now and you can't go around scaring your mother. She thinks you…"

"…drowned in the river," Joshua finished.

"Right. That's not taking care of her."

"I don't want to go back in there with the white doctor. Why do they have to come here?" He knew Marshall was going to repeat what he'd said before, but he just couldn't understand it. "Why do we need white doctors? Why can't the people take care of themselves?"

Marshall gave him a sad smile. "You have a point. So, I'll tell you what. Why don't you get the booster, so you can go to school? Then someday you can become a doctor and take care of the people." He reached for Joshua and hooked him under the arms, swinging him from the bed of the truck. "What do you say?"

"I guess, but when I'm a doctor, I won't make kids get boosters."

Marshall directed him back toward the meeting house. "How will you keep them from getting sick then?"

Joshua shot a look up at him. "I'll give them medicine on chocolate chip cookies instead."

Marshall threw back his head and laughed, making Joshua smile.

* * *

17

Jake Ryder sat on a table at the back of the conference room. Before him were four chairs arranged in a semi-circle. A curvaceous, young Hispanic woman, Maria Sanchez, stood before the chairs, holding up a piece of paper in each hand.

In the first chair was Big Bill Simons, a bear of a man whose hands looked like paddles. Next to him was his partner, Nathan Cho. Cho always looked dwarfed by his massive partner, but Jake avoided him. There was something quick and deadly about the man.

To Nathan's left lounged Marco D'Angelo, a GQ model who chose to strap on a gun rather than a thong. All six foot four of him oozed a raw sexuality that made women flock to him like a Greek god, hence Jake's nickname, Adonis.

To his left sat Jake's housemate, Peyton Brooks, with her mass of black spirals and compact frame, not pretty in the classical sense, but her mixed blood made her exotic. Combined with three inch heels to compensate for her lack of height and a leather jacket, she was an enigma who had stormed into his life a year ago and redefined it in ways Jake still didn't understand.

"Okay, I got a dead woman in an upscale condo on Russian Hill or a dead bum in the BART station on Market," said Maria.

The four cops exchanged looks, then three of them opened their mouths to say something, but Peyton held up her hands to stop them. "Hold on a minute. Cause of death?"

Maria looked over each piece of paper. "Russian Hill got her head smashed in, no murder weapon found. BART station got shot in the back of the head, execution style."

Cho leaned forward, biting his lower lip. "IDs?"

Maria looked up from the paper. "Nope. Woman's head burst like a pumpkin, and the other's a bum."

Simons shifted his bulk in his chair and eyed his competition. Then he pointed a finger at Maria. "I got two tickets to the Giants' game on Thursday, third base side. It's souvenir bat day."

Maria considered his offer. Cho and Simons leaned forward. "Location of the seats?"

Simons deflated. "Upper deck."

"Nope." Maria shook her head.

Jake rolled his eyes toward the ceiling.

Peyton elbowed Marco in the ribs. He braced his arms on his thighs. "I've got a lobster feed at Sacred Heart on Friday."

Maria gave him a sultry look, pursing her lips in a kiss. "And my date?"

Marco hung his head. "I only have one ticket."

"Ooo," said the other four.

"Swing and a miss," said Simons.

Marco glared at him.

Maria turned to Cho, who continued to bite on his lower lip.

"I've got dinner at the Marriot and two tickets to *Rigoletto*." He gave her a wag of his dark brows.

The others held their breaths.

Maria considered. "*Rigoletto's* opera?"

"Yes," said Cho, leaning forward urgently.

Maria shook her head. Cho and Simons slumped in defeat.

She turned to Peyton with a world-weary sigh. "Your turn."

Peyton leaned back in her chair and folded her hands on her belly. Jake could see the smirk curving the lines of her mouth. "I have…"

They all listened with interest.

Jake found himself leaning forward. The moment he realized it, he corrected his posture, but shit, he was getting caught up in this mess.

"I have…" repeated Peyton, "…a photo of Marco and his brother Vinnie at last year's 4th of July barbecue in Golden Gate Park…"

Maria's eyes widened and Marco swung around to glare at Peyton.

"…with their shirts off."

Maria held out one of the papers immediately. "Sold to the woman with the terminal case of bed-head."

"Ah," said Cho and Simons together, slapping their hands against their thighs.

Peyton leaned over and kissed Marco on the cheek, then jumped to her feet and grabbed the paper, waving it triumphantly over her head. Marco just shook his head, fighting a smile, as Cho and Simons cursed. Maria patted Marco's shoulder as she sashayed out the door.

Jake crossed his arms over his chest in disgust as they headed in his direction.

"Jake, you're with us," said Peyton.

"Hold on a minute," said Simons, crumpling up his paper. "We get him first. The BART station's on the way to Russian Hill."

Peyton gave a dramatic sigh. "Fine. I'll text you the address of the condo. Hurry up with the bum and get over there pronto, Ryder."

Jake just looked at the four of them without moving. "What you just did is not only unprofessional, but it's also immoral."

They gave him various expressions of disgust.

Cho poked a finger at Jake. "Look here, Preacher, in a few minutes, we get to look at dead meat. Let us get our kicks however we get them."

"Preacher?" Peyton nudged Cho with her shoulder. They were nearly the same height. "I like that. Mind if I use it."

"It's yours. You got to live with him."

"I know, right? You should see him at home. It's always you didn't say grace over the meal or you shouldn't be sleeping with men outside of the marital bed." They started walking together toward the door.

"Uptight shit," commiserated Cho, "Sleeping outside the marital bed is one of my favorite things."

Jake realized his mouth hung opened. Simons punched him in the shoulder, chuckling. Jake looked back and found Marco fighting another smile. "I never say anything about who she sleeps with. Besides that, she hasn't had anyone over in months."

Simons and Marco exchanged a look. "So you are keeping a tally," Marco said, turning toward the door.

"I'm not keeping a tally," answered Jake, climbing off the table, and hurrying after them. "Freakin'-ass cops," he muttered under his breath.

*   *   *

Jake slipped under the yellow crime scene tape and surveyed the area. He liked to have a visual before he walked into anything. The body lay on the ground, face down. The BART tunnel platform stretched away behind them, smelling of urine and cold, damp concrete. One of the vic's hands rested in the yellow warning track before the trains, but the trains had been moved out of this tunnel for the police. Jake glanced over the edge and studied the track for as far as his eyes could see, which wasn't far. Light wasn't a priority on a BART platform.

He settled the camera bag and his evidence case on the ground, then pulled out the camera. For the past six months, he'd taken night classes at City College in Administration of Justice. The precinct offered their own rudimentary crime scene classes, but he figured if he was really going to do this, he needed an AA degree. Captain Defino was happy with his decision and even offered to pay for it, a perk he readily accepted because he now had a relic of a car to maintain.

Peyton and Marco kept riding him about getting his own car. Jake had never owned a car the entire time he'd lived in the City, but it was one thing to take transit when he worked at the bank. It was another to take it when he had to lug all of the crime scene equipment.

Still, he didn't have much money, so Marco suggested he go to a police auction where they auctioned off the impounded cars that had been used in a crime. He told Jake he could get a good deal there. Well, Jake supposed most people could, but he could only afford a 1982 Dodge Omni, painted bright purple with a yellow daisy on the side doors. He wasn't sure what crime had been committed inside of her, but the paint job sure as hell qualified as a crime. To top it off, she was a stick shift and in San Francisco, a standard transmission was its own version of hell. He was always stalling her out on the hills, terrified he was going to roll back into someone.

Which brought him back to the color. He worked with cops. They just couldn't leave him alone about the freakin' color. Peyton called it the Purple People Eater, which was the kindest thing anyone said about it. Marco called it the Lazy-ass Daisy, but the worst had been when Abe Jefferson, the Medical Examiner, proudly declared he could now enter it into the Gay Pride Parade. Marco hadn't laughed outright, but he got that shit-eater grin on his face that Jake absolutely hated. Smug bastard.

"Ryder!"

Jake blinked at Bill Simons and realized he was daydreaming, stalling before he had to face the body. He began taking wide pictures of the entire scene, working his way toward the plastic markers the first cops on the scene had set out. Then he worked his way over to the body. Lying on his belly, the bum's head was turned to the right, his eyes staring straight ahead down the train tunnel, which meant the shot had come from behind him. His hands were on either side of his head, as if he'd been forced to his hands and knees before being shot. A large hole opened the back of his skull, the hair matted and compressed with blood. Someone had put the muzzle right up against his head. Leaning over, Jake could see the exit wound in his forehead.

The bum wore a bulky outer coat and multiple layers beneath it as most homeless people did. It was easier to keep all of your possession on you at once than try to lug them around. It also helped stave off the chill of foggy coastal nights on the street. His sneakers both had holes in the front of the sole, just behind the toes, and the back was cut down the seam, another trick people used when they couldn't afford the proper sized shoe. When he'd fallen forward on the concrete, the back of his coat had ridden up, exposing his torn and filthy jeans. The left pocket was gone, but in the right, Jake saw a white piece of cardstock sticking out. It was so white compared to the rest of the man that it couldn't be missed.

"Simons?" called Jake.

Simons turned.

"Grab my case, please."

Simons made a grunt of annoyance and picked up the case, hauling it over to Jake.

Cho followed him. "What you got?"

"Something's in his pocket." He settled the camera down and opened the case, reaching for his tweezers. He used them to pull the card from the man's pocket, then turned it over. Printed in bold red font were the words *Clean-up Crew*.

"Clean-up Crew?" said Cho. "What the hell does that mean?"

Jake shook his head, reaching for an evidence bag. "Never heard of it." He placed the card carefully inside.

"I'll go look it up on the computer," offered Simons and walked away toward the stairs.

"Anything else?" asked Cho, nodding at the body.

"You want me to search him?"

Cho gave him a smug look. "Have fun, Preacher." He moved back toward the uniforms, asking them more questions.

Jake grabbed latex gloves and began tugging them on. *Freakin' ass cops think they're so superior.* As he reached for the body, he wondered for the hundredth time what he was doing. A year ago, he'd been taking loan applications on million dollar homes, now he was searching a dead bum's pockets. And yet, when he thought of going back to the bank, he shuddered.

* * *

The condo was small, but luxurious. It had two bedrooms, two bathrooms, a walled off kitchen, and a dining room/living room combination. Brazilian cherry wood floors gleamed in the late morning sun shining through the floor to ceiling windows along the back wall.

The decorations were in bold colors, white leather sofa, green pillows, and pink throws. A thick burnt-orange shag took up the center of the floor. A zebra-wood coffee table and two end tables flanked the low-slung sofa and two glacial white egg-shaped swivel chairs rounded out the conversation area. A slate fireplace dominated the wall leading to the master bedroom. Next to it was a zebra-wood bar with a wine rack on top.

The vic lay at the base of the bar, on her back, staring up at the ceiling, or what was left of her did. The left side of her face had been smashed in, the skin torn and bloody, showing skull and if Peyton looked closely enough, brain between the skull fragments.

She closed her eyes and tried to fight back the bile. Officer Frank Smith put a hand on her shoulder to steady her. She looked up into his friendly face, the huge brown mustache and the mop of dark, shaggy hair, as she patted his hand. "Thanks."

He nodded.

"The perp was probably right handed," she said, nodding at the woman's head. Strands of blond hair lay soaking up the blood pooling beneath her.

"Looks that way."

"Any idea who she is?"

"We've got a call into the super, but he hasn't returned it. Both neighbors are out and we can't find any papers that have a name on them. Whoever did this was definitely beyond rage."

Peyton nodded and wandered toward Marco, where he was gathering information from the other uniform.

"Who placed the call?" he asked.

"Dispatch is looking into it. All we know is that he was a male and pretty shaken up. He just went silent in the middle of the call and hung up. They tried to call him back, but he wouldn't answer. We'll get a number for you as quick as we can."

"Who found her body?"

The uniform glanced at the clipboard he held. "The security guard in the lobby."

"What time did he come up here?" asked Peyton.

"He came in at 10:00."

"He couldn't identify her?"

"Apparently they've got a tenant list in a locked safe down there, but he was too shaken up to remember the code. He called his supervisor, but couldn't get ahold of him. It's a bitch tracking down anyone on a Sunday."

"Why is the tenant list locked up?"

The uniform shrugged. "How the hell would I know? To protect the tenants' privacy or something."

"We need to get the film from the security cameras."

"Aren't any."

Peyton exchanged a look with Marco. "What?"

"No security cameras in the lobby or the hallways. To protect the tenants'…"

"…privacy," finished Peyton. "What made the security guard come up here if there aren't cameras?"

"The fire alarm went off. He could pinpoint the floor and came up. That's when he found her door open."

"Where is he now?"

"One of our guys took him down to try the safe."

"We'll need to question him before we go," said Marco.

"On it."

"Thanks," Marco answered, turning to Peyton.

She nodded at the bedroom to their right. They entered the master bedroom and found a huge king sized bed, unmade, and a sheer robe discarded on the floor beside it. The curtains were drawn, blocking out the light.

"We need to take those sheets and see if we can get any DNA off them."

Marco nodded to a uniform to make a note of it. The young man wrote it on his clipboard. Peyton strolled around the room, frowning. Something wasn't right. She ran her fingers over a dressing stand and looked up in the mirror, viewing the room from a different angle.

"What?" asked Marco.

She pulled out a dresser drawer and found it empty, then she reached for the one below it. Despite a few pairs of feminine panties, it was virtually empty as well. "If the vic lives here, where's all her stuff? Jewelry boxes, perfume, tchotchkes – you know, feminine stuff?"

Marco looked around as well. Backing to the closet, he pulled it open and looked inside. A window at the other end allowed light to fall in the small room, but it was impossible to step inside. Boxes were piled up from the floor nearly to the ceiling.

"Looks like she planned to get out of Dodge," said Marco.

Peyton leaned into the closet and pushed up one of the boxes to look at it. "They aren't labeled. How strange. Most women would label the contents."

"Not if she was packing in a hurry."

"Hm. Have you seen a computer or anything?"

"No, have you?"

"Not a one." She moved toward the door. "Let's look at the other room."

They crossed the main room and pushed open the other bedroom door, finding themselves in a little girl's room. The bed was piled with stuffed animals and the dresser was littered with flower shaped jewelry boxes and trinkets. A whole row of fairies lined the shelves of a bookcase in the corner.

"What the hell?" said Marco, opening the closet. Brightly colored dresses, shirts, and pants hung from the railing, and lined up neatly along the floor were rows of shoes. "Do you suppose she didn't get to this room yet?"

Peyton didn't answer, her attention captured by something on the desk beneath the window. She picked up a flowered frame and stared at the picture inside. A pretty little girl with dark hair and huge black eyes stared back at her, and next to her was a man Peyton could only describe as beautiful. He was obviously Native American with high cheekbones and chiseled features. His long black hair lay in a blanket on his shoulders and his charcoal eyes glowed with sensuality. He was smiling, his teeth even and white, but there was something wistful about the smile that arrested Peyton.

"Holy shit," she breathed out.

"What?" said Marco behind her.

She turned and held the picture out to him. "Do you know who this is?"

He studied the man for a moment. "He looks familiar."

Peyton gave him a bewildered look. "Familiar? Are you shitting me? Every woman my age had his posters plastered all over her bedroom when she was a teenager. I had one that I'd kiss every day before I left for school. You don't know who this is?"

Marco held up a hand, giving her his annoyed look.

Peyton shook her head in disgust. "This, Marco Baby, this is the man that makes women weak in the knees. This is the man that makes them swoon. This, Marco Baby, is the sexiest lead singer ever to grace the microphone. This is…"

"Joshua Ravensong," he finished.

Peyton touched her nose with her index finger. "And I'll bet you dollars to donuts that the woman in the other room is his ex-wife."

* * *

Jake gave a low whistle as he came through the condo door. He took in the expensive furnishings and the artful décor. He'd always been partial to modern style, not that he could afford it, but he liked the minimalist approach. Then his eyes landed on the victim, lying at the base of a bar. Half of her head was smashed in and it was the half that faced him.

He settled his case on the floor and studied her for a moment. She had been pretty, blond hair, striking features, trim and fit. She wasn't naturally pretty like his wife, Zoë, had been; she was more artificial and affected. Her shirt was low-cut, showing an impressive amount of cleavage, and her jeans looked like they'd been painted on. Heavy makeup was smeared on the side of her face that remained, and she wore five inch heels.

His eyes tracked over the rest of the room, picking up little things that he'd been trained to spot, like the pressed down spot in the burnt orange rug where the sofa had been moved, the splatter of blood on the wall beside the bar, the two glasses on the bar with a few fingers of bourbon in the bottom.

Peyton and Adonis came out of a room on the left side of the condo. Jake could just see the pink walls and the frilly bed-skirt behind them. He bent over and took out his camera as Peyton stopped in front of him.

28

"You're finally here," she scolded. She didn't like sharing him with the other detectives, but he wasn't her private photographer; although truth be told, he'd rather work for her than anyone else in the precinct.

"Yes, Mighty Mouse, it was traumatic seeing a guy with the back of his head blow in, and thank you for being so concerned about my state of mind, especially walking into this little shop of horrors." He motioned at the dead body.

She smiled and Jake realized he enjoyed making her smile. Sure, he also felt guilty for enjoying anything now that Zoë was gone, but Peyton and this job made it hard for him to wallow in his loss. Once he wanted to hate her. She'd ruined his life, but six month ago, she'd also redefined it for him. Most days he wasn't sure the change was for the best, but he couldn't deny that life now was certainly not boring.

Adonis moved past them and went to talk with Smith. Smith was a hard-assed uniformed officer, but he was a solid guy. Jake liked him better than Holmes, who could never allow an opportunity to pass where he didn't give Jake grief about something, especially the Lazy-ass Daisy.

"Do we have an ID on her?" Jake asked.

"Nothing official. I can't find a purse or a computer of any kind, but I found a picture of Joshua Ravensong in the little girl's room."

"Joshua Ravensong? The rock star?"

"That's the one. I'm guessing this is his ex-wife and the little girl in the photo with him is his daughter."

"Where's the little girl?"

"Marco's talking with Smith about putting out an Amber Alert on her right now."

Jake studied the crime scene again. "She wasn't alone." He pointed the camera at the glasses on the bar.

"Yeah, I got that impression myself, seeing as I didn't think she bashed in her own brains."

Jake gave her an arch look. "Funny. Actually, what I meant was, don't you think it odd they were drinking this early in the day?"

"Maybe it was from last night?"

"Then why was she killed right there?"

"Good question."

"Any sign of forced entry?" He looked around again. "This place seems bare. Zoë always had bobbles and bits on every surface, but there's nothing here."

Peyton gave an approving nod. "I noticed that too. No, no forced entry. She must have let whoever killed her in, but when I looked in her closet, I found moving boxes, so I assume that's where her bobbles and bits went."

"It *is* odd that you didn't find a purse or a laptop. What about a cell phone?"

"Nothing."

"Hm, very odd. It really worries me that we don't know where the little girl is."

"Me too."

Smith and Adonis came out of the master bedroom.

"The uniforms have got an unidentified male sitting in a black Jeep Cherokee in the parking structure," said Smith, stopping in front of them. "They want you or D'Angelo to talk him down."

Peyton nodded, then turned to Jake. "Make sure you photograph every room."

"On it," he said and watched her head toward the door trailed by Adonis and Smith.

CHAPTER 2

"Joshua, this is my son, James, and my daughter, Jennifer."

Joshua gave the two children a once-over. The boy was big, raw-boned like his father with the same blunt features. He had blond hair that was cropped close to his scalp and the same overlay of freckles. The girl was small, younger than Joshua, blond hair pulled back in a ponytail. She swung back and forth on her father's hand, studying Joshua in return.

Dr. Connor smiled down at him, forcing Joshua to back into his mother's legs. He couldn't get over how big he was. The doctor turned his attention to Joshua's mother. "I'm so glad you came, Mary."

She smiled, smoothing down Joshua's hair with her palm. "I really appreciate you offering me this job. It will mean so much to both of us."

Dr. Connor shrugged. "I should be thanking you. There's a lot more work here than I originally thought and I really need someone to keep all the records and appointments straight."

Joshua ignored the kids and looked around the white doctor's new office. It smelled of paint and cleaning fluid. A wide white counter took up the north wall and a number of chairs in pastel colors lay scattered around the entrance hall.

"Why don't we let the kids play a bit out here and I'll show you the file room?" said the doctor, motioning to a door behind him.

Mary turned Joshua to look in his face. "Stay here with James and Jennifer, all right? I'll be back in a moment."

"I want to go with you." He didn't want her leaving him with the strange white kids.

"You're a big boy now. I need to learn about my new job. We talked about this, remember?"

"I remember."

She leaned forward and kissed his forehead. "Be good, all right?"

He rolled his eyes, but didn't answer.

"Be good," she said again, following the doctor across the room and to the door.

Joshua watched her go. They left the door open, but when they disappeared around the corner, he couldn't see her any more. It made him nervous, but he was determined he wouldn't show these white kids how anxious he was.

The boy leaned back against the counter and studied him. The little girl put her arms behind her and swayed back and forth, the skirt of her dress swishing against her legs.

"How old are you?" said the boy, sticking out his chin.

Joshua tore his eyes from the empty door and studied him in return. "Five."

"I'm eight. She's four." He motioned at the girl with his chin.

"I'm four," she echoed.

Joshua didn't respond.

The boy pushed away from the counter and walked toward him. He towered over Joshua, forcing Joshua to look up, but Joshua refused to back down. "You're small. You don't look five."

Joshua peered around him at the door, but it was still empty.

"You afraid?"

"Who's afraid?" Joshua shot back.

Behind the boy's back, the girl had disappeared around the counter. Joshua could see a chair rolling across the floor, then the girl climbed into the seat and from there, she scrambled onto the counter. Joshua's eyes widened, making the boy turn to see where he was looking.

"Get down from there!" the boy scolded the girl.

"I wanna color," she said.

Shaking his head, the boy went after her and she crab-walked away from him to the printer in the corner and pulled papers from it.

"Get down."

He grabbed her arm and she kicked at him, but he was stronger and pulled her off the counter, setting her on her feet. Then he reached up and grabbed a few pens from a cup on the counter and handed them to her. "Color on the floor."

She skipped around the end of the counter, her blond ponytail bouncing against her back and settled in the middle of the floor with her pens and paper. Joshua watched her draw enormous loopy lines down the center of the paper, her tongue pressed between her teeth in concentration.

When he glanced over at the boy, he'd disappeared beneath the counter. He came out a moment later, carrying a small, white ball with red stitching circling around the outside of it.

"You play baseball?" he asked Joshua, showing him the ball.

Joshua knew of baseball. Some of the older men got together and played softball, swinging sticks at a fat yellow ball. As for baseball, Marshall Youngblood had turned it on the television one night when April Youngblood had watched him while his mother went out. Marshall tried to explain it to Joshua, but Joshua grew bored with all of the rules. He still wasn't sure why the runner couldn't run to whatever base he wanted. It would make it harder to get him out if he could. Joshua just couldn't see any sense in both sides knowing exactly where the runner was going. It took some of the sport out of the game.

"I play soccer." He tried to puff up his chest the way the white boy did, but he didn't have much of a chest to puff.

"What's the name of your team?"

Joshua's face fell. Team? He didn't play on a team. They played in the empty lot by his house. "The Patwin," he

33

lied because he wasn't going to let this boy gain anything over him if he could help it.

"Never heard of it." The boy tossed the ball into the air.

Joshua's gaze involuntarily went back to the door where his mother had disappeared.

"You know what they're doing back there?" asked the boy.

Joshua shook his head.

"They're smooching."

"Smooching?" Joshua wasn't sure what that was, but it didn't sound good.

The little girl giggled and made a kissing noise with her mouth, then she went back to her drawing.

The white boy smiled. It wasn't a happy smile. "Yep, smooching. You know what that is?"

Joshua edged toward the door, anxious now for his mother. Based on the reaction of the girl, he could guess what it was and it worried him. "'Course I know."

"Let's play baseball." The boy tossed the ball into the air again. "Come on. They'll get mad if you spy on them."

"Who's spying?" Joshua shot back. His worry for his mother made his voice more antagonistic than he intended.

"Come on. You go over there." He pointed to the front door of the office. "I'll go back here." He moved past Joshua and blocked the door to the file room.

Joshua shifted weight from one foot to the other, wondering if he should push his way past the larger boy. "I don't feel like playing."

"You chicken?"

"Who's chicken?"

"Then go over there," said the boy, pointing to the front door.

Joshua realized the boy wasn't going to give up. He moved toward the door, positioning himself with an armchair to his left and a glass end table with a collection of magazines spread across its surface. An orange and yellow lamp sat on the outer edge of the table, closest to the window. This wasn't how he remembered the men playing softball, but who was he to argue with the older boy?

"Okay, I'm gonna throw the ball at you and you have to catch it, no matter how much it hurts. Got that?"

Joshua nodded, but he really wasn't sure he wanted any part of a scheme where the only rule was to play no matter *how much it hurt*, but maybe if he played the boy's game, he would let him go look for his mother.

The boy cocked back his arm and twisted his face into a grimace, then he launched the ball at Joshua, except it didn't go toward Joshua. It slammed into the lamp and ricochet into the window, then fell harmlessly to the ground. The lamp, however, teetered on the edge of the table. Joshua held out his arms to catch it, but he was too late and it toppled, breaking into sharp porcelain shards.

Joshua stared at it, uncertain what he should do. He looked at the boy and the girl, but they were staring at the broken lamp with expressions of shock on their faces. The boy looked like he might bolt and the girl sat with the pen poised above her paper. Behind them, Joshua heard the sound of running feet, then his mother and the white doctor skidded into the room.

"What happened?" said his mother, stopping in the middle of the room and taking in the scene.

"He broke the lamp," said the boy.

Joshua's mouth fell open and he stared at his betrayer in disbelief. He wanted to shout that he hadn't done any such thing, but the huge doctor was stepping around his mother and coming for him.

Joshua reacted on instinct. He knew he couldn't make it to the door, so he backed into the corner beside the door and curled in on himself, protecting his stomach and his face. Peeking out he could see the doctor's huge brown shoes come to a stop in front of him and he tensed, waiting for the blow.

A blow that never came.

He cracked open an eye and saw the doctor had squatted in front of him. His big hands were open and resting loosely on his knees and the look on his face wasn't anger, but rather concern. Lifting his eyes a little more, Joshua saw his mother and he wanted to go to her, but she looked frightened. He knew it was a look that said he shouldn't move too fast.

"What did you think I was going to do to you, Joshua?" said the man.

Joshua knew better than to answer silly questions like that. Questions without answers were fuel for more strikes, sometimes with a closed fist instead of an open palm.

When the doctor reached for him, Joshua pressed back into the corner, but rather than slap him, the man pulled him forward. Joshua opened his eyes in shock. The hands were firm, but they weren't hurting him.

"Look at me, Joshua." Another dangerous command, but Joshua knew that ignoring this one was worse. He forced himself to meet the white doctor's eyes.

"I would never hurt you," he said, and his gaze never wavered.

Joshua glanced up at his mother. She visibly relaxed, her breath leaving in a long exhalation.

"I would never hurt you, Joshua, ever."

Joshua realized he was shaking. The doctor turned his left arm and looked at a spot above his elbow. Joshua looked as well and saw the long scratch. He hadn't even realized he'd been hurt. A fat drop of blood was oozing toward his elbow and he watched it in fascination. Only then did it begin to hurt.

"That's a nasty cut. We need to clean it," said the doctor. His gaze went to the baseball sitting on the floor. "James, come here."

The white boy shuffled over, his hands twisting his pants at his sides. "Yes'm."

"You said Joshua broke the lamp. Is that the truth?" The look he leveled on the boy was severe.

Joshua tensed. He was mad that the boy had betrayed him, but he didn't want to see him get a beating either. "I did it," Joshua stammered, amazed he had the courage to say it.

The boy's eyes widened, but when his father continued to stare at him, he looked at the ground and cuffed the toe of his sneakers against the carpet. "No, I threw the ball and it hit the lamp. He didn't do nothing."

"So you lied?"

Oh, dangerous, dangerous question.

Joshua started to speak, but the boy interrupted him. "Yeah, I lied."

A sigh left the white doctor and he released his hold on Joshua. "I'm disappointed in you, James. How could you lie about that?"

"Don't know."

"Well, that will cost you, son. You've lost a week of TV privileges and you won't be able to go to your baseball game this weekend."

The boy hung his head, but didn't respond. Joshua was confused. Television? That was his punishment for lying? For breaking something? Television? He gave his mother a baffled look. She forced a smile for him.

"You owe Joshua an apology."

"Sorry," mumbled the boy.

"As for you," said the doctor and Joshua tensed. "You should never take the blame for something you didn't do, but I appreciate the gesture."

Joshua frowned at him. He didn't know what the heck the man was saying, but one thing was obvious – no one was getting hit for this. He wasn't sure how to process that knowledge.

Reaching up, the doctor ruffled Joshua's hair. "Come on. Let's get that arm cleaned up." He rose to his feet and held out a huge hand. Joshua reluctantly placed his own in it. "Come with us, Mary," he said to Joshua's mother. "I'd like to talk to you, all right?"

She met Joshua's eye, then she bent down and picked him up, pressing him against her. Joshua let her cuddle him, wrapping his arms around her neck. The rest of his fear bled away in her embrace, but he could feel how tense she was.

"No one will ever hurt you again," she whispered in his ear. "We're going to be all right now."

Joshua placed his head on her shoulder and looked back at the boy. He was watching Joshua in return, but Joshua wasn't clear on what emotion he saw on the boy's face.

* * *

Peyton rode the elevator to the lobby with Marco and Smith. She leaned against the mirrored back wall, watching the two men standing in the center of the elevator, their backs ramrod straight. Smith had his hands clasped behind him and Marco had his tucked into his pockets.

Peyton mulled over what she would say when they got to the car where the suspect sat. She knew that Marco would make her take point on this. He usually did. There was no one else she wanted at her back; therefore, she accepted that he made her do the majority of the cross-examination.

The elevator came to a bumping halt on the bottom floor and the doors swished open. Peyton pushed away from the mirrored wall and followed the men out. In order to get to the parking structure door, they had to cross the lobby. Peyton glanced over to see one of the security guards in a brown uniform, talking into the phone. A uniformed officer stood next to him. Peyton marked that there was no way to cross from the elevators to the parking structure without being seen by the security desk.

A heavy, fire door opened onto the parking structure. The echoing chamber stretched away, segmented by pillars to hold up the great expanse of floors above them. Each pillar was marked with a colored letter and number, designating the resident's assigned space. Cars were lined up in neat rows, many BMWs and Mercedes, but also a huge number of Priuses. This was San Francisco, after all.

As they moved away from the door, Peyton's heels made a sharp tattoo on the cement floor. Marco and Smith trailed a step behind her as they wove through the aisles and around the pillars. Turning a corner, they came upon the crime scene.

Uniformed officers encircled a black Jeep Cherokee, their guns drawn and pointed at the car. No one moved, no one said anything. Marco and Smith both drew their guns, but Peyton waited until they got close enough to see the man sitting in the driver's seat. She could only see his profile, but she recognized the spill of black hair over his shoulder and the sharp slant of his high cheekbones. He seemed to be looking at either the steering wheel or something in his lap, but he didn't move as the three of them edged up behind the other cops.

One of the uniforms glanced over as Peyton stopped beside him. "How long has he been sitting here?"

"'Bout five minutes. We told him to get out of the vehicle, but he didn't respond, so we called you."

Peyton nodded and glanced over at Marco. Marco didn't have his gun raised, but it dangled at his side.

"That's Ravensong, yes?" he asked, motioning toward the Jeep with his chin.

"Yes."

"He make any threatening moves at all?" Marco asked the uniform.

"Nothing."

Peyton squinted. The window seemed to be rolled down. "He say anything?"

"Nothing."

"He has to hear you. The window's down, right?"

"He doesn't act like he knows we're here."

Peyton exhaled and studied their perp. He wasn't even moving. A strange shiver raced up her spine. He *did* act

39

like he didn't know they were there, but how the hell could you miss seven cops surrounding you with guns?

"All right. I'm going in. You cover me," she said, reaching for her own weapon.

"You need a flak jacket," said the uniform.

"I don't think he's armed. He bludgeoned her with something, he didn't shoot her or stab her. I'll back away if he makes a move and you can take him out."

The uniform started to argue. He looked to Marco and Smith for assistance.

Marco ignored him. "Approach real slow, got it?"

"Got it." She thumbed the safety off her gun, but kept it pointed at the ground. Taking a step forward, she moved beyond the uniforms and eased toward the Jeep. She could see herself reflected in the rearview mirror on the driver's side, so Ravensong had to know she was approaching, but he gave no indication that he saw anything.

"Joshua Ravensong," she called loudly. "I'm Inspector Peyton Brooks from the San Francisco Police Department. I am approaching your vehicle. Do not make any sudden movements, please."

Stepping out away from the Jeep, she angled toward the open window. When she got close enough to where she could reach out and touch the door, she stopped and gripped the gun with both hands. Gazing in at him, she rose on her tiptoes to see if he held a weapon in his lap. She wanted to know what he was looking at with such intensity.

His hands were visible, resting palms up on the lower circle of the steering wheel. From her position by the door, she could see they were covered in blood.

"Joshua Ravensong, I am Inspector Brooks of the San Francisco Police Department..."

She hesitated as he slowly lifted his head. His eyes met hers, but there was no awareness in his dark gaze. Peyton opened her mouth to say something, but she faltered. She'd never seen eyes so blank or dead before. Then he blinked, dark lashes sweeping down to hide his stare.

When he looked at her again, his expression shifted to an expression of panic. His chest rose in a rapid pant and his head turned quickly, taking in the cops and the guns, then swinging back to her.

Peyton knew fear when she saw it, fear and confusion. She grabbed the badge out of her belt and held it up with her left hand. "SFPD, Mr. Ravensong. I'm Inspector Brooks."

His gaze swept over the badge, then focused on her again. "Inspector Brooks," he said in a voice she knew intimately, "I think I need help."

* * *

Peyton watched as Jake swabbed down Ravensong's hands. The knuckles on his right hand were swollen, the skin broken. Jake glanced up at her and made a pointed gesture for her to mark the damage. She nodded. She saw it. Unfortunately the evidence was mounting against the troubled rock star.

Ravensong was sitting outside the Jeep on the concrete, his back pressed to the passenger side door. Other uniforms were going over the car, searching for a weapon. Peyton didn't think it likely they'd find one. The weapon was probably back in the condominium or stashed somewhere in the hallway on the eighth floor. This was obviously a crime of passion and he would have gotten rid of the weapon the first chance he got.

After he'd told her he needed help, he hadn't said anything else. He'd allowed her to open the driver's side door, then he'd turned around and allowed her to search him. She confirmed his identity with his wallet, but it was only a formality. She knew this man on sight.

Her teen years had been spent listening to his smoky voice in her head phones, pretending he was singing directly to her. She knew every nuance of his songs with *Avalanche*, of the way he moved on stage, swaying, seducing his audience with his raw sexuality. And she knew the lines of his face, the sharp features, the velvet black eyes, the heavy lashes. Her hands had shaken as she searched him, fully aware she was touching the fantasy of her youth.

"Do you want to question the security guard who found the vic?" said Marco in her ear.

She blinked up at him, then reworked what he said in her head. "Yeah. Yeah, we should talk to him."

Marco frowned at her. "You okay, Brooks?"

"Fine." She stepped up behind Jake. "I'm gonna question the security guard while you finish up."

"Got it," said Jake, distracted by his work.

Ravensong lifted his head. He'd been watching Jake work on his hands obsessively. She could only describe his expression as confused, shocked. He hadn't asked her anything. In fact, he'd been oddly subdued, submissive even.

"I'll be right back," she told him.

He just stared at her without responding.

She backed away from him and turned, hurrying to Marco's side.

"When do you plan to ask him what happened?"

"I want to get him back to the precinct first."

"He acts like he's stoned."

"I know. Jake will do a breathalyzer next."

"He's not drunk, Brooks."

She ignored that and started across the garage.

"Brooks?"

"We'll get a urine and blood test when we get back to the precinct." She quickened her steps. For some reason, she didn't want to discuss Ravensong with Marco. He matched her with his long stride.

Pulling open the door, they crossed the lobby and stopped before the security desk. Both the security guard and the uniform were going over a list. The uniform looked up and Peyton read the nametag on his chest. Bryce Williamson.

"Officer Williamson, I guess we got the safe open, yes?"

"We did." He took the list from the security guard. "The resident in the apartment on the eighth floor is listed as Terry Ravensong."

Peyton couldn't deny a twinge of disappointment. She turned her attention to the security guard. "I'm Inspector Brooks, this is my partner, Inspector D'Angelo." She thumbed a card out of her pocket and laid it on the counter. "We understand you found her body?"

The security guard briefly closed his eyes, then nodded. "The bastard smashed in half her head."

"We know."

"Did you get him?"

"A suspect is in custody at this time," she answered. "Can you tell me your name?" She pulled her notebook out of her pocket and opened it.

"Carl. Carl Stein."

Peyton wrote his name. "Carl, what made you go up to the eighth floor?"

"The alarm sounded on the security door."

"I'm sorry. The security door?"

"Yes. Everyone uses the elevators. The doors to the stairwells are alarmed to prevent people from going in and out that way. We want to monitor all traffic through the lobby. The stairwells are just in case of fire."

"I see. What time did the alarm sound?"

Carl slid over to his computer and clicked with his mouse. "The first time was at 9:12AM."

Peyton frowned. "I thought you didn't find her body until about 10:00."

"That's right. I cleared the first alarm. It happens. Kids throw open the doors to make them sound. Or visitors open the doors by mistake."

"Got it."

"You always know what floor the alarm sounds on?" asked Marco, leaning on the counter next to her.

"Yeah, it indicates here on the screen."

"Was the first alarm on the eighth floor?" Marco continued.

"Yes."

"And what time was the second?"

"It registered at 9:56."

"Why did you go up the second time?" asked Peyton.

"Protocol. If an alarm sounds on the same floor twice, we have to investigate."

"Did you take the stairs or the elevator?"

"I took the elevator. Quicker."

Peyton made a note in her book. "After you exited the elevator, how long did it take before you found the open door?"

"Not thirty seconds."

"Okay, so you went into the apartment and you saw the body. What did you do then?"

"I got the hell out. I damn near threw up. Why the hell did he do that to her?"

Peyton shook her head. "Did you go back down the stairs or did you use the elevator?"

"Elevator. I got down here, called you guys, then tried to get my boss. He's out at church or something."

"Did you touch anything in the apartment?"

"No."

"Did you see anyone in the hallway?"

"No."

"And you didn't search the stairwell at all?"

"No, I called the cops and I stayed here. I don't have a gun or anything and I wasn't sure where the killer went."

He wasn't much worried about the safety of his tenants either.

Peyton shifted toward Marco. "We need to search the stairwell for the murder weapon and stop any garbage collection so we can go through it."

Marco motioned at the uniform for his radio and stepped away from the security desk to give the orders.

Peyton turned back to Carl. "Is it true there are no security cameras in the lobby or the hallways?"

"That's right, but there's a camera in the garage."

"We'll need a copy of what it recorded. Anything else you can tell us?"

"I don't know. I'm still shaken up. Dude, he bashed in her head."

"Yeah, I know." She pushed the card closer to him. "If you remember anything else, call me, all right?"

"Sure." He picked up the card. "You did get him though, right? You have him in custody?"

There was no reason to lecture him on the law, so she just nodded and stepped away from the counter. Even though everyone was innocent until proven guilty, it was hard to pretend that the evidence wasn't stacked up against Joshua Ravensong right now.

CHAPTER 3

Joshua watched the two boys throwing the baseball back and forth. He sat on the stairs of the porch, the screen door behind him. Jennifer had her dolls scattered over the stairs and one of them was driving a pink convertible up and down the front walkway.

"Come on, Josh. You aren't playing right. Bring your guy over here. He can go for a ride too."

He tore his gaze from the boys and glanced at her. She motioned to the doll dangling from his hand. He held it up and looked at it. The nose had been chewed off and one of the doll's blue eyes had been partially rubbed away, so he looked like he was squinting. This doll was a sorry excuse for the blond doll's boyfriend, but then the blond doll had a stripe of pink permanent marker running down the side of her hair, so he didn't think she could be any too picky.

Jennifer waited a moment more, then began driving the convertible toward the stairs, making alarming noises. On top of the pink stripe, the blond was a reckless driver.

The boys laughed at something, drawing Joshua's attention again, and the ball sailed through the air, smacking into James' glove with a satisfying sound of leather on leather. They were playing in the park across the street. Adam had allowed the older boys to cross the street by themselves, so they had more room to throw the ball. Joshua's mother hadn't wanted him to go, not that he'd been asked either.

"Come on, put your guy in the car too, Josh."

Joshua handed her the doll and watched as she bent its stiff legs and shoved it in the passenger seat. It got stuck halfway down, so Jennifer pushed hard on the head, denting the soft plastic. Joshua smiled, thinking the doll actually looked better with a dented head – it hid the scraped eye and bitten nose.

"Stupid, stupid man," hissed Jennifer, trying to push the head back into shape.

Joshua bent over to help her, but the sound of a car pulling up the curb distracted him. He glanced up to see a run-down Buick roll to a stop in front of the house. The car had once been black, but the paint had oxidized to a soapy-looking grey. Across the street, he could see that James and his friend had stopped playing baseball, making Joshua wonder who drove the car.

The driver's side door opened and a man climbed out. He had short black hair, parted in the middle and sharp cheekbones. As he leaned on the car, looking up at the house, he barely saw over the roof. He was a good deal shorter than Adam.

Joshua felt his heart stutter in his chest and he swallowed hard. He would never forget the harsh cut of those cheekbones, the wide-spaced black eyes, the sweep of dark hair winging back from a broad forehead.

"Go get your father," he said to Jennifer, never taking his eyes from the man.

As he spoke, the man looked down and a slow smile spread across his face. His teeth were even and white, his jaw smooth shaven.

"Who's that?" asked Jennifer without moving.

"Go get your father now," Joshua hissed. "Please."

She turned and studied him in bewilderment. Joshua thought to bolt inside himself, but he didn't want to leave her out here alone.

"Jennifer..." he pleaded.

"Come here, boy!" shouted the man, then he motioned with just the fingers of his right hand. "That's no way to greet your father."

Joshua pushed himself to his feet and pressed his back to the post on the porch. He clenched his teeth to stop their chattering. Jennifer was still sitting in the walkway, looking between him and the man, bewildered by both of their behavior.

"Josh, is he your father?"

Joshua tore his eyes from the man. "Go inside the house now, Jennifer. Now!"

She scrambled to her feet at the force of his tone and ran to the door, but she didn't open it. Joshua glanced back at her, but she seemed paralyzed.

"I said come here, boy!"

Joshua whipped back around. The man had made it to the center of the walk.

"Is this where your mother lives now? Pretty nice set up, eh? I drove a long way to see you, boy, and I'm not leaving until I do."

Joshua wanted to shout at him. He wanted to run to the house, but he couldn't do either. His fingers gripped the post so hard, he felt wood splinters press against his hands.

The man advanced. His sneakers didn't make any sound on the walkway, but Joshua wondered if that was because his heart was hammering so hard that he couldn't hear anything else. He willed himself to run, but he didn't.

The man grabbed him by the collar of his t-shirt and yanked him off the stairs. He stumbled into the walkway and fell on his hands and knees. He tried to scramble up and run for the street, but the man caught him before he could get away.

"Little bastard, disrespecting me!"

The man cuffed him on the side of the head. Pain exploded in his ear and he stumbled, landing on the walkway again. He tried to get up, but the concrete was tilting at a mad angle and his head rang with noise.

"I come all this way and you ignore me."

Joshua pressed his palms hard against the walkway, trying to force himself up, but he found his body listed sideways in an alarming way.

"Don't you run from me, boy!"

He staggered. He wasn't sure he was trying to run. He was just trying to find equilibrium. Something was off in his head, making his balance crazy. He stumbled and found himself landing on his side, the impact jarring his head again.

The man was shouting at him, screaming at him, then he hauled back his leg. Joshua tried to draw his knees into his chest, but he was too slow. The kick took him low in the stomach and pain exploded in his lower back. He tried to crawl away, but the pain was like a weight in the center of him and he had a crazy thought that the man might have kicked him in two.

He heard someone screaming and then a body launched over the top of him, slamming into the man and knocking him backward. Something was definitely broken in his head because it looked like James had landed on the man and had turned into a whirling mass of swinging fists and kicking feet.

The door on the house flew open and Adam loomed in the doorway, lunging down the stairs. The man pulled himself free of James and ran for his car. Joshua was sure Adam would follow him, but he dropped beside Joshua and placed his huge hand on his forehead.

Joshua flinched, but Adam just stroked Joshua's hair. "It's all right, son. Mary, call an ambulance!"

He heard running feet, then the screen door on the house banged shut. In the distance, he heard a car peel away.

"You okay, James."

"Fine, Dad. Will Joshua be okay?"

Adam looked down into Joshua's watering eyes. "He'll be fine. He'll be just as good as new in a few days."

Joshua didn't want to cry. He wanted to be as brave as James had been, but he hurt so bad, he couldn't help it. And he wanted his mother. Before the thought finished itself, she was there, covering him with a blanket and bending over him, folding her body around him as if that would be enough to protect him from harm.

* * *

The precinct had two interrogation rooms, but they mainly used the larger one. Jake had never been in this one. It was tucked in a back corner of the precinct, closest to the elevator that would take perps down to the holding cells in the basement.

A long conference table dominated the back wall and Jake took a seat on it, his feet dangling off the edge. He'd seen two dead bodies since breakfast and although he was getting used to the horrible things people did to each other, it still made him feel tired. Peyton stood at the one way mirror with her back to him, reading from a sheet of paper. He studied the wild tangle of curls at the end of her ponytail and wondered how much longer she would be able to handle this level of depravity. Marco leaned on the other end of Jake's table, closest to the door, his arms crossed in front of him as he stared at the man in the other room. Jake didn't think he expected anything more of humans than what he saw every day. He looked at each perp with the same resigned disgust, including the handsome one sitting on the other side of the glass right now.

Joshua Ravensong sat in a metal chair, facing the mirror. His hands were resting on his thighs. The blood was gone, but drops of it stained his jeans. His right hand was visibly swollen, the skin broken over the knuckles and beginning to darken with bruises. In front of him was a small metal table, which he seemed to be staring at with an intensity that bordered on madness. Jake had done the breathalyzer himself, so he knew he wasn't drunk. They'd taken urine and blood samples when he arrived, but they didn't have the result of those yet. Jake was certain, however, that they would turn up something more potent than booze.

Stan Neumann from Tech had processed the text messages from Ravensong's cell phone. Peyton was reviewing them now. Based on snippets she shared, Jake knew they didn't help Ravensong's case any.

The captain entered the room. "D'Angelo, Ryder," she said.

"Captain," they both responded.

Defino moved to Peyton's side. Katherine Defino was an inch or two shorter than Jake with a brown bob and a perpetual squint. She always looked like she was half pissed off. It had intimidated him at first, but he knew she was fair-minded and she'd given him a chance when no one else would, well, no one but Peyton.

Peyton handed her the paper and she read it over. Then she made a tsking noise and looked up through the window. "Damn, I hate this."

"I know," said Peyton. "I hate it too."

Defino turned toward Peyton, motioning at the window with the paper. "You know, Colin and I had our first date at an *Avalanche* concert. We almost didn't have our second. Colin accused me of being more interested in the lead singer than him." She leaned closer to Peyton. "He was right. No way any woman could see him strutting on stage and hear that voice, and not get all hot and bothered."

Peyton smiled and nodded at the mirror. "He was my first crush. I followed him when he was with his first band, *Blazes*. I'd listen to his voice and stare at his poster and my heart would ache."

Jake rolled his eyes.

"He really is the prettiest man I've ever seen," said Defino, looking through the mirror again.

"Yes, he is. Absolutely gorgeous."

Jake was flabbergasted. "Are you kidding me? What about Adonis over here? He's gorgeous."

Both Peyton and Defino turned and stared at him. Marco looked over, one dark brow lifting in question.

"Well, it's true," Jake protested, turning to Marco for help. "Isn't it?"

"I'm with you, son. The guy's clearly on something."

Jake pointed at the mirror. "He just bashed someone's head in and you're both going on like lovesick school girls. He's a murderer, not some pinup."

"Funny how quickly you forget what it's like to be on the other side of that window, Jake," scolded Peyton.

"Mmhmm," added Defino.

Jake felt his face color, but he ignored it. "This is the easiest case we've had in months and we could be wrapping it up, but you're sitting here ogling him like a piece of meat."

A smile touched the corners of Peyton's mouth and she leaned her shoulder against the captain's. Jake recognized the look. "Isn't it cute how they get six months under their belt on the force and they think they know everything?"

"It sure is. Cuter still when they spout off all this moral outrage over sexual equality."

Jake shook his head and looked to Marco.

He simply shrugged. "What you gonna do? Women never take us seriously. We're just playthings for them."

Jake glared at him. He wasn't helping.

"How are you going to handle this?" Defino asked Peyton.

Peyton took the text messages back from her. "I'm not sure I'll get much out of him. He's said only five or six words since we arrested him, but I'll give it a try."

"We need to find out where that little girl is. That's priority one."

"Got it." Peyton moved toward the door, but she stopped and glanced back at Jake. "By the way, I never ogle."

Jake shook his head, but he couldn't help the smile that teased at his lips. He couldn't stay pissed at her no matter what, and she knew it.

* * *

As Peyton entered the interrogation room, Joshua Ravensong lifted his head. The look on his face stopped her. For a moment, he didn't seem to recognize her.

"I'm Inspector Brooks," she reminded him.

He leaned back in the chair, his right hand resting on his thigh. She could see how swollen the knuckles were, the skin abraded and raw. Leather armbands wrapped around both wrists, held shut with metal buckles. They would have to take those away from him.

She moved to the chair at the end of the table, diagonal from him, and sat down, placing the paper with the text messages on it. "I need to know where your daughter is, Joshua." She figured using his first name might put him at ease, make it easier for him to confide in her.

"My daughter?"

"Yes, it's important."

He flexed the swollen fingers on his right hand. "She's with Elena."

"Elena?"

He narrowed his eyes on her. They were so dark, she had trouble telling if his pupils were dilated or not. They'd have to rely on the drug test for confirmation. "Elena Harris, my…" He paused and sighed. "My partner."

"Your partner?"

"She thinks it's stupid for grown people to have boyfriends and girlfriends." He lifted his left hand as if he would massage his wounded fingers, then stopped.

"Your daughter's with Elena?"

He nodded, staring at the table.

"Can I have her number?"

He rattled off the digits and Peyton shifted in the chair to look back at the mirror. A tap on the glass told her they got it.

Leaning forward, Ravensong braced his left arm on the table and pressed his forehead into his hand. "How am I going to tell my daughter her mother is dead?" The anguish in his voice touched Peyton.

"I can tell her."

He didn't move.

"It's sort of what we do," she added.

He canted a look at her, his expression disbelieving.

She decided not to pursue that topic any longer. "I need to know what happened, Joshua. I need you to tell me."

He shook his head. "I don't know."

Peyton fingered the paper, but she wasn't ready to use it yet. "You said your daughter's with Elena, right?"

"Yes."

"Are they at your house?"

He lowered his arm. "No, they went out to buy Tiffany a dress."

"Tiffany? Your daughter?"

"Yes."

"A dress?"

"Right. For court tomorrow."

"Court?"

"She's going to talk to the judge. It's the final step to granting me full custody."

"Why didn't you go with them?"

"I was going for a run, then I wanted to work on some music."

"At your house?"

He frowned at her. "Of course."

"Where is your house?"

"Marin."

"And yet you wound up in San Francisco?"

He closed his eyes briefly. "Yes."

"How?"

"I don't know."

Peyton leaned back in the chair. "Let's back up a bit, all right?"

He nodded.

"You said you were getting full custody, right?"

"Right."

"How?"

"Terry was signing custody over to me. Tiffany had been living with Elena and me for the last five months, ever since Terry's mother died."

"Okay, let me make sure I have this. Terry's mother died. After that, your daughter came to live with you full time, yes?"

"Yes."

"Terry offered to give you full custody and you were finalizing that through the court by meeting with the judge tomorrow?"

"Right."

"Why are you meeting with the judge?"

"He wanted to interview Tiffany and make sure she wanted this change to go through. I also had to take a drug test and prove that I'm clean."

Peyton absorbed that fact. If he was on something, he must have taken it this morning. "How old is Tiffany?"

"She turns ten in June."

"So Terry had primary custody up until now?"

"Yes."

"Why would she give it up now?"

"Her mother took care of Tiffany most of the time. Now that she's gone, Terry decided she was moving to Europe. She didn't want to uproot Tiffany."

Peyton flattened her hand on the paper. "But this morning she changed her mind."

Ravensong's head came up and he gave Peyton a confused stare. "What?"

She pushed the paper forward. "We have the text messages from your phone, Joshua. Terry changed her mind about giving you full custody and told you the deal was off."

He reached for the paper with his wounded hand and winced, but he picked it up and studied it. As he did so, she caught the raised pink scar snaking across his wrist, peeking out from beneath the leather arm band.

He lowered the paper and pushed it away. "I don't remember this."

Peyton wished for once that someone would just tell the truth. "You don't remember receiving those texts or responding to them?"

"No." He stared at the paper fixedly. "I don't remember any of it."

"Please understand my skepticism, Joshua. You were found at her condo, you had her blood all over you and your right hand is a mess, yet you expect me to believe that you don't remember receiving her texts and going over to her condo to confront her?"

His dark eyes pierced her. "I don't remember any of it. The first thing I remember is you, calling my name."

Peyton held out her hands, palms up. "Look, I get it. You're under pressure, you want your daughter to live with you, and you're so close to getting that, but at the last minute, Terry changes her mind. It would make anyone angry, Joshua. It would make anyone go over there to confront her. So what happened? Did it get ugly? Maybe she said some things that struck a little too close to home. You lost your cool and…" Peyton slammed her hand on the table, making Ravensong jump. "Suddenly she's dead."

The look on his face was stark. His eyes widened, his breathing accelerated, and his lips parted. She waited for him to do one of two things: confess or deny. After a moment, his eyes drifted to the paper.

"Oh God," he whispered. "I don't know. I don't know what happened."

Peyton frowned. "You don't know what happened? Are you going to stick with the memory loss, Josh, really?" She couldn't help the disappointment.

He shook his head. "I don't know. I don't remember. I'm not lying to you, I don't remember."

"How can that be, Joshua? How can you not remember?"

His gaze swung back to her, sharp, focused, stricken. "I'm a heroin addict, Inspector Brooks. No matter how long I've been clean, the damage was done. I have black-out sometimes and nothing I can do will ever get those memories back."

Peyton glanced at the mirror. "Are you saying you had a black-out today?"

"I remember saying goodbye to Elena and Tiffany. That's it. Until…." He closed his eyes and forced a calming breath. "Until you called my name. Everything else is blank."

Peyton tapped her fingers on the table. She needed to talk to a doctor, Abe probably, and find out if this was possible. She knew alcoholics suffered black-outs, but a recovered heroin addict? It seemed like too convenient a defense.

Pushing herself to her feet, she leaned on the table. He looked up at her with that vulnerable, confused expression she was beginning to expect. "You're gonna need a lawyer, Mr. Ravensong," she said, "a damn good lawyer."

When he didn't answer, she turned away, walking to the door. Smith met her on the other side and she stopped. "Put him in a holding cell downstairs and get a doctor to look at his hand. It might be broken." When he nodded, she started to walk away, but she hesitated and turned around again. She could see Ravensong framed in the doorway. He was reading the text messages once more. "And Frank, put him on suicide watch, okay?"

* * *

Peyton paused in the doorway of the break-room, her attention snagged by the corner of the front counter she could see. She lifted the coffee cup to her lips and took a sip. The bitter taste of the coffee was muted by the four tablespoons of sugar she'd put in it.

Maria was talking to a woman at the counter. She was shorter than Peyton by a good two inches, and that said something because Peyton didn't clear five four. She had brown hair, pulled back in a long ponytail. Her hair was curly and stray wisps fluttered around her face. She was pretty in a girl next door sort of way.

Marco stepped out of the front conference room and approached the counter. Maria placed her hand on his shoulder as if she was introducing him, but Peyton knew she

57

couldn't resist touching him whenever she got the opportunity.

He held out his hand to the woman and she accepted it briefly, then she clasped it around the handle on her purse again, holding on as if it were a lifeline. Peyton wandered toward them, taking another sip of her coffee.

"Why don't you come inside?" offered Marco, moving to the half-door and pulling it open. He stopped when he caught sight of Peyton. "Here's my partner, Inspector Brooks."

Peyton held out her free hand and the woman released her grip on the bag. Her hand shook in Peyton's.

"This is Elena Harris," said Marco.

Peyton nodded. "Maria, would you mind getting Ms. Harris a cup of coffee?"

"Tea, please, if you have it." Then she gave a strange little shiver. "It doesn't matter. Whatever you have will be fine." She tried to smile for Maria, but it came out odd.

"We have tea," said Peyton, giving Maria a pointed look.

Maria stuck her tongue out at Peyton behind the woman's back. "It's no problem at all," she said, then moved toward the break-room.

Elena Harris looked up at Marco. "You said Joshua was in some kind of trouble. Is he all right?"

Peyton took the opportunity to study her. She seemed genuinely afraid, her eyes brimming with tears.

Marco placed a hand in the middle of her back and directed her to the conference room. "Let's talk in here."

Peyton followed them into the room, crossing around the table, as Marco helped Elena into a chair. She placed the purse on her lap and gripped it with both hands. "I really need to know if he's all right."

"He's fine," offered Peyton.

Marco sat down beside the woman and turned so he was facing her. "We have him in a holding cell below us right now."

Elena nodded. Her green eyes glittered brightly, the tears hovering on the edge of spilling over.

"Do you mind if I call you Elena?" Marco asked.

Peyton wanted to roll her eyes at the gentlemanly side her partner was displaying. He'd basically convicted Elena's *partner* without a trial in his own mind, but he was all charm now.

"That's fine," she answered. "Please tell me what's going on. Why is Joshua here?"

Marco rested his left arm on the table and gripped the back of her chair with his right. "We found him at the condo of his ex-wife this afternoon."

"Terry? Why?"

"We don't know, but…" He paused significantly. "Elena, Terry is dead."

"What?"

The shock in her voice was real.

"Elena," said Peyton. "I need to know where Joshua's daughter is."

"Tiffany?"

"Yes, we need to check her welfare."

"She's home with the housekeeper, Martha. I wasn't sure what was going on, so I didn't want to bring her." Her face clouded over and the flood of tears broke. "Oh, God, how will I tell Tiffany about her mother?"

"We can discuss that in a moment, but I need a number for the house, so one of us can talk to Tiffany. It's important."

"You aren't going to tell her? Please don't tell her something like that over the phone."

Panic was beginning to sink in.

"No," said Marco. "Just give me the number and I'll make the call. I won't tell her what is going on."

Peyton reached into her pocket and pulled out her notepad, tearing off a piece of paper. She passed it to Elena, who fished a pen from her purse and wrote the number down. Marco took it and thanked her, then he left the room.

For a moment the two women just stared at each other, then Elena swiped at her tears and squared her jaw. "I want to see Joshua."

"I'll take you to him in a few minutes. We need to ask you some questions first."

Elena slumped back in the chair. She blinked at Peyton a few times in astonishment. "You think he did it? You think Joshua killed her?"

"It doesn't look good."

"What does that mean?"

"It means we found him in the parking garage below her building."

"And?"

"He had her blood on his hands."

Elena's hand flew to her mouth and the tears spilled faster. "Oh, God."

"The knuckles on his right hand are swollen and abraded as if he struck something."

Elena gasped as if she couldn't get enough air. She was fighting not to cry, but it wasn't working.

Peyton rose to her feet and went toward the door. As she stepped outside, Marco released the call on his phone and faced her.

"The little girl's fine," he offered, watching Peyton move to Maria's desk and retrieve the tissue she kept there.

"Thank God."

She couldn't help the wash of relief that swept over her. She could almost find a motive for murdering an ex-wife, but if he'd harmed his own daughter, that spoke to a depravity that Peyton didn't want to consider.

She returned to the room and set the box in front of Elena, circling back to her seat as Marco sat down beside her again. Elena grabbed a number of tissues and covered her face with them, her breath hitching as she fought to get control of herself.

While she did so, Peyton studied her. She wasn't at all what Peyton expected. Not that she wasn't pretty – she was, but she was small and ordinary pretty – not super model gorgeous. A man who looked like Joshua should have a Greek goddess for a girlfriend, not this rather studious-looking business woman. In fact, Peyton would have expected someone much more like his ex-wife than Elena.

Marco shifted and gave Peyton an aggravated look. Peyton smiled at his discomfort. No matter how much humans evolved, men would never be comfortable around a crying woman, but she knew Elena needed to get control on her own.

She wiped her nose and blinked her eyes a few times. Her breath was still coming too fast, but her eyes weren't overflowing any longer. "Did you get in touch with Tiffany?"

"I did. I didn't tell her anything."

Elena shook her head. "How am *I* going to tell her?"

"I can do it for you. I'll go out to the house with you when we're done here," offered Peyton.

Elena shook her head. "No, I don't want to scare her with police. This is horrible enough. She needs to hear it from someone she trusts."

"I'll leave that to you and Joshua."

"I want to see him. Please, let me go to him now."

Marco gave Peyton a bewildered look. Peyton knew what he thought. Why the hell would she want to see the man who had brutally murdered someone hours before?

"Let's get you calmed down and talk a little bit before we do that, all right?"

Elena leaned forward. "You don't understand..." She pulled up short and shot a look toward the door.

"What don't we understand?"

Elena twisted the tissue around her index finger. "He's tried to kill himself before."

Peyton relaxed. She'd been expecting a bigger confession. "We know that. We have him on suicide watch."

Maria entered at that moment and set the tea before Elena. "Here you go. I hope lemon is all right."

"Fine. Thank you." She didn't reach for it.

61

"No problem." Maria gave Peyton a sharp look behind Elena's back.

"Thank you, Maria. You can go," said Peyton, knowing it would piss her off.

Maria gave her a sarcastic smile, then reached out and ran her hand over Marco's shoulders where they strained against his striped shirt. With a flounce of her dark hair, she left the room.

Marco moved the mug closer to Elena. "Take a sip. It might help."

She forced a watery smile for his benefit and Peyton understood Joshua's attraction. This woman brought out protective feelings in men, something she herself had never done. Maybe it was the kick-ass boots she wore, or the fact that she carried a gun, but she'd never found a man who wanted to take care of her. Not that she'd let him. If any man treated her the way Marco was fawning over Elena, Peyton would castrate him on the spot.

"Elena, I need to ask you some difficult questions."

Elena sipped the tea, holding it with both hands. Slowly she lowered it. "You don't have to ask that. He's never once struck me or his daughter. Joshua would never do something like this."

Marco looked down, chewing on his inner lip. It was the standard statement all battered women gave and it meant nothing. Fear or intimidation often made them protect the very person who was beating them.

"Look, Elena, Joshua's in a lot of trouble right now and the only way we can help him is if you're completely honest with us."

Her jaw firmed and her eyes glistened with unshed tears. "I am being honest. I know what you're thinking and I know you think you're helping, but I'm telling you the truth. He's never raised a hand to anyone."

Peyton drummed her fingers on the table. She wasn't sure how to pursue this. "What was his relationship with Terry like?"

"She was a gold digger, Inspector Brooks. That and nothing more."

"She's also the victim here, Elena."

"Terry was never a victim in her life."

Peyton glanced at Marco. She was usually good at this, but Elena wasn't fitting the usual pattern.

Marco shifted toward her. "Elena, here's the honest truth. Joshua's drug addiction and past history with his ex-wife are going to go against him. The only chance he has of a reduced sentence is if we can find a motive for why he snapped. Temporary insanity…anything."

Elena stared at him in astonishment. "Both of you are sure he did this. You've already convicted him before he's had a trial. Is that what they teach you at the academy?"

"No, but here's the reality. All of the evidence, the motive, and the opportunity points to Ravensong and there just isn't any other possibility."

Elena pushed herself to her feet. "I want to see him now."

And just like that she closed the door.

Peyton sighed. "All right." She and Marco rose together. "We'll take you to him, but I hope you'll reconsider and talk with us before you leave. We really are trying to help."

"None of this helps, Inspector Brooks. None of it means a damn thing as long as you already believe him guilty. I'm not going to waste my time here. After I see him, I need to hire a lawyer, so we can get him out of here as fast as possible."

Peyton walked around the table and pointed out the door. "This way, then."

Elena grabbed her bag and followed her across the precinct. They took the single flight of stairs down to the holding cells and Peyton led her to a small conference room. It had no furnishings in it and the floor was bare concrete. There were no windows and the only opening was the heavy metal door. Peyton and Elena waited in the middle of the sparse room, while Marco stepped outside to talk to an officer.

Peyton reached for her card and held it out to Elena. "If you change your mind, you can call me any time."

Elena took the card. "If you change your mind, why don't you call me?"

Peyton crossed her arms and leaned against the wall. "Try to put yourself in our position, Elena."

Elena studied her a moment, then tucked the card into her purse. "Why don't you do the same?"

Marco led Joshua into the room. The difference in their heights was remarkable, but even in a prison jumpsuit, Ravensong exuded a powerful sexuality. He paused at the entrance and Elena turned to face him. Then they came together.

They never spoke, they simply fell into each other arms, pressing so tightly together that Peyton wondered if they thought they could meld into one person. Elena buried her face in his neck and sank her fingers in his dark hair. He folded around her, wrapping both arms around her back and closing his eyes.

Peyton glanced up at Marco. He shook his head in disgust and turned away, but Peyton couldn't deny she was moved. Here were two people who obviously loved each other, and despite the situation, that was something she envied.

CHAPTER 4

James halted in the doorway of the theatre and watched Joshua play the piano. A group of senior girls were gathered around the back of it and one was sitting on the bench next to him. The piano tinkled out a cheerful ragtime tune and Joshua's fingers flew over the keys, dancing away to the lively music.

He came to a flourishing finish and the girls all clapped, laughing in delight at his talent. The girl, sitting on the bench next to him, grabbed his arm and leaned into him, pressing her breasts to his side. James recognized her as Sarah Jameson, trouble. Joshua flashed a smile at her, but his eyes lighted on his brother at the top of the stairs.

"Gotta go," he said, sliding out from the bench.

The girls all protested and Sarah reached for him, catching his hand. "Don't run off. You said you'd play a slow one next."

He leaned toward her, his dark hair sweeping across his cheekbones. "If I don't go now, I'll have to walk home and I hate walking."

She pouted at him, but reluctantly let him go. Joshua grabbed his backpack off the edge of the stage and jumped down, jogging up the stairs. The girls all watched him, giggling at each other, and James felt his stomach tighten. No way should Joshua be hanging out with senior girls.

"What the hell are you doing?"

Joshua stopped and frowned at him. "Waiting for you. How was practice?"

"Forget practice." James kicked open the door and held it as Joshua stepped through. "Those girls are seniors."

"Yeah?"

"You're a freshman. You shouldn't mess with them, especially Sarah Jameson. She's trouble. She's seeing Luke Ames."

"So? He's a dick."

"He's on the football team. You screw with him, you screw with the whole team."

Joshua shot an aggravated look at James. "I was playing the piano. No big deal. Back off, okay?"

James reached out and caught his arm, stopping him. Joshua looked from James' hand to his face, but he didn't pull away. "Those girls are trouble, Josh. Leave them alone. You don't need to be messing with girls like that."

"I like girls like that."

"We all like girls like that, but it never works. You're gonna get your ass kicked and no stupid girl is worth it."

"Maybe they are. I'm not a priest like you, James."

"I'm not a priest, but I know better than to sniff around those girls."

Joshua shook off his hold and continued walking toward the parking lot. "I'll handle it."

"You stupid prick, you can't handle it. Luke Ames is a mean sonuvabitch, Josh. And he's not gonna come at you alone. He'll bring the whole damn team."

Joshua turned to face his brother, walking backwards. "It's a free country, James. If Sarah wants something different, it's her choice."

"The hell it is. She's playing with you. She isn't serious. She's never gonna be seen with a freshman." He closed the distance between them and tapped Joshua in the forehead. "Think! You don't need your insides rearranged again."

Joshua stopped walking and looked behind James where the girls were leaving the theatre. "You're right."

"Damn straight I'm right."

"They just look so good."

"Yeah, right up until you get a fist in your face." He grabbed Joshua's shoulder and turned him around. "Just don't look."

"That's not possible."

"Then look, but keep your distance." He shoved him forward.

"It isn't just the way they look."

"I know, but that's what gets us in trouble."

"I'm not sure I can avoid it, James."

James slung his arm across Joshua's shoulder. "I'm not sure you can either, but that's why I'm here." He ruffled his hair and shoved him away. "Someone's got to protect that pretty face of yours."

Joshua laughed and raced him to the truck.

*　*　*

Peyton eased her green Corolla into the parking lot and wound through the crowd to her parking space. Throwing open the door, she climbed out, almost smacking into the reporter who shoved a microphone in her face.

"Is it true that Joshua Ravensong's been arrested for murder?"

Peyton shoved the microphone away and glared at the man until he stepped back. Damn paparazzi! She locked the Corolla and pointed herself in the direction of the precinct door, then shoved and pushed her way through the crowd, ignoring their frantic calls for information.

She ran up the stairs. A uniform waited at the top and pulled open the door for her, holding it as she ducked inside. She didn't even have time to thank him before he yanked the door closed again, blocking it with his body.

Maria and Captain Defino were standing on the other side of the counter, watching the insanity in the parking lot.

Peyton drew a deep breath and released it, smoothing a hand over her ponytail. "If I find out who leaked this story, I think I'll shoot him."

"Get in line," replied Defino.

Peyton pushed open the half door. "So how *is* our rock star this morning?"

"You mean afternoon," said Maria with a smirk.

"It's only ten. I was here until late last night."

"Don't worry about it, Brooks," said Defino. "Our rock star had a quiet night. His lawyer showed up at 8:00AM and is pressing for a bail hearing, but other than that everything's fine."

"His girlfriend didn't waste any time, did she?"

Defino shook her head.

"Such a shame," murmured Maria, looking out the door.

"I know." Peyton couldn't deny she'd wished it had all been a bad dream when she woke up. It was hard to have a hero fall, especially one as special to her as Ravensong had been.

"He tried so hard to stay clean. And his life has been so difficult."

"Sort of self-inflicted difficult."

Maria shook her head. "He wasn't responsible for what his father did to him."

"What?"

"His father beat him as a kid."

"How do you know that?"

"He gave an interview a few years ago where he talked about it. He has a charity event every year against child abuse."

Peyton moved closer to the desk. "Can you find me that interview on-line?"

"I'll try."

"And see if Stan Neumann can pull up a CPS report for his daughter Tiffany or a domestic violence report from Terry." Peyton paused and thought for a moment, then tapped a finger against Maria's desk. "Also see if he can locate Ravensong's CPS report."

"On it."

"What are you thinking?" asked Defino.

"Elena Harris accused us of assuming Ravensong was guilty and not looking for other suspects. I just think we better cross all of our t's."

68

"Good thought. Devan's gonna want everything we can find to establish a pattern of abuse."

Peyton nodded. "Let me pull the drug tests from yesterday as well."

"Keep me in the loop," said Defino, moving toward her office.

"You got it, Captain," said Peyton, heading toward the back. She slowed as she came near her desk.

Abe, her favorite Medical Examiner, was sitting in a plastic chair with his feet propped on Marco's desk. Marco was leaning back as he usually did, talking to him. Peyton removed her coat and slung it across the back of her chair, adjusting her gun in its shoulder harness.

"Morning, Brooks," said Marco.

"Morning. What are you doing here?" she asked Abe.

He dropped his feet to the floor and swung around to face her. "I was hoping I'd get to see the delicious rock star you've got in stir."

Of course he was.

"And I brought Marco an apple scone." He waved an elegant, long-fingered hand over a brown fold of glistening, flaky pastry.

"You made an apple scone?"

"Yes. I took a drive to the foothills this weekend and picked some apples with my bare hands."

Peyton frowned at him. "You picked apples?"

Abe rolled his eyes. "Okay, I picked *an* apple."

"Yeah, and did you really make that?"

"Of course I made it. Sheesh." He sent his dread locks bouncing with a look of aggravation. "You have so little faith in me."

Peyton sank into her chair. "Come on, Abe. Admit it. You don't have one domestic bone in your body."

"I do so, and it's a very well-developed baking bone."

Peyton glanced at Marco. He was making an uncomfortable face. There was never a literal meaning to anything Abe said.

"Well, you know what hurts?"

"What?"

"You brought Marco a scone and you didn't bring me one. How could you do that to me?"

Abe gave her a pitying look. "You don't just make one scone at a time, you daft girl."

"You do if you pick only one apple."

"I made a tray. The rest are in the break-room." He pointed a finger at her. "But before you get one, you have to guess the secret ingredient."

Peyton let out her breath. "Give us a hint."

Abe glanced between them, the beads on the ends of his dreads clanking together. The beads were a new embellishment.

Marco shook his head at Peyton, but he stopped when Abe's gaze landed on him.

"It begins with L," said Abe jubilantly.

"Lard," said Marco.

Peyton beamed a smile at him. "Love."

Abe smiled too, his teeth struggling to be contained in his mouth. "Yes to lard," he said, pointing at Marco, "Yes to love." His finger jabbed at Peyton. "But I meant liqueur."

"Why did you bring him one instead of me?"

"He's prettier, darlin'. You know that."

Marco pushed his scone toward Peyton. "You can have mine. I avoid lard as a rule."

Abe pushed it back. "Do you really think I would give my Angel dead animal to eat? It's vegetable lard, gorgeous."

Marco broke off a bite and Peyton watched with longing as he put it in his mouth. She loved anything sweet and she meant anything.

Abe leaned back in his chair and reached into his pocket, pulling out a folded card. "Look what I got in the mail." He waved it in front of Marco.

Marco stuck another piece in his mouth and chewed. "What is it?"

"A birthday invitation." Abe waved it again. "For someone's thirtieth."

Marco's brows knit into a frown. Peyton couldn't help but smile. He snatched the card from Abe's hand. "What?"

"Did you get one?" Abe turned to Peyton.

"Of course."

"Damn Vinnie," muttered Marco.

"Vinnie D'Angelo." Abe leaned toward Peyton, cupping his hand against his mouth theatrically. "You know what I mean?"

"Oh yeah."

"Delicious."

"He certainly is," said Peyton, never taking her eyes off her partner. "Mama D'Angelo sure popped out some pretty babies."

"Uh huh."

Marco threw the card on the desk and reached for the phone in his pocket. "Excuse me," he said and rose to his feet, walking away.

"Brother Vinnie's gonna get an ear full."

"I don't think Vinnie cares."

"No, I guess not. So what are we getting him?"

Peyton leaned closer and dropped her voice. "Two tickets to the Niners, fifty yard line."

Abe reared away from her and gave her an admiring look. "How'd you pull that off?"

"We helped out one of the players a few years back, so I called in a favor."

"You slut." He slapped at her arm. "That earns you an apple scone, and I'll deliver it personally."

"I want coffee too. Three tablespoons of sugar."

71

"I know, I know," said Abe, rising to his feet and moving toward the break room. "Someday you'll make president of the Diabetes Club of America?"

"That's not a real thing."

"Sure it is. We meet in the morgue." He shot a pointed look at her and disappeared inside.

Marco turned off the phone and slumped back to his desk. "He never listens."

"You're having a party, so get over it. You only turn thirty once."

"I don't need to turn thirty at all."

"Well, I don't know about you, but the alternative is pretty unappealing."

Marco gave a laugh and watched as Abe settled a scone and a cup of steaming coffee in front of her. Peyton immediately tore off a bite and stuck it in her mouth. The flaky crust melted against her tongue to be followed by a blast of vanilla and the sharp woodsy flavor of the liqueur.

As Abe sank into his chair again, Marco pointed at both of them. "And no gifts." His finger stopped on Peyton when she was in mid-bite. "I mean it. No gifts!"

Peyton swallowed. "Of course not. Who buys gifts for a birthday party? Ridiculous."

Marco didn't seem convinced.

Peyton turned to Abe. "Out with it. Why are you here?"

"I told you. I want to see your rock star."

"That's a terrible reason. According to Jake, men are not for ogling."

"Ogling?"

Marco made a face. "Ugly word."

Abe nodded. "It is, Angel 'D, which is why I never ogle. I venerate."

"Venerate?" scoffed Peyton.

"Means admire."

"Yeah, I got that. It's still a no."

72

"Why not? He won't even know I'm there. This is my one chance to see him up close."

"Then he'll know you're there. Come on, Abe, why are you here? You wouldn't fight your way through paparazzi just to venerate or ogle either one."

Abe placed his hand in the center of his chest. "I'm hurt by how little you know me."

"Okay, so you would come to ogle, but there's something more." Her eyes narrowed on him. "You got our vic, didn't you?"

"Of course I did."

"And you found something?"

"I got back from picking apples…"

"Apple."

Abe acquiesced with an inclination of his head, his beads clicking. "I got back from picking *apple* too late last night, so I did the examination this morning. I still have an autopsy to perform, but I spent a few hours digging around in her brain."

Peyton stopped the piece of scone headed to her mouth and tossed it on the napkin. There went breakfast.

"And?" asked Marco.

"She was hit with some force, I'll tell you. Dented her skull into her brain. Pieces of bone were actually lodged in grey matter."

Peyton pushed the scone away.

"Whoever did this was beyond rage."

"We got that when we saw the body."

"But you don't have the murder weapon, do you?"

"We couldn't find it."

"Interesting."

Peyton leaned forward. "You know what killed her."

"I know what killed her."

"Spill."

"It was heavy, leaded crystal. A curio or something, maybe a paperweight."

"How could you know that?"

73

Abe's brow rose as he smiled cagily. "Parts of it broke off in her head."

"What?"

"Small glass fragments, slivers were lodged in her scalp and some were even pushed into her brain. I extracted as many as I could and sent it to the lab to be processed. Whatever he struck her with broke."

Peyton stared at the desk considering what Abe said.

"How much force would someone have to use to splinter something like that?" asked Marco.

"That isn't so strange. A defect in the glass, an air bubble, and you have a weak point, but the force needed to shatter her skull and shove it into her brain…" He gave a shiver and his beads made a tinkling sound. "That was something."

"Wait," said Peyton. "If the murder weapon broke off in the murderer's hand…"

Abe leaned over and tapped a finger against Peyton's forehead. "Now you're thinking."

Peyton swatted at him. "He'd have cuts, right?"

"Right. You need to check Ravensong's hands."

"The knuckles on his right hand are a mess, Abe."

"This would be on the palm and the finger tips. In fact, some might be pretty deep."

"Is there any way that slivers could have lodged in her scalp, but not cut his hand?" asked Marco.

Abe shook his head. "He'd have to be wearing the thickest gardening gloves ever made. There's just no way. And if he were wearing those gloves, where did they go?"

"And if he were wearing gloves, why did he have her blood all over his hands?" asked Peyton.

"Maybe it wasn't all her blood. It could have been his too if he cut himself," said Marco.

"Except wouldn't Jake have noticed if he cut himself? He processed his hands." She turned around and looked over her shoulder. "Where is Jake?"

"He's doing something for Simons and Cho."

Abe leaned back in his chair, stretching out his long legs. "So, do I get to see the rock star?"

"No, you get to go back to your lab and complete your autopsy."

Abe made a face. "I never get to have any fun. Now you want to send me back to that dungeon."

"You're not in the dungeon. They moved you up a few floors." Peyton pushed herself to her feet. "Come on, D'Angelo. Let's go look at our suspect's hands and get his drug test results."

Marco rose at well.

"If you won't let me see the rock star, can I take Jake back to the lab with me and have him take some more pictures of the vic?" asked Abe, looking up at her.

"Can't you take your own pictures?"

"His are better. He catches things I miss. Plus, I've also got Cho and Simons' bum to take apart. Jake can photograph both."

Peyton shrugged. "Ask him. I'm not his boss."

"You sure think you're mine," said Abe.

She caught his head in her hands and kissed him on the forehead. "Someone needs to keep you in line."

"No one can keep me in line, sister."

She released him. "That's the problem. Be good."

Abe turned and waved at Marco. "Bye, Angel."

"Later," said Marco, following Peyton toward the back of the precinct.

*   *   *

Jake returned to his desk and found Abe sitting in his chair. The tall, lean Medical Examiner was making a design with a paperclip. Jake leaned on the partition and watched him. He had long fingers with perfectly manicured nails.

"What are you doing?"

"Making a Star of David." He held it up for Jake to see. "What are you doing?"

"My job. Why are you making a Star of David?"

"The whys and wherefores of things matter less than the ability to do them."

"Deep. You're in my chair."

"I know." He continued to fold his paperclip.

"Why?"

Abe shot a look up at him. "That's a theme with you, isn't it?"

Jake didn't answer.

Abe dropped the paperclip. "All right. I want you to come back to the lab with me and take pictures of the two autopsies I'm doing."

"Why can't you take them?"

"You take better pictures."

Jake smiled.

"It wasn't a compliment."

"Of course it was. When you tell someone they do something better than you, normal people call that a compliment."

"Fine." He rose to his feet. He towered a good three inches over Jake. "Are you coming or not?"

"Yeah, just let me tell Maria where I'll be." He grabbed his camera from the lower drawer of his desk.

"How'd you like to ride in a real car instead of that gay-pride float you own?"

"At least I own my float."

Abe gave him a condescending smile. "I wouldn't list that as an accomplishment, if I were you. It's like taking pride in shopping in a thrift store. If you aren't careful, you'll be a middle aged hipster."

Jake frowned. Since he lost his job as a loan officer, he'd done his share of shopping in thrift stores, but he didn't do it *ironically*. He did it because he had no choice.

"Let's go out the backdoor and avoid the mayhem out front."

"Fine," Jake grumbled and pulled out his phone, sending a text to Maria.

76

They wound through the cubicles to the little used back door of the precinct. Abe shoved it open. A weak spring sun was peeking through the layer of clouds. They could hear the muted sounds of voices from the parking lot where the paparazzi had gathered. Abe pointed up the street and began walking.

They came to a Mini-Cooper squatting next to a parking meter. Jake stopped in mid-stride and frowned.

"What the hell is that?"

Abe pushed the remote button and unlocked the doors. "A real car that I didn't have to collect box-tops to buy."

Jake placed his hand on the roof of the tiny car. "You make fun of the Daisy, but this is a clown car, Abe. How the hell do you fold those long legs into it?"

Abe gave him a wicked smile and Jake wished he'd been more careful with his words. "I'll just bet you want to know, don't you, pumpkin?"

Refusing to take the bait, Jake opened the door and climbed down into the seat. Placing the camera case on his lap, he wrapped his arms around it, feeling as if his knees were pressed up beneath his chin. He watched Abe contort himself to fit behind the steering wheel.

With a laugh, he shook his head. "Oh yeah, this is so much better than my car."

Abe turned the ignition. "You just don't know style when you see it."

"One person's style is another person's torture."

"Deep," mocked Abe. "Now with all due sweetness, close your mouth and let me drive."

* * *

Peyton and Marco stopped at the counter to be processed into the holding cells. As they waited for the officer to sign them in, Peyton noticed Smith heading toward them.

"You're cleared," said the officer.

Peyton smiled at him. "Can you get me the results of Ravensong's drug test?"

"On it."

Peyton and Marco moved into the corridor and stopped in front of Smith. "Hey, Frank."

"Brooks, D'Angelo."

"What are you doing down here?"

"Came to see Ravensong."

"Why?"

Smith shrugged. "He bothers me."

"Bothers you? How?"

Glancing around, Smith shifted weight. "I know the evidence is stacked against him, but…"

"But?"

"Did you know I'm a recovering alcoholic?"

Peyton glanced at Marco. "No, I didn't."

"Yep. Been clean for six years now."

"That's amazing, Frank."

"Not so much. It's a constant struggle. Six years and I still think about it, wishing I could go into a bar and have a shot, drink a beer while watching a game. Some days it isn't so bad, but others…it's damn hard to get out of bed in the morning." He smoothed his mustache. "Here's the thing. I know what he's talking about – the black-outs. I had them too."

Marco gave a grunt of disagreement. "He says he has them when he's clean. Didn't you only have black-outs when you were drinking?"

"Yeah, but drugs are a different animal. This is the thing, though. The black-outs never worried me. I ignored them, until this one time."

"What happened?" asked Peyton.

"I woke up and I had my gun in my hand. I hadn't shot it, but…" He released his breath. "I could have killed someone and not even remembered doing it. I joined AA the next day."

Peyton and Marco waited for him to continue.

He looked down toward the holding cells, then back at them. "I know what he's feeling. I know how scary it is to have this blank spot in your head. And I know what it feels like to think you could have done something unspeakable."

Peyton reached out and touched his arm. "Thank you for telling us, Frank. It helps us with a motive."

"I'm not sure it helps anything, Brooks. This whole thing sucks for everyone involved."

Peyton squeezed his arm. "I know."

"No, you don't, but that's good. I wouldn't wish addiction on anyone. Go easy on him. You have the evidence you need. You don't really need a confession. He might give it to you just because he doesn't remember what happened. You've got enough for a conviction already. You don't need to break him anymore than he is."

"I wasn't going to go for a confession, but I'll keep your advice in mind."

"Thanks," he said, giving a nod to Marco and moving toward the exit.

Peyton and Marco shared a look. "Wow," she breathed.

"Yeah, your rock star is getting to everyone. What the hell power has this guy got?"

The officer appeared behind Marco. "Inspector Brooks, here's your report." He passed Peyton a piece of paper.

"Thank you," said Peyton as she took it. She read the report, then gave a short whistle, holding it out to Marco. "Take a look at this."

Marco read it, then stared at it hard. "He's clean?"

"Apparently."

"I know he was on something, Brooks."

"Well, you were wrong. We both were." She motioned down the corridor. "Let's go check his hands."

They found Ravensong sitting on his cot, his back to the wall, his feet braced on the floor, his arms crossed over his chest. Peyton motioned for the officer at the holding desk to let her into the cell. As he pressed the automatic lock and the door slid back, Peyton studied Ravensong.

Even in prison garb, he was handsome. His hair lay over his shoulders and framed a face that was both masculine and border-line pretty. His high cheekbones and darkly lashed eyes were almost perfectly proportional. Although he wasn't nearly as tall as Marco, he was fit, his shoulders straining the lines of his jumpsuit.

The door clanged as it stopped and Peyton entered the cell, taking a seat on the cot next to him, while Marco loomed in the entrance. Shifting, Peyton placed the paper on her lap and faced their prisoner. "How are you holding up?"

He gave her a disbelieving stare. "How am I holding up? Are you serious?"

"To be honest, I'm not exactly sure how to open a conversation in here."

"That's obvious."

She held up the paper. "We got your drug test. You're clean."

"I know. Ten years, 264 days, 8 hours."

"Hours?"

"When I stopped counting minutes, I considered that progress."

Peyton's gaze was drawn to his hands. He had them folded against his chest, but the right one was on top and his knuckles were still raw and swollen. "Did a doctor check out your hand?"

He flexed his fingers. "Nothing broken."

"Well, that's something."

His eyes narrowed on her. "Something?"

Peyton shrugged. She guessed he had a right to be contentious in his predicament. "It's something good."

"How is any of this good, Inspector Brooks? Elena had to tell my daughter her mother is dead and I wasn't there. It was my responsibility, but I wasn't there. No, you're wrong. Nothing's good."

"Okay."

"No, it's not okay. Do you know what it's like sitting here thinking that maybe I killed someone?" He shook his head violently. "Not someone. The mother of my child. I might have killed her and I don't even remember it. I don't remember a damn thing."

He was getting worked up.

Peyton put her hand on his arm and he focused on that to the exclusion of everything else. "Look, Joshua, we found out some information a little while ago and I'd like to follow that lead."

"I don't know what you're talking about."

"You're sure you don't remember anything from yesterday?"

"Not a thing between my house and when you called my name."

Peyton folded the paper. "The Medical Examiner had a chance to look at Terry's body this morning."

Ravensong closed his eyes.

Peyton pushed on. "It turns out Terry was bludgeoned with a leaded-glass object, perhaps a paperweight. Do you remember seeing anything like that in her condo whenever you visited?"

"Visited?"

"Picked up Tiffany maybe."

At the mention of his daughter, he leaned forward, hugging his arms around his waist. "I never went into the condo. We did our exchanges in the garage."

Which explained why he returned to the garage after the murder happened. It was familiar, safe.

"Okay. Well, here's the thing. This glass curio or whatever it was broke on impact."

Ravensong flinched when she said that. "Broke?"

"Yes, pieces were lodged in Terry's scalp." She deliberately didn't tell him they were embedded in her brain.

"What does this have to do with anything?"

"The killer most likely cut his hand when the curio broke, maybe many times."

Ravensong's dark eyes swung up to Marco. "What are you saying?"

"I need to see your palms, Joshua. I need to see if you have any cuts."

He leaned back again, considering both of them. Peyton waited as patiently as she could, which wasn't very patient.

When he didn't respond, she added, "We can get your lawyer in here to observe if you'd feel better, but if necessary, I can get a search warrant."

He still didn't move as if he was contemplating the situation, then without warning, he unfolded his arms and held out his hands, palms up. Peyton was struck first by the horrible scars that ran down from the base of his palms to his forearms. He'd sliced through both veins in his wrists. She wondered how he hadn't done nerve damage. Then she focused on his palms and his fingers.

Reaching out, she took his hands and pulled them into the light shining through the cell door. He grimaced when she brushed his raw knuckles, but he didn't pull away. Peyton turned his hands every direction she could to shine light on them.

"D'Angelo?"

He stepped into the cell and also inspected the rock star's open palms. "Shit," he muttered and met Peyton's gaze.

"What?" said Ravensong.

Peyton released him. "You have no cuts, Joshua. Not one single blemish. How the hell is that possible?"

CHAPTER 5

The sunlight streaming through the bay windows created a nimbus around him. He looked almost insubstantial in the glow, as if I could blink and he'd disappear. He was facing the window, but he was looking at his hands, reading the papers I'd printed for him. He said he needed it in print, he couldn't really get a feel for it on the cold, impersonal screen of the laptop. I understood that. I needed to print things out myself, I needed the solidity of paper in my grip. Technology was wonderful for so much, but it definitely distanced you from everything…including people.

Today he wore a printed shirt, but the tails hung down around his hips. The boots had been traded for converse sneakers, but the bands of leather still swathed his wrists. I knew about the scars they hid, even though we hadn't gotten to that part of the story yet. Still, I'd done my research. This was a man who'd tried to kill himself. A man who'd nearly succeeded. It made the strange glow of sunlight around him all the more surreal.

We'd spent hours together over the last week. I was becoming comfortable with the quiet side of him, the side that talked in that low, smoky voice, but I had also seen the side that looked at his own life with a wry sense of humor. Then there were the times when he tensed and shut down. Those moments scared me for him as if there were secrets too dark to share. I had to admit what had started as a crush was morphing into something more – that age-old obsession all sensible women had for the bad boy and the desire we all harbored to save them.

He turned and I caught my breath. Would he like what I wrote or had I gone too far, put too much of him into it?

Coming forward, he laid the papers on the desk and stared down at me with those dark eyes. *Oh yes*, I thought, *I definitely wouldn't mind trying to save you.*

"It's good."

I let out my breath and felt myself relax. His praise, simple as it was, fell over me like a blanket. I really shouldn't want his approval. It was inappropriate. As I'd said before, I considered myself a professional, but he made the lines blur. Yep, I was falling in love with him.

"So, are you ready to continue?"

He sank into the chair and folded his hands in his lap. "How do you make it seem so rational? Everything I've told you, none of it seems rational."

"I'm not sure I understand."

"That's probably not the word. I'm not sure what I mean, but I tell you a bunch of memories and you pull it together." He twisted the band on his wrist. I was coming to recognize that as a defensive mechanism when he was agitated, but whatever he needed to do, I figured, if it kept him from doing something far more destructive. "You make those memories fit together like a puzzle. When I read it, I can't help but wonder…" He trailed off and sank back against the chair.

"Wonder what?"

"How I didn't see it, how I didn't know where things would go. And if I had seen it, why couldn't I prevent it, stop it from happening?"

"You were too close to it. You know that saying, hindsight is 20/20. I don't think anyone really sees the pattern of their own lives or the warnings."

He studied me, sitting silent and still. These moments, and there were a lot, unnerved me, as if I was the one we were psychoanalyzing. Then he shook himself and a faint smile lit up his face. "You're right."

I felt myself relax again. He brought out strong emotions in me, but I was smart enough to realize he was exhausting. Being with him on a more intimate level would be emotionally draining.

I focused on my notes and picked up a pen. "When you were here last, we were talking about high school. You were a freshman and James was a senior." I tapped the pen against my lower lip. "You and James became very close over the years, didn't you?"

He considered that. "Close, yeah. At some point it didn't matter that we had different parents, we were brothers, family. Still are. It's the same way with Jennifer. I don't know how it happened. Maybe it was everything we went through together, everything I put them through, but they've always been there for me."

"That's important, isn't it? Having people at your back?"

He stared at the paper on my desk. "Important? Yeah, it's important, but it's hard too. If there's no one at your back, then you have no one to disappoint. No one to betray." His voice dropped, but I still heard him. "No one to hurt."

*   *   *

Mark Edwards threw out his arm, stopping James, and pointed toward the quad. James could make out a group of seniors standing around in a circle. One was Luke Ames and some of his teammates, and across from him was Sarah Jameson and her closest girlfriends. Standing between them was Joshua. James couldn't hear what they were saying, but he could tell from the postures that it wasn't anything good.

He dropped his baseball bag on the ground, reaching for the handle on his bat and tugging it out. Mark did the same, grabbing his own bat. Together they advance on the group as quickly as they could.

Before James could close the distance, Luke shouted something at Joshua and shoved him. Joshua staggered back, but he didn't swing, didn't shove him back. He made no move to retaliate.

"Leave him alone, Luke!" said Sarah.

Luke spat a string of cuss words and started for Joshua again, but James managed to close with them, holding his bat against his side. Luke pulled up short and took in the two ball players spoiling to enter the fight.

"Stay out of this, Connor." His eyes tracked down to the bat and back again. His teammates moved close behind him.

James didn't really want to fight Luke and his two friends, and he figured if he had to use the bat, he'd probably be expelled. But he only had a few months left anyway and he didn't plan on going to college, so what the hell. "Leave him alone."

"Tell the little prick to stop sniffing around my girl."

"I don't think he's been the one sniffing around, Ames."

Luke lunged forward, but one of his friends held him back. He puffed up his chest, trying to make himself bigger. James' fingers tightened on the bat, but he didn't bring it up. He really didn't want to use it.

Luke pointed over James' shoulder at Joshua. "He comes around her again and he dies."

"Then tell the bitch to stay away."

"I'm serious, Connor. Keep him away." He feinted at James, but James held his ground. When he saw he couldn't intimidate James with his size, he made a motion with his chin at the girl. "Let's go!"

She hesitated. James could see her out of the corner of his eyes.

"Sarah!"

She hurried to his side and he slung his arm around her shoulders, possessively. Then he backed away with her, finally turning and striding out of the quad with his friends. Sarah's girlfriends trailed after them, looking back at James and Mark as they went.

James eased his hold on the bat.

"Dick," muttered Mark.

James nodded. "Thanks."

Mark shrugged. "Hate those football pricks."

"Yep."

"Later," said Mark, turning the way they'd come and catching up his bag as he jogged toward the parking lot.

"Later," called James. "Let's go, Josh." He retraced his steps to his bag and shoved the bat inside, then he swung it over his shoulder. When he straightened again, he realized Joshua hadn't followed him.

He turned around. Joshua had moved deeper into the quad and had taken a seat at one of the picnic tables that littered the area. James went after him, dropping the bag on the table.

Joshua had his back turned, facing a planter bed. Jasmine vines trailed over the sides of the raised bed and the smell was cloying as it hung in the late autumn air.

Joshua's arms were braced on his thighs and his hands were clasped before him.

"I told you Luke Ames was a prick. Why didn't you listen?"

Joshua didn't answer, didn't even turn. James crossed around the table and sat down next to him. "I don't think he'll mess with you again, but you've got to stay away from that bitch Sarah."

Joshua still didn't answer.

James socked him in the shoulder. "We've also got to teach you how to fight. Especially if you're gonna mess around with girls like that."

"I know how to fight."

James stretched out his legs and folded his hands on his belly. "Right."

Joshua looked up at him. "I know how to fight."

"Then why'd you let that asshole shove you around?"

He looked away again.

"Josh?"

He leaned back. "Mrs. Clark gave us this article the other day."

"The health teacher?"

"Yeah."

"What the hell does that have to do with Luke Ames?"

Joshua chewed on his lower lip. "Forget it."

James forced himself to be patient. He'd had plenty of years learning to be patient with his brother. Joshua didn't talk much, but when he did, you'd better listen. "Tell me."

Joshua pushed a pebble with the toe of his converse. "The article was about abused children."

James went still. They didn't often talk about Joshua's father, but it was always there between them. "Yeah?"

Joshua chewed his lip again. "About how some percentage, I think it was 30% of abusers were abused themselves as children."

James shrugged. "Okay? What does that have to do with you?"

Joshua stared at James as if he couldn't believe he was so stupid. "I did some research on my own. The statistics are bad. Adults who were abused as children commit more violent crimes than those that weren't."

James tried to laugh and ease the tension, but it came out strained. "Okay, so there's some statistic. Who the hell cares? You aren't your father. You don't even see him anymore." Suddenly, he looked hard at Joshua. "Is that why you wouldn't fight Luke Ames? You're afraid you'll become him."

Joshua's gaze was unwavering. His dark eyes pierced into James, looking through him. "No, I didn't fight Luke Ames because while you were standing there hoping he didn't make you use that bat…" His eyes narrowed and his jaw clenched. "I was standing there thinking that if I took a swing at him, I wouldn't stop until his head broke and his brains spilled out."

* * *

Jake lowered the camera. "I think I got everything."

Abe pulled on a pair of latex gloves. "You wanna stay while I do the autopsy and take some more."

"Not so much. This is bad enough." He tried not to look directly at the woman, but it was like watching a car wreck, it was hard to look away. "I'll never understand how people can do something like this."

Abe moved to the table and leaned over, looking at the wound where the left side of her face had been. "This one makes a little sense. It was obviously done in the heat of the moment. He lost control and let her have it with whatever was handy." Abe canted a look up at Jake, his beads tinkling. "Now your other body is a lot more confusing. Why execute a bum?"

"I thought you wanted me to take pictures of him too."

"Yeah, I do."

"Why do you have to do an autopsy on her? It's pretty obvious what killed her."

"Have to be thorough. The D.A. wants all t's dotted and i's crossed."

Jake took a step away from the autopsy table. "She was pretty, wasn't she?"

He felt Abe's gaze on him. "You okay?"

Jake gave a strange laugh. "I was a loan officer. I didn't like the job, but I didn't have to look at dead bodies."

"So go back to it."

"I can't now. I don't like seeing dead people, but I like feeling like I'm doing something." He held up a hand and let it fall. "It's just this...this seems so senseless. Two lives are ruined over this – well, more than that. There's a little girl without a mother or a father now."

Abe grabbed the sheet and pulled it over the body. "Look, think of it this way. You're still doing something. Maybe this isn't the best outcome, but at least for her, we're giving her some closure."

"Really? Do you believe that?"

Abe shrugged. "Sure. Why not? Besides, can you see me making loans to people?"

Jake laughed. "No, that I cannot see."

"Come on. Let's go take pictures of the bum and then I'll buy you a liquid lunch."

"Liquid lunch?"

Abe gave him a condescending look.

"Oh no, I'm not going to lunch with you. I remember the last time I drank with you."

Abe moved toward the door. "That guy just wanted to dance with you, but you panicked."

"Damn straight I panicked," said Jake, following him. "He made two of me and he wasn't in the mood to take no for an answer."

They walked into the hallway and turned left.

"I saved you," said Abe, stepping to the next door over and pressing the button to open it.

"Yeah, by telling him I was your boyfriend."

Abe gave a wicked giggle. "It worked, didn't it? Besides, think of the sacrifice I had to make." He gave Jake a serious once-over. "You are *so* not my type."

"But Adonis is?"

"My Angel is everyone's type." He waved his arms and the lights came on.

The air conditioner rumbled overhead and Jake rubbed his arms against the cold. The body lay on a table similar to the other one with a drape pulled over it.

"How come you got both of them?"

"I do most of the work for the precinct. Thank God medical deaths are the bulk of our business and the other M.E.s usually take those. Boring, if you ask me. It's just carving up fat guys who die from heart attacks."

"You're really compassionate, aren't you?"

Abe grabbed the drape and pulled it back. "I'm honest, that's all."

The body was shrunken and grey. Without the many layers of clothes, the vic looked small and frail. Jake couldn't understand why anyone would want to shoot him in the back of the head. The exit wound sat nearly in the middle of his forehead, the edges blackened, but if he peered closely enough, he could see bone fragment and brain matter in the gaping hole.

Jake lifted the camera and snapped off a number of pictures. "What kind of gun do you think it was?"

"By the powder burn on the back of his skull and the size of the entrance hole, I'd say a Colt, maybe Smith & Wesson."

"Any other wounds?"

Abe pulled back the sheet completely. The bum's chest was sunken, his arms and legs wiry and thin. Jake scanned him quickly. In some ways, this emaciated corpse was worse than the woman. He'd been barely holding onto life and yet someone had felt even that pitiful existence was worth stealing.

Jake snapped a few more pictures, but as he turned to move around the foot of the table, he hesitated, looking at the man's ankle. A thin, black snake wrapped above the bone on his ankle and ended at the top of his foot. It was poorly designed, amateurish.

"Abe, look at this."

Abe leaned over and studied it. "Looks like a prison tat."

"Do we have a name on him?"

Abe moved back toward the vic's head and picked up a clipboard, looking at it. "We found a scrap of paper from Glide Memorial. He stayed there last month. Under name it said Kimbro."

Jake reached into his bag and pulled out his computer tablet. He thumbed it on and typed in the public records website for California. Clicking on the criminal record link, he keyed over to *Name*. "Kimbro must be a last name, right?"

"Don't know."

Jake typed it in, then pressed enter. A moment later he got a list of all Kimbros in the records. "Anything else on the ticket you found?"

Abe bent under the table and pulled out a sealed bag. In it were the man's clothes, the note Jake had found with the words *Clean-up Crew* on it, and a smudged ticket. Abe turned it and pressed it flat. "It might be a U or a W. I can't tell."

Jake scanned down the list. "W? There's a Wayne Kimbro." As he clicked on the name, Abe came around the table and looked over his shoulder. An arrest record scrolled across the screen and on the right side was a mug shot. Both Jake and Abe glanced at the body. The man on the mug shot was a bit heavier, younger maybe, and clean shaven, but it was obviously their vic.

"That's him. What'd they get him for?" asked Abe.

Jake scanned the arrest records a few times, then frowned, lowering the tablet. "Child molestation," he said.

Suddenly, all sympathy he'd been feeling bled away.

* * *

Peyton set her hamburger down.

Marco looked up from his own meal. "Not hungry?"

She shrugged. "Why doesn't he have cuts on his hands?"

Marco picked up a carrot and bit off the end. "Maybe Abe was wrong."

"When has Abe ever been wrong?"

Marco held up a hand in acquiescence. "There's always a first time. What's the alternative, Brooks? We have the text messages, so we know she planned to take their daughter out of the country. Motive. We literally have her blood on his hands. Evidence. And we can place him at the crime scene. Suspect. We've got all three legs of your daddy's stool. So one part of it doesn't fit. I don't think Devan is going to be worried about that when he takes it to the Grand Jury."

Peyton picked a piece of lettuce off the burger and placed it in her mouth. "I know."

Marco gave her a strange look.

"What?"

"This is definitely bothering you. You just ate something green."

Peyton grabbed a fry and threw it at him. He caught it and placed it in his mouth.

"Brooks?"

Peyton looked over her shoulder. Maria was standing in the doorway. "Hey, sweetcakes, did you want to share my lunch?"

Maria glared at her. "I'd rather die of starvation." She gave Marco a smoldering once over. "However, I'll share your lunch anytime, Marco baby."

"Aw, you just keep playing hard to get and it makes me think we don't have any future," purred Peyton.

Maria ignored the remark. "The girlfriend is here and she wants to see you."

"Ravensong's girlfriend?"

"No, yours."

Maria's eyes widened as soon as she realized what she'd said, but Peyton smiled wickedly. "You're the only girlfriend I have, sweetie."

"She wants to talk to you. What do I tell her?"

Peyton pushed herself to her feet. "I'm coming."

When Marco started to pick up his lunch, Maria motioned him back down. "She asked to see Brooks alone."

He frowned.

Peyton gave him a sympathetic pat on the shoulder. "I know it's hard to believe that a woman wouldn't want to see you, D'Angelo, but then again, look who she's got sharing her bed."

"I don't know why you women get all hot and bothered around him."

93

Peyton halted beside Maria and glanced back at him. The two women exchanged a look, then they both laughed.

"What?"

"It's sad, really," said Peyton to Maria.

She nodded. "It's all right, baby, I still think you're a close 9."

Marco frowned as the two of them left the room.

Peyton found Elena and another young woman standing in the lobby. The other woman was in her late twenties, blond, blue eyed and pretty. She would have made a perfect stereotypical cheerleader at any high school.

Elena looked tired. She wore no make-up and her eyes were red-rimmed. Her hair was neatly combed back in a bun, but it only emphasized the bleakness of her expression. She wore a pair of jeans and a loose sweater that looked about two sizes too big.

"Hey, Elena. Maria said you wanted to see me."

Elena nodded.

Peyton stopped on the other side of the counter. "What can I do for you?"

"Can we talk in private?"

Peyton reached for the half door and pulled it open. "Sure, come in." She motioned to the conference room, then followed the two women inside. Elena took the first available seat and the young woman sat down at her side, clasping Elena's hands with both of her own.

"This is Joshua's sister, Jennifer."

Peyton reached out her hand and the young woman accepted it. "I'm Inspector Brooks." Her eyes shifted to Elena. "How can I help you?"

"Joshua's lawyer, Drew Steinberg, got bail set and Joshua's scheduled to be released tonight. Hopefully when the media frenzy has died down."

"Good. How did Tiffany take the news?"

"She's devastated. She keeps asking for her father." Elena pressed her hand against her temple as if she fought back tears, but her eyes were dry. Peyton figured she'd

94

probably done a lot of crying over the last day. "Here's the thing, Inspector Brooks. I need your help."

Peyton frowned. "With all due respect, Elena, I'm surprised you asked to see me. I thought our last conversation didn't go as well as I'd hoped."

Elena flattened a hand on the table. "I don't have anyone else I can go to."

Jennifer stirred. "Please listen to her, Inspector Brooks. It's important for all of us."

"I'm listening."

"Joshua is checking himself into a psych facility as soon as he's released."

Peyton blinked in surprise. She hadn't expected that. "I see."

"He's convinced he's capable of murder. You convinced him."

"I don't think I convinced him, but even so, I'm not sure what you want me to do."

"Talk to him. Tell him to go home where he belongs."

She drummed her fingers on the table. She hated it when people asked her to intervene in their lives. "Here's the thing, Elena. I actually think it's a good idea. I think he's smart to make this decision."

Elena's eyes widened and Jennifer looked like she'd been slapped. "How can you say that? How can you believe this is a good thing?"

"He's trying to protect you and his daughter. I think it's for the best and I'd leave it alone if I were you."

Elena's face hardened. "How can you believe he's capable of something so horrible? As a woman, I expected you to be more open-minded, more sympathetic, but you aren't considering any other possibility, are you?"

Peyton leaned forward. "I wish it was different, Elena. I really do, but you've got to see where we're coming from. There just isn't any other explanation, any other suspect. Everything points to him." She deliberately left out the lack of cuts on his hand. She really didn't think it meant anything and even if it did, all other evidence pointed to Ravensong. "He doesn't even deny it."

"Because he can't remember what happened!" She slammed her fist on the table. Fighting for composure, she held up a hand. "He isn't a violent man, Inspector Brooks. He's never hurt anyone in his life."

Peyton tried to keep her voice neutral, but it was hard. Why were women so blind, such idiots for love? "His knuckles are raw, Elena. Come on. He obviously struck something. Everybody has a breaking point and he reached his. He's right to commit himself. He's doing the sane, responsible thing."

Elena didn't respond. Her jaw clenched. Then she rose to her feet.

Jennifer rose with her. "Where are you going?"

"I'm going to call his lawyer. See if there's anything he can do." She glared down at Peyton. "I'm certain you feel you're doing your job, and I'm certain this seems like an easy win for you, but you are ruining countless lives with your inability to look beyond what is right in front of you. Not everything is exactly as it seems."

"And yet, sometimes it is exactly as it seems, Elena. I really am sorry."

"That doesn't help," she said, tossing her hand up and backing to the door. "That doesn't help a damn thing."

Jennifer moved to go after her, but she stopped and turned back around. Peyton rose to her feet and braced herself for a dressing down. "You don't know my brother, Inspector Brooks. You don't know anything about him." She stepped back into the room and faced Peyton. "If he *broke* as you say, he wouldn't have hurt Terry."

Peyton sighed. What was the point of arguing this madness?

"I've never told anyone this, and I ask that you keep it to yourself."

Peyton nodded, feeling a knot form in her stomach. Maybe here would be answers, confessions, secrets revealed. Anything to explain this murder, and moreso, this loyalty. Jennifer was clearly not Ravensong's biological sister, but that didn't seem to matter to her.

"I was there the first time he tried to kill himself."

"When he slashed his wrists?"

"No." Her eyes were unwavering. This one was strong. No useless tears for her. "I was at the window of the car before he drove it into a tree. Everyone else thought he lost control because he was drugged out of his mind, but I know better. I saw his face, I looked into his eyes. I knew the minute he decided that he had to end it. He didn't do it for himself. He did it for us, to save us from him."

Peyton felt the knot get tighter. One thing they taught in the academy was to not let a perp get under your skin, to keep objectivity. Joshua Ravensong was screwing with her objectivity.

"I was also there when he held his daughter for the first time and I saw his face then, and I knew he would never do anything to hurt her, no matter how bad it might get." She pointed at Peyton. "That's the man my brother is, that is the man who would never hurt his daughter so terribly by taking her mother away from her." She let her hand fall against her thigh. "So you remember that when you decide you're sure of his guilt."

Peyton followed her out into the lobby. Elena had her phone pressed to her ear. She gave Peyton a withering glare, then closed the phone. Outside the doors, the paparazzi milled about, waiting to pounce on anyone who left the precinct. Jennifer moved to Elena's side and put her arm around her, and together they pushed open the doors.

Reporters and photographers descended on them, swooping in like mechanical vultures, snapping away as both women ducked their heads, pushing their way through the throng. Peyton watched them from the safety of Maria's desk, wondering if she shouldn't have offered them an escort to their car.

After they disappeared from view, she looked down. Maria was also watching after them.

"Did you find that article about Ravensong's father for me?"

"Yep, I sent it to your email."

"What about the CPS reports?"

"Nothing for his daughter, and only one for him." She shook her head. "Almost makes you want to cry. I sent you the link for that as well."

"Thank you." She glanced out the doors again. "Do you think you can find anything on his car accident? The one where he apparently drove into a tree."

"I remember that. Yeah, I can find it."

"You remember him driving into a tree?"

Maria kept her eyes fixed on the parking lot. "While you had a crush, I was obsessed. I devoured everything about that man."

"What's bothering you, Brooks?" came Defino's voice. She was leaning on the doorjamb to her office.

"A lot. I hate this case. It makes me feel sick inside."

Defino stepped back. "Come in and debrief me."

Peyton followed the captain into the office and took a seat on the other side of the glass desk. Defino sat down opposite her.

"What's going on?"

"I don't know. Maybe Marco's right and I'm caught up in Ravensong's charisma, but the case just seems too neat and tidy."

"We always second-guess those cases, but we should be grateful for them. They are few and far between. We have a motive, he was at the scene with her blood on him. It's enough for a Grand Jury." She leaned her elbows on the desk. "And let me tell you, Devan is going to be calling either today or tomorrow, expecting it to be released."

"I think we need more time."

Defino shook her head sadly. "For what?"

Peyton scooted forward in her chair. "Abe believes the murder weapon was a heavy-leaded crystal something, maybe a curio or paperweight."

"Okay?"

"The weapon broke in the murderer's hand. Abe believes there's no way the killer would have escaped deep cuts on his palm or fingers."

"And let me guess? You checked Ravensong's hands."

"Yep, there's nothing there."

"Hm. Where is the murder weapon then?"

"I don't know. We didn't find anything. We held the dumpster at the condo and her own garbage. The evidence department is going through it today. Maybe something will turn up."

"Ravensong was at the scene. He was covered in her blood. His right hand is a mess. What other explanation could there be?"

"There isn't one, but Abe is sure about the murder weapon."

"Maybe he's wrong about the suspect's injuries though?"

"That's what Marco thought."

"But?"

"But, Abe's never wrong."

"If you could give me another theory...anything. I might be able to hold Devan off, but he's going to want something compelling, Brooks."

"This is a man whose life is at stake here, Captain. More than that, his daughter only has one parent left. Both her grandmother and mother are dead now. She needs her father. Don't you think we owe it to her to spend a little more time on this case?"

Defino considered Peyton's request for a moment. Peyton stayed stock still, waiting. Finally, the captain sighed. "Okay, what do we know?"

"We know that Terry had promised Ravensong custody of his daughter. Terry's possessions were packed and Tiffany's were not. At some point on the day of her death, she changed her mind and sent Ravensong a text telling him she was taking their daughter with her. He was upset and went to her condo to confront her."

"Where did she plan to move?"

"Somewhere in Europe. I'm not sure which country."

"Europe's expensive. How did she plan to afford such a move?"

"I'm not sure about that either."

"Then start where we always do once we have a suspect."

Peyton smiled.

"Follow the money," they both said together.

"Get a warrant for her bank records. Maybe something will show up there. That should give me enough to hold off Devan for a few days."

Peyton rose to her feet. "On it." She turned toward the door and stopped. "Thank you, Captain."

"You're thanking me because you're doing your job?"

"No, thank you for not questioning why I want to investigate further."

Defino leaned back in her chair. "I know you, Brooks. There was no way you couldn't get personally involved with this one."

Peyton hesitated. She wasn't sure what the captain meant, but she figured it was probably best not to question it. "Right," she said and pulled open the door.

CHAPTER 6

James heard the vibration of the keyboard, the electronic hum of the notes. He eased down the stairs, peering between the spindles on the banister. The band equipment was set up just as he'd left it, the drum set tucked back under the stairs, the bass guitar on its stand, the amplifiers and microphones each where they had been. Reaching the bottom of the stairs, he turned, then hesitated.

Joshua was sitting on a bar stool beneath the half-window, his fingers a blur of motion over the keys. Sunlight filtered through the dusty window and landed on him. Before him was the score that James and the others had penned just yesterday, and Joshua seemed to be playing it.

James felt a rush of annoyance. He'd been given the basement as his sanctuary away from the other kids, especially now that his father and Mary had a freakin' litter. The twins and Susan weren't allowed down here because of the stairs and Jennifer had been forbidden by James himself. Joshua had his piano upstairs and James never touched that, so why the hell was he down here on the keyboard?

He stepped over the tangle of cords and around the amplifiers. Once he'd graduated from high school, his father had made him take classes at the local J.C., but he was simply playing at it. He took Art History and Musical Theory, but really he was waiting for his music career to take off. A year ago, he'd permanently traded the baseball bat for a microphone and never looked back. After playing together all through high school, his band, *Blazes*, finally had a record label interested in them and as soon as they got that one perfect song, they were out of here.

He started to shout at Joshua, then stopped. Joshua was playing their song, but not really. He'd done something to it, something different.

Joshua stopped playing and glanced around, sensing someone at his back. The moment he saw James, he scrambled off the stool and backed up. It pained James to see the momentary fear that crossed his features, so he reached for his own guitar and plugged it into the amplifier.

"I'm sorry, James," Joshua stammered.

James nodded at the keyboard. "Play that again." He adjusted the guitar strap on his shoulders and strummed his fingers across the strings. Then he stopped, frowning down at the guitar. Strumming again, he tilted his head and listened, then went through a run of chords. Lifting his head, he speared Joshua with a look. "What did you do to it?" He'd never heard it sound like this before.

Joshua still hadn't taken his seat again. In fact, he had the stool in front of him as if he thought it offered him protection. "It was out of tune."

"Out of tune?"

"Bad."

"You tuned it?"

"Yeah. I'm sorry. I shouldn't have touched it, but it was so bad. So bad."

James smiled and ran through his chords again. "Wow, it sounds…I don't know what."

"In tune."

"I guess, but more."

"That's because you've never heard it in tune before."

James glanced up at him, then they both broke into laughter. "Okay, okay." He nodded at the keyboard again. "Play what you were playing before I came down."

Joshua's smile dried and he didn't move toward the instrument.

"What's wrong with you? Play it."

Joshua dropped his eyes and chewed at his lower lip.

"Josh? What the hell? You've already been caught. Just play the damn song."

"I changed it."

"I know."

"I shouldn't have. It was your song."

"Just play it for me, okay? Shit. Don't make me beg. And stop looking at the ground. I hate it when you do that."

Joshua raised his eyes. "You sure? You're not mad?"

"You're pissing me off somethin' awful right now, but no, I'm not mad. That song is gonna get me out of this circus. I need it to be the best we've got or the producer won't even listen to it."

Joshua gave him a ghost of a smile and edged back to the keyboard. James tried to be patient with him, but sometimes his quirky ways annoyed the hell out of him. He'd never struck his brother, never even in play, so why did he act skittish as a cat all the time? His annoyance dissipated in the next moment, however.

Joshua started to play, a haunting, melodious ballad that captivated James where he stood.

"Holy shit," he breathed and forgot to play himself.

* * *

Marco pulled the Charger into the parking lot of the M.E.'s office and turned off the ignition. As he set the brake, he looked over at Peyton. She was staring at the back of the building.

The podium where the guard once sat had been dismantled and moved inside. They needed an ID card to get through the door now.

Marco reached over and covered her hand. "You okay?"

Peyton forced a smile for him, but she suspected it looked strange. "Yeah."

He squeezed her fingers. "You don't have to go inside. I can do it."

She squeezed him back. "I can do inside. It's getting to the door that's a bitch."

He opened the Charger's door. "Come on. Best not to think about it over much."

"That your philosophy of life?"

He ducked his head back in the car. "Gotten me to thirty, ain't it?"

She smiled at him and opened her own door. Climbing out was okay. She could do that. Shutting the Charger door, got it. Turning toward the building is where it got a little complicated. Marco came around the back of the car and put his arm around her shoulders, propelling her forward.

"Come on. It's like sex the first time. No one enjoys it, but it's gotta be done."

Laughter bubbled out of her and she leaned into him, letting him support her as they walked to the door. Without letting go of her, he pulled his ID card out of his pocket and swiped it across the sensor. The lights on the sensor blinked, then the lock clicked open.

They entered the white, austere hallway and halted by the podium. Six months ago, during their gangbanger case, the guard, who had been stationed outside, had been shot when Peyton had left the building. After he recovered, he'd decided it was time for retirement. This new guard was middle aged, built like a marine and had a nearly shaved head. He slapped a clipboard on the edge of the podium without speaking and pointed to the spot they should sign.

Marco released Peyton and signed them in, then motioned down the hall for her to precede him. Peyton felt a little calmer as she navigated the familiar hallway toward Abe's lab. Peering through the glass window in the door, she could see him fussing with a microscope. She pressed the button for the automatic door and waited as it slid open.

As she and Marco stepped through, Abe looked up and beamed a smile at them. "If it isn't the prettiest cop in San Francisco, and his adorable little sprite of a partner. How are you this wonderful spring morning?"

Marco gave a sarcastic nod, but he didn't respond. He'd learned a long time ago that response only encouraged more flirtation.

Abe's dark chocolate eyes fixed on Peyton. "You okay, soul sista?"

"I am now."

He patted the table and she moved to the stool across from him, taking a seat. "The first time is always the worst."

"What the hell kind of sex did you two have the first time?"

Abe gave her a puzzled look. "I wasn't talking about sex, but if you want to talk about sex, I'm game." He leaned forward, his dreads swinging around his jawline. "I'll tell you about mine, if you tell me yours." He winked up at Marco.

"We won't be doing that!" said Marco. "No, we won't be doing that."

Peyton and Abe laughed.

"So, what's up?" Abe asked, moving the microscope aside.

"Joshua Ravensong doesn't have any cuts on his hand."

Abe braced his chin on his fist. "Ah, interesting."

"Yeah. Here's the thing. Could you have been wrong?"

Abe arched one brow. "Wrong? Me?"

"I know. Ridiculous, huh? But is there any way he could have struck her with the glass curio and not gotten cut? Maybe it wasn't as sharp as you thought?"

Abe swiveled in his chair and picked up an evidence bag. Peyton could see shards of leaded glass in the bottom of it. He carefully opened it, then grabbed a set of latex gloves and pulled them on. Picking up a pair of tweezers, he reached into the bag and snagged a shard of glass. It was larger than Peyton had expected, easily seen with the naked eye.

"Grab me a piece of printer paper, Angel D'," he asked, motioning to the printer with his chin.

Marco retrieved it and handed it to him. Holding the paper in the air between them, Abe used the tweezers and scored down the center of it. It parted, allowing Peyton to see a pink bead on the end of Abe's hair through the gap.

He lowered his hands. "Still think I'm wrong?"

Peyton let out her air. "No. Shit."

"Now what?"

"Yesterday afternoon we subpoenaed her bank records. Hopefully, we'll have them by tomorrow."

He placed the glass shard in the evidence bag and sealed it. Then he pulled off his gloves. "Come on. I'll treat you both to lunch at the Cliff House. The sea air will do you some good."

Peyton glanced at her watch. "Okay, but no drinks."

"Of course not," said Abe, tossing the gloves into the trash. "It's not even noon yet."

* * *

"Morning, Brooks," said Marco, glancing up from his computer.

"Morning, D'Angelo," she answered, settling her coffee on the desk and pulling out her chair. "Pizza and beer tonight at my place?"

"As long as you've got the game on, I'll be there."

"You know it'll be on." Her father, when he was alive, had been an ardent Warriors' fan. She'd never missed a game if she could help it. "Abe wants to come over."

Marco made a face. "He's gonna wanna talk all through the game."

"He can talk to Jake."

"Ryder too? How come we can't just watch the game the two of us anymore?"

"We could have watched it at Vinnie's if you weren't fighting with him over your birthday party."

"I'm not fighting with him."

Peyton gave him an arch look and sat down.

"Ravensong made bail."

"I know, and promptly checked himself into a psych facility."

"Probably for the best."

"Elena didn't see it that way."

Marco leaned on the desk. "Explain it to me. Why do women go for guys like that?"

"How should I know?"

"'Cause you're no better. You were drooling over him the other day too."

"He's gorgeous."

"And an addict and a murderer."

"Suspect."

"Whatever. Face it, Brooks, you're no better."

She acquiesced. "If we knew why we liked his type, we'd be able to avoid his type. That's just the way it is."

"It's stupid."

"So is chasing after every bimbo in a mini-skirt, but men still do it."

Marco ducked back behind his monitor. "Not the same thing at all. I can tell you why I like a bimbo in a mini-skirt, but you can't tell me why you like a drug-addicted murderer."

"Suspect."

"Whatever."

Smiling, Peyton opened her email and clicked on the message Maria had sent her the previous day. The first link led to an interview Ravensong had given where he talked about his father and the abuse he suffered as a child.

The elder Ravensong had a serious drinking problem and battled with bouts of rage. Knowing that didn't make Peyton feel any better about their current case. Maybe Marco was right and the apple didn't fall far from the tree. The predilection for substance abuse had certainly not skipped a generation.

She closed that window and clicked on the CPS report. It had been scanned into the computer, so parts of it were smudged, but she was still able to make out the majority of it. She let out a whistle and picked up her coffee, taking a sip.

"What?" came Marco's disembodied voice.

"I'm reading Ravensong's CPS report from when he was a kid. His father really did a number on him. Concussion, broken pelvis. Why the hell wasn't the bastard arrested?"

"Probably was. Got a few months, some parenting classes and presto, he's fixed."

"Not by half. What a brutal son-of-a-bitch. No wonder his son is a mess." She read through the entire report and kept it open.

"Hm," mumbled Marco.

"What?"

"We just got the warrant to access Terry Ravensong's accounts."

"Great, take a look while I finish this," she said, distractedly.

She went to the final link Maria had sent her. Maria had found the actual police report with photos of Ravensong's car accident. The car had been totaled and by looking at the angle of the shot, it had plowed head-long into the massive tree, folding the front end around the trunk. The photographer had even backed up and taken a picture of the street, the car, the tree and the yard. There were no skid marks to indicate the brakes had ever been applied.

Scrolling up to the report, she scanned it. The responding officer had even remarked that Ravensong hadn't appeared to brake. He chalked it up to the high level of narcotics in the rock star's system, but Peyton didn't think that was the cause. Jennifer had been right. Ravensong had clearly been trying to commit suicide. Based on the look of the car, he'd damn near been successful.

"Uh, Brooks, come here a moment."

Peyton glanced up. "What did you find?"

"I'm not sure."

Peyton rose to her feet and crossed around to his desk. "What?"

Marco used the mouse wheel to scroll through a long list of numbers, large numbers. "See all these?"

Peyton squinted and leaned closer, putting her hand on his shoulder. "Yeah."

"They come regular. First of the month, then the fifteenth. Over and over again."

"A lot of money goes into that account."

"Yeah, but it's all regular and most of the time it's the same amount or thereabouts."

"You think it's child support payments from Ravensong."

"They all have the same account number linked to them, so I'm guessing that's his. But look here." He released the mouse and pointed at a spot on the screen. A deposit in the amount of $250,000 had suddenly appeared.

"What's the date on that?"

Marco clicked on the link and a window dropped down. Peyton glanced at the date, then reached for her phone and thumbed it on, pressing the calendar. The deposit had cleared Terry's bank almost a full week before she was murdered.

"Do you think Ravensong was paying her off to keep his daughter in the country?"

Marco shook his head, still staring at the screen. "Look at the account numbers. They're not the same, and there's very little information listed on this one. In fact the account numbers aren't similar at all." He glanced up. "Where's Ryder?"

Peyton straightened. "Jake?" she shouted.

Jake popped up from behind his partition. "You bellowed?"

"Come here a moment."

Jake ambled over and Peyton moved back to give him room.

"Could this be from the same bank as all the rest of these?"

Jake studied the numbers, then reached for the mouse and scrolled up and down. He passed the cursor over the quarter million amount and then stood up. "Nope. That's an off-shore account."

"From where?"

Jake shrugged. "I don't know. I'd have to look up the codes, but I'd guess the Cayman Islands, or someplace like that. Someplace where you don't want people to know you're stashing money."

Marco wheeled around in his chair and looked up at Peyton. "Do you think Ravensong has an off-shore account?"

"He might. If he has a savvy accountant."

"Maybe," said Jake.

"What?"

"It's just usually businessmen, CEOs, that have accounts like that. I don't remember one single entertainer who had one the entire time I worked at the bank. They usually aren't that savvy and their accountants are usually crooks."

Peyton and Marco exchanged a look. "Then who is paying her such massive sums of money? Will the bank give us the name on the account?"

"That's the problem with off-shore accounts. The countries who house them are reluctant to divulge any information. You can try subpoenaing the records, but they'll drag their heels and unless the feds are involved, they may even go so far as to ignore you."

"So now what?" asked Marco, shaking his head.

"Clearly we need to know more about Terry Ravensong and the only one I can think of to ask is her daughter."

"Ravensong will never allow that."

Peyton went around her desk and grabbed her jacket. "Well, I'll just have to convince him to let me give it a try."

"I guess I'm coming."

Peyton hesitated. "Let me go. I think he'll respond better to me."

Marco gave her a sly smile. "You just want to be alone with him."

Peyton rolled her eyes, but didn't answer.

"What about the game?"

"Go on over. I'll be home as soon as I can. It shouldn't take too long."

"Be good. Don't do anything I wouldn't do."

Peyton smiled over her shoulder. "Well, that leaves my options just wide open, dunnit?"

*   *   *

The psychiatric facility sat at the top of a hill, overlooking the whole of the City. Peyton could see all the way out to the ocean. Checking in at the front desk, she was directed to the common room off to the left of the lobby.

As she stepped into the room, the sound of a piano filled the space. The notes were clear, airy, rollicking, the song upbeat and joyful. Ravensong had his back to the door and in front of him were a bank of windows that overlooked the hill, framing the view of the ocean with pleasant navy blue curtains.

She glanced around the room. A fireplace occupied one wall, and overstuffed couches and arm chairs were arranged around a blue and silver rug, covering the dark hardwood of the floor. The piano was a black baby grand and a few lighter arm chairs were arranged in a semicircle around it. In the corners were tables, spread with board games, chess and checkers, and a bookshelf housed a collection of hardbound books to the right of the door.

Ravensong's black hair fell down to mid-shoulder, spreading over his back like a blanket. He had a grey sweatshirt on and a pair of jeans. His converse sneakers worked the pedals on the piano rhythmically, but Peyton marked that the shoes had no laces.

She walked across the floor and stopped on the side of the piano, leaning against it. His fingers continued across the keys without faltering, but he looked up with no hint of surprise in his expression. She could see the bruised knuckles on his right hand and when he shifted, a glimpse of the scars on his wrists. A round hoop earring peeked out of the fall of his hair. She was surprised they hadn't taken that from him.

"Didn't take you long to find a musical instrument, did it?"

He continued playing. "I'm drawn to them. Funny thing is I didn't want to take lessons when my mother suggested it. I wanted to play baseball like my older brother, but the first time I sat down and touched the keys, it was magic. There's something soothing about it."

"I get that."

"You play?"

Peyton smiled. "Not a whit. I am the most unmusically inclined person you've ever met."

He stopped playing and shifted on the bench. "I have to say, Inspector Brooks, I didn't expect to see you again."

"Peyton."

"Peyton?"

"My name is Peyton." She ran her hand over the piano.

"Peyton," he repeated. "Interesting name."

"My father was a fan of Walter Payton, hence the rather unfeminine choice."

He shrugged. "I like it. Different, unique. Suits you."

Peyton didn't want to go down that route. She wasn't immune to his charm and this felt a little too much like flirting. And if she were honest, she suspected she'd started it. "Look, Elena came to see me."

"Ah. She wanted you to stop me from checking in here?"

"Yes."

"I'm not changing my mind."

"I agree with you. I think this was a wise decision."

He considered her a moment, giving her time to study his features. He might be a murderer, she still felt there was little doubt of that, but he was also exceptionally charismatic. "You're here for a reason though."

She nodded. "I'm here for a reason."

He turned his hand over and showed her his unmarked palms. "The glass thing?"

"That and we subpoenaed Terry's bank records."

"So?"

"So, she received a large deposit one week before she died. Did you give her money?"

"I give her money every month on the first and fifteenth. How large a deposit are we talking?"

"Quarter of a million."

Ravensong whistled. "That's large, all right."

"Did she work?"

"Work?"

"Did she have a job?"

"Yeah, her job was milking me."

"I meant a more legitimate form of employment."

"No."

"Did she have a boyfriend?"

He rubbed the scar on his left wrist with his right hand. "She and I rarely talked, we did our exchanges in a garage, and generally we stayed out of each other's lives. She probably had a lot of boyfriends."

Peyton shifted weight. "Look, I'm about to ask something of you and I want you to hear me out before you say no."

He frowned at her.

Peyton continued. "I want to talk to Tiffany."

"No."

Peyton gave a grim laugh. "That's not exactly hearing me out."

"I don't want you talking to my daughter."

Peyton leaned on the piano, bringing herself closer to him. "Listen, Joshua, the D.A. is going to demand we turn the case over to him for a Grand Jury hearing. Once that happens, I can't help you. I have to have some reason to continue working this case."

His eyes narrowed on her. "You have doubts, don't you?"

"I didn't say that. I still think the evidence stacks up pretty strongly against you, but there are a few loose ends I don't like."

"You have doubts, not loose ends. Doubts."

"I haven't given you any reason to believe that."

"But you have. You told me to call you by your first name. You wouldn't do that if you'd written me off as a murderer." He leaned forward, touching a hand in the center of his chest. "I can't remember what happened. It's like there's a gaping hole where my memory is, but I can't see myself striking her either. Now that could be because I can't accept I'd do something like that, but shouldn't I have some memory, some fragment of something if I had done something so horrible."

"I'm not sure that's true, Joshua. You may have blacked the memory simply because you couldn't accept you're capable of doing something like that. The evidence still all points back to you."

His expression fell, shifted inward. He stared down at the piano keys.

Peyton took a seat next to him. "Look, I don't want to get your hopes up, I don't want to give you the wrong idea, but here's the thing. I can't explain why you don't have cuts on your hand and I can't figure out who gave Terry that money. I want to investigate this further. Please let me talk to Tiffany."

"I can't put her through that."

Peyton played her final card. "In the last year, she's lost her grandmother and her mother. I don't want her to lose her father too. I'll be careful with her, I won't push. I'll

114

just ask general questions and if she gets upset, I'll stop. Elena can be with us the whole time."

He lifted his right hand and put it on the keys, compressing them.

"I wouldn't do this if I didn't think it was important."

He gave a distracted nod. "Okay, but you have to promise me you won't upset her or speak badly about her mother."

"I won't do that. I promise you."

He exhaled. "All right, you have my permission."

Peyton suppressed her smile. "So, show me how to play this thing." She settled her fingers over the keys. Ravensong reached around her and covered her hands with his own. She could feel the muscles in his chest shift against her back, and he smelled like soap with a faint hint of saddlewood aftershave.

Closing her eyes, she sucked in a deep breath, trying to still the instant rage of hormones through her body. His touch was warm as he compressed her fingers on the keys, playing a simple melody.

Peyton resisted the impulse to lean back into him, reminding herself he was a murder suspect and a taken-man, but it was hard to concentrate with his arms wrapped around her and the warmth of his breath brushing her cheek.

*　*　*

Peyton opened the door and tossed her keys onto the sofa table. Pickles scrambled over to her as she shrugged out of her jacket and hung it on the rack by the door. Unhooking her gun, she hung that over the coat, then bent to untie her boots.

Marco and Jake were sitting on the bar stools at the counter, the basketball game was on the television, and Abe was in the kitchen, messing with something. It felt homey and comforting. She was happy they were there.

"Hey, Mighty Mouse," said Jake.

"Hey," she answered.

Marco swiveled on the barstool. "How'd it go?"

"He agreed," she said, kicking off her boots. Bending over, she picked up Pickles and cuddled him. He covered her face in delighted doggy kisses.

"He's had dinner and been out already," said Jake.

"Thank you." She checked the score on the game. The Warriors were up by ten, start of the second quarter. She carried Pickles to the bar and climbed onto the stool. "Did you order the pizza? I'm starved."

"It should be here in fifteen minutes," answered Jake.

"Did you set up the meeting with the little girl?" asked Marco, taking a sip of his beer.

"Yeah, Elena agreed to let us come out at 11:00AM tomorrow."

Abe gave her a smile. "You look tired."

She shrugged.

"He got to you, didn't he?" said Marco.

Peyton didn't want to answer that. He got to her in more ways than one. It was so hard to keep her objectivity. Well, to be honest, objectivity had always been a difficult part of her job, but Ravensong was especially hard. He tripped so many of her buttons. He was tied to her adolescence. He was handsome, and charming, and talented, and worst of all, tormented. Peyton couldn't deny she had a weakness for tortured people, which is why Jake Ryder was still living in her house.

Abe watched her as he quartered slices of lemon on a wooden cutting board. "You should let me go with you next time. I want to lust after a hot rock star."

Jake made a choking sound, but Peyton ignored him. "Can we talk about something else?"

"Sure. Let's talk about my latest creation," said Abe.

The three of them watched as he bustled over to the refrigerator and pulled it open. He took out a tray and carried it to the kitchen counter. It was filled with tall glasses and inside was an orange liquid with a swirl of red rising through the center. Crowning the ridge of each was a cherry pierced by a toothpick and topped with a crepe paper raspberry. Peyton studied them in appreciation. She usually avoided Abe's drinks like the devil, but this one was pretty.

"What's it called?" she asked.

Marco and Jake shot her quelling looks, but Abe smiled like a cat in the cream. "I call it Sex at Sunrise."

Peyton's brows rose and she gave him a slow nod.

"It's a Tequila Sunrise with a twist," he finished.

Before she thought better of it, she asked, "What's the twist?"

"Peyton!" Marco and Jake shouted in unison.

She shot a smile at them as Abe rolled his eyes.

"The twist is a twist of lemon," he said innocently, then he leaned toward the two men, placing his chin on his hand. His eyes gleamed with wicked delight. "All sex should come with a twist."

Marco's gaze narrowed on him in a glare, but Jake blushed and looked down. Peyton couldn't help but laugh. They were too funny.

"Give me one," she said bravely.

Marco's stunned gaze shot to her.

She shrugged as Abe pushed the drink across the counter. "Hey, you gotta take some risks sometimes. Man up, D'Angelo," she said as she lifted the glass to her lips.

CHAPTER 7

James tried to hide his excitement as they finished the song for Phil Rowlands, the music producer who'd taken an interest in *Blazes*. Since they didn't have the recording equipment necessary to lay down a good track, Phil had agreed to hear them live in a small studio in East L.A. This had to be the best they'd played this song, especially with Joshua's improvements.

Evan Brown, the bassist, gave him a thumb's up. He beamed a smile at him and watched as Phil rose to his feet and went to the glass door between the control room and the vocal booth, pulling it open.

"Sounds good, guys," he said.

James tried to tamp down on his excitement. "So what do you think, Phil?"

"You're good. You're real good."

James face fell. He could hear the lack of enthusiasm in his tone. "What?"

"Do you have a gig tonight?"

"Yeah, we're playing a pizza parlor tonight."

"Give me the address. I'd like to come out and see the crowd's reaction."

James glanced at his band mates. Evan was staring at the ground and Ben was fiddling with his drumsticks. "I thought we had a deal."

Phil shifted weight. "Look, I like you guys. I think you have something. It's just you don't have that…I don't know. That one thing that would make you unique. This is a bitch of a business, kid. Playing good music isn't enough. You need that one thing that will bring people out in droves, that one thing that sets you apart from the other good bands."

James sighed. "Okay. I'll get you the address."

Phil patted his shoulder. "Good. I like your spirit." He turned to go.

"Tell Josh to come in and help us pack up," James told Ben.

Ben climbed off the stool and went to the door, pulling it open. "Hey, we're ready to go."

Joshua came into the room, glancing around. James shoved a guitar into his hands and grabbed the amplifier cord, winding it around his arm.

"How'd it go?" Joshua asked as he knelt and settled the guitar into the case.

James shrugged. "Not great." Glancing up, James noted that Phil had stopped with his hand on the handle of the door. He turned around and gave Joshua a close once-over.

"James, come here a minute."

Everyone stopped and looked up at him. James laid the cord down and rose to his feet, stepping around the rest of the equipment and crossing toward him. Phil opened the door and stepped into the control room, holding it open for James.

Once James was inside, Phil closed the door and moved to the control panel, staring out at the band. They had returned to packing up the equipment. Pointing at Joshua, Phil looked over his shoulder at James.

"Who's that?"

"My brother, Josh."

Phil gave him a puzzled look. "Brother?"

"Step-brother."

"How old is he?"

"Sixteen."

"He ever play with you?"

James shrugged. "One time. He was thirteen and Evan talked me into letting him sing a song for us. We were just playing a girl's birthday party."

"How'd it go?"

"Okay, I guess, but he's just a kid."

Phil studied Joshua for a moment. "He's gorgeous."

James frowned, shifting uncomfortably. "What?"

"Look at him. He's absolutely gorgeous. I'll bet girls piss their pants when he's around."

"He's sixteen."

"He's your ticket."

"What?"

"Can he sing? He's got a great talking voice."

"You only heard him say a few words."

"I know a voice when I hear one. Can he sing?"

"I guess."

"Doesn't matter. Look at him. He could shriek like a banshee and girls would piss themselves."

James shifted weight again. "Look, Phil, this is making me uncomfortable. He's my kid brother."

"He's also exactly what you need, James. Trust me. He is your ticket to stardom." Phil turned around and placed a hand on James' shoulder. "Let's try something, okay? Tonight, you bring him out. Let him sing a few songs. Does he know your music?"

He wrote most of it, thought James, but he didn't say that. "Yeah."

"Okay, let him sing a few songs with you and let's see how the crowd reacts. Don't bring him out until the middle of the show, so we can get a good gauge of the audience's reaction, but I'm pretty sure I know what they're going to do."

"I don't know. Our mother isn't going to like it."

"Is she here?"

"No, she's home, but the only way she would let him come with me is I promised to look after him."

"I'm not seeing the problem. He'll be where you can keep an eye on him and he'll be occupied. Better him singing on stage, than picking up some chick backstage, right?" He looked out at Joshua again. "I'm telling you that kid is your answer. He's the thing that will make you big."

James looked closely at Joshua for the first time. All he saw was a timid, scrawny sixteen year old who would be eaten alive in the music business. He knew Mary would have a fit if she found out. She wanted Joshua to pursue classical piano, not rock-n-roll. Still, if Phil was right and this was their only chance, James had to take it.

"Okay, we'll do it your way," he said reluctantly.

Phil smiled. If James had been more experienced, he would have recognized the smile for what it was.

* * *

Marco parked the Charger in front of a massive white house, whose front porch was supported by Greek columns. Ivy climbed up the front of the house and spread across the façade, softening the lines. A black, wrought iron fence separated it from its neighbors. This was not the house Peyton expected from a rock star.

"This is so…so normal."

Marco laughed. "What did you expect? Neon lights and a shag rug leading to the entrance."

"Yeah, I guess I did."

Marco opened his door. "Come on. I'll bet you find your shag on the inside."

Peyton climbed out after him and they made their way to the gate. Marco unhooked it and they went up the walk. The front yard was covered in juniper with a large redwood dominating the center of it. Cedar tanbark spread beneath the plants, giving of a rich, earthy scent, but even here they could smell the salt from the ocean.

Ringing the doorbell, Peyton glanced around the porch. A pink bike with streamers on the handlebars lay propped against the house. A bistro set was arranged next to it, a potted lily resting in the center of the table. Definitely not a bachelor's pad.

The door opened and a huge black dog barreled out. He careened into Peyton first, knocking her back into Marco, but the moment he saw the man, he launched himself at him and rose up on his hind legs, putting his paws on Marco's shoulders and kissing him smack on the lips.

"Oh God, I'm so sorry. Wolf, no!" came Elena's voice and she scrambled out onto the porch, grabbing the dog's collar and trying to pull him off.

Peyton laughed and scratched behind the dog's ears. "Good lord, what is he?"

"Part Mastiff, part Lab, or so I'm told. A regular beast, but he's just a big lover." She tugged ineffectively.

Marco eased him down, but continued stroking his wiggling body.

"I'm so sorry, Inspector D'Angelo."

"No problem. I love dogs."

Once she realized Marco had the animal under control, she straightened. "Thank you for coming out." She motioned inside the house.

Peyton led the way, but the dog brushed past her, zipping around the entrance hall, his tail whipping back and forth excitedly. A little girl stood in the arched opening.

Peyton hesitated, watching as the dog pressed tight against her side. The girl was about ten with dark hair and the largest, most stunning eyes Peyton had ever seen. Tiffany Ravensong had taken the best of both her parents and already showed signs that she would be a heart-breaker someday.

Elena went to her and placed her arm across the girl's shoulders. "Inspector Brooks, D'Angelo, I'd like you to meet Tiffany, Joshua's daughter."

Peyton held out her hand. "Nice to meet you. I'm Peyton and this is my partner, Marco."

Marco held up a hand in greeting.

The girl shook Peyton's fingers, then released her, wrapping her arms around Elena's waist. Elena hugged her briefly, then motioned into the other room.

"Please come in."

They followed her into a huge great room. The entire back wall was comprised of windows, which offered a panoramic view of the ocean. A fireplace occupied the left wall and centered on the windows was a large red leather couch. An armchair sat to the right of the couch, and Joshua's sister Jennifer was occupying it. She rose at their entrance, but she didn't come toward them.

"Hello, Inspector Brooks, D'Angelo."

"Hello, Jennifer," said Peyton, then she took in the view. "My God, that's impressive."

"Yes," said Elena. "Please take a seat."

"Can I get you something to drink?" asked Jennifer as they made their way to the couch.

"Nothing for me."

"Or me," echoed Marco.

"Elena?"

"I'd love a cup of tea."

Jennifer nodded and moved toward a door behind them. Tiffany took a seat on the end of the couch and Elena sank into the chair beside her. Peyton sat in the middle of the couch closest to Tiffany with Marco beside her. The moment Marco sat down, the dog came over and climbed into his lap.

Elena started to go after him, but Marco waved her off. "I really don't mind," he said, trying to balance the huge animal.

"He's Joshua's baby. I think that's why he's behaving so badly." Elena shot a glance at Tiffany.

Peyton did as well. The little girl was staring at her clasped hands. Scratching the dog's ears, Peyton smiled at Tiffany. "I have a dog." She reached into her pocket and pulled out her phone, thumbing it on. "Do you want to see a picture of him?" She tilted the phone, so Tiffany could see her wallpaper. Pickles stared back at her with his ears pricked and his head tilted.

A faint smile touched the girl's lips. "What's his name?"

"Pickles."

"Pickles?"

"I know. Silly, huh? My friend Abe named him, said he wasn't any bigger than a pickle."

That got a full smile. Elena smiled as well.

"I saw your dad yesterday," Peyton said, placing the phone in her pocket.

"How is he?"

"He's doing all right. He was playing the piano."

"He does that a lot."

"I know. He said it calms him."

Tiffany nodded, but she didn't say anything else. Peyton glanced at Elena and she nodded that she should continue. "I asked him if I could come talk to you and he agreed, but he told me I could only do it if you were okay with answering my questions."

"Questions about what?"

"About your mom."

Tiffany glanced over her shoulder at Elena and Elena leaned forward, covering her hands with her own.

"He told me I have to stop if you don't feel like continuing. If I ask you something you don't want to answer, all you have to do is tell me, okay?"

"How does this help my dad?"

Good question. "I'm a detective. You know what that is?"

"You investigate crimes."

"Right. See, we look at clues, kind of like a puzzle and we try to find out the truth."

"What does this have to do with my mom?"

"Well, some of the clues aren't fitting too well, so we need to know something more about her." Peyton reached into her pocket and pulled out her notebook. "I like to write things down when I talk to people, so I don't forget." She opened the notebook and showed the little girl a page. "Do you mind if I do that now?"

Tiffany shook her head.

"Okay. So are you all right with me asking you some questions?"

"If it'll help my dad, yeah."

"Good. So I know the last few months have been different for you, but you've been staying here most of the time, right?"

Tiffany glanced at Elena, then nodded. "Since school started, yeah."

"How often did you see your mother?"

"Sometimes on the weekends. A couple times a month."

"Good. When you were with your mother, what things did you do?"

"What do you mean?"

"Did you go anywhere, do anything special with her?"

Tiffany shrugged. "We watched T.V., saw a movie sometimes."

"You didn't go anywhere with her?"

"Not with Mama. Grandma used to take me places."

Peyton smiled. "Where did she take you?"

"The zoo or Fisherman's Wharf. I liked seeing the street performers."

"Your mama didn't take you to those places?"

"No, we stayed at home mostly. Maybe to the grocery store, but that's all."

"Okay. What about company? Did your mom have people over when you were there?"

"No. It was just the two of us."

Peyton felt a wash of disappointment, but something else occurred to her. "When we were at your mother's condo, we noticed she was packing. Did you know where she was moving to?"

"She said Europe."

"Was she moving with anyone?"

Tiffany sighed and tightened her hold on Elena. "She said something about me maybe coming with her, but I didn't want to leave."

"Okay. Anyone else?"

"No."

"Did she say why she was moving?"

"She was sad after Grandma died. She said she needed a change."

Peyton looked at her notes. "Tiffany, this might be a hard question, but did your mom have a boyfriend?"

"No, she didn't say anything about one."

"Okay," said Peyton with a sigh. This obviously wasn't getting them anywhere. "I appreciate you helping me out."

A frown creased Tiffany's brow. "There was one time."

Peyton stopped in the midst of putting her notebook away. "Go on."

"One time I was there, Mama said she had someone coming over. She said he was coming to study the *Bible* with her."

"The *Bible*? Did your mom belong to a church?"

"I don't think so. At least not when Grandma was alive, but she said he was coming over and that I needed to go to my room and watch a movie."

"And did the man come over?"

"Yeah, I heard the doorbell and then they were talking. She told me not to come out, that it was important I didn't interrupt them."

Peyton's eyes lifted to Elena. The other woman swallowed hard.

"Did you stay in your room like your mama asked?"

"Yeah, I fell asleep, but when I woke up, I had to go to the bathroom, so I peeked out the door."

"Did you see the man?"

"No, they weren't in the living room, so I came out and went to the bathroom. It was weird though."

"What was?"

"She said they were studying the *Bible*, but there was wine on the table."

"Do you think the man was gone when you went to the bathroom?"

"No, he was there."

"How do you know?"

"Her bedroom door was closed, but I could hear them. I could hear him. He had a deep voice."

"What was he saying?"

"*Bible* things."

Peyton sat back. "*Bible* things?"

"Yeah, about God and stuff."

"Tiffany, was the man there the next day?"

"No, Mama said he was gone."

"Did she tell you his name?"

"No, she just told me he was a preacher man. That's all."

"And you never saw him?"

"No."

"Did he ever come over again or did she talk about him to you?"

"No, that was the only time I remember someone coming over. She never said anything about him again."

Peyton made a note in her tablet, then replaced it. "Thank you, Tiffany. You've been a big help."

She nodded.

Peyton rose to her feet and watched Marco extricate himself from the dog. Immediately the dog crawled over to the little girl and placed his head in her lap. Peyton gave him a pat, then the two of them headed toward the door. Elena followed them.

"Inspector Brooks?"

Peyton stopped and turned around.

"Does any of that help?"

Peyton put out her hand and grasped Elena's elbow. "I'll look into it, but we really have nothing to go on – no name, no description. I don't want to get your hopes up, Elena. The D.A. is going to be breathing down our necks in a few days, demanding we hand the case over to him."

"You don't really believe Joshua did this, do you? You wouldn't be here if you did."

Oh, the two of them were perceptive, she had to give them that. "The evidence points to him."

"That's not what I asked you."

Peyton didn't know how to give them hope, and yet maintain her objectivity. "I know. You don't want me to answer that, Elena, do you?"

"Yes, I want the truth."

Peyton glanced to where Tiffany sat. She didn't think the little girl could hear her. "I think the evidence all points to Joshua. I'm sorry."

Elena's jaw firmed. "I don't believe that. That's just what you have to tell me." Her gaze shifted to Marco. "You wouldn't be here if you didn't have doubts. You wouldn't be looking into anything."

Peyton knew it didn't do any good to pretend otherwise, but she wasn't going to encourage a false hope. There just wasn't enough evidence to believe Joshua Ravensong was anything other than doomed. "I wish I could tell you differently, but I can't. Please take care of yourself. That little girl needs you right now."

With that, she and Marco left the house.

* * *

Jake flipped through the pictures on the camera as he made his way back to his cubby. Funny how it bothered him less and less to see a dead body. He didn't really like taking pictures for Abe, especially the way the M.E. flayed the bodies open, but even that wasn't as upsetting as it once was. He was gaining a detachment about it that was necessary if he was really going to make this a career. Still he was careful not to tell his sisters this. They already didn't understand why he'd left the bank, or stayed in San Francisco for that matter.

He stumbled to a stop and stared at the man sitting in his chair. The man was in his late fifties or early sixties with thinning grey hair. He lounged back in Jake's seat, his hands dangling off the arms. In one hand he held a pair of dark sunglasses, on the other was a large ring. A shadow of beard lined his cheeks and he had a cleft in his chin. His face wasn't handsome, but rugged, a man's man. He wore black combat boots and a pair of faded jeans. A red flannel shirt stretched across a chest that still maintained a muscular physique.

"Hello?"

"Hey there." The man nodded at the camera. "Nice piece. Must have set you back a bit?"

Jake nodded, then glanced around. No one else was in this area. In fact, all of the other officers seemed to be out on calls. "I'm Jake."

"Chuck, Chuck Wilson. You took my job."

Jake frowned. He was fairly certain the guy before him was Bob Anderson, who had quit because Peyton criticized his work. "I'm sorry?"

"Back about five years, I was the crime scene investigator. They let cops do that then." He gave a deep laugh. "Relax, kid. I retired."

Jake did relax. He set the camera on the desk and eased the bag off his shoulder, placing it at his feet. Then he held out his hand. "Nice to meet you, Chuck."

Chuck shook it, then released him. "Sorry to invade your space, but I was just curious about how things worked now."

"No problem." Jake leaned against the partition. "Actually, I'm not certified yet, but I'm taking a couple of classes at City College."

"Good for you. What'd you do before this?"

Jake cuffed his toe against the tiled floor. "I was a banker. Loan officer."

Chuck laughed. "How the hell did you wind up taking pictures of dead meat?"

"My wife died and doing a job for money just didn't seem that important anymore."

"Sorry." Chuck leaned forward in the chair. "My wife died too. Waited thirty years for me to retire, then she dies

129

first year I'm free. We planned to buy an RV and see the country. We didn't even get out of the hospital parking lot."

"Wow, that's bad."

"Yeah, so you got any interesting cases right now?"

Jake smiled. "Yeah, but none that I can talk about."

"On-going investigations, eh?"

"Yep."

"So how you like the job?"

"Funny thing," said Jake, running the strap of the camera through his fingers. "I was just thinking that I'm getting used to it. I didn't think I would, but I kinda like feeling like I make a difference."

Chuck narrowed his eyes, then he pushed himself to his feet with a grunt. Sliding the glasses over his eyes, he dropped a hand on Jake's shoulder. "And that's the problem. Don't start thinking you're making a difference, boy, 'cause you ain't. You keep cleaning up the shit out there and there's more right behind it. It never ends. You solve one case and there's another. It's like holding back the tide with a bucket."

Jake wasn't sure how to respond to that. It seemed so cynical. "Did you come to see anyone in particular?"

"Naw. Most of the cops I knew are retired or dead. That's another thing that gets old, going to cop funerals. Depressing shit, that." He lowered his hand. "Just came by to flirt with Maria. She's a looker, isn't she?"

"I guess."

Chuck laughed. "Take some time and look at her. In the end, that's the only thing that matters. A pretty girl. Everything else is bull shit."

He punched Jake in the shoulder and headed toward the front. Jake turned and watched him walk away. Once he reached the front, Jake could hear Maria giggle. Shaking his head, he reached for his camera and dropped into his chair, swiveling it toward the computer. Whatever Chuck said, Jake was just happy he wasn't clocking hours messing with other people's money.

*　*　*

Peyton and Marco returned to the precinct. Taking off her leather jacket, she slung it across her chair and sank into it. For some reason, meeting with Ravensong's daughter upset her more than she thought it would. She wished they'd gotten something more, but a vague reference to some suspicious *Bible* study hardly qualified as significant.

Marco slung his jacket over his chair as well. "Want a soda?"

"Yeah," she nodded distractedly.

"And a candy bar?"

She gave him a half-smile. "Did you have to ask?"

"It's one of those things men do to make women know we're thinking of them without having to say we're thinking of them. Just accept it, Brooks, and don't make me explain."

"No one's making you explain. You're choosing to explain. And it's not like women don't already know what you're explaining. You men aren't that complicated."

Marco gave a chuckle. "Even when we try to do something nice, we gotta get shit," he grumbled as he walked away.

"Hey, how'd it go?" Jake came up beside her and took a seat in the extra chair Abe had drug over when he was there.

Peyton braced her head on her fist. "Not great."

"She didn't know anything or she wouldn't talk to you?"

"She talked, she just didn't know anything. She hasn't spent much time with her mother since her grandmother died."

"Now what?"

Peyton shook her head.

"You could subpoena the bank for the strange deposit."

"How long will that take?"

"Couple weeks, probably."

"And then no guarantees that they'd cooperate, right?"

"Right."

"Ravensong doesn't have that long." She took out her notes and thumbed the cover open. "I just wonder if we missed something when we inspected the condo."

"Like what?"

"Like the murder weapon. Where the hell is it?"

"Maybe in the garbage."

Peyton picked up a pen and tapped it on the pad. "Yeah, I need to check on that and see if they've processed it all." She closed the pad. "So what have you been doing?"

"Processing the pics I took with Abe two days ago." He leaned back in the chair and braced his ankle on the opposite thigh. "I did get a strange visit though."

"Visit?"

"Some retired cop named Chuck Wilson. He was sitting in my seat when I came back to my desk."

"Chuck Wilson? Hasn't he been retired for a while?"

"He said five years. Do you remember him?"

"Remember who?" asked Marco, reaching over Jake's shoulder to give Peyton her soda and candy bar.

"Chuck Wilson."

"The crime scene investigator?"

"Yeah."

Jake pointed at Peyton's snack. "Where's mine, Adonis?"

"In the machine. What about Chuck Wilson?" He took a seat and popped open his own can.

"He paid Jake a visit."

"What for?"

Jake shrugged. "I think he's lonely. His wife died the year after he retired. He said he just wanted to see how things were running now. Oh, and flirt with Maria."

"Man has good taste," said Marco.

Peyton threw her wadded up wrapper at him.

He deflected it and it landed in the trash by his desk. Looking up, he gave her a wicked smile, but the smile dried. "In coming," he said cryptically.

Peyton looked over her shoulder, then wished she hadn't. Devan was coming toward her with that long-legged lawyer gait of his. Even when he was headed to the bathroom, he moved with a purpose.

Jake dropped his leg and moved his chair closer to Marco as Devan loomed over Peyton. She faced forward again, fighting to pull her composure around her. This was so not what she needed after their disappointing morning.

"Marco," Devan said.

"Adams," Marco answered, lifting his soda can and taking a swig.

"Peyton."

Peyton forced herself to look up at him. She couldn't deny some part of her still felt a flutter when she saw him. His clean-cut, sleek style, his dark eyes and coffee-colored skin, his neatly cropped hair – he was handsome in a pressed and polished way that was universally appealing.

"Devan." She tried to keep the bite out of her voice. So he'd dumped her? So he hadn't given her a chance? That was water under the bridge and they had to work together still. And yet, she rankled at the way he looked at her, so detached, so professional. Trying to divert the sting, she held out a hand toward Jake. "You remember Jake Ryder."

Devan shot a look at Jake and away. "Yes."

Not exactly polite, but then he was a lawyer. Economy of energy seemed to be a hallmark.

"I want to talk to you about this Ravensong case."

Peyton bit her lip, shifting her gaze to her partner. Marco picked up the soda can again and took a deliberate gulp. She knew there wouldn't be any help from that quarter. "It's a bit premature to talk about it. We're still in the first stages of investigation."

"It's Thursday."

Clenching her jaw, she resisted the impulse to say, *Look at you, reading a calendar.* "I know."

"The murder happened on Sunday."

"Right."

"That's four days."

"Five if you count Sunday."

His face grew even more serious, if that was possible. Marco turned the can up and started reading the ingredients on the side. Jake suddenly found a piece of loose rubber to pull on his shoe.

Opening his mouth to retort, he stopped himself and made a visible shift. "I understand there are no other suspects?"

"You understand no such thing. I don't believe we've discussed the case with you."

"So there are other suspects?"

Peyton wasn't going to answer that. She also didn't like the way he loomed over her. He was already a good six inches taller than her in her heels, so this really put her at a disadvantage. She pushed her chair out and stood up.

"Oh shit," muttered Marco, putting down the can.

Jake looked like he might bolt.

"I said the case was still being investigated. That should be enough."

"It isn't." He was clearly not intimidated.

"Care to elaborate."

"I understand you have one suspect, who not only had a motive, but the evidence all points to him, possessing no alibi and has, in fact, committed himself to a psych facility to prevent another such murder from occurring, so I guess I question what more there could be to investigate."

"Right now, I'm trying to investigate why you're such an assh—"

"Okay!" interrupted Marco, coming to his feet. "Look, Devan, not all of the evidence matches up. The vic was killed with a leaded glass curio that broke in the murderer's hand, but Ravensong doesn't have any cuts. Not

134

to mention that a week before she died, a large sum of money was deposited into her account from an off-shore bank, so although four…or five days may have passed, we need more time."

Devan took it all in, then he turned toward Peyton and held out a hand. "See, that wasn't so hard…"

Peyton took a step toward him, but Marco came around Jake's chair and grabbed him by the shoulders, propelling him backward and stepping between them.

"Now that, *that* was just mule-ass stupid," he said.

"I was stating a fact."

"Yeah, some facts do *not* need to be stated," commented Marco, turning Devan toward the door and marching him forward.

Peyton glared after them until they disappeared around the corner, then she backed up and sat down. Jake reached over and pushed the half-eaten part of her candy bar at her.

"It'll help."

"Smug sonuvabitch."

Jake nodded vigorously. "He is."

Peyton shifted her gaze to him and they both burst into laughter. "That was very unprofessional of me."

"Well, he deserved it. He's a prick."

"He is, isn't he?" She picked up the candy bar and took a bite. "Problem is he's right. We've got nothing."

Jake leaned toward her. "You've got your instinct and that's saved one sorry sonuvabitch already now, hasn't it?"

Peyton smiled at him and took another bite.

CHAPTER 8

The pizza parlor had a main room where the booths were located, a counter where the pizzas were delivered, and a back room filled with arcade games, a small wooden dance floor, and a dart board. A number of pub tables were arranged around the edges and neon signs for various beers cast everything in an electrified, phosphorescent glow.

Joshua sat on one of the barstools, watching James and the band run through their usual collection of songs. The music producer, Phil Rowlands, sat next to him, his fingers curled through a mug of beer.

The crowd was small, maybe twenty people and most of those were guys busy playing a game of darts in the corner. *Blazes'* music drifted out into the main part of the restaurant and Joshua could see people nodding their heads and shifting around to watch them through the wooden spindles separating the two rooms, but it just wasn't enough to draw them in.

Joshua didn't really know why. They all had good voices, Evan in particular, and James played a mean guitar, still Joshua knew instinctively that this wasn't the reaction the music producer wanted. He didn't want pubs, he wanted stadiums, and *Blazes* wasn't going to deliver that.

As the heavy bass of the song died away, James turned to Evan and the two of them began a whispered conversation. Phil took the opportunity to lean toward Joshua and nudge his elbow with his beer mug.

"I told him to let you sing. You know the lyrics, right?"

Joshua gave a bark of laughter. "You told him what?"

Leaning closer, Phil dropped his voice. "This is all they'll be, kid. They need something different, something captivating. They need you."

Joshua looked at him skeptically. "They just need exposure."

"Get an earring, a couple of tattoos, grow out that hair, and you could be a rock star."

Joshua smiled wryly. Oh, his mother would love that.

"Here." Phil pushed the beer over to him.

Joshua didn't even have time to react. James loomed at the table, catching the beer before it crossed mid-point. "He's sixteen."

Phil laughed, but he took the beer back. "So you gonna let him sing?"

Joshua frowned. The crazy bastard was serious. Still there was no way James would agree...

"You wanna?" He gave Joshua a pointed look.

"This is your thing, James."

"Do you wanna sing the next song or not? You know the lyrics, you wrote the damn thing."

Joshua looked around the parlor. Did he want to sing? He wasn't sure. He'd never sung in front of this many people before. Playing the piano was one thing, he could disappear behind the instrument, but singing meant he'd be out in front, exposed to everyone.

"You did it before."

"That was just a stupid birthday party."

"So?"

So?

Drawing a deep breath, he held it, then he exhaled, rubbing his hands against his thighs. He couldn't look at Phil. He could feel the man's anticipation and it almost made him sick. Finally he nodded, that and nothing more.

James clapped a hand on his shoulder and drew him forward. Later Joshua wasn't sure how he walked across the floor or stepped up on the silly, wooden dance floor. Evan gave him a tight smile as he took his place behind the microphone. His heart was pounding so loudly in his head, he wasn't sure he'd be able to hear the music. The neon lights created prisms of color in his peripheral vision, dancing just beyond his sight.

Then James counted off the beat and the band launched into the song, a heavy pounding rhythm with a slow melody. Joshua almost panicked. He preferred the faster, harder songs. The bass drum could hide a less than stable voice, but not this song. This song he'd penned himself, a ballad he'd named *The River*. It was his silent tribute to his own people, to the Patwin people, and deeply personal. Not even James knew what it really meant.

He gripped the microphone, hoping the cold of the metal against his palm would ground him, and he studiously ignored the men playing darts. Picking a poster on the wall of a mountain stream, he focused on it and let the rest of the parlor fade from his mind.

When the melody started, he sang. He'd known his voice was pleasant, but the voice that drifted through the microphone was haunting, smoky, low and smooth like the heavy flow of water over rocks. Closing his eyes, he drifted with the music, let the notes fill him up, merge with him.

James didn't know how much he missed the reservation, the quiet, the shelter, the familiar. He missed the flow of time on the reservation, the community, the connection. He'd learned to adapt in the bigger world, the world of television and fast moving cars, but a part of him always felt that he didn't really belong either place. No matter how much Adam and the kids made him a part of their family, he was different, he was separate.

The song slowed to an end and he held the final note, let it drift away naturally, let it slide into a memory. Opening his eyes, he was surprised to see people standing in the entrance to the back room, peering through the spindles. In the corner, the men had stopped playing darts, and Phil...Phil was smiling.

* * *

Peyton opened the break-room refrigerator and peeked inside. She was hoping to find some left over cake or pie for breakfast. She'd gotten up late and hadn't had time to grab anything before heading to work. Marco had the day off for his birthday, so she planned to spend her time reading through the articles Maria had found for her about Ravensong. A piece of cake was just the thing to make her reading complete.

"Hey, Brooks," came a voice behind her.

She glanced over her shoulder. Nathan Cho had come in the room and was headed for the coffee pot. "Hey, Cho."

"What ya looking for?"

"Something for breakfast, but there's nothing here. Maria's off her game."

Cho laughed and poured a cup of coffee. "Want some?" He held up the pot.

"I already had a cup on my way in." She closed the refrigerator and wandered over to him. "How's your case?"

Cho shook his head. "We've got nothing. The Preacher and Abe figured out the guy had a record, but that's about all we've got. No family to speak of. Parents both dead, never married, no kids. He has a sister, but she wants nothing to do with him. Won't even arrange a burial."

"What's he got a record for?"

"Child molestation."

Peyton tilted back her head. "I guess that's why the sister is avoiding him, eh?"

"Probably." He brought the mug to his lips and took a sip. "Can't even find a witness."

"Weird. You'd think someone would have heard something in a BART station at night. He can't be the only bum sleeping down there."

Cho started to answer, but he was distracted by loud shouting coming from the lobby. Peyton looked over her shoulder, but she couldn't see anything from where she stood. Stepping out of the break-room, she moved toward the front of the building with Cho on her heels.

A crowd was gathered in the lobby.

Smith and Holmes were trying to restore order, while Maria stood behind her desk, looking anxious. Jake had wandered over from his cubby, but he didn't seem inclined to get involved. At first Peyton thought it was paparazzi that had found a way into the building, but then she caught sight of Elena hovering in the background.

A tall, stocky blond man was shouting at Smith and pointing his finger toward the back of the precinct. "I'm not messing around anymore. You tell me what the hell is going on!"

Peyton glanced at Defino's door, wondering why she hadn't come out, but the door remained closed. Drawing a deep breath, she knew this was her problem to sort. She missed Marco at her back because people typically calmed down when they saw him looming behind her, but this blond dude didn't seem like he gave ground easily.

She came up behind Smith with her most intimidating cop stance. "What the hell is going on?"

The blond man stopped shouting and stared at her.

"Inspector Brooks, this is Ravensong's brother. A cop from L.A.," said Smith derisively.

Cop? Peyton vaguely remembered something about that. Maybe she should pay more attention to what she read, instead of gawking at the photos of Ravensong.

"Sergeant," the blond man corrected, bristling with hostility. "Not cop."

"What is the problem, Sergeant?"

"I demand to know what's being done to exonerate my brother. It's been nearly a week and instead of being home with his daughter where he belongs, he's locked in a mental facility."

"Of his own accord," said Peyton in her most reasonable voice.

"The hell it is." His eyes narrowed on her. "Brooks? So you're the incompetent idiot who told him he was guilty."

"James!" This came from a shorter woman with dark hair.

"James, I don't think this solves anything," said an older man.

"The hell it doesn't. Look, Dad, you don't know what we're dealing with here."

"I don't think insulting the officer investigating the case is going to do us a bit of good."

"Really? 'Cause if someone doesn't step in here and take control, Josh is gonna wind up convicted of murder. You think they didn't coerce a confession out of him, and I'll bet they didn't even let him have a lawyer."

"We didn't coerce anyth—"

"And don't for a minute believe that they're really going to look into this. It's open and shut as far as they're concerned, save the tax payers some money, we've got a suspect, let's convict his ass before someone else gets murdered and we might have to do our jobs. I know how this place works, Dad."

Peyton shared a bewildered look with Holmes and Smith.

"James, please, don't do this. We don't need enemies," said the woman.

"Enemies? Look around you. They're all enemies. They just want someone to hang for this murder and it doesn't matter who, especially if it's a celebrity. Oh, they'd love to bring down a celebrity. They get extra points or something without having to do a damn thing. This frickin' city couldn't wipe its own ass if the state didn't tell it how. It's a rainbow hued fairyland where they lock up law abiding people and dance under the moonlight with murderers."

Okay, now that went too far.

"Just a damn minute," Peyton said, pushing between the two uniforms. "These aren't the mean streets of L.A. and we aren't some prancing ponies. In this City we talk to people with respect and we ask questions, we don't run around spouting off like an arrogant prick."

"Now you listen…" he began.

Peyton took a step toward him and lowered her voice. "I'm gonna tell you just one time and one time only. Shut the hell up, calm the hell down, and sit your ass on that chair, or I will kick your balls into your stomach, slaps some cuffs on you, and haul you downstairs to a holding cell until you can speak like a civilized human being."

He opened his mouth to say something, but Peyton took another step toward him, reaching for her cuffs. Backing up, he sat heavily in a chair and blinked at her.

"I have got to learn how to do that," said Elena with admiration.

"Now, will someone tell me who we all have here in a calm, rational voice?" When James started to speak again, Peyton pointed at him. "Not you!"

Elena eased to her side. "This is Joshua's mother, Mary," she said, indicating the dark haired woman. "And his step-father, Adam." She motioned to the tall older man. "You've already met Jennifer and now James."

Peyton shifted her attention to a woman in a severe navy blue suit with dark rimmed glasses. She had short cropped hair and overly large brown eyes. She held a leather notebook in her hands and the strap of a purse hung over her shoulder. She gave Peyton a nervous smile.

"This is Joshua's psychologist, Emily Staddler."

Peyton leaned toward Elena. "His what now?"

"Psychologist."

At that moment Defino's office door opened, emitting both her and Devan. She surveyed the gathering with her usual squint eyed stare. She used her glare for intimidation, but really she couldn't see and refused to wear glasses or contact lenses.

"What the hell is going on out here?"

Peyton swept the gathering with her hand. "This is Joshua's family."

"Well, part of it," offered Elena. "He has a sister and twin brothers at home."

"Why the shouting?"

"These people are his parents, his sister and…"
Peyton gave James a snarky smile. "His brother James, who is a sergeant with the Los Angeles police force, Captain."

"Really?"

"Yes, oh and his psychologist."

"His what?"

"Psychologist."

"And a partridge in a pear tree," quipped Jake behind them.

Peyton almost barked out a laugh, but Defino glared in her direction. Well, in all fairness, she glared at Jake, but she couldn't see him very well.

Coming forward, she positioned herself in front of a chastised James. "Sergeant, let me make something amply clear."

"Yes, ma'am," he said, ducking his head.

"If you ever shout in my precinct again, I will have you arrested. Is that clear?"

"Absolutely."

"Now what was it you wanted?"

"I wanted to know the status of the case. We've gotten very little information and I'm worried he was coerced into admitting guilt. He's a recovering drug addict…"

"I'm aware of that."

"…and he doesn't always remember what happened, especially if it's a stressful situation, but he would never hurt the mother of his child. He would never strike anyone."

"Which is why we are still investigating?"

James' gaze lifted to Devan. "With all due respect, ma'am, I recognize a district attorney when I see one."

For the first time, Peyton felt for him. He really was scared for his brother.

"And we have just been discussing why my people need more time with this case, Sergeant. I cannot divulge the particulars of an ongoing investigation, but I assure you we will not turn over the case until we are satisfied the evidence holds up under scrutiny."

143

James leaned forward, bracing his forearms on his thighs. "I want in on the case."

"I can't allow that, any more than a hospital would allow a doctor to operate on his own kin. Go back to your brother's house and give us a little space."

"I need you to take this seriously."

Defino's eyes narrowed. "I'm going to assume you didn't mean that the way it sounded, Sergeant. I'm going to assume you are talking out of fear and frustration, and meant no insult."

He stared up at her. Peyton wondered if he would be smart enough to back down and let them handle it. He held up a hand to her. "Of course. I'm sorry. I'm just scared for my brother."

"Then take care of your family and let us take care of the rest." She didn't wait for an answer, but turned and headed to her office. Peyton watched as James rose to his feet and turned toward his father, who clapped a firm hand on his shoulder and guided him to the door. With his other hand, he supported Joshua's mother.

Elena touched Peyton's elbow. "Please call me if you find out anything."

"You know I will."

Elena hesitated, then she followed Joshua's family out of the precinct.

Peyton wished she could give Elena better news. She wished she could give them all better news. It was refreshing to see a family standing by one of their own.

She felt Devan's eyes on her, so she looked up and met his gaze. Then she turned away.

*   *   *

Peyton passed the card over Jake's shoulder as he sat at his desk, messing on his computer. "Sign it."

He took the card and read it, then swiveled in his chair, so he could see her. "Are you sure I'm invited?"

"Yes, now sign it. We're already late."

He accepted the pen from her and scribbled his name below Abe's. "What did we get him?"

Peyton held up the two tickets. Jake took them from her and inspected them, then let out a low whistle.

"These are two tickets on the 50 yard line, lower deck."

"I know."

"How the hell did you afford this, Mighty Mouse?"

"We helped a player a few years back with a case."

"You still must have paid a fortune."

She grabbed them from him and placed them in the card, then put the card in the envelope. "None of your business. Now grab your coat and let's go."

He rose to his feet and reached for the coat hanging from the footboard on the bed. "Let me help you."

"With what, Jake?"

"I have some money."

"I've got it." She went to the front door and grabbed her own coat, slipping it on. She took down her gun and wrapped the shoulder strap around it.

"Here." He handed her a couple of twenties. When she shook her head, he snapped them at her. "Come on. I want to contribute. You let Abe, didn't you?"

"Yeah, but he's got money."

"Take it."

Peyton took the money more for his sake, than hers. She knew he wanted to pay his way.

"I'll drive," he offered.

"No you won't. I've got a reputation to maintain and the Daisy doesn't cut it." She picked up Pickles and deposited him on the couch, then pulled open the door.

"Your car isn't much better," he grumbled, but he followed her down to the driveway.

She peered at herself in the rear view mirror just long enough to smooth down her wild curls.

145

The ride to Vinnie's house didn't take more than five minutes. He lived in the Avenues near Peyton in a pretty pink house with two huge windows on the front that looked like eyes. Peyton found a place to park a few doors down.

A wrought iron gate usually closed off the arched entrance, but someone had braced it open with a potted red geranium. She and Jake climbed the stairs to the front door, which was also open. Peyton peeked inside.

Marco's mother, Mona, caught sight of her and hurried to the door, pulling her inside and wrapping her in an embrace. "Come in, come in." She pressed her hands to Peyton's cheeks. "It's been too long since I saw you. You have to come to dinner on Sundays from now on."

Peyton laughed and hugged her back. "I'd love that." She pulled Jake up beside her. "Mona, this is my housemate Jake Ryder."

Mona hugged him too. "I'm so glad to meet you. Marco tells me about you."

Jake gave a skeptical look. "That can't be good."

"Nonsense," she said, hooking her arm in Jake's. "Let me introduce you to everyone." And she pulled him in the direction of the kitchen where the sound of laughter and loud voices wafted out.

Peyton crossed the living room to the circular black coffee table and laid Marco's gift on it. The living room was a perfect square with real wood parquet floors and a semi-circular fireplace in the corner. A large white leather sectional and two leather recliners lay arranged around the table, and family photos littered the walls. Most were of Vinnie and Rosa's two kids, Cristina and Antonio, sporting the D'Angelo's height, striking bone structure, and blue eyes.

As she turned toward the kitchen, two boys raced out of the right hallway and sprinted out the front door. Peyton thought it was Emilio and Sergio, Franco's sons, but she wasn't sure. Just as she started moving again a third boy careened into her. She caught him and he laughed.

"Sorry."

"Michel?"

"Yeah."

"Good lord, boy, you've grown a mile. How old are you now?"

"Six." He danced in her grasp. "Gotta go."

She released him and watched him race out the door. Glancing into the hallway, she didn't hear any more thundering feet, so she walked to the door of the kitchen. It was by far the largest room in the house with vaulted ceilings and an island in the middle. A full dining table was laid out with dishes and food to the left, and everyone was gathered around it and the island.

Rosa, Vinnie's wife, saw her first and came over, grabbing her in a hug. She was plump and pretty with dark hair and eyes that always looked like she was smiling. "Peyton," she said, kissing her cheek.

"Thank you for inviting me, Rosa," she said, then she was captured in a bear hug by Vinnie.

All the D'Angelo men were tall and handsome. Marco was the prettiest, but they all could have easily made their mark in modeling if they had chosen. The three oldest brothers had advanced college degrees and worked in business. Vinnie was an architect and restored old Victorians.

She hugged Vinnie in return, then greeted Franco and Bernardo. She didn't know them as well as Vinnie, but she'd been to many family functions. Franco's wife Sofia was cooking with Mona and she waved from the stove.

"Hey, Peyton."

"Hey, Sofia."

Serena, Bernardo's wife, handed her a beer. "Here you go, sweetheart," she said. "Drink one for me." She rubbed her swollen belly.

"How much longer?" asked Peyton, taking a sip.

"Another month."

"Boy or girl?"

"Boy, of course."

Marco came up and pulled her out of the crowd, wrapping her in his arms. He bent down and kissed the top of her head. "You're late, Brooks."

"I know. It's Jake's fault."

"Hey!" shouted Jake from the other end of the room.

Peyton looked around Marco and smiled at him. He was sitting between Abe and Marco's father, Leo, at the table. Leo patted the empty chair beside him.

"Come sit here, Peyton."

She crossed around the table and took the seat he indicated. He hugged her and she hugged him back. "How are you, Leo?"

"I'm doing great. How are you?"

"In the pink." She smiled at Abe. "You okay?"

Abe gave her a dreamy look. "Are you kidding me?"

Peyton didn't ask for elaboration. She knew Abe thought heaven smiled on the D'Angelo family. Looking around, she noticed Vinnie's son Antonio and daughter Cristina occupying stools at the island. "How's school, you guys?"

Antonio flashed dimples at her. At seventeen, he was already developing the D'Angelo charm. "Good. Running track to get ready for summer football."

"Any colleges looking at you?"

"They can't talk to me until schools out in June."

"Got it."

Mona handed Peyton a plate heaped with food. "Eat something."

Marco looked over her shoulder. "Where's mine? And there is definitely not enough sugar on there for Brooks."

Peyton stuck her tongue out at him. "Thank you, Mona," she said, accepting the plate. She turned her attention to Cristina, Vinnie's youngest. She had her mother's plumpness, but a mane of glorious black hair framed a very pretty face. "How about you, Cristina? How are you?"

"Fine," she said shyly.

"She's got a boy chasing after her. Asked her to prom," said Antonio mischievously.

"Tonio!" scolded Rosa. "Leave your sister alone."

"Of course she does," said Marco, kissing her on the forehead. "She's the prettiest girl at that school."

She beamed at him, wrapping her arms around his waist.

Mona handed him a plate. "Here's for my birthday boy."

He took it. "Thank you, Mama," he said, bending and kissing her cheek.

Peyton loved coming to a D'Angelo party. As an only child, she couldn't deny there was something seductive about a big family. They took everyone in and looked out for each other. She didn't even mind the chaos and the noise. Kids raced through underfoot, grabbing food off the table. The adults milled around, laughing loudly and hugging…there was a lot of hugging that went on with the D'Angelos. Peyton was content to sit back and watch, absorbing it all.

After the food was eaten, people wandered into the other rooms. Peyton stayed in the kitchen, listening to Leo talk about his work as a PG&E technician during the earthquake in '89. Finally, Mona scolded him for monopolizing Peyton and told him to get their present for Marco from the car. He winked at Peyton and left the room.

Bernardo handed her another beer and she got up, walking into the living room to find Jake. He and Abe were sitting on the floor by the couch and Jake was telling Abe about her confrontation with Ravensong's brother.

Vinnie and Franco were listening.

"She told him to sit his ass down and he did it," said Jake.

The men laughed.

Marco was sitting on the arm of a recliner, while Serena was stretched out in the seat, her hands around her stomach.

Peyton leaned against him. "You okay?"

He put his arm around her waist. "I'm great."

"You weren't so sure about turning thirty and having a party, remember?"

He gave a grunt. "Yeah, but look at this."

"And then she said she'd kick his balls into his stomach and slaps some cuffs on him." Abe and Jake peeled off into laughter.

"How can I be upset around this madness? I've got my family, a job I love…"

"And me."

Marco squeezed her. "And you and the craziness you bring me." He pointed his beer at Abe and Jake.

"Time for presents," said Rosa, bustling into the room. Everyone came from the kitchen and gathered around, perching on the arms of the chairs. Rosa and Sofia carried some of the kitchen chairs out with them, and Rosa placed one next to Marco and sat down. She patted the seat next to her. "Sit with me, Peyton." Peyton sat on the edge of it, balancing precariously, but Rosa didn't seem to mind. "Pass your uncle his presents, Tonio."

Antonio gave him a small bag and Marco settled his beer on the floor next to the chair, reaching for the card. "This is from Bernardo, Serena and the boys." He pulled out a Niners baseball hat and immediately put it on.

From there, he got a Niners t-shirt that looked too small to Peyton, a pair of socks in red and gold, a picnic blanket with the Niners logo on it, and from his parents, a Niners jacket. Abe gave her a wink. Obviously, there was a theme to the gifts and hers fit right in there.

Finally Antonio handed over the envelope. Marco pulled out the card and opened it, then he just sat still and didn't move for a moment. Peyton shifted nervously. She couldn't believe how badly she wanted him to like it.

His eyes lifted and he stared at her, but he didn't speak.

"Well?" said Franco, "What is it?"

Marco held up the tickets. "Niners tickets…"

Everyone gasped.

"Fifty yard line…"

"Holy shit," said Franco.

"Lower deck…"

Vinnie sat forward. "There had better be two tickets there."

Slowly Marco separated the two tickets.

Vinnie leaped to his feet and scrambled over all the legs to Peyton. He grabbed her face in both hands and kissed her on the cheek.

Peyton laughed. "It's from Abe too."

Abe stood up. "Yeah, where's mine?"

Never missing a beat, Vinnie swiveled around and planted a kiss on Abe's cheek too. The room erupted in laughter and Abe pretended to faint.

"And Jake," Peyton added.

Vinnie moved toward him, but Jake held up a hand. "I'm good. I'm good."

Peals of laughter filled the house, but Rosa pushed herself to her feet. "All right. Come on. It's time for cake. Everyone back in the kitchen."

There was a mad scramble to follow her. Peyton waited until the room had mostly cleared, then she rose to her feet. As she turned to go, Marco grabbed her wrist. He hadn't budged from his spot on the arm of the recliner.

"Did you hear her? She said cake."

"I heard her." He tugged Peyton back to him. "How much did this cost you?"

"Remember that linebacker we helped a few years ago. I contacted him and he gave me a great deal. Abe and Jake also helped out."

He ran his thumb across her inner wrist. "You didn't have to do this, you know?"

She straightened his ball cap. "I did have to do it. I love you, D'Angelo," she said and kissed his cheek. "You know that."

He smiled. He was so damn pretty when he smiled.

"Did you not hear her say cake?"

He chuckled. "I heard her."

She tugged him to his feet. "Then come on."

He didn't budge. "Peyton?"

She looked over her shoulder at him.

"Thank you."

She came back and wrapped her arms around his waist, laying her head on his chest and hugging him tight. He hugged her in return and bent, kissing the top of her head as he always did. She couldn't believe how happy she felt, but it also made her ache to know she would never have this with her own family again.

CHAPTER 9

"Okay, now, unbutton the jeans and act as if you're going to pull them off, so we can get a shot of the briefs." The camera snapped frantically, flashes going off like gunfire. Joshua closed his eyes and turned away. He just couldn't do this anymore.

The flashes stopped. "Phil, brooding is good, but we're getting boredom here," said the photographer.

"Okay, okay," said Phil. "Give me a minute."

He circumvented the lights and cords, grabbing Joshua's bare shoulder and motioning for him to follow him to the side of the studio. Joshua hooked the jeans around his waist and trailed him, wishing he could retrieve a shirt as well. He felt exposed and self-conscious walking around bare foot and bare chested.

A table had been set up along the wall with cookies and donuts and pastries soaking in their own sugar. Phil stopped beside it and motioned to the fare. "What would you like?"

Joshua hadn't eaten yet today, but he just couldn't stomach anymore sweets. "Nothing."

Phil poured a glass of juice, then held it out. "Drink this. You look tired and tired doesn't sell underwear."

Joshua took the cup. "Why am I selling underwear? I'm a musician, Phil. The other guys don't do this shit."

Phil caught him under the chin. "None of them look like this either. You are the face and body of the band. Accept it. If you sell underwear, they sell records."

"I hate this." He said it through clenched teeth. "This isn't what I agreed to do."

"Do you like the condo? The Mercedes?"

Joshua set the cup down. "Not as much as you think I do."

"Then do it for your brother, 'cause he sure as shit likes it, doesn't he?"

Joshua closed his eyes and rolled his head back.

Phil's fingers gripped his shoulder, digging into the muscle. "Look, I know this sucks. No one wants to parade around like a piece of meat, but that's the business. The music doesn't bring out the girls, but you in your briefs, that brings them in droves."

"I'm so tired," he said, staring at the ground. "We play until late at night, then you have me up at dawn for this stupid shit. I'm just so damn tired."

"I know, but this is the life, Josh. You picked this. You said you wanted it."

"I wanted to play music." He leaned against the table. "I wanted to write and sing and that's all. I'm eighteen, Phil. I shouldn't feel tired all the time. This shit isn't worth it."

Phil looked over his shoulder. No one was paying any attention. "I know you're tired. You'll get a break soon. You'll get to go home for Christmas. Four weeks off, doing nothing, sleeping in. We've just got to get through 'til then."

Joshua frowned. "That's weeks from now. Are you even listening to me? I'm dying here."

Phil glanced around again, then he reached in his pocket and pulled out a brown prescription bottle. He turned his back, so only Joshua could see what he was doing, and unscrewed the top, then he shook something into his hand.

"Take these." He held them out. Two little royal blue pills lay in the palm of his hand.

Joshua backed a step away. "What is that?"

"Nothing really. It'll just give you some energy, make you less tired. You'll hardly notice it, but it'll get you through the day."

"I'm not taking that."

Phil recapped the bottle, hiding the pills in his palm, then he shoved the bottle in his pocket again. "It's nothing. My doctor gives them to me. It's no more than caffeine." He picked up the juice and held it out. "Take it. We've got to get through this shoot and it'll help. You won't feel so self-conscious either."

154

Joshua leaned close to him and lowered his voice. "I don't want your pills. I want this other shit to stop."

Phil sighed. "Here's the thing, Josh. I didn't want to say anything, but the band just isn't that good. You aren't going to go any farther with them. They're holding you back."

"That's bull shit."

"No, it's the truth. They just don't have that spark, but you do. You could be a megastar."

Joshua tilted his head. "If what you say about the band is true, then I see no reason to do this crap anymore."

"Except for this. You can pull them along behind you. You can make them great. You have that star quality, that brilliance. You are their only chance. I know it doesn't mean anything to you, but it means a whole lot to your brother. You're his ticket, his one way pass. And this…" He motioned around the studio. "This is the only way to get it for him."

Joshua wanted to walk away, he wanted to call his bluff, but he knew James wouldn't understand. James did want this worse than he did.

Phil held out the pills and juice again.

Joshua rubbed a hand over his jaw and shifted weight. He knew this was how so many people got in trouble, how it all started. He wasn't stupid and he wasn't naïve, but he was tired, so damn tired.

And even though he knew better, he reached for them.

*   *   *

Peyton jogged up the steps and opened the door to her house. Jake was coming out of the hallway with Pickles in his arms. He stopped and took in her running attire.

"You went jogging?"

"Yep," she said, bending over to untie her running shoes.

"How could you go jogging? A marching band is hammering in my skull." He set Pickles down and the little dog ran to Peyton.

She picked him up as she kicked off her shoes. "I didn't drink as much as you. I drove, remember."

"I was trying to keep up with the D'Angelos."

"They're twice as big as you," she said, bending over and picking up her shoes.

"You know it's Saturday, right?"

"Yep." She passed him on her way to her bedroom. He followed her and leaned against the door jamb as she settled Pickles on the bed and opened her closet, chucking her shoes inside.

"Saturday, a day of rest. A day to sleep in."

She grabbed a clean pair of jeans and went to her dresser, pulling out a t-shirt. "It's 11:00AM, Jake. You slept in."

He leaned forward and glanced at the alarm clock on her dresser. "Well, shit."

She came to him and pushed him back into the hallway. "I'm gonna take a shower now. Go take some aspirin, then eat some bread. It'll help."

He stood there as she closed the door in his face.

Twenty minutes later, she found him in the kitchen eating cereal. Going to the sofa table, she grabbed her keys, the small bi-fold that held her license and ATM card, and her lip gloss. She slipped everything but the keys in her pocket and grabbed her coat off the rack.

"Where going?" he mumbled around a mouthful.

"To tidy up some loose ends on this case. I should be back by dinner, but don't wait for me."

"Got it. Pickles and I are gonna take a nap."

"You do that." She reached for her hair, gathering it in one hand.

"Don't do that."

"What?"

"Tie it up. It's better down."

She frowned at him, but she released it. The heavy weight settled on her shoulders, curls tickling her face. "It's annoying."

"And yet you don't cut it off."

"Maybe I will. Good idea."

He waved her away. "I'm too hung over to play today. Just leave the hair alone. It's your only good quality right now."

She laughed and grabbed her gun, wrapping the shoulder strap around it. "Take a nap, Grumpy." She pulled open the door and stepped outside. Sunlight was peeking through the clouds, and the trees were rustling in a cool ocean breeze. She unlocked the Corolla's trunk and hid the Glock in the spare tire well, then climbed behind the steering wheel. Last time she went to the psych facility, she'd worn the gun, but she didn't think it was a good idea. Best not to give mentally ill people an opportunity if it wasn't necessary.

She started the ignition and pulled out of the driveway. Rolling down the window, she enjoyed the wind as it blew past the car, sending her curls to dancing.

When she'd visited Ravensong last time, she'd let him off too easy about Terry. She needed to be firm with him today. He had to know more about the woman's life than he let on. If she was sleeping with this preacher man like Tiffany said, wouldn't the little girl have told her father and wouldn't any father be concerned about a strange man around his ten year old daughter? If not, she needed to know how their marriage ended, if there had been more than words between them.

The same receptionist waited at the front desk when she arrived. She was a large woman with man sized hands and blunt features. Her brown hair was curled tightly in a bowl cut and she wore bright red lipstick, but when she smiled, her expression seemed genuine and kind.

"Inspector Brooks," said Peyton, showing her the badge.

"I remember." She placed the book for her to sign on the edge of the desk. "Right here, dear."

Peyton signed her name. Like last time the woman didn't ask if she carried a weapon. This surprised Peyton a bit, but she dismissed it. "Is he at the piano?" She pointed to the door of the common room.

"No, I haven't seen him today. Too bad. Listening to him makes the hours pass quicker."

"I bet looking at him doesn't hurt any either."

The receptionist giggled. "Not going to deny that."

Peyton smiled at her. "Do you know where he is?"

"Well, being Saturday, if he isn't in the common room, he's likely in his room. No therapy today."

"I see. Can you direct me to it?"

"Take this hall behind me and go right. He's in room 34. He's got one of the nicer views."

"Thank you." Peyton moved beyond her desk and took the first right. A man passed her in the hallway, muttering to himself. In another room, she could see a woman sitting in a chair, but as Peyton passed, she threw her hands into the air and whooped. Peyton wasn't sure this was the place to be if you were struggling to maintain your composure.

She came to the room marked 34 and knocked. Nothing happened. She looked down the hallway again. The man had turned around and was wandering back toward Peyton. He appeared to be having an animated conversation with someone she couldn't see. She kept one eye on him and knocked a second time.

"Go away." The muffled voice came from beyond the door.

Go away? That didn't sound like the man she knew. Even when most stressed, Ravensong had maintained a sort of spacy charm. She reached for the doorknob and turned it. The door opened and she peered inside.

Ravensong was sitting in a chair before the window, gripping the arms with both hands, his eyes closed. His hair was damp at the temples and the mouth of his shirt was open, sweat glistening on his chest. She crossed the room to him and knelt by the chair. He opened his eyes a slit and glared at her.

"Not a good time, Inspector Brooks."

"I can see that," she said, reaching out her hand and touching his cheek with the backs of her fingers. His flesh was feverish to the touch. "What's going on?"

"It's called withdrawal," he gritted out between his teeth. He moved his right hand from the chair arm and wrapped it around his middle, sucking in a painful breath.

"Let me get someone."

"No."

"No? You clearly need help."

He reached out with his left hand and caught her wrist. "Their form of help involves a needle and drugs. I've had enough of that help in my life, don't you think?"

She covered his fingers with her own. "Okay. Let me call Elena then."

"No."

"And why no?"

"I don't want her to see me like this."

Peyton was pretty sure Elena wouldn't agree, but she understood pride, even if it was stupid. "Okay, no help." Gently extricating herself, she went to the bathroom and found a washcloth. It was the smallest, sorriest washcloth she'd ever seen, but she guessed it was too small to make into a noose. Turning on the water, she let it run cold, then soaked the washcloth and wrung it out. Returning to his side, she laid the cold compress over his forehead. He glared at her, but she pressed it against his temples. "This helps me when I have a migraine."

He closed his eyes again and clenched his teeth.

She sat on the edge of the bed. It brought her close enough to him to touch him, but give him space. Glancing around, she found the room rather sparse and utilitarian. No decorations on the wall, no dangling light fixtures, no cabinets or closets. His clothes were stored in a tub on a shelf, and the few toiletries he was allowed amounted to shampoo, conditioner, and toothpaste. He didn't even have a toothbrush or a comb. A shadow of stubble marred the hollows beneath his high cheekbones, and she felt certain they would definitely not give him a razor.

Completing her look around, she turned back to the window. Beyond his room was a fenced-in yard of ferns, redwoods, and baby tears – a veritable garden of Eden in green. She gave a low whistle. "The receptionist wasn't kidding. You've got a great view."

He squinted at her beneath the washcloth. "I like to sit out there." He gasped and tightened his hold on his stomach. Instinctively Peyton reached out and took his other hand. His fingers squeezed hers, but she didn't let go until the spasm passed.

"How often does this happen?"

"Less often than it did, and this one is mild compared to the others."

"Great." She knew her voice didn't sound convinced.

"You don't have to stay. I'd prefer it if you left actually."

"Well, if you won't let anyone else help you, I guess I'm what you get."

He tried to laugh, but it became a moan of pain. After a moment, he looked at her again. "How is Tiffany?"

"She's amazing. You know you're going to have your hands full in a couple of years, right?"

"Meaning?"

"She's a looker. You're going to have to fight the boys off."

"I know. That's why I got the dog."

"That's not gonna help. I met your dog."

Joshua nodded stiffly. "You're right. I named him Wolf to give him ideas, but it didn't take."

"I also met the rest of your family. Well, most of them. Apparently, the twin boys and a sister didn't come."

"James?" He gave her a worried look.

She smiled, still holding on to his hand. "Oh, I met James all right."

"He means well."

"I know that. It's just wading through all of the threats and insults that's a bitch."

He gave a chuckle again, but his fingers tightened on her hand. She waited until his hold eased.

"They love you dearly, you know?"

"I know."

"That's hard on you, isn't it?"

"What do you mean?"

"Knowing how much they love you. How much they want to protect you. Even Elena. I know you adore her, but it's hard."

"Having a family is hard, Peyton, because you're bound to hurt them, disappoint them, worry them, but without them, what are you?"

"Alone."

He opened his eyes and studied her. "That sounds personal."

She shrugged.

"If you're going to stay, you have to tell me about your family. Your chatter helps."

"Chatter? Where's that famous Ravensong charm? You're starting to sound like James."

He laughed again. "I'm in pain here, Peyton. How much charm do you think I can muster?"

She reached for the washcloth and found it hot to the touch. "All right. Let me wet this again, then I'll tell you about my dysfunctional family. That ought to get us to the other side."

He didn't respond because he was too busy grappling with another wave of agony. Watching him, Peyton felt her protective instinct go into overdrive.

* * *

The buzz of her cell phone catapulted Peyton out of a sound sleep. She sat up quickly and dragged it out of her pocket. Sometime in the night she'd fallen asleep on Ravensong's bed. Looking around in a daze, she saw sunlight was streaming through the window, encircling him in his chair. He moaned and screwed his eyes shut tighter.

She thumbed it on and put it to her ear, swinging her legs to the floor. "Hello," she whispered.

"Where the hell are you!"

Jake.

"Jake?"

"Are you all right?"

She held the phone away from her face and looked at the time. Shit! "Yes, I'm fine."

"I was worried sick, Peyton. I didn't know if something had happened to you."

"I know. I'm sorry. I got busy and just decided to stay here." For some reason, she was reluctant to tell him where she was. She rose to her feet and stretched the kinks out of her back.

"You slept at the precinct?"

She glanced at Ravensong. His eyes were still closed and a frown darkened his brow. *Sure, let's go with that,* she thought. "Is everything all right? Is Pickles okay?"

"You scare the shit out of me and you ask me about Pickles? Thanks a hell of a lot, Peyton."

"Okay, stop scolding me. I'm sorry, all right?"

"You could have called me, sent a text message, anything."

"I know. You're right. I was completely wrong."

"Damn straight you were."

Okay, Preacher, this is going a bit far. "I didn't mean to worry you, but I won't do it again. I'll be home in a few hours, okay?"

"Fine. We'll talk more then."

Wonderful, she thought. "Bye."

"Bye."

The phone went dead and she put it in her pocket, taking a seat on the edge of the bed again.

Ravensong cracked open an eye. "Boyfriend?"

"You'd think, huh? No, just a housemate. An uptight, over-protective housemate."

"I guess with your job that's understandable."

She thought about it. He had a point. It was kind of nice having someone worry about her for a change. "How are you?"

"If I don't move, I'll be fine. The worst is over, now it's just the hangover."

"That's shitty. No fun, but all the suffering."

His laugh turned into a moan. "You don't help when you make me laugh. What time is it?"

"7:00AM."

He squinted at her. "You're kidding, right?"

"Nope." She looked around the room. "It's kinda strange that no one came to check on you in all that time."

"With enough money, you can buy a great deal of privacy. Most of the people here are not here voluntarily, but I came here with the understanding that they leave me alone for the most part."

"Yet they won't let you have a toothbrush."

"I can have a toothbrush if they watch me. It's a concession I make."

"What exactly can you do with a toothbrush?"

"Sharpen the end of it."

Peyton reared back. She hadn't thought of that. "Well, okay then."

He forced a smile for her. "I haven't been suicidal since my daughter was born, Inspector Brooks. It's all a precaution."

"So you don't do the therapy sessions?"

"I have my own psychiatrist."

"Yeah, I met her."

He frowned. "Is there anyone you didn't meet?"

163

"Nope. I pretty much got the whole Ravensong experience." Her phone vibrated again and she pulled it out, looking at the display. Marco's name flashed across the screen and she thumbed it on. "Hey."

"Peyton, I need you to come down…" His voice trailed off and she could hear other voices in the background.

"Marco?"

"Peyton, look, I need you to come to Saint Francis Memorial."

Peyton felt her heart slam against her ribs. "Saint Francis? The hospital?"

"On Hyde, yes. I need you to come now."

Her grip tightened on the phone. "Marco, what's wrong?" Her mouth felt suddenly dry.

"Tonio was in an accident last night. Bad." His voice had dropped and she had to strain to hear him.

"Oh God," she breathed. "Is he all right?"

"He has a head injury and a compound fracture in his left leg. They're prepping him for surgery right now. There was another boy in the car, Billy Miller. He's in a medically induced coma." His voice trailed away and she could hear other sounds in the background, a PA system, loud talking.

"Marco?"

"I need you to come down, Peyton, please."

"I'm on my way."

"Thanks. I'll meet you here. Seventh floor, ICU, okay?"

"Okay. I'll be there."

"Thank you." Then he was gone.

Peyton held the phone in her hand for a moment, trying to still the frantic pounding of her heart.

"You okay?"

"I have to go. I'm sorry."

He leaned forward in the chair, grimacing in pain. "No worries. Go. You've done enough for me."

She hesitated. She wanted to offer him some comfort, some platitude, but she didn't think he'd appreciate it. Mostly she wanted to tell him she wasn't giving up on the case, that she was still looking into it, but that seemed small and petty. The reality was without some break, he would be tried for his ex-wife's murder and she couldn't stop it.

"I'll check up on you in a few days, okay?"

He took her hand in his. "Inspector Brooks, you don't owe me anything."

But she did. She owed him the truth, even if that meant the worst for him. He deserved to know. Damn but he was making it hard for her to see him as a murderer.

She squeezed his hand and rose to her feet. "It would help if you weren't so damn charming."

He laughed. "You'd better go."

She released him and backed toward the door. "You're gonna be okay, right?"

He gave her a smoky look and Peyton felt like she was half-in-love with him. "I'm fine," he said, but it wasn't convincing to either of them.

With a short wave, she turned and hurried to the door, pulling it open. She didn't allow herself to glance back as she shut it behind her.

*　*　*

The Saint Francis Memorial Hospital was an imposing grey building in the heart of the City. Peyton parked in the garage on Pine and hurried to the main hospital entrance. A security guard directed her to the information desk and Peyton found an older woman sitting behind it with cat-eye glasses perched on the end of her nose and held in place by a beaded chain.

"ICU?"

"Sign in, dear," she said, pointing to a spot on a register.

Peyton quickly signed.

The woman handed her an oval shaped visitor's badge and pointed an arthritic finger behind her. "Take those elevators to the seventh floor."

"Thank you." She hurried to the elevators and pushed the button. As she paced before them, she wished she'd had time to grab a cup of coffee and a shower, even use the restroom, but she'd raced right over the minute she left the psych facility.

The elevator opened and Peyton stepped inside. The back wall was mirrored, so she tried to smooth down her hair and straighten her clothes as she waited for it to climb. Turning around, she studied the numbers above the door, then noticed a glass covered box. Peering at it closer, she marked that it was a camera. Made sense. She was sure there were cameras all over the hospital, watching everything people did.

The doors opened and she hurried out, coming to a glass door that blocked her from going any farther. Located beyond the doors was a nurse's station and a young Asian man in scrubs buzzed her through. She pushed open the door and hurried to the counter.

"D'Angelo?"

"They're in a waiting room down that hallway on your left."

"Thank you." She walked as quickly as she could down the hallway. It was white and austere with no decorations on the walls. A bank of windows looked out over the City, but the only view she saw was a covering of fog shrouding everything.

She came upon the waiting room and turned in the doorway. Marco glanced up at her from where he sat in a chair by himself. He had his hands clasped before him, but he rose immediately. She marked that Vinnie and Rosa sat in chairs on the other side of the room, next to Mona and Leo. A television flickered on the wall above Marco's chair, but the sound had been turned down.

She stepped forward to meet him and wrapped her arms around his waist. He enfolded her and pressed his cheek to the top of her head. "Thank you for coming," rumbled his voice beneath her ear.

After a moment, she pulled away and went to Vinnie and Rosa. Rosa fell into her arms, tears racing down her face. Peyton held her and reached out her hand to take Mona's. Mona kissed the back of her fingers.

Peyton held Rosa off and smoothed back her hair. "It's gonna be all right," she soothed. "Where's Cristina? Do you want me to take her to my place?"

"She's with Franco and Sofia," said Vinnie.

Peyton nodded. "Is Tonio in surgery right now?"

Rosa wiped her eyes. "Yes, they had to operate right away or he might lose his leg. They're worried though because he has a brain injury and the surgery might increase the swelling."

"Was he conscious?"

"Yes, but he doesn't remember anything that happened."

Peyton turned and hugged Vinnie. "Can I get you guys anything?"

He hugged her in return. "Just being here is enough."

Marco touched her back. "I need to talk to you." He motioned to the hallway.

Peyton quickly went to Leo and kissed his cheek.

"Thank you for being here for my family, bella," he said, patting her shoulder.

"Always," she answered and followed Marco into the hallway.

He was leaning against the window sill, his arms crossed. His eyes were bloodshot and he hadn't shaved.

"You okay?"

He nodded, his gaze drifting to the waiting room. "I need you to do something for me."

"Anything."

"I need you to look at the police reports from last night."

"Okay. What happened, Marco?"

Marco held up a hand and let it fall against his arm. "He and this Billy Miller kid went to a party near George Washington. Tonio was driving. He doesn't remember what happened, but somewhere around midnight he slammed the car head-long into a tree on the corner of the school."

"Where?"

"Thirtieth, right on the corner of Balboa."

"You said Billy Miller's in a medically induced coma?"

Marco swallowed hard. "The crash severed his spine. If he lives, he'll be paralyzed."

Peyton felt tears burn her eyes. "Okay." She fought to choke them back because she could see Marco's eyes were glistening too.

"I need you to get the police reports and take a look at the car. They moved it to the impound yard this morning, so I didn't get a chance to see it."

"Was he drinking, Marco?"

"I don't know. They took blood, but they didn't tell us the result."

She nodded.

"Peyton, if he was drinking and if this Miller kid dies, they'll try him for manslaughter."

"I know. I'll get the reports, then Jake and I will go see the car."

"I'd help, but…" He motioned to the waiting room.

"No, you stay here." She thought for a moment. "You said Balboa and Thirtieth, right?"

"Right."

"Was he turning on Thirtieth and lost control?"

"I don't know. He doesn't remember anything."

"I'll take a look at the crash scene too. I'm just having a hard time picturing the accident."

"So am I."

She came forward and he lowered his arms, so she could wrap her arms around him. He folded his body around her, resting his forehead on her shoulder, and she simply held him, running her hands across his back to soothe him.

"You'll keep me updated?" she said.

"You know it."

"Let me know as soon as he's out of surgery, okay?"

"Yeah." He lifted his head and kissed her cheek. "Thank you."

She leaned back and gave him a watery smile. "You don't need to say that."

"I know."

She kissed him in return and stepped away. "Tell Vinnie and Rosa I'll be back as soon as I can."

He nodded and watched her walk away.

CHAPTER 10

I wandered to the window and back toward my desk. Most of the time, he did the pacing, but this part of the story worried me. We'd gotten to something deep and dark, something I wasn't sure I was ready to broach. Up until now, everything he told me made him the victim, but this would change things, this would cast him in a different light.

Maybe I could stop. Maybe I didn't need to go on. I had enough for the book, didn't I? I didn't need to delve any deeper. His life until now was interesting, tragic, compelling. Did people need to know more, know the man who was weak and flawed and flat out stupid?

There's where it was. I wanted people to feel sympathetic toward him. I wanted them to love him. I didn't want them to see him as just another junkie, a drug addict, master of his own destruction. Here's where the story would change, would paint him in a light that wasn't flattering because there was no way to not hold him responsible for his own fall.

"You're wearing a hole in the floor."

That voice, sexy, smoky, like dark chocolate. It flowed over me and made me stop pacing.

He had his back to me, his hands clasped on the chair arms, the damn leather bands like shackles. I could only see his dark hair, the edge of a royal-blue sleeve rolled to mid-arm, exposing the bands as if they were his brand, his mark of shame.

Ah, a writer's mind is a playground of words. Some came so easy, but some were hard. Some didn't want to be said, written. That's what took courage. Writing what shouldn't be written. Like confession, it hurt, but the pain was necessary to get to the truth.

I didn't know how to answer him, so I didn't.

"You wanted to do this project. You asked me to cooperate, but now you're backing out," he said.

"I'm not backing out. I'm just wondering if we have enough. If we should stop?"

"That's not it."

I wanted to argue, but there wasn't any point. We both knew I was flirting with cowardice.

"If I continue telling you, things change and you don't want that. You're afraid to go there. Afraid to hear how easy it is."

"Easy what is?"

"To slide."

To slide. And there it was. I couldn't ignore it, I couldn't pretend we hadn't arrived at this point, I couldn't bury the truth. He connected it and it was done.

"You know people may not feel the same way about you after we write this."

"I know."

"The adulation, the worship, it will be tarnished."

"I know."

"It's one thing to read about it in the abstract, but this won't be abstract, this will be real."

"A confession."

"Yes."

"I know."

"Why do it? Why tell this? Why not let people have their fantasy?" I came around the chair, so I could see his face, his dark eyes, high cheekbones, perfect bone structure. "Why not let them pretend?"

He gave me a grim smile. "We make gods out of lesser things. We make gods out of shallow, two-dimensional people and we shower them with riches and adulation. Why? Why do we do this?"

"Because it makes our lives seem less mundane. We can live out a fantasy through them."

"And all the while we rot inside. We have more substance abuse than at any other time. Maybe we should stop living the damn fantasy and take a look at ourselves. Maybe we should start living for real."

I stared at him. I could wax on poetic about seeing him, really seeing him for the first time, but that would be more author chicanery. Instead I just nodded. That and nothing more. After a moment of staring at each other, I went and took my seat again.

∗   ∗   ∗

The roar of the crowd echoed in Joshua's head as he pushed through the roadies and band members backstage. He needed just a moment to himself, a moment to gather his thoughts. Pushing open the backdoor of the club, he eased out into the alley. A single light illuminated the area over the door, so he moved a few steps to the left, deeper into the alley and the shadows. The night was cold and he leaned against the brick of the building, allowing the breeze to cool the sweat on his body.

This was the biggest concert *Blazes* had done to date – two encores and the fans had continued to scream for more until the management brought the house lights up. Joshua's modeling had done exactly what Phil promised, it had catapulted them into the spotlight and soon these sorts of clubs would be too small. Now he wanted Joshua to accept a cameo in a movie. Joshua wasn't ready for that yet. He wasn't an actor, he wasn't a model, he was a musician. Why the hell wasn't that enough?

Hearing voices at the other end of the alley, he edged back the other way, closer to the street. He didn't want to see anyone, talk to anyone, but it was unavoidable. Three people blocked the opening to the street. He almost missed them since they were crouched against the building, huddled in a circle, but they looked up when he got close. The one nearest to Joshua rose to his feet. He was young, dressed in baggy jeans and an oversized black jacket. Tattoos covered the side of his neck and lined the top of a white tank top beneath the jacket. His hair was cut in a Mohawk and bright green.

Joshua recognized the other two, the singer and drummer from the band that had played before *Blazes*. Light from the bulb over the door caught on something metal as they shifted to hide what they were doing.

Joshua took a step back. He didn't want to get mixed up in whatever they were doing. Turning on his heel, he headed back for the door and had just grabbed the handle when he heard footsteps behind him.

"Hey," a rough voice called.

Joshua glanced over his shoulder. The guy with the tattoos had followed him. "What?"

"You're that singer in the last band, right?"

Joshua nodded, but kept his hand firmly curled around the handle.

"You got some pipes, man." He gave Joshua a once over. "Kinda surprised me, your voice."

"Why?"

"Just did." He glanced back at the other two. "You interested?"

Joshua frowned. "Interested?"

"I can hook you up, you know?"

Hook him up? Suddenly it dawned on Joshua what he'd seen. The bit of metal had been a syringe. "No. No thanks." He pulled open the door.

"Hey," said the guy. "What I got is better'n what you're taking."

"What?"

His eyes lowered to Joshua's leg. "I know the twitch, man. I know it."

Joshua tried to fight it, but the pills made him jumpy. The only thing that helped were the white pills Phil gave him, the downers. He turned toward the door again.

"I'm not kiddin', man. What I got will take that away. It'll make everything smooth."

"Smooth?"

He held up a clear vial. "Smooth, man."

Joshua let the door close. "What is it?"

173

"China white."

"China white?"

The guy nodded. "Best you can buy."

Joshua's gaze shifted to the other two musicians. They were leaning against the building now, their bodies slack. He didn't need that. He needed energy and then he needed sleep. He didn't need oblivion.

The guy held the vial out in the palm of his hand. "Take it. Free sample." He took a step toward Joshua.

Joshua pulled open the door. "No, I don't think so."

The guy slipped the vial in his pocket, pulling out a scrap of paper. "Take my business card then." He held it out to Joshua. "When you get tired of the twitches, call me."

Joshua shook his head. Phil was bad enough. He wasn't dealing with a common two-bit drug dealer.

The guy came forward and grabbed Joshua's hand, shoving the scrap of paper inside. "You got some pipes, man. You got some pipes." Then he turned and jogged down the alleyway, jumping over the musicians' legs and disappearing around the corner.

Joshua glanced at the number, then crumpled it up. He started to throw it into the alley, but he caught sight of his leg, the strange twitching he couldn't control. Closing his eyes, he shoved the number into his pocket, then went back inside.

* * *

Peyton leaned on the back of the little blue Ford Escort. The front of the car looked like an accordion, only so much twisted, collapsed metal. The driver's side door had been pushed nearly to the passenger seat and where the passenger seat had been was a twisted bit of crumpled cushion. Looking at the car, Peyton was amazed anyone had survived.

As she folded out the printer paper, she could hear Jake taking pictures behind her. She'd gotten the on-scene officer to fax her his report as she'd hurried to pick Jake up, then they'd come straight to the impounds yard. This was the first time she'd had an opportunity to look at what he sent and she dreaded what she'd find. She liked Antonio. He was a good kid, but even good kids did stupid stuff sometimes.

The ride over had been tense. Jake was warring with his anger that she hadn't called the previous night and she was anxious to do what Marco had asked her, so they spoke little to one another. Abe called on the way, so she handed the phone to Jake. He gave Abe a terse explanation of what was going on, then hung up. Peyton half expected him to complain about her, but he hadn't said anything and handed her phone back without looking at her.

As soon as they'd been directed to the car, Jake had begun taking pictures, so she left him to that. She already apologized enough and she wasn't about to tell him what really happened, so there was nothing more to say on the subject.

She didn't examine why she was reluctant to explain where she'd been. Nothing had happened between her and Ravensong, yet she felt a need to protect him and she didn't really want anyone else knowing what he'd been going through when she found him. Of course, that brought up a host of other issues – for one, her need to protect people that were accused of doing really bad things. No one understood that, not Marco, not her captain, and certainly not Devan. It had cost her one serious relationship and she wasn't sure even Jake would understand it, despite the fact that it had helped him directly.

Forcing herself to focus, she read through the report. The on-scene officer estimated Antonio's speed at 60 mph, far too fast for a residential street. He'd been coming down 30th Avenue, turning right on Balboa when he lost control of the car. He'd smashed the little Escort into a bank of trees that bordered the soccer field. The cop attributed the damage to both doors from impact with the trees.

Peyton turned around and studied the interior of the car. Although the passenger side was badly damaged, the greatest damage had occurred on the driver's side. The driver's seat had been shoved nearly into the area where the passenger was. If he was turning right, lost control and jumped the sidewalk, wouldn't the first impact have come on the right side?

Jake was taking pictures of the front of the car, trying to shoot over the dashboard. The deflated airbags blocked the view, so he angled around to the driver's side door to shoot the interior. With a heavy exhalation, he glanced up at her.

"How the hell did they survive this?"

Peyton shook her head. "Modern cars are made to crumple like that."

"Yeah, but look where the driver's seat is."

"I know. According to the report, the side damage was caused by trees, but I don't understand how that works if he was turning right. Most of the damage is on the left side."

Jake continued taking pictures. "Was he drinking?"

Peyton spread the papers out on the trunk and continued reading. "His blood alcohol level was below the legal limit, but…"

"He's a minor."

"Right. It doesn't matter. Any amount is illegal."

"Shit." Jake hunkered down by the car and continued snapping. "What did Marco say about the other kid?"

"If he survives, he'll be paralyzed."

"Damn. There's just no good outcome to this, Mighty Mouse."

"I know." She scrutinized the car again. "Why is so much damage on the left side, Jake? How come I can't get a visual of this?"

"Didn't the officer include a diagram?"

"Yeah, but it doesn't make sense."

"Well, we'll just have to go out there and canvas the scene ourselves. I'm almost done here."

Peyton read over the report again, searching for something she missed. Neighbors across the street heard the crash and came running out. They called 911 within a few minutes and paramedics were on the scene in less than five. No one witnessed the actual crash, but many of them reported hearing squealing tires just before impact.

"Peyton?"

Peyton glanced up.

"Come here a minute."

Peyton folded the report and edged around the back of the car. Jake was kneeling by the dent in the driver's door.

"Look here," he said, pointing to a spot in the twisted metal.

Peyton hunkered down beside him and studied where he pointed. She could see where the blue paint had been scraped away, down to the metal, but just to the right of it was a streak of white.

"That didn't come from no tree," said Jake.

Peyton fingered the paint. A bit flaked off on her hand. "No, so what the hell else did he hit?"

*   *   *

Jake reached for his camera bag as Peyton pulled the Corolla up in front of the houses that bordered George Washington High School. They could see the accident scene roped off with yellow caution tape up ahead, but except for a couple walking their dog in the street, no one else was around. Late afternoon sun shone through the trees, casting a dappling of shadows on the road.

Opening the door, Jake climbed out. He set the camera bag on the Corolla's hood and removed the camera. He began taking pictures as they walked toward the scene. Peyton angled out away from him, walking into the middle of the street.

177

Skid marks from the Escort were clearly visible as if Antonio had tried to break before making the turn. They carried up and onto the sidewalk, then disappeared as the cement gave way to the loam beneath the trees.

Jake stepped into the trees and continued taking pictures. Damage to the trunks was extreme and pieces of metal were strewn about the area. A tree on the right had been uprooted and tilted backward precariously and the one right in front of Jake, closest to the soccer field had a huge chunk taken out of the center of it where he presumed the front bumper had made its final impact.

Turning back to the street, he noticed that Peyton was squatting by the skid marks. Behind her, a man stood in the driveway of his home, watching them. Jake snapped off a picture of her, then wandered in her direction.

She glanced up when he stopped in front of her. "This must be from the Escort." She laid her hand on a set of narrow tread marks that angled directly into the trees.

"Yeah, I'm sure it is."

She moved her hand and touched a second set of skid marks. These angled to the right and were wider, the tread a different pattern. "Then what the hell are these?"

Jake frowned. "Old marks?"

Peyton shook her head. "They're as dark as the first ones."

Jake lifted the camera and began shooting the different marks. "Doesn't the department have an expert who can look at the tread marks and identify the car?"

"Yep, so make sure you get a good shot of each of them."

Jake lowered the camera. "What if this is where the white paint came from? Maybe he sideswiped someone?"

Peyton shrugged, then swiveled to look at the houses. She spotted the man standing in the driveway and pushed herself to her feet. Reaching for her badge, she walked over to him. "Inspector Brooks with the San Francisco Police Department," she said, holding out the badge.

He looked at it, then nodded. "There were cops out here last night and this morning again. Did the kids make it?"

"They're in intensive care right now." She looked up at the house. "Do you live here?"

"Yeah."

Jake surreptitiously snapped off a picture of the house. It was the third one down the block from Balboa, a cream colored single home with curved windows all across the front.

"Did you see anything last night?"

"I was in bed. All of a sudden I heard tires squeal and then a loud crash. My wife started hitting me in the shoulder, telling me to get up."

"Did you come out?"

"Yeah, I called 911 and ran over to the car, but I couldn't get them out. The firemen had to use those cutty things."

"The jaws of life?"

"Yeah."

"How long did it take you to get out here?"

The man shrugged. "I was asleep, so I had to put on some pants and find my shoes. Maybe two…three minutes." He gave Peyton a puzzled look. "It was a couple of teenagers, right?"

"Yeah."

"So why all the cops?"

"Just making sure we have all the details. When you got out here, was there only the blue Escort?"

"What do you mean?"

"No other car, maybe a white one?"

"No, just the Ford."

Jake lifted the camera and took a picture of the building next door to the man's, a pale blue duplex. It also sported an entire front wall of windows. He wondered if anyone might have seen something from there. They were even closer than the man in the cream-colored house.

Peyton must have thought the same thing. "Who lives next door?" She pointed to the duplex.

"The one on the right is empty. Older couple, wife died and the husband couldn't keep it. I think it's for sale, but the one on the left is two gay guys."

"Are they usually home this time of day?"

"Naw, they're on a cruise or something. We're getting their mail for them. They won't be back until Tuesday, I think. I'll have to ask the wife."

"Thank you." Peyton reached for one of her ubiquitous business cards and handed it to the man. "If you remember anything else, will you let me know?"

"Sure."

Jake lowered the camera and pressed the button to view the pictures he took. He thumbed back through them to make sure that he got everything he needed. He was particularly concerned about the tread marks. They looked clear in the viewfinder, so he hoped they'd be even crisper on a computer screen. Thumbing back in the other direction, he stopped at the blue duplex.

Something caught his eye near the eaves on the left side. He pressed the picture to zoom in and squinted in concentration. The dark spot beneath the gutter looked like a lens. Lowering the camera, he glanced up at the house, then walked across the street until he was standing in the far left driveway. Tilting back his head, he could just make out a camera mounted above a window.

"Inspector Brooks," he called.

She strolled down the street until she was next to him.

He pointed. "Isn't that a camera?"

"It sure is." She turned around and tracked where it pointed. "It looks like it's directed right at the school."

"Yep," said the man. He'd followed them over to the driveway. "Chase, the guy who owns this place, was sick of all the kids drinking under the trees, so he installed it to show the principal at the school."

"Is it on all of the time?"

"Far as I know."

Peyton removed a second card. "Do you have a pen, Jake?"

"Hold on." He jogged over to the Corolla and opened the camera case. He kept a pencil in the inner pocket and he fished it out. Peyton and the man had wandered over to him while he searched for it.

Handing her the pencil, he watched as she wrote something on the back of the card, then handed it to the man. "Will you give this to Chase and ask him to call me as soon as he gets back from vacation? We need to see that tape."

The man tapped the card against his palm. "Got it."

"Thank you." She held out her hand and the man shook it. "I appreciate the help."

"No problem. Just hope the kids are okay."

Peyton smiled at him as she reached for her car keys. "So do I," she said, "so do I."

*   *   *

Jake wanted to return to the Saint Francis with her. They checked in at the visitor's desk and waited by the elevators. She hadn't heard from Marco again and she felt anxious. Not to mention the mixed bag of information she had to give him. Unless Antonio or Billy Miller could tell them what happened, everything hung on the possibility of a surveillance tape.

"I hate hospitals," muttered Jake.

"I'm sure you do."

He shifted nervously.

"I'm glad you're here, though."

A grunt was her only response.

She canted a look sideways at him. "Still hate me?"

181

He rocked on his heels. "No one makes me as mad as you do. Frickin' assed cops always think they're invincible."

She smiled and bumped him with her shoulder. A moment later, the elevator opened and they waited until a couple with two little children exited. Stepping inside, she leaned against the back wall. It was nearly 6:00PM and she was tired. Besides a bag of chips she'd grabbed at home, she'd had nothing to eat all day.

Jake pushed the button for the seventh floor, then reached out to stop the door as it slid closed. The door opened again and a young man pushed through the opening, punching the button for six.

"Thanks," he said and Jake nodded.

Peyton glanced up at the numbers as the door closed again. They couldn't stay long. Pickles was waiting for dinner and he would definitely need to go out in a few hours, but she hated to leave Marco alone here.

As the floors began climbing, Peyton shifted her attention to the black box she'd noticed earlier. Frowning, she moved closer to it. "Jake, does every elevator have a camera?"

Jake glanced up as well. "I think so. For security in case the elevator stalls. That's why they have a phone. Why do you ask?"

"People have cameras everywhere now. Street corners, houses, but that condo building on Russian Hill didn't have anything except in the garage."

"Right."

"What about the elevator?"

The young man looked over, but Peyton ignored him.

Jake shrugged. "I'll bet the elevator had one. Still, what will that prove? We know Ravensong was in the building."

"Ravensong? The rock star?" said the young man. "I read something about that."

Peyton moved closer to Jake, dropping her voice. "Maybe it'll show us if he had the murder weapon. If I saw the murder weapon in his hand, I'd be more certain…" She trailed off and glanced over her shoulder at the young man.

The elevator came to a halt on the sixth floor and the doors opened, but the young man hesitated to get off. Peyton narrowed her eyes on him, trying to intimidate him. He blinked in surprise, then exited, the elevator door shutting behind him.

"It's worth a look," said Jake.

The elevator accelerated, then came to a halt at the next floor. Stepping out, they came to the glass door and waited for a blond nurse to buzz them inside.

"How can I help you?"

"I'm looking for the D'Angelo family."

She checked the monitor in front of her. "Only family members are allowed in the ICU, but you can go to the waiting room down the hall and I'll let them know you're here."

"Thank you."

"Can I show you where it is?"

"I know, but thank you," said Peyton. She motioned Jake to follow her and headed down the hall where she'd been that morning.

Marco was sitting on the opposite side of the room across from the television and to Peyton's surprise, Abe was sitting beside him. The television was off and they were the only ones there. Marco looked up as she entered. When he started to rise, she motioned him back down, taking a seat on his other side.

Reaching over, she took his hand. "Any news?"

"He's out of surgery and in recovery."

"Is that where everyone is?"

"Yeah. They limit the number of people who can go in."

"Have you heard how Billy Miller is?"

"Same."

183

Peyton tightened her hold on his hand. She really didn't want to give him the information she had. Jake took a seat in the chair beneath the television, giving Abe a nod of greeting.

Marco shifted toward her. "Don't stall, Brooks. Tell me what you found out. Did you get the police report?"

"I did."

"And?"

"The cop estimates he was going about sixty. He came down 30th and was trying to turn right on Balboa when he lost control, crashing into the trees on the corner."

Marco closed his eyes briefly. "Did you see the car?" He looked up at Jake.

Jake nodded.

"And?"

Peyton and Jake exchanged a look.

"Peyton, please. Whatever it is, tell me."

Peyton exhaled. "Okay. Here's everything." She told him about the car, the white paint, the two skid marks, and the camera.

He listened without expression, then he tightened his hold on her hand. "Was he drinking, Peyton?"

Funny how she hated when he called her by her first name. He only did it when he was mad at her, or when something was wrong. The worst time was six months ago when he had a gun pointed at the back of his head and she couldn't do anything to stop it.

"He was below the legal limit."

"There's no legal limit for minors."

"I know."

Marco stared at her without speaking for a long time. She found it hard to meet the probe of his blue eyes. Then he released her and rose to his feet, stalking out the door. Peyton started to go after him, but Abe placed a hand on her arm.

"Let me," he said.

Peyton watched him follow Marco outside, then she got up and eased to the door, peering out. Marco stood in front of the windows, his hands braced on the window sill. Abe leaned on the sill beside him.

"He's going to need a lawyer, Angel'D."

"I know."

"I'll bet Devan knows someone."

"My brother and sister-in-law won't be able to afford anyone Devan knows."

Abe reached into his jacket pocket and pulled out a check. He held it out to Marco. "Here."

"What's that?"

"A check."

"I know it's a check."

"I wrote it out when I heard what happened."

Marco faced him. "I'm not taking your money, Abe."

Abe reached for his hand and pressed the check into it. "I make more money than I need cutting up dead bodies that died by other people's hands. Let me do something good with that money, okay?"

Marco looked at the amount. "I can't accept this."

"You can and you will because your nephew needs a lawyer. In this, there is no pride. Take the money for Antonio and don't argue with me."

Marco's fingers tightened around the check. "I don't know what to say. I'll find some way to repay you, Abe, I promise."

Abe laughed. "Are you kidding me? Looking at your pretty face all these years is payment enough."

Marco gave him a faint smile. "Thank you."

Abe cupped a long fingered hand against his cheek and kissed the other one. "Anything for you, Angel." Then he released him and went to Peyton, throwing his arms around her. "Take care of him," he whispered in her ear. "And call me if you need me."

She hugged him back. "Thank you."

He kissed her as well and then waved to Jake as he took his long legs down the hallway and around the corner.

Peyton walked over to Marco and slipped her arm through his, resting her head on his shoulder. "I'll bet you haven't eaten anything all day."

He laughed, folding the check and putting it in his pocket. "No."

"Let's find the cafeteria and get something, okay?"

"Yeah."

"Just let me give Jake my keys, so he can go home and take care of Pickles."

When Marco nodded, she walked back into the waiting room, trying to shake off her own weariness. No matter how tired she was, she wasn't leaving him sitting in that room by himself.

CHAPTER 11

He only had ten lines, then he would be blown away with a machine gun and he could leave. Ten lines. One of them was "I did it for love." Cheesy as hell, just like this movie.

And yet, he couldn't remember them. He couldn't remember a single one. The director was getting pissed and he was one scary bastard. Whenever Joshua flubbed a line, he threw his hands in the air and shouted that he was a retard. The casting director would remind him that Joshua wasn't there to act, but to provide the eye candy. Joshua didn't know which term he found more insulting.

The lines should be so easy, but they made him begin shooting at 6:00AM and he played with *Blazes* until after midnight. The pills were clouding his concentration. The blue pills helped him get here at dawn, and the white pills let him catch a few hours of sleep. He was in a loop and he knew it, but no one seemed to give a damn. Phil had promised him a break around Christmas. Joshua had intended to get off the pills then, but this movie had come up ruining that plan. While James and Evan were home with their families, Joshua was here, shooting this crappy assed cop thriller.

Eva Sterling, the B-grade actress who was the star, came over to where he sat and grabbed the script from his hands. She tossed it on the table before him and then put her hand on his knee, stopping the bouncing of his leg. He stared at her hand. He hadn't even been aware he was twitching until she touched him.

"You know how I learn lines?" she purred, her hand tightening as she sat down on the couch beside him.

Joshua looked up at her. She was beautiful, dark hair, hour-glass figure, but lines fanned out from her eyes. He knew she was at least twenty years older than he was. "How?"

"I get someone to run them with me. If you can picture it, it sticks in your mind better."

Joshua didn't think that was going to help. None of this movie was hard for him to picture, it was that stupid. His problem was the pills. "Thanks for the advice. I'm just not an actor."

She smiled and her smile made her seem youthful. "It seems to me that when you're in a movie, you have to pretend to be an actor and darlin', you're not pretending very well."

He looked down at the script. She had a point.

She reached out and took his hand. "Come on. I can help."

He let her pull him up, then she grabbed the script off the table, tugging him after her. "Where are we going?"

"To study."

The director turned as she moved across the sound stage behind him. "Eva?"

"We're going to study," she called theatrically.

A bunch of snickers followed in their wake.

Eva led him to her trailer. He hadn't been given a trailer. He got a chair in make-up and that was it. She tossed the script on the couch and went to the little kitchenette, opening a cabinet overhead. She pulled down a bottle of scotch and two glasses.

"You need to relax. Let's have a drink first."

Joshua shook his head. "I don't think that's a good idea." He was trying hard not to combine the pills with booze. He didn't really want to wind up dead. That would kill his mother.

"Okay." She poured herself a drink and sipped at it delicately as she studied him. "Why did you agree to this? You obviously hate it."

"My manager said it would help the band."

"I see."

He looked around the trailer. It had seen better days. The fabric on the couch was circa-1960 and the paneling looked worse. Who the hell was going to see a movie this low budget?

"So, what are you taking?"

He glanced back at her. "What?"

"Drugs, darlin'. You're obviously on something." She looked pointedly at his leg.

"It's like caffeine."

She laughed. "Right. How old are you?"

"Eighteen."

"Eighteen. God, I hardly remember eighteen." She set the drink on the counter and walked into the back. Joshua peered after her, trying to see where she went. She turned into a little room and opened a glass cabinet. The bathroom. Taking something from the cabinet, she walked back to him, holding up a bottle. "This is better than whatever you're taking. I promise you, it'll get rid of the shakes."

He studied the bottle. Oxycodone. What the hell did that do?

She opened the cap and shook one into her hand. "Be careful with these, though. Only one at a time, darlin'."

"What does it do?"

"It relaxes you."

He swallowed hard. "I don't need to relax. I need to stay awake."

She placed the pill in his hand. "You need to relax. That's why you can't remember your lines. Just try it." She reached back and grabbed the scotch, holding it out to him.

He stared at the oblong white pill. God, he wasn't stupid. This was another step down the ladder and he knew it, but he had to get through this damn movie somehow. Lifting his hand, he tossed the pill into his mouth and reached for the scotch. It burned as it went down and he coughed, closing his eyes.

She took the glass from him and set it on the counter behind her. "You know what else helps a person to relax?"

He opened his eyes and looked at her. "What?"

The smile she gave him should have been another warning, but he ignored it as she reached for the buttons on his shirt.

*   *   *

Tuesday dawned bright and beautiful, spring in full regalia in San Francisco, but Peyton wasn't enjoying it. She made it to the precinct on time after downing two cups of coffee before she left the house. Jake was already gone, said he wanted to get the pictures of the crash scene processed, then he wanted to take the tire treads to Forensics himself and see how they went about matching them up. She'd hung back a little to walk Pickles. The poor Yorkie was feeling abandoned.

She'd spent Monday at the hospital with the D'Angelos. Antonio slept most of the time, recovering from his surgery. He was in so much pain, he couldn't talk with anyone. Late in the day, she and Marco had tried to see Billy Miller, but his parents refused a visit. The father, a tall handsome man with dark skin and weary eyes, had informed them he'd gotten a lawyer. Poor Marco looked so stunned, Peyton had led him away by the hand.

Jake was right. She was beginning to hate hospitals. They made you feel so helpless and useless. There was nothing you could do while you watched a loved one fight for his life. Jake thought they were an alternate reality because time just seemed to pass that much slower in a hospital than in the real world.

She took her seat at her desk and turned on the computer. Marco wasn't coming in today, but she needed to get back on the Ravensong case. Devan was not going to be put off much longer. On Sunday night while she and Marco grabbed something in the cafeteria, she stepped outside and placed a call to the security guard at the condo building on Russian Hill. He led her to the elevator company. A few strings pulled and she got someone who agreed to get her a copy of the video from the day Terry died. It was the only thing that had worked out during this entire case.

Lifting her hand, she rubbed her eyes. She'd been staring at the computer screen for five minutes and realized she couldn't remember her log-in. Last night Marco had made her leave about eight o'clock, but even then her sleep had been filled with dreams of cameras following her everywhere she went. The world was filled with cameras, recording every intimate detail of people's lives, but right now, when she needed them, she didn't have access.

Pushing away from the desk, she rose to her feet and walked to the break-room. Pulling open the refrigerator, she found half of a chocolate cake from someone's birthday on Friday or Thursday, she couldn't remember. Oh, shit, it had been Thursday, the last day Marco was here, for his birthday.

She pulled it out and carried it to the counter. It was probably stale, but she didn't care. She opened the top of the box and grabbed a plate out of the cabinet, then she cut off a slice. She made sure to get one of the yellow roses decorating the edge. Carrying her cake to the coffee machine, she poured herself a mug, then automatically reached for the sugar. She hesitated a moment, studying the cake, then she dumped a tablespoon into the steaming liquid and stirred it. There, that was moderation.

Carrying both back to the table, she took a seat and reached for a plastic fork they kept in a Styrofoam coffee cup in the center of the table. Digging into the cake, she placed a huge bite in her mouth. The outside was a bit stale, but the inside was still moist, flooding her taste buds with chocolate bliss.

She'd wolfed down about half of it when Maria appeared in the doorway. Peyton stopped with a bite nearly in her mouth and lowered it. Reaching for a napkin, she wiped stray crumbs off her lips and sat back, picking up her mug and taking a sip. Bitter warred with sweet in her mouth and she grimaced.

Maria came forward and took a seat across from her, sliding an envelope over the table. Peyton lifted it and gave Maria a questioning look.

"From the elevator company," she said.

Peyton laid the envelope on the table and flattened her hand on it. For some reason, now that she had it, she felt sick to her stomach. She pushed the cake away.

Maria followed her motion with her eyes. "How's Marco?"

Peyton almost wished she'd make some comment about her getting fat, or her hair – her hair was always a target for Maria. "He's…Marco. Tough Italian not willing to show his feelings, but he's hurting inside."

"Will his nephew be all right?"

"He'll live, but his leg was mangled pretty bad. A football scholarship is out of the question now. He doesn't remember what happened and they've been too afraid to tell him about his friend."

"How is the friend?"

"Still in a medically induced coma. They performed an emergency operation on him when he got to the hospital to take pressure off his spine, but they don't think he'll ever walk again."

"When I was in high school, some kids went to a party out in the Sunset."

Peyton nodded.

"They were drinking, you know, and the cops broke it up. They ran out the back door. Four of them got in this car, Mustang or something big. Drove it right into the median on Highway 1. All four died." Maria met Peyton's eyes. "I was supposed to go with them, but my mama wouldn't let me." She gave a little laugh. "I hated her for that."

Peyton pushed the fork against the cake, flaking off some crumbs. "We do stupid shit as teenagers, don't we?"

"Yeah. I always thought about the kid who threw the party. I didn't really know him, but I always wondered if he's walking around carrying the guilt all these years."

Peyton drove the fork into the center of the yellow flower. She'd thought about that a lot over the weekend – how would Tonio accept the guilt for crippling his friend?

"I was thinking we might start a fund or something for the two families? Do you know how we do that?"

Peyton looked up at her. This was probably the most she and Maria had ever talked. "Jake will know. He worked in a bank. Ask him."

Maria nodded. "I'll do that."

"I think that would be really helpful, Maria."

"Yeah, well, it doesn't put lives back together, but it might help."

"Yeah."

Maria pointed to the envelope. "You afraid to look at that?"

Peyton sighed. "How'd you guess?"

"Because I'd be. What if he's holding the murder weapon?"

"Exactly."

"It's hard to think of him as a murderer, isn't it? He's like the first love I ever had."

"Tell me about it, sister." And Maria hadn't spent the night with him, trying to get him through withdrawal.

"Glad that's your job, not mine." She pushed herself to her feet, leaning over the table. "By the way, that one rose…" She pointed to the yellow bit of frosting. "…has about a million calories."

"A million?"

"Yep, and it's all made out of lard." Maria tilted her head and a mischievous light twinkled in her eye. "But go ahead and scarf it down. When your ass is as big as a hippo's, I'll have something besides your hair to make fun of."

And there it was. Peyton smiled, leaning back in her chair. "So you do watch my ass when I walk by, eh, Maria? I thought so."

Maria's lips tightened in frustration, then she turned away from the table. "Tell Marco Baby I send my love," she called over her shoulder as she walked out the door.

Peyton laughed, then she grabbed the cake and stood, taking it to the garbage can. She really didn't need an ass as big as a hippo's, although she liked hippos. When she returned to the table, the envelope was waiting for her.

Before she could change her mind, she snatched it up and went to her desk. This time she remembered her log-in. Sparring with Maria had cleared her mind. While she waited for the computer to boot up, she tore the end off the envelope and shook the contents into her palm. A zip drive slid out.

Inserting it into the computer, she waited for it to read, then a folder popped open on the desktop. Only one file was visible. She leaned back in her chair and pushed her fingers into the curls beneath her ponytail. No going back now.

She reached into her pocket and took out her notebook. Flipping to the Ravensong case, she searched for the interview with the security guard. What time had he said the alarm went off? She found it. 9:56.

Clicking on the file, she waited while the video loaded. The date stamp in the corner listed Terry's date of death. The guy at the elevator company had simply given her the entire day from midnight on. She hit the pause button, then moved the bar across the bottom until she got to 9:30 in the morning. That should give her a big enough window. If not, she could go back farther in increments of five.

Nothing happened for the first five minutes. The elevator climbed the floors, once or twice someone got on, but it was no one she recognized. The camera distorted the image a bit, made it look like the elevator was a fishbowl and the mirrored back wall sometimes made it look as if the same person was really two. Why did every elevator have a mirrored back wall? She suspected it was to make the elevator appear larger for claustrophobic people.

Squinting at the screen, she noticed a strange green blur in the mirror above the people's heads. She stopped the video and leaned closer for a better look. Suddenly it dawned on her what the blurry green light was. The floor number reflected into the camera from the mirror.

She started the tape again. Nothing for another five minutes. Maybe she needed to go back further. The security guard found Terry's body at 10:00AM, the alarm sounded on the stairwell door at 9:56. Maybe they fought for a lot longer than she figured before Ravensong struck her with the curio.

She reached for the mouse, but stopped, her heart slamming against her ribs. Ravensong had entered the elevator. There was no mistaking him with his mane of dark hair and his collared shirt with the sleeves rolled up, showing the two leather bands on his arms.

Peyton released the mouse and covered her lips with her hand as she watched him pace back and forth in the elevator, back and forth like a caged animal. He was clearly agitated. Facing the door, he looked up at the numbers, giving the camera a clear shot of his face, then he raked a hand through his hair.

Suddenly, he dropped that hand and punched the wall beside the door. Peyton jumped, then fumbled for the mouse to stop the video.

Slumping back in her chair, she stared at the screen. His image had blurred as he slammed his fist into the wall. She realized she was breathing hard. That was where the injuries to his hand had come.

Reaching out, she backed up the video and pressed play. Again he faced the door, raked his hand through his hair, then pounded his fist into the wall. And they said he wasn't violent? What the shit?

She played the tape again and again. Over and over again, he slammed the wall.

195

"Whoa," came a voice behind her.

She hit pause and swiveled around to see Jake standing at her back. "Yeah. Whoa is right." Her voice shook.

"Play it again."

She did what he asked, but she couldn't watch it any more. She watched Jake instead.

His brow knit into a frown. "That's how he hurt his hand."

"I know, but they all told me he wasn't violent. He never hurt anyone."

Jake gave her a strange look. "Peyton, that's what men do when they don't want to go around punching people. We punch inanimate objects."

"Walls?"

"Yeah, better that than people, right?"

"Walls, Jake?"

He held out his hands. "I'm just telling you how it is. Men punch inanimate things when we're pissed."

She stopped the video, shaking her head. "That's a bunch of crap. This is a man with violent tendencies."

Jake shifted weight. "Listen. When I found out Zoë had that warfarin stuff in her system, I lost it. I went into the bathroom and tore it apart, looking for the pills. That wasn't enough. I came out and started punching…"

Peyton swiveled around to look at him again. "Punching?"

He dragged his teeth over his lip. "The bed."

Peyton's brows rose. "You punched the bed, Jake?"

"And the pillows."

Peyton couldn't help but laugh. "You're all kinds of bad ass, aren't you, Ryder?"

"Okay, but listen, that's what men do to blow off steam, to calm ourselves so we don't go around punching women." He nodded at the image of Ravensong on the screen. "I'm just not certain he killed her, Peyton. Especially after seeing this."

Peyton shifted back and pressed the play button. After punching the wall, Ravensong flexed his wounded fingers, then glanced up as the elevator came to a halt. When he stepped out again, she could see the number 8 reflected in the glass on the mirror. She and Jake continued watching, until the security guard entered at 9:59 AM. Ravensong never appeared again.

Peyton drummed her fingers on the desk. "Okay, so how do I prove he didn't kill her and if he didn't do it, who the hell did?"

Jake shook his head, his eyes still on the computer screen. "That's why you're the cop and not me, Mighty Mouse."

*   *   *

Elena sat in Peyton's chair watching the computer screen as Peyton played the video. When they came to the part where Ravensong punched the wall, Elena jumped as Peyton had done and her hand flew to her mouth. Peyton stopped the video.

"I've never seen him do something like this."

Peyton gave her a moment to collect herself.

She shifted toward Peyton. "I swear to God, Inspector Brooks, he's never struck me or his daughter."

"I believe you." She tilted her head toward the video. "I have it on good authority that this is what men do when they don't want to hit someone."

"They punch walls?"

"I know. My point exactly."

Elena looked back at the screen. "What are we going to do now?"

Peyton placed her hand on the back of Elena's chair. "Look, Elena, I actually think this is good. We know how he hurt his hand and it wasn't punching Terry, right?"

She nodded, but her eyes were swimming in tears.

"I need to know everything you know about Terry."

"I hardly ever spoke to her. I didn't really know her."

"How long have you been with Joshua?"

"Almost two years."

"Did he ever talk about her? Tell you how they met."

Elena leaned back in the chair. "She was a groupie. I guess she followed the band around for a while."

"When he was with *Blazes*, right?"

"Yeah. He married her when he joined *Avalanche*."

"How long did that marriage last?"

"Three years I think."

Peyton swiveled Elena's chair so they faced each other. "Elena, who ended the marriage? I can get the divorce decree, so it doesn't do any good to lie to me."

"Why would I lie?"

Peyton shot a look at the screen again. "Because you love him and you're praying like hell he didn't do something like this."

A tear ran down her cheek. "He filed for divorce."

"Why?"

"He caught her in bed with another man. He came home early to see his daughter and surprised her."

"Who was the man?"

"A CEO of some company here in San Francisco. I can't remember which one." She wiped the tear away. "I'm trying hard not to speak ill of the dead, Inspector Brooks, but that woman was a gold digger. She was always extorting money out of him so he could see his daughter and then she always had some other wealthy guy waiting in the wings to take Joshua's place." She clasped her hands in her lap. "I probably shouldn't tell you this, but she told me once she expected him to go back on drugs. She just didn't believe he'd stay clean, and she needed someone to take his place when that happened."

"Take his place?"

"Money."

"Okay. Do you know who this preacher man is that Tiffany mentioned? Did Joshua or Terry tell you she was seeing someone new?"

"She got erratic after her mother died. She came up with this scheme to move to Europe. I don't think her mother had been dead more than a week before she started talking to Joshua about him taking full custody."

"And how was that going to work?"

"We had to go before the judge and have him sign off on it. He didn't like the idea of Joshua having full custody, but it helped that I was in the picture. Ultimately, he couldn't block it because both of her parents agreed and there was nothing to show Joshua unfit."

Peyton rubbed the back of her neck. She needed a vacation. "Then why would she have changed her mind?"

"I don't know. Joshua didn't tell me what was going on when he went over there. I thought he was staying home. I didn't even know…" She caught herself and her eyes widened.

"You didn't know what, Elena? You have to tell me everything. You have to tell me the truth. You've got to believe that I'm on your side or I would have handed this case over to the DA by now."

"I didn't even know he'd left the house. He never texted me."

Well, that wasn't good. It meant he hadn't wanted her to know. So what had he planned to do when he went to Terry's? Bribe her. Seduce her. Kill her.

Peyton's phone vibrated in her pocket. She fished it out. Marco's number flashed across her screen. "I'm sorry. I have to take this."

Elena nodded.

Peyton swiped her thumb over the display. "Hey?"

"What are you doing?"

"Talking to Elena."

"Can you take a break and come down to the hospital?"

"Yeah, did something happen?"

"Tonio's lucid for the first time and I want to ask him some questions, but I really want you here when I do."

"Is he up for it?"

"I think so. He's able to sit up and eat a little, although he's got a raging headache." His voice trailed off. "That guy with the camera call you?"

"Not yet. It's still early. Who knows when they get back from their vacation?"

"Yeah. Can you come down? You know I'm not very good at this. You've always been better at interrogation."

Peyton's gaze zeroed in on the monitor. She needed to go out and question Ravensong about his ex-wife again, but she couldn't deny Marco anything he asked. "I'm on my way," she said.

*   *   *

The whites of Antonio's eyes were red from the impact and he couldn't open them all the way because the light hurt his eyes. His leg was in traction and IV tubes ran into his arms. They had the bed raised, but he didn't seem able to sit up on his own. Looking at him, Peyton wasn't sure this was a good idea. The kid looked horrible, although she guessed it was a good sign they'd moved him from ICU.

His parents didn't look much better. Rosa wasn't wearing any makeup and she wore a baggy sweat suit with running shoes. Peyton didn't remember ever seeing her in anything but the most fashionable attire. Vinnie's blue eyes were blood-shot and circled in exhaustion. He had on a crumpled t-shirt and jeans.

Not that Marco looked much better. She'd never seen his jaw covered in so much beard and he had his dark hair pulled back severely in a ponytail.

Rosa vacated the chair by the bed as he and Peyton entered. Sinking into it, Marco clasped his hands between his thighs, giving Antonio a sideways look. Antonio could hardly look his uncle in the eye.

"How's the headache?"

"Bad."

Rosa leaned against Vinnie and he put his arm around her shoulders, pulling her close. Peyton reached over and took Rosa's hand.

"Look, Tonio. I need to ask you some questions. Your dad said you're up for it."

"Yeah, I guess." He rolled his head on the pillow and looked squarely at his uncle for the first time. "Is it true about Billy? Is he paralyzed?"

Marco met his look, but he didn't answer right away. Peyton felt Rosa's fingers tighten on hers.

Antonio narrowed his eyes. "Tell me the truth, Uncle Marco."

"We don't know yet. He's still under medication, but the doctors are pretty sure he'll be paralyzed."

"When are they going to let him wake up?"

"I don't know."

Antonio rolled his head the opposite direction. "It's all my fault, isn't it?"

"I don't know, Tonio. I need to get more information."

"He was fast, Billy. He could run the mile under five."

Marco studied his hands, then he swiveled and looked back at Peyton. The pain in his eyes almost made her want to cry. She nodded at him to continue.

"Tonio, I need to know where you were Saturday night."

The boy tried to shift in the bed, but it was almost impossible with his leg in the sling. "We went to a party." He shot a look at his parents. "For the track team. We made sections."

"Where was the party? On 30th?"

"No, it was at Derek Kelly's house. He lives on Shore View."

Marco wiped his hands down his pants legs. "Tonio, I need you to tell me the truth now. You can't lie to me."

The boy didn't answer, he just studied his uncle's face.

"Was there booze at the party?"

The boy held up a hand and let it fall on the bed. "Someone brought a couple bottles of champagne to celebrate. They got it from their parents' wine fridge."

"That's all they had? Champagne?"

"Yeah, that's all I saw."

"Did you drink any?"

His eyes flickered to his parents and away. "I drank a few swallows. They were passing the bottles around."

That accounted for the alcohol in his blood. A few bottles wouldn't go very far at a party.

"Don't lie to me."

"I'm not. That's all there was. The party was lame, so Billy and I decided to leave."

"Where did you go?"

"Driving. We thought we'd cruise down Market, but there wasn't anyone out."

"The accident happened on 30th. How did you wind up back there?"

"Billy wanted to go back to the party. There was a girl there he liked. He thought he could get with her."

Get with her? Peyton wondered if that meant what she thought it did.

"You were coming down 30th when the accident happened. That's going away from Shore View, Tonio. Why were you on 30th?"

Antonio blinked his red-rimmed eyes.

"Tonio?"

"I don't know."

Marco sat up straight. "What do you mean you don't know? You told me you were going back to the party on

Shore View, but you wound up going the opposite direction. Why?"

"I don't know."

Peyton could see Marco's jaw harden.

"Do you have any idea how much trouble you're in? That kid is going to be paralyzed and you're telling me you don't know?"

"I don't know." His voice was rising.

Peyton released Rosa. She could see Marco was getting agitated.

"How can you not know? You said you were going back to the party. Did you? Did you make it back to the house on Shore View?"

"I can't remember."

"You can't remember? Tonio, you had alcohol in your system. They're going to charge you with reckless endangerment, driving under the influence, and who knows what else. You have to tell me what happened."

"I don't remember."

Peyton started toward Marco, but he rose to his feet. "You remember going to the party, you remember cruising on Market and you remember going back toward the party again. What happened after that? Why were you on 30th?"

"Marco!" said Vinnie, but Marco ignored him.

"Tonio, answer me!"

"I don't know!" screamed the boy, bursting into tears. "I don't know. I don't remember! I don't remember anything!"

Peyton grabbed Marco's arm, startling him. He took a shuddered breath, staring at his nephew.

"I'm so sorry, Uncle Marco. I'm so sorry. I didn't mean for this to happen."

Marco touched Peyton's hand and she released him. Then he took a seat on the bed and gathered his nephew into his arms. The boy clung to him, burying his face against his chest, sobbing. Marco stroked the back of his hair.

"It's okay, Tonio. It's okay."

"I'm sorry, I'm so sorry."

"Shh," he whispered, "it's gonna be okay."

Peyton fought back the tears as she watched her partner cradle the injured boy, promising him things she didn't think they would be able to deliver. Sometimes it wasn't okay and there was nothing you could do to fix it.

CHAPTER 12

Joshua let his head fall back against the couch and closed his eyes. Evan had *Blazes'* music blaring in the hotel room and he was singing to it, swilling down a beer. Ben, the drummer, had his sticks out and he was banging on the table. Both had girls draped over them. Joshua wanted to go into his room and sleep, but he knew he'd never be able to with this racket next door.

James kicked him in the leg, forcing Joshua to squint up at him. His brother had his arm around the shoulders of a pretty blond whose boobs were nearly falling out of her cut-off tank top. She wore a mini-skirt and fishnet stockings that ended in stiletto heels. Her eyes were rimmed with eyeliner and she had bright red lipstick on her mouth. She reached up and grabbed the beer out of James' hand and took a drink, but her eyes never left Joshua.

"Go get some sleep," James ordered. He snatched the beer from her and drained it.

Joshua knew James was drinking too much, but who was he to say anything?

Evan levered himself off the couch next to Joshua and slapped him on the leg. "Don't go to sleep. Wanna beer?"

"No." Joshua watched him stagger over to the hotel refrigerator and bend over to pull it open.

When he saw there was nothing inside, he looked over his shoulder at James. "We're all out."

"Go tell that roadie, Mark, to get some more."

Evan staggered to the other end of the room where a couple of roadies were chatting up some girls.

James fell onto the couch next to him and the girl perched on his lap. "You should get some sleep."

"Yeah, and you should stop drinking." He took the empty bottle away from his brother and set it on the floor.

James broke into drunken laughter, nearly knocking the girl off his lap. She wrapped her arm around his shoulders, but she continued to stare at Joshua. Across the room, the roadie extricated himself from the tangle of bodies and went to the door. Evan dropped into his place on the floor.

"That was one bitchin' concert tonight, huh?" said James, leaning on Joshua. "You see how many people were there." His words slurred.

"Yeah."

He didn't seem to realize he had the girl on his lap or else he was too drunk to care. "Can you believe what we've done in just a few months? We're actually headliners now."

"Yeah."

"Tell you what. Tell you what." He slapped Joshua's leg. "'Nother year and we gonna be doing stadiums."

"Great."

"Yep, s'great." He shook his head drunkenly. "S'great."

Looking around the room, Joshua had a hard time seeing the great. Beer bottles lay on every surface, old pizza boxes, and half-clothed girls without names. The more success they got, the more chaotic it became. So many places, so many rooms, so many faces that all meant nothing. He loved the music, but he wasn't sure he loved this.

He pushed himself off the couch and stepped over sprawled legs and trash until he came to the bathroom, then wedged himself past a roadie to get inside. He didn't bother to shut the door. What the hell did it matter? There was no privacy left.

Leaning on the sink, he turned on the cold water and splashed some on his face, then reached back and grabbed a towel off the rack. Drying the water away, he dropped the towel over the sink and reached into his pocket for the baggy filled with oxycodone pills. He shook four into his hand and tossed them in his mouth, then bent over and drank water from the faucet to wash them down.

"That's a hell of a lot of pills," came a feminine voice from the doorway.

He straightened and looked into the mirror. His brother's blond was standing there, but the minute he acknowledged her, she came into the bathroom and closed the door. He swallowed the pills, then turned around, leaning on the sink.

"You always take so many?"

He shrugged. He wasn't going to answer that for a girl who came into a band's hotel room of her own free will. She moved until she was so close, her breasts brushed against his chest with every exhalation.

Her black-rimmed eyes searched his face. "You're almost pretty. You know that."

"I thought you were with my brother."

She put her arms on his shoulders and began toying with his hair. "He's not pretty."

Joshua braced his hands on the sink. He couldn't deny he felt a sense of loyalty to his brother and didn't want to upset him, but he wasn't sure James gave a damn. He had to know the girl had followed him into the bathroom. "You got a name?"

"Yeah." She brought her mouth near his until they almost touched. "My name's Terry."

*   *   *

As soon as Peyton got to work the next day, she hauled out the white board and set it up behind Marco's desk. She listed everything about Ravensong's case into two columns – those things they knew and those they didn't.

For instance, Ravensong was in Terry's apartment around the time of her death and he had her blood on his hands. Then there were the text messages showing that the two of them had been arguing about Tiffany. Those were all things they knew.

What they didn't know was where the murder weapon was and why he didn't have cuts on his hands when the weapon broke.

She tapped the grease pen against her chin. The evidence that muddied her whole system was the video. Clearly he had a temper, but he'd struck a wall, not Terry, so the injury to his hand was now explained. Which column did that go into?

She circled back to her desk and took a seat, pulling up the video again. She had it keyed to the exact spot she needed and she leaned forward so she could see better. She wasn't sure what she expected to find, but there had to be something she was missing.

When Ravensong struck the wall, he actually seemed to calm himself, regain control. How odd. She couldn't understand how someone could be so angry one minute, but appear perfectly rational the next.

She played the video again.

"Now that's interesting."

Peyton grabbed the mouse and stopped the video, then jumped to her feet and threw her arms around Marco where he stood behind her chair. He hugged her back.

"Glad to see you too, Brooks."

She leaned back so she could see his face. "Why are you here?"

"I work here, right?"

"Right, but how is Tonio?"

"Resting. I couldn't do much there, so I thought I'd come in for a while." He pointed at her computer screen. "What the hell is that?"

"That's Ravensong punching the wall on his way to see Terry."

"Play it again."

Peyton returned to her seat and clicked the play button. She'd seen it so many times it was engrained in her memory, but it always made her jump when he struck the wall.

"Hmm," said Marco, bracing one hand on the back of her chair and the other on her desk.

She looked up at him. "You ever hit something like that?"

"Lots of times."

"Like what?"

"Punched a locker when we lost a football game once. Socked Franco's door when we got in a fight over who was taking the car." His brows rose. "Punched a car once too."

"You punched a car?"

"Yeah. The night we found that little girl in the dumpster."

Peyton would never forget it. She looked back at the screen. She was beginning to see the merit in punching inanimate things. "Jake punches pillows."

"Figures," he said. He straightened and looked at her board. "Now we know how he hurt his hand." He'd shaved since the previous day and he ran his hand over his chin. "I don't know. The evidence seems to stack up, but that video makes me wonder."

"What do you mean?"

"I mean it looks like he got his anger out in the elevator before he went inside."

"But what if she sent him back into a rage again once he was with her?"

"Yeah." He didn't sound convinced.

"It's the cuts, isn't it?"

"Abe just isn't wrong about stuff like that."

"I know, but if he didn't do it, then who did?"

"Do we have anything at all on a second suspect?"

"Nothing except what Tiffany said about the preacher man."

"Doing *Bible* studies in the bedroom, yeah, I remember. We need to ask Ravensong."

"I agree, but he wouldn't even talk about Terry with me the last time I tried."

Marco started to say something, but his eyes went past Peyton toward the lobby. Peyton didn't need to turn around. She could hear the click of dress shoes on the tile.

"D'Angelo," Devan said, stopping behind Peyton.

"D.A."

"How's your nephew?"

"Better."

"Good." Peyton could feel his eyes shift to her. "Peyton, how are you?"

"Great." She didn't bother to turn around. She didn't want to discuss this case with him.

"Look, I've been to see Captain Defino again. She wouldn't turn the case over to me until I get your confirmation."

Peyton swiveled around and looked up at him. "Well, you don't have it. We're not done with the case yet."

Devan glanced at Marco, but he simply shrugged. Leaning on the desk, Devan brought himself closer to Peyton's height. "I know you want to tidy up all the loose ends, but this is ridiculous. The case is done. It's obvious who committed the crime. You only have the one suspect and even he's convinced he did it."

"The case is not done. We have an unreliable suspect, a weak motive, and next to no evidence. We aren't ready to give him up yet."

"So you have other suspects? Who are they?"

She wasn't about to say the *preacher man* because she knew how that would go over with Devan. "We have other suspects."

"Tell me."

"I don't have to tell you. I don't work for you."

"In a way you do, so consider this pulling rank."

Marco let out a low whistle and retreated to his chair.

Peyton rose to her feet. "You're pulling rank on me? Who the hell died and made you King of San Francisco?"

"It's just an expression. I was trying to be funny."

"Of course you were, because telling a woman that you out rank her is always amusing."

"Look, I admire you as a cop. You do a good job, but..."

Marco closed his eyes.

"But?"

"But you get all worked up over these cases."

"Worked up?" She turned to Marco. "You hear that. I get worked up. Silly little woman."

"Here it comes," muttered Marco.

She faced Devan again. "Silly little woman, right? Getting all worked up."

"Peyton…"

"Why don't you go ahead and ask me if I'm on my period!"

Devan threw his hands up in surrender. "Look, I'm just stating a fact. God damn it, Peyton, you can't rescue every single person that comes through those doors."

Peyton went still and stared at him. "You mean like uptight lawyers."

He started to respond, but nothing came out.

She went toe to toe with him. "You can be sure I won't make that mistake again." She threw herself down in her chair and turned it away from him.

Devan held out his hands to Marco. "Talk some sense into her, will you?"

Peyton glared at him, waiting to see whose side he was going to take.

Marco's lips drew tight against his teeth. "Talk some sense into her?"

"What? Now you too?"

"You come in here and you throw your uptight lawyer ass around thinking that we're your lackeys, while you sit in your air conditioned office, surrounded by your legal books and neatly stacked folders."

Devan took a step back. Peyton could hear the captain's door open and she glanced around to see everyone watching them. Maria had her mouth open, Jake grinned from ear to ear, and behind him stood Holmes and Bartlet looking like they were ready to throw Devan out in the next minute.

Marco slowly rose to his feet. "If my partner tells you we aren't finished with the case, you're going to nod politely and walk away because when it comes down to it, D.A., we're the ones putting our asses on the line, so you can sit behind your desk and think up clever repartees."

Devan held up his hands again. "Okay, okay. Don't go all De Niro on me. I'll check back with the captain in a day or two." With that, he walked away.

Peyton waited until he left the precinct and everyone had started to disperse before she turned back to Marco. He'd taken his seat again and was busy messing with his keyboard. "You okay?"

"Smug bastard pisses me off."

"Clearly."

He shot a look around, then gave her a narrow-eyed stare. "He pisses you off too, Brooks."

"Absolutely, but then he did dump me."

Marco gave a bark of laughter and returned to typing on his computer.

Peyton picked up a pencil and tapped it against her desk. "You know we don't have air conditioners in San Francisco, right?"

"Right."

She nodded. "Okay then."

He looked up and the smile he gave her could melt anyone; she was so damn happy to see it.

She started to tell him, but her phone rang. She grabbed it, but she didn't recognize the number. Thumbing it on, she pressed it to her ear. "Brooks?"

"Inspector Brooks, this is Chase Alreed on 30th Avenue. I got a message to contact you."

"Yes, Chase, I'm so glad you called. You have a video camera set up outside your house, pointed at the high school across the street."

"Yes. I pulled the video as soon as we got in."

"You did? Did you see anything on Saturday night?"

"I viewed the whole thing…and, Inspector Brooks, I think you should come down here whenever you've got a minute. There's something you really need to see."

*   *   *

Peyton pulled the Charger to a stop in front of Alreed's house and set the brake. Beside her, Marco stared out the window at the yellow caution tape and damaged trees. She watched him for a moment, then she reached over and covered his hand with her own.

"You okay?"

He nodded, but he didn't look at her. "When he started to drive, I took him to the impound yard and made him look at the busted up cars. I told him that everyone who had been in those cars died in them. I wanted to scare him, make him understand how dangerous they were. We talked about how he didn't have the right to take anyone's life, even his own."

"He's a kid, Marco. We all did stupid things when we were a kid. We think we're invincible."

"I watch my brother and sister-in-law and I see the pain they're going through. They can't make this better for him. They can't take it away. I just don't think I can do it, Peyton. I don't think I can ever be a father." He turned and faced her, staring into her eyes. "This world is filled with so much horror, so much pain and suffering."

"We just see it, Marco. We see the brutality and the cruelty so much, but there's good out there as well."

"What? Tell me one good thing you've seen this week, Brooks. One thing that gave you hope that we aren't doomed."

213

She tightened her hold on his hand. "I saw a man take a seat on the edge of a hospital bed and gather a wounded teenager into his arms, holding him while he cried. To me, that was an absolute good, Marco."

His eyes searched her face, then he lifted his free hand and cupped her cheek, leaning over to kiss her on the forehead. "What would I do without you, Brooks?"

"That's what I keep saying."

He laughed and reached for the car door. "Come on. Let's get this over with."

She caught his elbow and held him back. "This might be really hard, Marco. I could go view the tape and you could wait here."

He patted her hand. "I need to do this. I'll be all right."

She let him go and reached for her own handle, pushing the door open. Walking up to the gate, Peyton looked around for some way to let Alreed know they were there. A buzzer beside the gate caught her eye and she pressed it. A moment later, the door at the top of the stairs opened and a young man with neatly combed blond hair jogged down to greet them.

"Inspector Brooks?" he said as he began unlocking the gate.

"Yes. This is my partner Inspector D'Angelo. Are you Chase?"

"The one and only." He pulled open the gate and held out his hand. Peyton shook it, then reached for her badge and showed it to him. "Thank you." He motioned them inside and shook hands with Marco as he passed him. "Please come up."

Peyton let him lead the way into a pleasant living room with minimalist furnishings and eggplant painted walls. She'd never have the nerve to do this, but she liked it. He motioned to a desk set up before the windows.

"I'm sorry I didn't call yesterday. We got in late last night."

"I understand. How was your vacation?"

He smiled at her. He had a kind, open face. Lifting a glass frame from the desk, he passed it to her. Two beaming young men stared back at the camera from the deck of a cruise ship. "The Bahamas are beautiful."

"Looks like you had fun."

"We did. Best vacation we've taken. You should try it sometime."

Peyton didn't remember when she last had a vacation. It sounded good. "Is your partner here?"

"He had to go to work."

"I appreciate you seeing us on such short notice."

"No problem." He took a seat at the desk. "I went through the whole day and narrowed it down to the accident. Well, I'm not sure it's an accident anymore." He motioned for Peyton and Marco to gather around him. "I also put it on a zip drive, so you can have a copy of it."

"Thank you. What do you mean you're not sure it's an accident?"

"See for yourself." He clicked on the file and waited for it to load on the screen.

Two vehicles tore down 30th, going too fast for the narrow street. One was the blue Ford Escort, but the camera didn't catch who was driving because the little car was shadowed by a much larger white pick-up truck. Just as the two vehicles neared the intersection, the truck swerved into the path of the Escort, forcing it up and over the sidewalk and into the trees. The truck skidded to a stop, paused for a moment behind the Escort, then squealed away, turning the corner going left on Balboa.

Peyton didn't speak for a moment, staring at the screen. Behind her, she heard Marco breathing heavily. Reaching back, she grabbed his hand and felt his fingers tighten on hers. "Play it again, please, Chase," she said.

"Sure." He clicked the file.

Once more the two vehicles careened down 30th and the truck swerved into the Escort, actually hitting it and forcing it over the curb. When the truck came to a bouncing halt, Peyton touched Chase's shoulder.

"Stop it there."

He did as she requested.

They stared at the truck. It was impossible to see the driver, but it looked like only one person was in the cab.

"Can you read the license plate number?" she asked.

Chase squinted at the screen, then shook his head. "The video's too dark and grainy for that."

"Maybe Stan will be able to enhance it?" she said to Marco. Stan Neumann was the precinct's tech genius who could work wonders with a computer.

Marco didn't respond, just stared at the screen.

Chase held up the zip drive. "The footage is on here. Let me know if you want the original."

Peyton closed the drive in her fist. "Thank you. I really appreciate this."

"I wish I could do more." He pushed himself to his feet. "I know it's not the best quality."

"It tells us a lot." She glanced at her partner. "More than you can imagine."

Chase gave Marco a puzzled look.

Peyton pushed Marco in the stomach to back him up. He blinked at her and then acknowledged Chase. "Thank you," he said in a tight voice.

"No problem."

Peyton led the way to the door and opened it. "If you ever need anything, please use my card."

"Thank you, Inspector Brooks," he answered, leaning on the door as they went down the stairs.

Once they were on the street again, Marco walked over to the crime scene. Peyton followed him, but she waited on the sidewalk while he walked through the destruction.

"I blamed him for this. I yelled at him when he couldn't remember what happened."

"It was a natural reaction, Marco."

He turned around. "If there hadn't been a video on that house, Tonio would have carried the blame for that accident for the rest of his life."

"Maybe not. Jake found white paint on the Escort when we saw it in the impound yard. And he took photos of the tire treads to be analyzed by Forensics. The video is just quicker."

Marco strode back to her. "Brooks, I was sure Tonio was responsible. I jumped to that conclusion without looking at the evidence."

"Okay? What's your point?"

"What if I've been wrong about Ravensong?"

Peyton started to answer, but both of their phones went off at the same time. "Hold that thought," she said as she pulled the device from her pocket. "Brooks?" She stepped away from Marco and into the street.

"Inspector Brooks?"

"Yes."

"This is Emily Staddler, Joshua's psychiatrist."

"Yes, Dr. Staddler?"

"I was wondering if you could come to the psych facility. I have an idea of how to jar Joshua's memory about the day Terry died and I'd like to run it by both of you."

"Sure. I have to finish up something, but I'll be over there in an hour."

"Great. See you then."

The phone went dead and Peyton replaced it in her pocket, turning back to Marco. He had his back turned as well and the only thing she could hear was "Uh huh" over and over again. Shifting sideways, he glanced back at her. "Okay, I'll be there. Yes, 30 minutes. Okay."

Lowering the phone, he closed the distance between them. "That was Billy Miller's father. They brought him out of the coma and he wants to talk to me."

"The boy does?"

"Yeah. The father says his son remembers what happened."

"Do you want me to come?"

"What was your call about?"

"Dr. Staddler, Ravensong's psychiatrist, has an idea to jar his memory of the day Terry died and wants to discuss it with him and me, but I can reschedule if you want me to go with you."

"No. We can't stall any more about that case. Devan is going to demand we hand it over to him pretty soon. Let me drop you off at the precinct and then we'll meet up tonight and compare notes."

"Got it." She tossed him the keys to the Charger. "You drive. I want to send the captain a text message and tell her what we've got."

* * *

Peyton watched Marco pull away, then she jogged up the stairs to the precinct and pulled open the door. Jake was waiting for her by Maria's desk with the captain. She tossed him the zip drive and he caught it with his free hand. His other held a couple of photos.

"Take this to Stan for me and see if he can get a license plate number off it," she told him.

"All right, but I got the tire analysis from Forensics."

"Okay?"

"The second set of tires belonged to a truck of some kind."

"Yep, a white pick-up. It's there on the zip drive."

"What the hell? Why didn't you tell me that?"

"I wanted to make you feel useful."

"Freakin' assed cops," he muttered, turning away and walking toward the back of the precinct.

Defino smiled after him. "You could stroke his ego a little, you know?"

"Oh, come on, Captain. When have you ever done that for a man?"

218

"Point taken. What's happening with the Ravensong case?"

"The psychiatrist wants to meet with me. She's got an idea to jog Ravensong's memory."

"Okay, but I want to be debriefed when you get back. Where's Marco?"

"On the way to the hospital to meet with Billy Miller. They brought him out of the coma and he asked for Marco."

"You okay handling this on your own?"

Peyton held up her hands. "I'm fine. Unless, you'd like to come out with me and see our rock star for yourself?"

Defino hesitated just long enough to surprise Peyton, then she glanced at Maria and shook her head. "You do it. I'll man the fort here."

"I'll go," piped up Maria.

"That's okay. I think he's been put through enough already."

Maria glared at her. "Well, then I don't know why you keep torturing him with that hair."

Defino didn't say anything, just shook her head and retreated to her office.

Peyton left the precinct, taking her little green Corolla, and made the drive to the psych facility. The late day sun played over the hills and dappled the sidewalk in shadows, but from the top of the psych ward she could see all the way over the City to the bay. Checking in at the desk, she found it manned by an older security guard with a completely bald head.

He directed her to an office to the right of the lobby and she entered to find Ravensong already sitting in a chair before a massive cherry wood desk. He glanced up at her as she entered and she was glad to see he looked much better than the last time she saw him. He still wore the non-descript grey sweat suit and sneakers without the laces, but his hair lay in a glistening blanket about his shoulders and the dark circles under his eyes were gone.

She closed the door at her back and sat down next to him. "Hey."

"Hey." He gave her a crooked smile and she noticed the beauty mark above his upper lip for the first time. Damn the man was sexy, even in sweats.

"Do you know why we're here?"

"When Emily's involved, I never know."

Peyton looked around the office. It had a very masculine feel with heavy wooden paneling and leather desk chairs in burgundy. The desk was cleared of papers, but a silver metal schooner hung suspended from a fulcrum to Peyton's left. In the center was a leather pen cup and calendar. To the right, a desk lamp and a bowl of chocolate candies.

"Did Elena tell you about the video from the elevator?"

He involuntarily flexed his hand. "Yeah. I don't remember doing that."

"Well, I guess it's something men do."

He narrowed his eyes on her. "Meaning?"

"Meaning it must be a trait common to testosterone-laden humans." When he still looked confused, she held up a hand. "Every man I've talked to can relate at least one incident of punching something inanimate."

"And?"

"Women don't do that."

"You don't punch things, or you don't punch inanimate objects?"

"Pretty much both."

"I see."

"Apparently, it's very understandable if you have…" She caught herself and glanced at him from the corner of her eyes.

He shifted in the chair, so he faced her, a smile tugging at the corners of his mouth. "Have what?"

"Have…chutzpah."

He laughed. "I have never heard it called that before."

She wasn't going to touch that. Not with him, not when being next to him made her heart do funny little flutters. She was glad her skin was dark enough to hide the blush that tinged her cheeks.

"You are good for me, Inspector Brooks. I don't know of anyone else who makes me laugh as much."

She wasn't sure that was a compliment. Frankly, she'd rather make him feel as fluttery as he made her. Reaching out, she set the schooner in motion, watching it pass through its wide arcs, the light from the desk lamp reflected off its sides. It was almost mesmerizing, the way it swung back and forth, back and forth, rhythmically, until the arc gradually got less and less.

She blinked and glanced over at him. He was staring at it, his eyes wide and fixed, completely absorbed in the motion. Leaning forward, she caught it and forced it to stop. He gave a little start and blinked.

"Sorry," she said.

He released his held breath. "Uh, yeah."

The door opened and Emily Staddler stepped through, going behind the desk and taking a seat. She had her glasses perched on the end of her nose and she wore a crisp charcoal grey business suit. "Forgive me for the delay. I had to take a call." She hesitated and looked between the two of them, noticing the strange energy. "Is everything all right?"

Peyton didn't want to explain what had happened. She didn't think Ravensong would appreciate it. "Just a little sexual tension," she said. She meant it as a joke, even though she hadn't thought it through all the way, but Ravensong's breath escaped in a half-laugh.

The doctor frowned at her from above the glasses.

Chewing her lip, Peyton wasn't sure what to say now. Reaching across the desk, she grabbed a piece of candy, unwrapped it, and popped it in her mouth. "Oh, that's good." She grabbed one and handed it to Ravensong. "Try it."

He took it, giving her a half-bewildered, half-amused look.

Peyton swallowed, facing the doctor again and plastering a smile on her face. What the hell was it about this man that had her babbling like an idiot?

Dr. Staddler continued to watch her with a skeptical look on her face, then she deliberately flattened her hands on the desk. "I have an idea on how to spark Joshua's memory. I want to show him the video from the elevator."

Ravensong shifted in his chair and Peyton could see his shoulders tense from the corner of her eyes. Automatically she reached over and put her hand on his wrist. He glanced down at it, then covered her fingers with his own. The doctor frowned fully now, but Peyton didn't move her hand. This doctor hadn't been there the night he fought his way through withdrawal.

"I don't think that's a good idea."

"Why?"

"What makes you think it'll work and if it does, to what end?"

Staddler held up a hand. "To the end of this whole mess. To Joshua's freedom."

Or conviction, thought Peyton.

"I'll do it."

Peyton glanced over at him. "Joshua, think about it."

"I have." His grip tightened on Peyton's hand. "I have to know. I need to know if I did it and if this is the only way, then so be it."

Peyton gave him a sad smile. "Okay. I'll make the arrangements for tomorrow. If you're sure?"

He met her gaze, the velvet dark of his eyes beckoning her in. "I am."

Well, okay then, she thought. Nothing more to argue about. "Fine, I'll set it up." She released him and pushed herself to her feet. "If you'll excuse me, I've still got a lot to do today."

She turned for the door and pulled it open, feeling the psychiatrist's eyes on her. Glancing back, she smiled for Joshua. "See you tomorrow."

He nodded and she left the room, hurrying down the hall to the lobby. She'd just made it past the reception desk when Staddler called to her. Peyton stopped and slowly turned around. She knew the entire exchange in the office had been weird, but she wasn't going to discuss it with this woman. The night of Ravensong's withdrawal was theirs and no one else needed to know what he'd gone through.

"Inspector Brooks, I'd like a word with you."

"Of course."

She came to a halt in front of Peyton, her hands clasped around a file. The cut of her business suit was professional, but stiff and formal, at odds with the more bohemian style of her patient.

"Inspector Brooks, I'm certain you understand that Joshua is in a delicate place right now."

"Of course."

"He's vulnerable and probably not thinking as clearly as he should."

Peyton frowned. Was there a point to this?

"He has a tendency to misread situations."

"Dr. Staddler, I don't have a fancy college degree, so if you don't mind, I'd appreciate it if you'd speak a bit more plainly for me."

The doctor glanced over her shoulder, then moved closer to Peyton. "Joshua has an addictive personality as you may well be aware and that extends to everything."

"Meaning?"

"Meaning he tends to get emotionally invested with people and right now he's in a committed relationship. Were something to happen that affected that relationship, he would come to regret it very much, but he might not be able to stop himself before it's too late."

"What?"

"In the past, Joshua has entered physical relationships, believing them to be emotional ones; however, to be honest, the only real relationship he's had is with Elena. He truly loves her, but he might fixate on someone else if he feels she offers him solace and safety. And if that confusion were to evolve into a physical encounter, it would be very destructive to the wellness he's been building for so many years now."

"What exactly are you saying, Dr. Staddler?"

"Okay, here it is. I get the feeling that you are personally invested in this case, and while I appreciate how that can happen, I'm just wondering if Joshua wouldn't be better off with someone less emotionally attached."

Peyton clenched her jaw and moved close enough to the doctor that their shoes almost touched. "Right now, you'd better be grateful for my emotional attachment because it's all that's standing between him and arraignment, and with the way the evidence stacks up in this case, I'm his best chance to beat a conviction, so let me just ask you, Dr. Staddler, how much you want to pursue this train of thought because when you start accusing people of impropriety, you might just want to take a look in the mirror yourself. A lot of people might question why a psychiatrist comes all the way up from L.A. to treat one of her patients."

Dr. Staddler's nostrils flared and she took a step back.

Peyton narrowed her eyes. "Do we understand one another?"

"Yes."

"Good. Then I will see you and Joshua in my precinct tomorrow at 9:00AM."

"On the dot."

"Excellent. Have a pleasant evening, doctor."

"You too, Inspector Brooks."

"Oh, I most certainly will."

CHAPTER 13

Joshua gripped the microphone so hard he could feel the edge of it dig into his fingers. Closing his eyes to block out the crowd, he tried to think of the song, but he couldn't concentrate. All he could hear was the pounding of the drums, beating inside his chest, and the wail of the guitar filling his head with noise. He snapped open his eyes and the crowd swam before him, a kaleidoscope of colors and motions, blurring in trailing tails of light.

Releasing the microphone, he stepped back. He nodded at James to take center stage and moved further away from the spot lights. James gave him a strange look, but he stepped up and automatically launched into his guitar solo.

Joshua turned then and headed backstage, pushing through the roadies and groupies lining the wings. He made it to the open, near the concession table, and leaned on it, trying to gather his thoughts, trying to chase back the panic.

"What the hell are you doing?"

He turned and faced Phil. Sweat slid down the planes of his chest and ran down his spine. It stung in his eyes, making his vision swim. "I just need a moment."

"You need a moment? What the hell do you mean you need a moment? We're playing a packed house."

"I know. I just need a break."

"A break?" The look on Phil's face spoke volumes. Joshua knew it sounded ridiculous. "What is this? A panic attack?"

"I can't remember the lyrics."

Phil tilted his head as if he didn't hear him right. "You can't remember the lyrics?"

Joshua shook his head. "No, I can't remember them."

"What the hell do you mean you can't remember them? You wrote the damn things!"

"I know!"

People turned and stared at them. Joshua realized they were both yelling.

Phil came forward and grabbed his shoulder, pushing him further away from the stage and prying eyes. "What the hell are you talking about?"

Joshua lifted a hand and let it fall against his thigh. "I'm almost out of the pills and I…I can't think straight without them."

"The pills? The ones I gave you?"

"No."

Phil pulled him closer, dropping his voice. "What pills then?"

"Oxycodone."

"Oxycodone?"

Why did he keep repeating everything Joshua said?

"How many do you take?"

Joshua shrugged. "Too many. I don't know."

"How many do you have left?"

"Only two."

"Two?"

Joshua nodded. "I've been trying to save them, but when I don't take them, I can't think straight. All I hear is the drum and the guitar, and the people…" He closed his eyes.

Phil's grip tightened. "Okay, listen. We've got to get through this concert tonight. You hear me?" He shook Joshua. "Do you hear me?"

Joshua opened his eyes. "Yeah."

"Okay, good. Now listen, take the pills you've got, and tomorrow, I'll take you to a doctor, okay?"

Joshua straightened. "Doctor?"

"Yeah, a doctor."

It scared him to think of telling someone else what he was doing, but he knew he needed help. He couldn't continue like this, popping pills every few hours just to keep the panic away. A doctor would be able to help him. There had to be a way to get off the drugs. There had to be something a doctor could do.

"Okay."

Phil patted his cheek and smiled. "Good boy. Do you have the pills on you?"

Joshua fished them out of his pocket and held them out in the palm of his hand.

"Okay." He grabbed a bottle of water from the concession table. "Take them now 'cause you've got to get back out there."

Joshua popped the pills in his mouth and swallowed a sip of water to wash them down.

"Good." He hooked Joshua by the back of the neck and pressed their foreheads together. "Now, don't worry about anything. The pills will start working and you'll remember the lyrics. Tomorrow we'll go get help from the doctor."

Joshua forced a few deep breaths into his lungs. "Okay. Tomorrow."

"Right, tomorrow." He slapped Joshua lightly on the cheek. "See, I take care of my star, don't I?"

"Yeah."

"Good. You got this, right? You got this!" He pushed Joshua toward the stage and he stumbled, but a roadie caught him and set him on his feet again.

Joshua hesitated on the edge, fighting the panic, but he clung to the idea that tomorrow there would be a way out of this hell, tomorrow he'd stop the spiral he was on. He had to believe there was a way back.

*   *   *

Marco stepped off the elevator and waited to be buzzed into the ICU. Just as he was about to ask the nurse on duty for the Millers, Billy's father turned the corner and moved in his direction. Marco let the man approach, trying to corral his own emotions. The ride over hadn't done much for his state of mind. A combination of guilt and worry gnawed at him. What did Billy Miller want to say and how

227

were they going to find out who was driving the white truck? He hadn't even told Vinnie or Rosa about that yet.

"Mr. Miller," he said, holding out his hand.

"Inspector D'Angelo," said the man, taking it with both of his own. "Thank you for coming down." In his early forties, Billy's father was a tall, handsome man with very dark skin and surprisingly white teeth.

"How is your son? You said they brought him out of the coma?"

"Yes." The man's eyes filled with tears, but he blinked them back. "He's stable now, but he still has no feeling in his legs. He did move his hand though. The doctors say that's a good sign."

Marco didn't even know how to answer the pain in the man's voice. No words would ever be good enough to make this better. "I don't know what to say, Mr. Miller. I'm so very sorry."

"Bill, please." He released Marco's hand. "Thank you. That helps."

"Bill, I need to tell you something before I go in."

"All right, but my son says he has something important to tell you as well. About the accident. He wouldn't tell us. He just kept saying it had to be you."

"I understand. Here's the thing, Bill. One of the houses across the street from the school had a video camera attached to the front of it. It caught the entire accident."

Bill's expression grew grave. "You saw the accident?"

"Yes."

"What did you see?"

"The boys were coming down 30th, going way too fast for that road. It looked like they were trying to turn right on Balboa. The thing is they weren't alone. A white pick-up was coming down beside them and just before they reached Balboa, it swerved into them, sending them over the curb and into the trees."

"What do you mean it swerved into them?"

"I mean it smashed into them."

228

"Did you get a license?"

"We're working on it."

Bill took Marco's elbow. "I think you better talk to my boy then."

Marco allowed the man to lead him down the hallway and to a glass enclosed room at the far end of the corridor. A woman with fair skin and pale brown hair sat in a chair by the bed and in the bed was the boy.

Tubes went in and out of him, machines beeped and burred around his head, and he looked small and fragile in the huge hospital bed. His eyes were sunken and bloodshot and the fingers of his right hand twitched on top of the bed covers. Although he wasn't as dark skinned as his father, his flesh had a grey cast to it that was alarming.

As Marco approached, the woman rose to her feet and took his hand.

"Inspector D'Angelo," introduced the man. "This is my wife, Heather."

Marco clasped her hand in both of his own.

"Thank you for coming, Inspector."

"My pleasure." He released her, then went to the side of the bed and gently squeezed the boy's fingers. "Nice to finally meet you, Billy." Seeing him now, Marco remembered watching him jump hurdles at one of Tonio's track meets. The memory almost made Marco sick.

"You too, sir," said the boy in a rough voice. He had a nasal cannula going into his nose and patches for a heart monitor covered his chest.

"Take a seat, Inspector," said his mother, placing a chair behind Marco.

Marco sank into it, releasing the boy's fingers. "Your father called me and said you wanted to talk."

The boy tried to nod, but it was hard with so many tubes going into him. "He told me that Antonio couldn't remember what happened."

"That's right. The doctors don't think he'll ever get the memory back."

"But I remember."

"All right. Do you mind if I ask you some questions? That might be the easiest way to do this."

"Sure."

Marco shifted in the chair, bringing himself closer to the bed so he could hear the boy more easily. He'd never been one to take notes when questioning someone, but he wondered if he should now. "Tonio...Antonio told me that you went to a party at a house on Shore View. Is that right?"

The boy nodded. "For the track team."

"Right, because you made sections."

The boy nodded again.

"Antonio said someone brought a couple bottles of champagne that got passed around to everyone."

"Robbie Malloy did."

"Did Antonio drink anything?"

"A couple of sips. There wasn't much there."

"Okay." It wasn't necessary to ask if Billy drank. He wasn't the one driving. "Antonio said the party got boring, so you left."

"Went cruising."

"That's right. On Market?"

"Yeah, it was dead."

"So you went back toward the party?"

Billy shot a look at his parents, then focused on Marco again. "There was a girl there..." His voice trailed off.

"I got you," said Marco. He knew the boy didn't want to elaborate with his parents in the room. "Did you make it back to the party?"

Billy's fingers tightened on the blanket, balling it in his fist. "No. When we got off Market, Antonio got lost. We were trying to get back to the Avenues, but he was turned around."

"Do you remember what street he got on?"

"We finally circled around to Van Ness and I told him to go left on Geary, but he cut this guy off. We almost smashed into him in the intersection."

"What intersection?"

"I don't remember. I think it was O'Farrell."

Marco adjusted his shoulder harness. "Was the guy driving a white pick-up?"

Billy's eyes searched his face. Then he nodded. "It scared us bad. Antonio kept saying that his dad would kill him if he caught him anywhere near Market. We just wanted to get back to the party."

"Did you turn onto Geary?"

"Yeah, but the guy was right behind us. He kept pulling up on our bumper and flashing his high beams. Then once we got on the part of Geary that's two lanes, he kept swerving around us and getting in front, slamming on his brakes."

"Did you guys think about calling the police?"

"We were freakin' out, sir, but Antonio, he says we've got to get the guy's license plate number. He remembered you telling him that or saying something about it."

Marco leaned closer to him. "Did you get it?"

"I started trying to climb in back and get Antonio's backpack. I got a pen out and found a hamburger wrapper from earlier. I started taking down the license plate number."

"Then what happened?"

"Antonio turned on 30th. He thought we'd lose him, but all of a sudden the guy was there again." Billy gave a strange gasping sound. His mother started forward, but his father held her back.

Marco reached out and took the boy's hand. "It's over, Billy. He can't hurt you again, but I want to make sure he doesn't hurt anyone else. What do you remember happening when you got on 30th?"

"He slammed into us. He slammed his truck into us. Next thing I know, the paramedics are cutting me out of the car. That's the last thing I remember until yesterday."

Marco released his held breath. "What you just did, telling me about the accident, was the bravest thing I've ever seen anyone do."

Billy tried to smile, but his eyes filled with tears. "He tried to kill us."

"I know."

"Just because we cut him off. He tried to kill us. Who does something like that?"

Marco tightened his hold on the boy's hand. "I don't know, but I promise you I will make sure he doesn't do it again."

Billy gave him a nod.

Marco released him and pushed himself to his feet. He moved toward the door and Billy's parents followed him.

"What now?" said his father.

Marco turned to face them. He could see the small figure of the boy silhouetted in the doorway. "I'm going to look for the partial plate Billy took and see if we can get a hit on the white truck."

"If you find it, can you arrest the driver?"

"You better believe I can."

Billy's mother came forward and took his hands, pressing them to her breast. "Please, please find him. I'm begging you for my son, please."

Marco nodded and she released him. "I'll keep in touch," he said, backing away from them.

As he walked down the corridor, the tragedy of it all weighed him down until he felt like he was walking through syrup. Even if he caught the guy, it would never bring back what Billy Miller had lost.

* * *

Peyton took a swig of her beer and set it down. "Then she accused me of being too emotionally attached to him."

Jake bit into his pizza slice and rolled it into his cheek. "Are you?"

Peyton frowned at him. "No."

Abe snorted into his glass of wine. It was the tamest thing Peyton had ever seen him drink, but then he only had two choices at the pizza parlor and neither of them met his unique tastes. Wine was the lesser evil, he said.

"What does that mean?" she demanded.

The two men exchanged knowing looks.

"You'd get emotionally involved with a grizzly bear if he was your case," said Jake.

"And this one's got you bad, girl." Abe slapped her arm. "You know we like pretty men, honey. I don't entirely blame you."

Peyton rolled her eyes and took another drag on her beer.

Jake pushed the pizza over to her. "You'd better eat something. That's your third beer."

"Keeping tabs, Ryder," she snapped.

"Oowee, this one's got you real bad," said Abe, picking a pepperoni slice off his piece and sticking it in his mouth. "Why don't you let me meet him and then I can tell you whether he's worth your career or not?"

"Worth my career? What do you think is happening? You sound like that stupid psychiatrist."

Jake and Abe exchanged another look, then Jake leaned toward her. "Just where were you the night you didn't come home?"

"She didn't come home?"

Peyton kicked Jake under the table before he could answer. When he looked at her in shock, she glared at him and shook her head. He grabbed his beer and took a swallow, so he couldn't answer Abe.

Abe gave her an arch look. "You better not kick me, sister. Did you spend the night with the rock star?"

"It's not what you think."

"What do I think?"

Peyton set her beer on the table. "Really, Abe? Really. Do you need me to tell you what you always think?"

"I guess I do."

"Sex!" said Peyton and Jake at the same time. Then all three of them broke into laughter.

Marco appeared at that moment and slumped down into the booth next to Peyton, taking a long pull on his beer. He lowered it and sighed. "Who's talking about sex?"

"Who do you think?" asked Jake, shoving more pizza into his mouth.

Marco's gaze shifted to Abe. "Forget I asked."

Abe studied him over his wine glass. "You look tired, Angel."

"Yep." He took another swig.

Peyton rubbed his shoulders. "What happened?"

"Billy Miller said Tonio cut off the guy in the white pickup and the guy followed them from O'Farrell to 30th, tailgating them and cutting them off. Tonio thought he'd be able to lose him on Balboa, but the guy sideswiped them before they could get away."

Jake paused with his pizza halfway to his mouth. "No shit?"

"No shit."

"Stan's working on the video," offered Peyton.

"Billy says he got a partial on the plate. I just need to get clearance to go through the evidence bags."

"I can get it tomorrow," said Peyton. "That way we don't have to worry about conflict of interest."

"Thanks." He lifted the beer again.

Abe dished him up a slice of pizza and laid it in front of him. "Eat something, Angel. This is good news, isn't it?"

Marco lowered the beer. "I guess, except you didn't have to stand there and listen to a 16 year old boy tell you how he lost his legs to some bastard with road rage."

None of them responded because there really was nothing anyone could say.

* * *

234

Peyton picked up her phone and pressed a finger against the text message. *Just what is it you think I think that isn't what I think? Abe.* He wasn't going to leave this alone. She'd diverted the topic when Marco showed up last night, but she knew Abe. When he got a juicy bone, he was definitely going to keep gnawing it.

But was he right? Was she risking her career here? It was one thing to feel responsible for destroying Jake's life, or wanting to help Venus escape prostitution, but no one was going to appreciate her getting emotionally involved with this rock star.

"Inspector Brooks?"

Peyton blinked and glanced over. Ravensong sat beside her and on his other side was Emily Staddler. They were both staring at her strangely. They'd arrived promptly at 9:00AM and Peyton had set up the computer in the conference room to play the video. They were waiting for her to show it when Abe texted.

"You okay?" Ravensong asked.

"Sure." She shoved the phone in her pocket without answering. "Why?"

"You seem distracted."

She studied his features. Although she didn't want to admit it, her feelings for Ravensong were more complicated than they'd been for her other cases. He reminded her of her youth, he was sexy as hell, and she wouldn't be opposed to a liaison...well, except for Elena and her career. Joshua Ravensong offered a temptation she really didn't need right now.

"Here's the thing, Joshua. It's been brought to my attention that I may be too emotionally involved in your case."

"Who brought that to your attention?"

She didn't answer, but her gaze shifted to Staddler involuntarily. He picked up on it.

"What did you say?"

235

She held up a hand. "I said I thought it might be better for you if you had someone a bit more detached."

"Detached? What are you saying?"

"You know your history, Joshua. You tend to confuse physical encounters with emotional ones."

He frowned at her. "Well, here's something I'm not confused by. I'm facing a murder trial, Emily, and the only person I want handling that is sitting next to me right now, so back the hell off."

Staddler's mouth opened in surprise, but she didn't say anything.

"She might be right, Joshua. It might be better if I turn this over to someone else."

"Why would you say that?"

"I don't think I'm objective anymore."

"Meaning what?"

"If I play this video and you remember what happens, I'm duty bound to arrest you."

"Are you saying you wouldn't do it?"

No, she'd arrest him, but it would hurt like hell.

"Peyton?"

"I'd arrest you."

"Then I don't see what the problem is." He turned back to face the computer and extended his hand toward the screen. The sweatshirt pulled back, exposing the rope of scar tissue on his arm. "Let's get this over with, Inspector Brooks."

Peyton reached for the mouse and clicked on the file. The video loaded to the spot she'd keyed that morning. Shifting in her chair, she watched Ravensong as he watched himself. When he struck the wall, the man beside her flinched. Peyton stopped the video.

He lifted a hand and covered his mouth, his eyes fixated on the screen.

"Joshua?"

He didn't answer.

"Play it again," said Staddler.

Peyton rewound the video. She had the exact spot engrained in her memory as she hit play. The video ran again, but beyond a narrowing of his eyes, Joshua didn't show any recognition. Peyton stopped it.

"Do you remember that, Joshua?" said the psychiatrist.

"None of it." He turned his hand over and looked at the scabs on his knuckles. "How can I not remember doing that?"

Peyton chewed her lower lip, but didn't answer. She hated seeing the confusion on his face.

"Play it again," said Staddler.

Peyton released the mouse. "Just what do you think that will do?" She tried not to sound aggravated, but this woman was pissing her off. What the hell kind of therapy was this?

"Just play it. Sometimes the mind needs to see something multiple times before it makes a connection."

"And sometimes the mind just makes shit up when there are no connections to make," Peyton snapped.

"Play it again, Inspector Brooks."

Peyton slid the bar back to the original spot and let the video run. Halfway through a loud voice filtered through the doorway from the lobby. Both Ravensong and Peyton looked back.

"James," said Ravensong.

Peyton recognized that voice.

"Ignore that. Play the video again, Inspector Brooks."

Peyton sighed. There was no use arguing with this woman, but she was beginning to wonder if Joshua was the one who needed a psychiatrist. She grabbed the mouse and drew the bar back on the video, but James' voice cut into the room, demanding to see his brother.

Peyton released the mouse and shifted in her chair. "He's going to make me arrest him yet," she told Joshua.

Joshua gave her an anxious smile.

"The video, Inspector Brooks," demanded Staddler.

Peyton gritted her teeth against her irritation and punched play, but she'd taken the tape too far back and the elevator was empty.

"That's too far back."

"I know. Give me a second." She reached for the mouse and started to move the bar, but the elevator door opened and a tall, blond man stepped in. Peyton went still, staring at the screen.

"Inspector Brooks, this is too far back."

"Quiet," Peyton snapped. Her eyes shifted to the time stamp in the upper corner. 9:03AM.

The man wore a finely tailored business suit, his blond hair was parted on the side and feathered back from his brow in perfect waves, and when he looked up into the camera, Peyton caught her breath. The cleft in his chin was visible.

He didn't pace as Joshua had done, but he fidgeted with the lines of his jacket and his watch, glancing up at the numbers above the door repeatedly. When the door to the elevator opened, Peyton stopped the video and leaned forward, squinting at the green number displayed in the mirror on the back wall of the elevator.

He got off on the eighth floor.

Peyton backed the video up until she caught him staring into the camera, then she shifted to look at Joshua. "Do you recognize this man?"

He squinted at the screen. "He seems familiar." Then recognition dawned. "O'Shannahan, right?"

Peyton gave a grim smile. "Right. The Reverend Jedediah O'Shannahan." She slumped back in her chair. "The preacher man."

CHAPTER 14

"Okay, you can put your shirt back on."

Joshua reached for the t-shirt and pulled it over his head.

The doctor went to the sink and washed his hands. "Well, I can't find anything wrong with his back. I can send him for some physical therapy, but I don't even feel tense muscles and there doesn't appear to be a herniated disc."

Phil pushed himself away from the door and moved closer to the doctor. "Physical therapy is great and all, but he's in so much pain, he won't be able to perform."

Joshua climbed off the exam table and slipped his feet into his sneakers as he watched the exchange. The doctor gave Joshua a pointed look, then faced Phil. "I didn't get the indication he was in pain when I examined him."

"I can assure you it's quite severe." Phil pulled his wallet out of his back pocket and opened it, taking out a number of bills.

Joshua tried to see the denomination as he pulled on his jacket. This wasn't at all what he'd expected to happen when he agreed to this. He'd planned to ask the doctor for help, but Phil had insisted on coming in with him. He didn't really want to admit his pill usage in front of *Blazes* manager. He was afraid it would get back to James somehow.

"I honestly can't recommend medication without some sort of indication of pain. I didn't find anything."

Phil held out a number of bills. "The kid can hardly walk, he's so stiff. And he barely made it through the concert last night."

The doctor's eyes shifted from the bills to Joshua and back again. "I could lose my medical license for this. What exactly are you suggesting I give him?"

"Oxycodone."

"Oxycodone? Do you know how addictive that is?"

"It's just to help him for a little while. Just until we get these shows finished."

"I could lose my medical license."

"For helping a kid in pain? How?" He waved the money. "We just need to get through the rest of the shows, then he'll be able to rest up and get that physical therapy. We just need something to tide him over."

The doctor sighed heavily and reached for the bills. "Oxycodone is bad stuff to mess with. He's liable to overdose if he isn't careful."

"I'll keep an eye on him."

The doctor looked at Joshua. "It's highly addictive. You keep taking it and you won't be able to stop."

"We'll stop. We've got a break coming up soon," said Phil.

The doctor sighed again and went to the cabinet against the wall, pulling open a drawer. He took out a prescription pad and began writing. "Where do you want the prescription filled?" he asked, pocketing the money.

"The pharmacy on Vine."

The doctor tore the paper from the pad, holding it out to Joshua. When Joshua tried to take it, he held on and met Joshua's gaze. "I'm not kidding about addiction. You'd better be damn careful."

When he released the paper, Joshua folded it and put it in his pocket, then he backed toward the door. The doctor followed him with worried eyes until he was on the other side. Phil was right on his heels and he threw his arm around Joshua's shoulder, pulling him against his side.

"I told you I'd take care of you," he said.

Joshua wanted to push him away, but he didn't. If this was taking care of him, it felt an awful lot like being used.

* * *

"They told me my brother was here and I want to see him."

Peyton threw back her chair and went to the door, pulling it open. James was standing on the other side of the counter, shouting at Maria. Smith had come to help her and just as Peyton stepped out, Captain Defino's door opened.

"Officer Connor," said the captain, then she faltered when she saw who was standing behind him.

Peyton walked over to Maria's desk, transfixed. Elliot Evans, the guitarist from *Avalanche*, was standing in their lobby. She couldn't remember how many times she'd played air guitar with him, while listening to Joshua's earthy vocals.

"That's…"

"I know," breathed Maria.

Captain Defino gave herself a visible shake, then she moved toward the counter. "Mr. Evans, it is a pleasure to have you in our precinct."

"Thank you, ma'am," he said, ducking his curly brown head.

Joshua appeared in the doorway and James immediately focused on him. Crossing to the half-door, Joshua started to open it, but before he'd even gotten to the other side, James had him in a bear hug.

Joshua hugged him in return, then Elliot was there, pulling him into his embrace. The captain gave Peyton and Maria a wide-eyed stare when Ravensong appeared, her mouth dropping open.

"I didn't know he was here," she breathed.

Peyton offered her an apologetic smile.

Smith turned around and gave the three women an aggravated look. "I guess I'll go back to my desk."

They didn't even acknowledge his departure.

"Why won't you let me see you?" said James, holding on to Joshua by the arms.

"James, I was arrested for murder. I don't want any of you around me right now."

"That's stupid. We're your family. Mom and Dad are worried sick."

"I know, but I can't take a chance on anything."

"What the hell are you talking about?"

"I don't want to talk about it here." He looked around. "Please."

"Okay, but I want to come to the hospital and talk to you. All right? And Mom needs to see you too, Josh."

"Okay, bring her, but just her. I don't want Tiffany or Jennifer seeing me there."

"Done."

Elliot pulled him close again and said something in his ear that Peyton couldn't hear. She couldn't believe Elliot Evans was in her precinct. He and Ravensong had been the staple of her teen years. She'd always been smitten with Ravensong, but Elliot Evans was a close second in her heart.

Ravensong hugged his friend in return, then motioned Peyton forward. "Elliot, I'd like you to meet Inspector Peyton Brooks, the best damn detective in San Francisco."

Peyton felt her cheeks heat with pleasure and she came to the counter to shake Elliot's hand.

"Nice to meet you, Inspector," he said.

"The pleasure is mine," she answered, beaming at him. Glancing over her shoulder, she beckoned the captain over. "Joshua, this is Captain Defino. I don't believe the two of you have met."

The captain gave Peyton a breathless smile as she accepted Ravensong's hand. "Mr. Ravensong, we finally meet in person."

"Yes, ma'am."

"I wish the circumstances were better."

Joshua offered her a grim smile. "So do I, ma'am."

"Joshua, we need to get back to the hospital," said Staddler from the doorway.

Joshua nodded, but his eyes lifted to Peyton.

"I'll contact you tomorrow," she promised him.

"Great," he said, reluctantly turning away.

As always Peyton wanted to offer him some comfort, but she couldn't. She watched him leave the precinct flanked by his brother and Elliot. Dr. Staddler paused as she moved to the other side of the counter.

"I wish the video had been more helpful," she said, "but I guess that memory is lost for good."

Peyton didn't know how to answer that.

"How much time does he have before you have to turn this over to the D.A.?"

Glancing at the captain, Peyton lifted her chin. "That isn't my decision, Dr. Staddler, but I will inform Joshua when that happens."

She looked down and nodded, then she walked stiffly to the door.

Peyton turned to Defino. "Something happened in there and I need to tell you about it."

Defino motioned to her office. "Come in."

They walked into the dark interior and Peyton took a seat as the captain went around her desk. For a moment, they simply stared at each other, then Defino chuckled and shook her head. "I can't believe I had Joshua Ravensong and Elliot Evans in my squad room."

Peyton smiled.

Forcing her features to be serious, Defino folded her hands on her desk. "So tell me what happened in the conference room."

Peyton scooted forward in her chair. "When James started shouting, I took the video too far back on accident. I took it past where Ravensong was in the elevator."

"And?"

"Someone else got on at 9:03AM and got off on the eighth floor."

"Who?"

"Jedediah O'Shannahan."

Defino's features grew grim. "Are you sure about this?"

"I can show you the video myself, Captain."

"How do you know he got off on the eighth floor?"

"The numbers are reflected in the mirror on the back wall."

Defino stared down at her desk.

Peyton waited while she thought, but it wasn't easy. She hated the captain's melamine chairs. They didn't conform to the body and she wasn't very good at sitting still either. A crystal bowl, with paperclips in it, sat on the edge of the desk. Peyton started to reach for it, but Defino moved it before she could touch.

Peyton closed her hand into a fist and brought it to rest on her leg.

"You're going to tell me you want to go out and question him about this case."

"Yes."

"And you know the minute you do, I'll get a call from the mayor."

"I know."

"He's going to accuse me of doing this deliberately."

"I'm sure he is."

"You know O'Shannahan is a huge contributor to the mayor's campaign fund."

"Yes, that came up last time we talked to O'Shannahan."

"Why can't we investigate people who aren't tied to the mayor?"

"Why can't the mayor tie himself to people who aren't corrupt?"

Defino's eyes caught Peyton's. "Point taken." She fixed her hand under her chin and shook her head. "This is going to be nothing but trouble."

"I'm sorry, Captain."

"You're going to have to show me the video."

"I will."

"Where's Marco?"

"He went with Jake to search the evidence bags from Antonio's accident."

"I don't want you going out to O'Shannahan's alone."

"Okay."

"Take a uniform."

"I'll take Smith."

"Fine." She squinted at Peyton. "Tread carefully here, Brooks. I'm willing to go to battle with the mayor again, but I have to know it's worth doing. He isn't going to like us questioning O'Shannahan, especially for the benefit of a drug-addicted rock star."

"I understand."

"You remember how O'Shannahan is? You remember how easily he gets under your skin?"

"I remember. That is one thing I will never forget, Captain." Jedediah O'Shannahan was a very powerful man and like most powerful men, he wasn't opposed to using that power as long as it benefitted him.

* * *

Marco pulled on the latex gloves, then bent down and lifted two full bags of garbage onto the table.

"Jesus Christ," breathed Jake. "What did that kid use his car for?"

"Apparently a trashcan." Marco pushed the bags over on their sides. Wrappers and burger boxes filled the interior. "Let's get sorting."

Jake took a seat across from him as Marco opened the first bag. A stainless steel table spread between them and Marco began inspecting each item, placing it in different piles based on what it was. Jake began doing the same thing.

"Yeah, this is way more glamorous than being a banker," he groused.

Marco smiled, but kept sorting.

"So, Adonis," said Jake conversationally. "You ever think of having kids?"

Marco turned a wrapper over in his hand, searching it. "I will never have kids."

"How can you say that? Never's a long time."

"Because I know. I never want kids." He set the wrapper aside. "You want kids?"

"I did. I couldn't imagine anything better than having a baby with Zoë, but that's gone now."

"Maybe you'll meet someone else."

"Maybe."

Marco inspected a soda cup, but he knew Billy Miller had said he wrote the license plate numbers on a burger wrapper.

"So how come you're so sure you don't want kids?"

"Just am."

"Maybe you haven't met the right girl."

Marco's eyes lifted to Jake's face. "I've met her, but I ain't having kids with her either."

Jake narrowed his eyes in question. "Who?"

"None of your business."

Jake went back to sorting. "Well, if you've met the right girl, what are you going to do if she wants kids?"

"Nothing. It's not an option."

"What do you mean it's not an option? Did you get a vasectomy or something?"

Marco gave him a chilling look.

Jake barked out a laugh and held up his latex-covered hands. "Okay, sorry."

Marco tossed another blank wrapper on the pile and drew a deep breath. "It's just…" He stopped and shook his head.

"What?"

"It's not worth it. Having kids. You worry and agonize and lie awake afraid, then something like this happens and you think you're dying inside. I don't want to go through that."

Jake stopped sorting and sat there staring at him. Marco glanced at him. "What?"

"What do you think you're doing right now?"

Marco looked down and smoothed out the next wrapper. What was he doing? Since the accident, he'd been angry and afraid and sick at heart, and Tonio wasn't even his kid.

"You don't always have to be such a hard-assed cop, you know?"

Marco tossed the wrapper aside and grabbed another. "Why don't you stop talking so much and get to sorting? I don't want to be here all frickin' day."

Jake gave him a smile, then grabbed another piece of trash. He turned it over and smoothed it on the table. "Adonis, take a look at this." He passed it over the table.

Written in a scrawling hand was the beginning of a license plate number: 2DLS. Marco's fingers tightened on it and he nodded his head. "Good job. Good job," he said.

*   *   *

Peyton rode with Smith in his patrol car to O'Shannahan's house. After they parked and climbed out of the car, Peyton stood on the sidewalk and stared up at the enormous mansion. Smith moved to her side.

"Sure doesn't seem right that religion can get you all this."

Peyton shrugged. "I'm not sure you can call what O'Shannahan does religion. He's subverted the purpose of faith to his own benefit."

"Someone's buying what he's selling."

"I haven't been back to this house in six months. I didn't think it would bring up so many memories."

Smith bumped her with his shoulder. "You okay?"

"Yeah, but I can still see Rafael Peña with his gun to Marco's head. If he'd pulled the trigger…"

247

"He didn't. Marco's fine. You got to put some of this stuff in boxes, baby girl, or you're gonna go crazy."

She smiled at Smith. He'd never called her that before. If anyone else had, she'd have gutted him, but with Smith it was nice. "Look, O'Shannahan is…"

"An ass."

Peyton gave a surprised nod. "Nuff said."

"I got this."

"All righty then." They climbed the stairs to the house and Peyton knocked on the door. She could hear someone moving around inside, but the door didn't open. She knocked again.

Finally Kristin O'Shannahan, the reverend's wife, opened the door a crack and peered out. Peyton pressed her badge to the crack.

"Inspector Brooks from the San Francisco Police Department, Mrs. O'Shannahan. We'd like to talk to your husband."

She pulled open the door a bit more. "He's not here."

Peyton took in her charcoal grey pencil skirt, white button-up sweater, loafers and grey tights. Her hair was pulled back with a black headband; however, the string of pearls was gone from her neck and her face was scrubbed clean of all makeup.

"When will he be back, Mrs. O'Shannahan?"

"I'm not sure."

"Where did he go?"

"He's out of town."

"Where?"

"Dallas, I think."

"How long has he been gone?"

"A week."

"And you don't know when he's coming back?"

"I'm not sure. I think it's tomorrow or the next day."

Peyton moved closer to the door. "Do you mind if we come in, Mrs. O'Shannahan? We'd really like to talk to you."

"I can't allow that, Inspector Brooks. The last time you were here, you did so much damage to our master bedroom that the whole thing had to be remodeled."

Damage? A man died in that room. "Fine. Will you come out? I'd like to ask you a few questions."

"About what?" She was using the door as a barrier.

Peyton exchanged a look with Smith. They didn't have a warrant, so they couldn't force their way inside. "Won't you come out and I'll tell you?"

"I don't feel that's necessary, Inspector Brooks."

"Fine," Peyton acquiesced. "I'm here to ask your husband about Theresa Ravensong. Is that name familiar to you, Mrs. O'Shannahan?"

"Theresa Ravensong? Wasn't that the poor unfortunate girl who was murdered by her ex-husband? Some rock star with a drug addiction as I heard it."

"Well, we're trying to figure out who murdered her. So her name is familiar to you?"

"Yes, I heard about it on TV."

"Did your husband have anything to do with her? Know her in any way?"

"I'm certain he didn't."

Peyton frowned. She'd answered rather quickly. "Are you sure of that, Mrs. O'Shannahan?"

"Quite."

"Then can you explain why I have a video tape of your husband going up an elevator in her building and exiting on her floor?"

"My husband counsels his parishioners, Inspector Brooks. If I remember right, there's a young man in that building who is asking for help with conversion therapy."

"Conversion therapy? He's gay?"

She pulled her head back in surprise. "Oh, no, he's feeling the temptation of the devil, but he's trying to turn away from it."

Peyton realized her mouth was hanging open. She wondered how Abe would respond to this assessment. "Your husband feels he's qualified to counsel anyone on this matter?"

"Of course he is. My husband is a vessel for God."

He's a vessel for something, thought Peyton. Then she remembered what Kristin had said a moment before. "Hold on a minute. You said your husband was counseling a young man in Terry Ravensong's building. In fact, her very floor. Is that right?"

"Right. You asked me why he was in the elevator of her building and I told you why."

Peyton tilted her head. "But I didn't tell you what building she lived in."

Kristin made an airy wave of her hand. "I told you I saw it on TV."

"And you recognized the building as one in which your husband has clients?"

"Followers."

"Right. Doesn't that just seem a little too convenient? He goes to the eighth floor of the building to see a young man wanting conversion therapy at around the time of a murder."

"What are you suggesting, Inspector Brooks?"

"Did he see anything, Mrs. O'Shannahan? Hear anything?"

"I'm certain he didn't. He's very dedicated to his parishioners."

"What does that mean?"

"He's focused when he's on a job."

Hm. Focused was an interesting way of putting it if he'd been the man *studying* the *Bible* in Terry Ravensong's bedroom.

"Can you tell me the name of the young man he counsels on the eighth floor?"

"His counseling sessions are private."

Of course they were.

"Can you call him and find out his name? I'd like to ask the young man if he heard or saw anything."

"I'm not certain what my husband is doing at the moment and I would hate to interrupt something important."

"Mrs. O'Shannahan, I have to say I'm a little surprised that you know so little about your husband's whereabouts."

"What do you mean?"

"You aren't sure where he is, you aren't sure when he'll be back, and you're really not certain how long he's been gone. Why should I believe that you know what he was doing in Terry Ravensong's building?"

"I find your tone insulting and I don't have to answer these questions."

Well, that about ended the conversation.

Peyton reached into her pocket and pulled out a card, passing it through the crack. "Please have him call me when he gets back into town."

"I don't know what you think you're investigating, Inspector Brooks, but wasn't the last time bad enough? You disrupted our lives and violated our house. I think you should leave us alone."

"Violated your house? We took out a criminal, one your own husband reported."

"But what are you after now? You have your drug-addled rock star. Let it go. You have no need to bother my husband with this."

Let it go? What a strange thing to say.

"I can't talk to you any more, Inspector Brooks. Have a nice day." With that, she closed the door in Peyton's face.

*   *   *

Peyton found Captain Defino waiting by Maria's desk. She squinted at Peyton as she pulled open the precinct door and stepped into the lobby, followed by Smith. Aggravation made Peyton wish she could just slink into the break-room and grab a soda without explaining her conversation with O'Shannahan's wife. Ravensong was running out of time and there wasn't anything Peyton could do to save him.

"Well?"

Peyton pushed open the half-door, holding it for Smith to pass through. "He wasn't there."

"Where was he?"

"Dallas or maybe not." She exchanged a look with Smith.

"What does that mean?"

Peyton leaned on the counter across from Maria's desk. "We talked with Kristin O'Shannahan, the good reverend's wife. She wasn't really clear on where he was."

"Or when he'd be back," offered Smith.

Peyton held out a hand toward him.

"What do you mean she wasn't clear?"

"She didn't know. Maybe today, maybe tomorrow. Maybe Dallas, maybe not."

"How long has he been gone?"

"About a week."

"Really? How convenient."

"Isn't it."

Defino crossed her arms. "Now what?"

Peyton shook her head wearily. "I just don't know. I wish there was some way to connect him to Terry Ravensong. Some proof that he knew her, that she belonged to his church or something. Kristin O'Shannahan swears he didn't know her, that he was counseling someone else in that building, on that very floor, but she couldn't give me a name.

Without a direct connection between O'Shannahan and Terry, we're dead in the water."

"Maybe not," came Devan's voice from the captain's office.

Peyton gave Defino a questioning look.

"He wanted an update. I was buying Ravensong time."

Devan appeared in the doorway. As always he looked pressed and polished, not a speck of lint, not a crease, not a molecule out of place.

"What are you thinking?" asked Defino.

"Search on-line. I know he has a website. I'll bet he has a published list of the parishioners on there."

"Why would he do that?" asked Peyton. "Isn't that a violation of their privacy?"

"Ego. That way he could show off how many followers he has."

"Wouldn't they protest him using their names that way?"

"Why? People are very big on church affiliations. They even put their religions on job applications. Give it a shot. What have you got to lose?"

Ravensong.

"He's got a point," said Defino.

Peyton's gaze shot to Maria.

"I'm on it," she said, reaching for her mouse.

Peyton crossed around her desk and leaned over her shoulder as she searched for O'Shannahan's website. She found it within a few clicks and the website spread open across the screen. Well, O'Shannahan did, his arms encompassing one side to the other, his mouth open in a beaming smile.

"Oh lord," breathed Peyton.

Maria scrolled the cursor across the top until she came to a drop-down menu, labeled simply *Flock.* As she clicked, the website shifted to a new screen where a list of names was displayed against the backdrop of a massive white church.

Peyton pointed to the alphabet across the top. "R."

Maria scowled at her. "I see it." She clicked the "R" drop-down.

They scanned the first page, but found nothing. Maria clicked to advance the page. At the top of the second page was Theresa Ravensong.

"I'll be damned," said Defino.

Peyton's hand closed into a fist. How the hell were they going to get him? Straightening, she faced the captain. "Now what?"

"That's enough for me to put a uniform outside his door until he comes home."

"He'll just lawyer up, Captain."

Defino smiled slowly. "Then that will be cause to get a warrant and search his house now, won't it? Officer Smith, will you make the arrangements and make sure the on-duty officers report directly to me."

"With pleasure, Captain."

Peyton exhaled and watched Smith walk away to arrange the stakeout.

Defino drew Peyton's attention back to her. "I'll let you know when I think it's best to go question him. I really wish he'd lawyer, so I'd have probable cause to get a search warrant for his bank accounts. I'd like to get a look at his books, see where all that money comes from."

And goes, thought Peyton, remembering the huge deposit into Terry's account before she died.

"Take D'Angelo with you the next time. We've got to keep this above board."

"Got it."

"Good work, Brooks," she shot over her shoulder before she disappeared inside her office.

Devan leaned on the door jamb and watched her. Peyton shifted uncomfortably. "Thank you for your help."

"Peyton, you do know we're on the same side, right?"

"Right." She didn't add that it didn't feel that way most of the time. Why pick a fight now? "I appreciate it."

"Be honest. You just don't want me to have Ravensong."

"If you get O'Shannahan, he'll make your career. Better than Ravensong will. Fair trade."

"You've got a point. The jury just might be sympathetic to your rock star, but O'Shannahan is another matter." He chuckled. "See you in a couple of days."

CHAPTER 15

The Marina Green is a beautiful expanse of lawn that runs along the edge of the bay from the Presidio to Fort Mason and has some of the most stunning views in all of San Francisco. Park benches line the sea wall and the crowning spectacle is the rust-red towers of the Golden Gate rising in the distance.

He took me to this spot and I knew it was our last day together. The fog had rolled in from the ocean and cut the bridge in half, stray wisps trailing through the park, curling around the benches, and billowing in chilling whiteness with each pulse of the waves.

He sat down on a bench along the sea wall and the waves crashed against the rocks below him, spray gathering in his dark hair. I wrapped my sweater tighter around me and sat down next to him. The breeze blew my hair into my eyes and I clawed it out, pushing it behind my ears.

I could see his profile. He was staring at the bridge, his arms braced on his thighs, the leather bands in place on his wrists. Sitting at the angle I was, I could see the scars, snaking down toward his forearm, thick and raised.

I didn't want to talk. I just wanted to sit. We'd spent so much time talking, so much time going over everything. There was only one thing I didn't know, but I wasn't sure I wanted to know it any more. I wasn't sure it mattered.

He could be so still, it warred with what he'd told me, what I knew myself. A man whose life had been filled with so much chaos shouldn't be able to find such inner peace.

I watched the waves, fighting the sadness that rose inside of me. I hadn't known that what started as an exciting project, interviewing a famous rock star, would become something more, but it was impossible to know so many personal things about a man and not feel something, not feel a connection.

"I've always found the fog depressing."

"Then you're looking at it wrong."

I gave him a wry smile. "How's that?"

He pointed to the bridge. "Look at the way the fog cuts it in two. It hides the cars and the bustle, and all you can see are the towers, supporting it, connecting everything." He looked over his shoulder at me, dark hair sliding down his back. "It cocoons you, brings everything in, shuts out the turmoil." He tilted his head as he listened. In the distance, I could hear the fog horns, the splash of the waves against the rocks. "The noise."

I let myself relax, let myself see it as he did. We sat for a while, enjoying the silence.

Then his voice rippled against the stillness, vibrating in that smoky way he had. "Do you really think you can avoid asking me the one thing you haven't?"

"I don't know what you mean."

He smiled his slow, crooked smile. "You aren't a coward. You can't just leave this, let it end without knowing."

"I know enough. It makes sense, how it compounds, how each new step is really just an extension of the previous one. Like those nesting dolls, you keep adding layers until what was once a tiny thing is now monstrous."

He shifted and faced me, laying his arm along the back of the bench. "It's not like that at all. Pills are one thing. We take pills all the time. We take pills from the time we're children. We associate pills with medicine, with taking away our pain. Putting something in our mouth and swallowing it is easy, we're not involved with it, it's not personal." He slowly tapped his fingers on his thigh. "What you want to know is how you go from pills to putting a needle in your arm. The needle…that's an invasion."

I stared at him, transfixed. I *did* want to know, but then again, I didn't and the conflict was making me anxious. This is what being with him was like. It wasn't easy, it wasn't simple, it was always fraught with doubt and anxiety. And yet he was intoxicating.

"A needle is bloody and violent and you can't do it without knowing exactly what you're doing."

I sat there and fought myself. I needed to complete the story, that's what the writer in me wanted, but I didn't want to hear it. I didn't want to know the truth, I didn't want to admit that he was responsible for it all. You could blame the business, you could blame the drug dealer, you could even blame the manager, but when all the blame was done, you had only him and he was the one who put the needle in his arm.

"Then tell me. Tell me how you get to that point where it's even an option. How can you make that monumental leap from pills to heroin?"

His eyes had drifted away, but they came back to my face, focusing on me. "It's not that great a leap. Not nearly as far as you think." He tapped his fingers on his thigh again as if he were making a point. "It's getting back that's the problem."

* * *

Joshua stepped into the auditorium and watched the band playing on the stage. Phil was sitting on a stool before them, listening. The singer was about seventeen, younger than Joshua now, with spiky blond hair and a voice that hadn't quite made the complete shift to manhood.

Behind him stood a guitarist and a bassist and a guy on keyboard. The drummer didn't look like he was more than fourteen. Joshua frowned and let the door close at his back. For the past two years, Phil had represented *Blazes*. He didn't remember Phil saying he was managing anyone else.

The heels of his boots made a strange noise against the concrete of the auditorium floor, causing the singer to stop and Phil to turn around. His face registered surprise, then he shifted back to the band.

"Take five, guys," he said, sliding off the stool.

The band members watched him move toward Joshua, then they dispersed.

Phil took Joshua's arm and directed him back toward the door. "It's not a good time right now, Josh. I'm right in the middle of something."

"Who the hell are they?" Joshua asked, shaking off his hold.

Phil shrugged. "Just a new band I'm looking at managing. No big deal."

"Does James know what you're doing?"

"Why would I tell James? What has he got to do with it?"

Joshua dismissed the issue. He didn't care what Phil did with his time as long as he kept getting gigs for *Blazes*. "Look, Phil. I need your help."

Phil stopped moving at the door and turned to face him. "What's up?"

Joshua leaned closer and dropped his voice. "I'm almost out of the prescription you got me."

"All of it? The refills too?"

"Yeah."

Phil's attention drifted back to the band. "How the hell many pills do you take a day?"

"It doesn't matter. I just need you to get that doctor to refill it. The pharmacy says he refuses."

Glancing back at him, Phil shook his head. "I don't think I can do that, Josh. You're really asking me to go out on a limb." His attention drifted away again.

Joshua turned and marked where he was staring. The singer had come out and was messing with the microphone.

Suddenly it all came clear. "Are you shitting me? You're replacing us with this crap."

"Look, Josh, it's not like that."

"The hell it isn't." His head lifted in understanding. "You're getting a younger band."

"That's what pulls in the teenage girls, Josh."

"I'm not even nineteen yet, you bastard."

"Now hold on a minute. I've done good by you and *Blazes*. You'd be nothing without me. And we still got a long run ahead of us, but let's be realistic. This is a fickle business, Josh. Fads come and fads go. You gotta stay fresh, you gotta stay young, or you're done."

"And I'm done?"

"You're gifted, Josh. No doubt about it. You've got the looks, the voice, and a butt-load of talent, but the pills are affecting you. You've lost about fifteen pounds, your face is gaunt, and the clothes hang off you. Teenage girls want a fantasy, kid, and…" He looked beyond Joshua to the other singer. "He's more the fantasy right now."

Joshua wasn't sure what to do with any of this. He took the pills because Phil made him work brutal hours, modeling or acting during the day, playing with *Blazes* at night. He'd promised him help, but when he'd been ready to get help, Phil had gotten him more pills instead. If he didn't look the way he once did, it wasn't intentional.

"What are you saying?"

"Go home, kid. Get yourself straightened out and then call me." He patted Joshua's cheek. "With your pretty face, middle aged women are going to be panting after you as soon as you put on a few pounds."

"Go home?" Where was home now? He couldn't go home. The minute Adam saw him, he'd know what Joshua was doing. There was no hiding his addiction from a doctor. "You bastard."

Phil grabbed his shoulder. "Don't do this, Josh. Don't burn bridges with me." His fingers tightened. "Let me tell you, that isn't smart at all."

Releasing him, he walked away, headed toward the stage and his latest conquest. Joshua watched him, watched him pull the kid close and tell him something that Joshua couldn't hear. Staring at the boy, Joshua felt like he was seeing himself before everything got out of control, when it had just been about the music, about the chance to share it with others.

He walked toward the door and threw it open. The Southern California sun blazed down on him, forcing his pupils to contract. He leaned against the brick wall beside the auditorium door and stared out at the traffic. What the hell was he going to do? He had four pills left and then they were gone. There was no way to get any more.

Sinking down to a sitting position, he braced his arms on his knees and stared at his hands. They shook uncontrollably. No matter how much he concentrated, he couldn't stop the tremors. And it would only get worse. Once the last of the pills were gone, the shaking and the panic would begin to overtake him.

Closing his eyes, he tried to think, but that was hard. Once he could reason things out, but so much of the time, he felt like he was walking around in a fog. And if he wasn't in a fog, he was anxious, nervous, shaking.

Pulling out his wallet, he opened it. A scrap of wrinkled paper poked out of the bill section and he drew it out, smoothing it on his thigh. The numbers were faded, but he could still read them. He remembered watching the two musicians huddled in the alley, trying to hide what they were doing. *When you get tired of the twitches, call me.* Joshua could still hear that voice, see the tattoos on the man's body. *When you get tired of the twitches...*

Closing his eyes, Joshua reached for his phone.

*   *   *

Peyton and Maria searched the rest of O'Shannahan's website, looking for anything that might indicate where he was or what he was doing, but they found nothing. The website was an ego-maniac's wet dream with testimonials and eye witness accounts of all the miraculous things O'Shannahan had done for his *flock*.

A short while later, Peyton received a text message from Marco, saying that they'd returned and were with Stan

Neumann. Peyton left Maria still searching the website and went to find them.

Stan Neumann's office had once been the closet that housed the computer for the precinct during the late 80's when computers took up entire rooms. Peyton didn't visit him very often because it made her claustrophobic, but he seemed particularly proud of it. His walls were covered with posters that Peyton frankly didn't understand. They all displayed some type of tech device and said things like *How many computer programmers does it take to change a light bulb? None, it's a hardware problem* or *Hand over the calculator. Friends don't let friends derive drunk.* Not only did he have a desktop, but he had a laptop and a tablet going all at the same time. And the noise of fans made spending time in there uncomfortable.

She peeked in the door. Stan glanced up over the top of his computer monitor and his eyes widened behind his glasses when he saw her. Marco leaned on a table to his right, looking over his shoulder at what he was doing, while Jake sat on a table behind both of them, swinging his legs back and forth like a little boy.

"You found something?" she said, stepping into the room.

Stan had his table turned so he could see down the hall, but there was only a little passage through to the other side. With three men occupying that area, Peyton was just as happy to remain on the outer edge.

"Billy Miller only got a partial plate, but Stan's going to put it into the system and see if it brings up anything," said Marco, his gaze riveted on Stan's screen.

Peyton had never seen him so intent on anything before.

"Hey, Peyton," said Stan, beaming a smile at her. "Cool to have you come down here. You haven't been to my office in a long time."

"I know." She looked at his posters and his display of collectibles arranged wherever computers weren't. "You've really done a lot with it, haven't you?"

"Yeah. I think about half of this stuff is new since the last time you saw it."

Peyton nodded.

At his back, Jake continued to swing his legs, but a smile was hovering at the corners of his mouth. Peyton refused to look at him. He was enjoying Stan's divided attention.

"Stan," said Marco, pointing at the screen.

"Yeah, sorry." Stan tried to concentrate.

A strange cardboard box attracted Peyton's attention and she picked it up, studying it. An action figure occupied the box, but the box had to be more than thirty years old.

"You like that?" asked Stan. "I bought it on-line. It's an authentic Storm Trooper from the original movie, never been out of its box."

Peyton set it down, not sure how much a toy like that might cost. "Star Wars, right?"

"Right." His eyes tracked from the box to her and back again. "You've seen Star Wars, Peyton?"

"Of course. A million times."

"Really? You like it?"

"Who doesn't? It's one of my favorites."

Stan's look grew besotted.

"Stan," said Marco, scowling at Peyton.

He blinked. "Sorry. Let me just punch in the partial and then we'll narrow the search to California and once again to San Francisco. Then we press this button and it'll pull up every vehicle that begins with those letters."

"Who's your favorite character?" asked Jake, a grin teasing at his lips.

"What?"

"Your favorite character? Star Wars? You said it was one of your favorites."

Peyton gave him a cutting smile. "Princess Leia because she kicks ass."

Stan's eyes snapped to her.

263

Jake's grin got broader. "She also wears a metal bikini." His gaze traveled over Peyton.

Stan's mouth dropped open, but Marco whirled on Jake, giving him the death stare.

Jake had the grace to duck his head, but he was still grinning. "Just saying."

Turning back to Stan, Marco exhaled loudly. "Stan." When Stan continued to stare at Peyton, Marco pushed him in the shoulder. "Stan!"

He visibly shook himself and looked down at his screen. "There it is. 300ᵗʰ Block of Fern. Registered to a Bryce Everton. I'll send the address to your phone."

"I'm going with you," she told him.

"Fine." Marco rose to his full height. "I'll drive. You call dispatch and get some uniforms out there, so he can't get away."

Peyton nodded, but her attention shifted to Jake. He was looking at his cell phone, then he glanced up at her and pushed himself off the table. "I've gotta go too. See you at home, roomie."

"See ya," she called after him as he squeezed his way out the door.

*   *   *

Jake pulled the Daisy to a stop before the hostel on Isadora Duncan Lane. A sign read rooms for the night, $13.00. The very definition of a flop house.

Patrol cars blanketed the entrance and cops had roped off the stairs with yellow crime scene tape. Jake grabbed his evidence case and camera, and climbed out. Even though the place was crawling with police officers, he locked the Daisy's doors. She might be the ugliest car on the road, but she was his.

Ducking under the crime scene tape, he jogged up the stairs and into the lobby of the hostel. Officer Holmes was talking to the clerk behind the counter, but Bartlet, the young cop with the boyish face, spotted him and came over.

"They're back here," he said, leading the way into a hallway to the left of the lobby. Dark wood paneling ran from floor to ceiling and the carpet was a print so threadbare, the pad showed through. It reminded Jake of the apartment he'd rented in the Tenderloin before Peyton rescued him.

"Here it is." Bartlet paused in front of an open door to the right of the hallway and motioned inside.

Jake stepped into a one-room box with bunk beds on either side. Directly in front of him was the single window, covered in metal bars and ragged orange and brown curtains, allowing sunlight to seep through the dirty glass panes. Swinging from the ceiling fan between the two bunk beds was a man, a noose around his neck, his face purple and swollen, his eyes bulging.

Jake stumbled to a halt and sucked in a wild breath. Nathan Cho peered around the man's dangling legs and gave Jake a displeased scowl. Without a word, Jake ducked back into the hallway, pressing his back to the wall where he came face to face with the bearish figure of Bill Simons.

"Nice of you to show up, Ryder."

Jake forced himself to breathe, in and out, in and out.

"Bit of a shock, eh?"

Jake could only nod.

"Well, pull yourself together. You gotta take pictures."

"What? Why? That's clearly a suicide."

"Ya think?"

"Yeah, I think."

Simon's gaze narrowed. "Then I'm guessing you didn't notice his hands were tied behind his back?"

Jake blinked in surprise, then he leaned around the door jamb and peeked into the room. Sure enough, the victim's hands were tied behind his back with a belt.

"That's not the only thing," said Simons, stepping into the room. "You need to see this."

265

Jake forced himself to follow the large man across the room. Simons angled around behind the victim, staring at his bound hands. Jake edged up beside him to take a look. A white card was just visible, cupped in the victim's hands. Jake felt sure he recognized it.

He looked up at Simons. "Is that…"

"You tell me. That's your job, not mine."

Jake set the evidence case on the ground beneath the man's dangling feet and hunkered over it, unhooking the buckles that held the top in place. He pushed it open and searched around for a pair of latex gloves and the tweezers, trying to gain control over his raging emotions. His hands shook as he pulled on the gloves, but he forced himself to pick up the tweezers.

Angling around behind the man, he used the tweezers to pry the card loose. Turing it over, he studied the red lettering. *Clean-up Crew.* A shudder raced down his spine and he held it out for Cho and Simons to see.

Cho's lips pulled back against his teeth, while Simons blew out air.

"What does this mean?" asked Jake.

Simons and Cho both met his gaze, but Simons was the one to answer. "It means we have a serial killer."

Jake's expression fell. "Oh shit," he answered.

* * *

Marco pulled the Charger to a stop and looked up at the house. It squatted over a two car garage, boxy and nondescript. He pulled the keys from the ignition and climbed out without a word. Peyton followed him.

Smith met them on the sidewalk. "Over here," he said, guiding them down to the driveway. Pressing the button on his shoulder radio, he spoke into it. "Open'er up."

Peyton and Marco watched as the garage door creaked into motion, revealing a set of tires, a bumper, and the white bed of a pickup truck. As soon as the door came to a stop, Marco walked into the garage and around the front of the vehicle to the right side. The front bumper was smashed into the wheel well, tenting the metal outward.

Peyton sidled through between a shelving unit and the pickup on the right side. Squatting down, she ran her fingers along the dent, coming away with a dusting of blue-tinted powder. "Frank, can you have the CSI take a sample of this paint?"

"They already did."

She levered herself to her feet and looked up at Marco. He was staring at the damage, his expression difficult to read. She squeezed through to his side. "You okay?"

"Yeah."

"The driver's inside. They've already read him his rights," said Smith.

Marco walked to the inner door and Smith opened it for him. Peyton followed on his heels, worried he might not be able to resist punching the ass who'd hurt his nephew. They climbed a flight of stairs and found themselves in a living room with an orange, shag carpet and a tweed patterned couch.

Bryce Everton sat in a recliner before the windows, his hands clasped on the chair arms. He was a slight man with a receding hairline and watery brown eyes. He was arguing with a cop Peyton didn't immediately recognize. "That ain't my car."

"Why's it in your garage?"

"I don't know."

"Then why's it registered in your name?"

"That ain't my name."

"Show me some I.D."

"I lost it."

The cop threw up a hand and turned, finding Marco standing behind him. Peyton recognized him as Drew Logan, a sergeant from the Civic Center precinct. He gave Marco a sympathetic look.

"Do you mind if I try?" Marco asked, surprising both Logan and Peyton. Marco hated interrogation.

"Sure."

Marco moved closer to Everton until he leaned over him. Everton was clearly intimidated by Marco's size and proximity. "Let's start again. Okay?"

Everton started to speak, but Marco held up a hand. "Don't give me any shit. We both know that's your pickup in the garage. Don't make me prove it with the registration."

Everton eyed him, taking in his size. "Okay, it's my pickup."

"And it's been in an accident."

"Not with me. It was stolen from my garage."

Marco drew a deep breath and slowly released it. "That's another lie." The low, deadly quality of his tone was more terrifying than if he'd been screaming. "There's a kid in the hospital who'll never walk again and another one with a crushed leg and a head injury."

Everton squirmed in the chair. "I didn't mean to hurt anybody."

"But you did."

"I just wanted to scare them."

"Why?"

"They're punks. They think they own the world, going around intimidating people, taking things. They cut me off on O'Farrell, and they didn't even care. Damn near crashed into me. I just wanted to scare them, make them think, but they didn't care. They think they own the road, they think nothing can touch them. I'm sick of it. I'm sick of being afraid."

"They're sixteen years old."

"Doesn't matter. Gang bangers and hoods. They take everything from us. Make us afraid to leave our houses at night."

Marco loomed over him and Everton pressed back in the chair. "The driver was my nephew. The other boy had a scholarship to run track in college. They weren't gang bangers."

Everton's expression grew alarmed. "I just wanted to scare them. That's all, just scare them the way they scared me. You should have seen the way they cut me off. Then I lost it. I didn't mean to hurt anyone, but they acted like they owned the damn road, as if they could do anything they pleased."

Marco bowed his head. "They were scared. They'd gone cruising on Market and were trying to get back to where they belonged before their fathers found out. They cut you off because they were scared."

The man's face crumpled and he braced his forehead with a hand. "I'm sorry. I didn't mean it. I just lost it. I was so damn pissed. I just wanted to teach them a lesson. I'm so sorry."

Marco sighed. "Well, you did. You taught them a lesson." He leaned close, steadying himself on the arm of the chair. "The worst part is, you ruined three lives that night. Theirs and…yours."

*   *   *

Peyton drove back to her house. Marco didn't say anything the entire way; he just sat with his hands braced on his thighs, staring out the side window of the Charger. Peyton wanted to say something, but they'd been together long enough that she knew sometimes he just needed the silence.

She pulled in the driveway and he climbed out. Together they walked up the stairs to her door and she unlocked it. She hadn't asked him if he wanted to go home. That wasn't an option for her, and she suspected he was glad to have her take the decision away from him. She'd pick up her Corolla in the morning. It would be safe enough at a police station.

Pickles came running when she opened the door, but he immediately sensed something was wrong and he walked to Marco with his tail between his legs. Marco bent and picked him up as Peyton turned on the lights. Reaching around her, he grabbed Pickles' leash from the peg by the door and snapped it to his collar, then he went back out the door. Peyton watched after him, but she let the two of them disappear around the corner of the house without following.

Tossing her keys and her license on the sofa table, she shrugged out of her leather coat, kicked off her boots, and hung her gun beside the door, then she walked into the kitchen and ordered a pizza from Marco's favorite pizzeria down the street.

Pulling open the lower cabinet, she grabbed the Jack Daniels bottle and two shot glasses, setting them on the counter. If there was ever a time for their ritual, this was it. Many years ago during a particularly difficult case, they'd made it up and they only performed it when the trials of their job began to tell on them.

Picking up Pickles' food bowl, she filled it, then gave him fresh water. She was just pouring the first shot when Marco and Pickles returned. He released Pickles from the leash and hung it by the door. A subdued Pickles padded into the kitchen and began eating.

Peyton finished pouring the shots and pushed a glass over to him as he took a seat on one of the bar stools. Lifting the glass, she said, "The Lord is my Shepherd; I shall not want. He maketh me to lie down in green pastures." She tossed back the shot, closing her eyes and bracing her hand flat on the counter.

"He leadth me beside the still waters. He restoreth my soul." Marco drank his and gave a shudder. "He leadeth me in the paths of righteousness for his name's sake."

Peyton filled their glasses. "Yea, though I walk through the valley of the shadow of death, I will fear no evil, for thou art with me." She brought the glass to her lips again and let it blaze its path down her throat. As she lowered it, the door opened and Jake walked through.

He took in the scene with weary eyes as he tossed his keys on the sofa table and shrugged out of his coat. Peyton and Marco watched him hang the coat next to hers, then he walked over to the counter and climbed on the stool next to Marco.

Peyton reached down and grabbed a shot glass for him, filling it with Jack Daniels and sliding it over to him.

"Where are you?"

"Thy rod."

He thought for a moment, then lifted his glass. "Thy rod and thy staff, they comfort me." Slamming back the shot, he banged his fist on the counter. "Oh, God that burns."

Peyton and Marco shared a smile.

"Thou preparest a table before me in the presence of mine enemies." Marco tossed his back.

Peyton refilled. "Thou annointest my head with oil." She sucked in cold air after the shot, trying to ease the burn.

"My cup runneth over," said Jake. His fingers closed around the shot reflexively as he brought it to his mouth. His lips pulled back tight against his teeth as he swallowed.

"Surely goodness and mercy shall follow me all the days of my life, and I will dwell in the House of the Lord forever." Marco stared at the amber liquid a moment, then he released his held breath. Peyton could see his shoulders relaxing. Lifting the glass, he saluted her, then he downed it and slammed the empty glass on the counter again.

CHAPTER 16

Joshua pushed open the door to the studio and stopped. James, Evan and Ben were gathered around Phil. They hadn't seen the manager in more than a month as he went about promoting his new, younger band.

A flush of anger rose in Joshua's face, but it drained away a moment later. The drugs made everything seem so slow and liquid, he couldn't hold on to an emotion for long. He let the door close behind him and he walked toward his brother.

James threw his arm across Joshua's shoulders pulling him up against him. "Phil has some great news, Joshy."

Joshua met the manager's sheepish look. "I'll bet he does."

"Tell him."

Phil scratched at the back of his neck. Joshua could tell he was feeling uncomfortable. Well, he deserved more than discomfort.

"Yeah, tell me your news, Phil."

"I got *Blazes* a gig in Los Vegas. You'll be playing at one of the smaller casinos, but it's on the strip."

Joshua gave him a grim smile. "And just who are we opening for?"

"Opening for? You're the headliners." He beamed at them and held his hands out as if he wanted applause.

James and the others laughed and high fived each other, but Joshua wasn't fooled. He narrowed his eyes on the manager, but Phil wouldn't completely meet his gaze.

"So you guys gotta clean up that new stuff. It's amazing and they're gonna love it, but you gotta set down those riffs, James. You've got two weeks to get it dialed in, then we fly out of here."

"I'm on it."

"I'll bring the contract by tomorrow."

James released Joshua and hugged Phil. The other band members gathered around, patting him on the back and shaking his hand. Joshua wandered away, taking a seat on the arm of the sofa they used to nap on when they played late into the night. Rubbing his arm, he watched them fawn over Phil as if he'd given them a kidney or something.

With another admonishment to get back to work, Phil extricated himself and headed toward the door, which brought him right by Joshua. James and Evan started talking about the future, while Ben went back to his drums.

"So what happened?" asked Joshua as the manager came alongside him.

Phil gave him that practiced smile. "I don't know what you're talking about."

"Sure you do. Where's your hot, young singer and his high school mates?"

His eyes tracked over Joshua. "He wasn't you."

A laugh rumbled out of Joshua's chest. "He wasn't me?" He leaned forward a bit unsteadily. "How stupid do you think I am?"

"Actually, I was wondering how high you are."

"What do you care? You have your new band."

Phil cast a look over his shoulder, but the others were too absorbed in the news he'd given them. "Why didn't you tell James?"

Joshua's gaze lifted to his brother. He'd wanted to, he'd intended to.

"I know why."

Joshua looked at him again.

"You didn't want me to tell him what an addict you are and you knew I would if you ratted me out."

Joshua gave him a slow, condescending smile. "It doesn't matter now. You're back, playing the hero, rescuing us from obscurity. Just tell me. Humor me. What happened to the other band?"

"Like I told you, the singer wasn't you. He didn't have the voice or the talent or the ability to write his own shit. Even stoned off your ass, you've got it." He reached out and tried to pat Joshua's cheek, but Joshua slapped his hand away. Phil didn't seem to care. "And he sure didn't have your pretty face. So I figured, I could try and make him something he wasn't, or I could come back to you. Here I am." His look grew cunning. "So tell me what you need, sunshine?"

Joshua pushed himself to his feet and bumped Phil with his shoulder as he walked away. "Not a damn thing from you, you backstabbing bastard," he answered.

*   *   *

Peyton took a seat on the coffee table, facing Marco. He was sprawled out on her couch, his hands folded on his belly, his head resting on the arm, sleeping. She'd put a blanket over him when he'd fallen asleep, but Pickles had made a nest in it, curling up on Marco's thighs.

"Hey, sleeping beauty," she called.

He blinked open his eyes, looking around in confusion, then recognition lighted in their blue depths. He rolled his head on the arm and squinted at her.

She held up a cup of coffee.

Scrubbing a hand across his face, he carefully eased out from under Pickles and sat up, reaching for the mug. She held out her other hand and when he extended his palm, she dropped two aspirins in it. He tossed the aspirins back with a sip of coffee.

"You are the best partner a man could want," he said, cupping his hands around the mug.

"I was going to present you with flapjacks, but Defino called."

"And?"

"O'Shannahan came back last night."

He sipped at his coffee.

"She doesn't want me to question him alone."

"Of course not." He looked around. "Just let me splash some water on my face and we'll go. You got any mouthwash?"

She smiled at him. "Go take a shower. We've got time. And there's mouthwash in the medicine cabinet. There's also a new toothbrush in there as well, still in its box. You can have that." When he gave her a frown, she shrugged. "I bought it for Devan."

He planted a kiss on her forehead as he levered himself to his feet, still holding his coffee. "His loss," he said, staring directly in her eyes, then he turned and headed for her room. He passed Jake at the entrance to the hallway and the two men gave a grunt of recognition, then he was gone.

Jake leaned against the arch, looking hung over. He wore a faded pair of sweats and a tank top, his hair disheveled. "Hey."

"Hey yourself," she said. "There's coffee in the kitchen."

He glanced over his shoulder at her closed bedroom door. "I'll get some in a minute. Why are you up so early?"

"O'Shannahan's back. Marco and I are going to question him." She started to rise. "Let me get you a cup of coffee."

"It's okay, Peyton, really. I need to talk to you."

Peyton sat down again. She hated when people said that. It never meant anything good. Maybe he was moving out. For some reason, that thought bothered her. She liked having Jake around. He livened things up, made the house seem less empty.

"I need to walk Pickles, but I won't be long."

He moved around the couch, casting a skeptical look at the dog. "I'll do it later. Pickles seems perfectly content to me."

And he was. He'd rolled over on his back, his paws folded against his chest.

Jake sat down in Marco's spot, directly across from her. "I really need to talk to you."

"Okay." She rubbed her hands on her jeans, wishing the aspirin would hurry up and kick in. "What's up?"

"Yesterday afternoon, I got a call to meet Simons and Cho at a hostel on Isadora Duncan."

Peyton blew out air in relief. He wasn't going to tell her he was moving out, unless he was moving to that particular hostel, but his apartment in the Tenderloin had to be more upscale than that. "Okay?"

"When I got there, I saw a man hanging from a ceiling fan."

"Hanging? As in suicide?"

"That's what I thought at first, but Simons pointed out the guy's hands were tied behind his back with a belt."

"I see."

Jake tented his hands, touching the tips of his fingers together. "Actually, you don't. I have to go back further. Do you remember when you got the call for Terry Ravensong's murder?"

"Yes."

"Well, I went first to a call at a BART station."

"I remember."

"Bum who'd been shot in the back of the head, execution style."

She nodded. "Cho said they didn't have any leads."

"They don't." Jake clasped his hands. "When I processed the scene, I found a card in his back pocket."

"Card?"

"Business card."

"Okay?"

"It said two words on it. Just two words."

"What words, Jake?"

"Clean-up Crew."

"And?"

"Last night, the dead guy had a card in his hands. It said…"

"Clean-up Crew," she added.

Jake nodded. "Peyton, when Abe and I were taking pictures of the bum, we did some research on him. He had a criminal record."

"Right. Cho said he'd served time for child molestation."

"Yeah." Jake pointed his clasped hands at her. "Last night I did some research on our latest guy. He also has a record."

"Let me guess. Child molestation."

Jake gave a short nod.

"You've got a serial killer here."

"That's what Simons said."

"Let them handle it, Jake. They're great cops. They'll get him."

Jake closed his eyes briefly and drew a deep breath. "Here's the thing, Mighty Mouse. Maybe they shouldn't. Maybe they should just let this guy do his thing. These men were child molesters. They deserved what they got and maybe we should let vengeance take its course."

Peyton straightened her back. "That's a dark place to go, Jake, a very dark place."

"How?"

"This guy is a murderer. He's not Batman. And this isn't what we do. We stop the killers, we don't make judgment calls about whether they are justified in what they do or not. Those decisions are for people like Devan to make. Lawyers, judges, juries, not us."

His look was intense. "Are you going to tell me that it hasn't crossed your mind just once that it would be so much easier if you just pulled the trigger, if you just took care of the problem yourself?"

Peyton leaned forward and grasped his forearm. "I'm not gonna lie and tell you the thought hasn't crossed my mind, but it's nothing more than a thought. My daddy used to say a cop didn't have the luxury of playing God. His job was containment and containment only. We stop the chaos, we stop the madness, we don't decide whether it is wrong or right. We have our laws and we must adhere to them, because anything else leads to anarchy."

Jake rubbed his hands across his face. "I know you're right, but it's so hard. How can anyone justify protecting a child molester, giving him due process?"

Peyton smiled sadly and ran her hand up and down his arm to soothe him. "Poor Jake. What did I do to you? I should have just left you in the bank, safe and secure and happy."

He covered her fingers with his own. "Not happy. I was never happy there." He shook his head. "Yeah, it might be hard and I might question it, but I think I'm actually doing something with my life for a change. Something beneficial."

She squeezed his fingers, then looked up as Marco threw open her bedroom door.

"Let's go shake down a preacher man," he said.

* * *

Peyton knocked on O'Shannahan's door for the second time in as many days. Kristin opened it a crack and peeked out. Today she wore a pair of khaki capris and a navy blue polo shirt with flat heeled loafers. Her brown hair was pulled back in a navy headband. She made an aggravated noise when she recognized Peyton.

"Inspector Brooks, my husband is just leaving for a game of golf in Redwood City. He has a long drive and he doesn't have time for this."

"We won't take much time, Mrs. O'Shannahan. We'll even walk him to his car."

"That won't be necessary. He has no information to give you. As I told you before, you have your man, Inspector. Let the dead rest in peace."

Peyton started to answer her, but O'Shannahan's voice came from beyond the door. "Let the inspectors in, Kristin. We have nothing to hide. As it says in Second Corinthians, 'Make room for us in your hearts. We have wronged no one, we have corrupted no one, we have exploited no one.' And we have nothing to fear, but fear itself." He pulled the door open and beamed a smile at them.

"The last part was a nice touch," said Peyton.

"Whatever do you mean, Inspector Brooks?"

"Combining the *Bible* with FDR."

O'Shannahan gave her a confused look.

"Nothing to fear…" She shook her head. "Forget it. Can we have a word with you, Reverend?"

"Certainly." He motioned them into the foyer.

Peyton started over the threshold, then she paused and looked back at Marco. This was his first time in this house since he had a gun pressed against his skull.

He gave her a wry look. "Man up, Brooks," he said, placing a hand in the center of her back and propelling her inside.

For the first time, she looked at O'Shannahan fully. He was dressed in yellow checked golf pants with a yellow polo, and he had leather gloves on his hands. Her eyes zeroed in on his hands immediately.

"I thought Mrs. O'Shannahan said you were playing golf in Redwood City."

"I am. Lovely little course in Woodside."

"That's a bit of a drive, isn't it?"

"Yes, but it's nice to get out of the fog."

Peyton gave him a tight smile. "I'm just wondering why you're wearing your gloves already, Reverend. Isn't that a bit premature?"

Kristin glared at Peyton, but when Peyton looked over at her, she dropped her eyes and stared hard at the toes of her loafers. Her arms were crossed over her stomach as if she were hugging herself.

O'Shannahan laughed and held out his hands. "These are Italian hand-tooled leather gloves, made to my exact measurements and shipped here directly from Italy." He beamed at Marco. "You'll be interested in seeing the workmanship of your people, yes?"

279

Marco scowled. "Why are Americans making gloves in Italy?"

O'Shannahan chuckled. "Anyway, they are so exact that they need more than an hour to warm to your body temperature, but once they do, they mold directly to your skin." He rubbed one against the other. "They're like butter. Exquisite."

Exquisite and convenient, thought Peyton, but she couldn't do anything about it without a warrant.

"How can I help you, Inspectors?"

"We're here about Terry Ravensong's murder."

His face made an alarming shift from genial to tragic, his mouth drawing down into a frown. "Horrible, horrible, that. I heard about it just before I left for Dallas. I was so relieved to know you had the murderer in custody, although I have to say he's a rather unfortunate man with a terribly troubled past. It's a shame someone couldn't have shown him a righteous path sooner."

Peyton felt her face flush with anger. He wasn't really saying anything about Ravensong that she didn't know, but she just didn't like him taking a superior tone. "Here's a funny thing, Reverend. I have a tape of you in Terry Ravensong's building. When I asked your wife about it, she said you were counseling a young man on the same floor, but I found Theresa Ravensong on the list of parishioners on your website. Can you explain that?"

"Of course."

"Go on," said Peyton, holding out a hand.

"Theresa Ravensong was a member of my parish and I wasn't counseling a young man on her floor, I was counseling her."

Peyton and Marco exchanged a look. "So you knew her?"

"I knew her very well. We met on a regular basis for the last six month. I think you'll see there are text messages back and forth between us and I'm on that video feed more than a few times."

"Your wife said…"

"My wife is very busy with her charities and all, and she can't keep focused on who is in the parish. As you probably know, Inspector Brooks, my congregation is quite large, impressively large, in fact."

Peyton wasn't sure what to do with this admission. She reached for her notepad, then thought better of it.

"Now, if you have no further questions, I do need to get on the road."

Desperation rose inside of her. She couldn't believe he'd admitted so much with such a cavalier attitude.

"I have a few questions," said Marco, rescuing her. "But I don't think they're appropriate to ask out here."

"My wife and I have no secrets."

The look Kristin gave him was interesting. Peyton stored it away.

"It's about the nature of your *counseling*. Aren't reverends bound by the same codes as psychologists, meaning you shouldn't reveal things to other people, including your wife?" said Marco.

"I see. Why yes, you are right." He stepped back and motioned into his study. "Won't you come in?" He glanced over his shoulder at his wife. "Kristin, you are dismissed."

Peyton shifted to look at her, but she refused to meet her gaze. Then she turned stiffly and walked to the stairs. Peyton watched after her as she followed Marco into the study. The same two arm chairs were arranged facing the bay windows and O'Shannahan's desk. He grabbed a spare chair and placed it in front of the arm chairs, taking a seat. He fussed with his gloves for a moment as Peyton and Marco sorted out who wanted to sit where.

"What were you counseling Terry Ravensong about?" asked Marco as he sank into the chair.

O'Shannahan crossed one leg over the other and clasped his gloved hands on his knee. "Her bad choice in men and why she felt she deserved abusive relationships. She suffered from terrifically low self-esteem and only felt better about herself when she was having sexual relations with strangers."

So much for discretion.

"Strangers?" asked Peyton.

"Yes, Inspector Brooks. She frequently took strange men to her bed. Very self-destructive behavior. She specifically joined my congregation to break from that lifestyle."

Hm, Peyton had to wonder if she'd succeeded or simply found a new, deadlier lifestyle. "Reverend O'Shannahan, you were admittedly with Terry Ravensong just before she was killed. Isn't that a bit coincidental?"

"Not at all. We were having a counseling session, when she received a text message from her ex-husband. I didn't want to leave, but she told me I had to. She said he had a temper and it would make it worse if another man was there."

Peyton narrowed her eyes. "She told you he had a temper and you left her?"

"A temper is one thing. You can imagine my surprise when I heard he'd killed her. Terrible. Terrible. I'll have to live with that the rest of my life. Ah, but as Romans tells us, 'Therefore, since we have been justified by faith, we have peace with God through our Lord Jesus Christ.' I did my best by that poor soul and I take comfort in that."

"I wonder if she'd feel the same," said Marco. He shifted and gave Peyton a pointed look. She knew what he wanted her to do. It was time to take the figurative gloves off with O'Shannahan.

"Look, Inspectors. I'm very sorry for what happened to that poor girl, but I'm not surprised. You go slumming with a drug addict and bad things are bound to happen to you. I did my best, but there was no saving her. Now if you don't mind, I do have a tee time I need to make." He started to push himself out of his chair.

"Just one more thing, Reverend, if you don't mind."

282

His polished façade cracked a bit, but he visibly smoothed over his features. "Of course."

"A large sum of money was deposited into Terry Ravensong's account about a week before she died. Unfortunately, we can't trace it because it was made through an off-shore account. Do you know anything about this?"

His smile faded. "Why would I know? She was in negotiations with her ex-husband for custody of their daughter. Maybe he paid her off."

"It wasn't him."

"Well, I can't imagine who it was. Now if you don't mind…"

"I'm not done, so why don't you just make a call and reschedule your tee time? You can take your Italian hand-tooled gloves off, while you're at it."

His brows drew down over his eyes and Peyton could see this wasn't a man used to being challenged. "I'm being very accommodating here, Inspector Brooks, but I'm afraid I don't like your tone. I would hate to call the mayor and complain about the treatment I've received from your precinct."

"Once I'm done with my questions, we can call the mayor together, Reverend O'Shannahan."

"What exactly are you insinuating?"

Peyton leaned forward, bracing her arms on her thighs. "I talked with Ravensong's daughter. She remembers an interesting incident, which oddly enough squares with what you were telling us about your counseling sessions with her mother."

He forced a smile, but it was strange and tense. "I have no idea what you're talking about. I've never met the child."

"No, you didn't. Her mother told her to stay in her room. You probably didn't even know she was there."

"The point, Inspector Brooks."

"Sometime in the night, she went out to use the bathroom and she noticed her mother's bedroom door was closed."

He shrugged. "So?"

"She heard a man's voice behind the door. She says he was quoting the *Bible*."

O'Shannahan uncrossed his legs. "Again, the point, Inspector Brooks."

"Well, to a nine year old girl, she might have thought she heard *Bible* quotations, since her mother told her she was going to be studying the *Bible*, but to a grown woman, I have to wonder if the *Bible* verses she heard were a man in the throes of passion."

"The *Bible* can be very inspiring."

"So can sex."

O'Shannahan launched himself to his feet. Marco and Peyton were up instantly. "You have no evidence to prove I was the man in that condo."

"You're right, except when the little girl questioned her mother about who was coming over, her mother told her the preacher man. Seems a bit specific to me."

O'Shannahan's smile was no longer affable, it was predacious, cunning, chilling. He moved beyond them and went to the door, pulling it open. "I want you to leave, both of you. I will be calling the mayor and reporting this abuse the moment you are gone."

Peyton and Marco strode toward him, but they didn't leave. He stood with his back against the door, pointing out into the foyer.

"Leave, Inspector Brooks. I command it."

"You command it? Fine, but know this, we'll be back, O'Shannahan, and when we return, you won't be commanding a damn thing."

"Just what are you saying, Inspector Brooks?" He moved so that he loomed over her.

Peyton refused to give ground. "I'm saying that I think you killed her."

His eyes narrowed and a muscle in his jaw bulged. "Titus 2:2, 'Teach the women to be 'self-controlled and pure, to be busy at home, to be kind, and to be the subject to their husbands, so that no one will malign the word of God.' You have strayed from the path of God, Inspector Brooks, you have ignored the proper place of women in our world."

"Funny how you have that quote memorized perfectly."

"Do not mock me, woman. Go back to your precinct and tell the D.A. to begin prosecution of that drug addict. You have no evidence against me, and you never will, so stop harassing me or I will see that you are stopped."

Peyton squared up to him, toe to toe, staring into his face. "Is that a threat, Reverend O'Shannahan?"

"Threat? Let me just say that I am a man who believes in the Old Testament and the justice it metes out. Do not overstep your place or I promise you, you will be sorry."

Before Peyton could respond, Marco grabbed the reverend and shoved him back against the door, his arm over his throat. "Go ahead. Take a swing at me. Give me a reason to put a bullet in your head!"

O'Shannahan made a gagging sound and grabbed for Marco's arm, trying to dislodge it.

Peyton wedged herself between the reverend and her partner, pushing on Marco's chest. "Let him go."

Marco slammed him back into the wall, then released him.

O'Shannahan made a dramatic coughing sound and rubbed his throat. "That's police brutality."

Peyton turned to face him, keeping a hand in the center of Marco's chest. "I have no idea what you're talking about. Do you have witnesses, Reverend? Do you have any marks?"

He glared at her, but he didn't respond.

"In fact, the way I remember it, you came at me, but trust me, that will be the last time you ever do. And the next time I come for you, it will be to haul your ass to jail."

"The only one going to jail is that heroin junkie, Inspector Brooks. Let's look at this logically. You found him at the crime scene with her blood on his hands. Even he believes he might have done it. And then there's me. What have you got on me? Nothing. Where's the murder weapon, Inspector Brooks? Without it, we both know you have no case. Now get the hell out of my house."

Peyton clenched her jaw, but he was right. Without a murder weapon, there was nothing but circumstantial evidence tying him to Terry Ravensong. She pushed Marco toward the door, backing up herself.

"I'll be back, O'Shannahan."

He gave her a slow, predatory smile. "You can certainly try, Inspector Brooks. You can certainly try."

* * *

They made it out to the Charger. Peyton stood staring at the handle, unable to open the door. Marco halted in crossing around the front of the car and walked back to her, but just as he reached her side, the garage door on O'Shannahan's house rose and a white Corvette convertible sped up the driveway. O'Shannahan sat in the driver's seat and he whipped the little car onto the street, then threw it in gear. As he drove past them, he lifted a hand and waved. He still wore the leather gloves.

Peyton and Marco watched him speed out of sight. Marco placed a hand in the middle of her back to comfort her.

"We'll get him."

"How? He's right. We don't have a murder weapon, we can't trace the money, and our eye witness is nine years old and didn't even see him." She looked up at Marco. "He's going to get away with it and Ravensong's going to prison."

"Peyton?"

She turned and faced Marco. "You know I'm right. He's going to prison and you know what's gonna happen to him. You know what they'll do to a man like Joshua Ravensong and he's not strong enough to take it. He'll commit suicide and there's nothing I can do to stop it."

"Peyton." Marco's voice was sharp. "We will find something. Besides that, all we need is to plant doubt in one juror's mind. One juror, that's all."

"And if we don't. If they convict him, O'Shannahan goes free and Ravensong gets brutalized. I don't think I can stand that, Marco."

Marco exhaled, dropping his hand. "I don't know what to say."

She looked up the street. The sun was breaking through the clouds, but she felt so lost and cold inside. "There's nothing to say. I've got to go see Ravensong. I've got to prepare him for this."

"I'll go with you."

She reached for his hand and squeezed it. "No, you go to the hospital. Tell Vinnie and Billy Miller's father that we got the guy who hit them. They deserve to know. I need to go see Ravensong by myself, anyway. I owe him that."

"Call me when you're done, all right?"

"Yeah. Just drop me at the precinct, so I can get the Corolla."

"Done," he said, squeezing her hand in return. He released her and went around the front of the car.

Peyton turned and looked up at O'Shannahan's house. Kristin was watching them from the upstairs window, but the minute Peyton saw her, she let the curtain close, blocking her from sight.

*   *   *

287

Peyton's favorite receptionist was manning the desk at the psych facility. She smiled brightly as Peyton approached her desk.

"How are you, honey?"

Peyton gave her a tired smile. "I've been better. How's our rock star?"

"He's doing real good. You should have heard him on the piano this morning. Like listening to angels singing."

Peyton swallowed the lump in her throat and nodded. There would be no pianos where Ravensong was going. She signed the book, trying hard not to let despair take her over, but it was hard. She wasn't sure how she was going to look into his dark eyes and tell him there was nothing more she could do to save him.

"Is he in his room now?"

"No, I think he's in the garden. There's a door at the end of the hall that will take you directly to it."

"Thank you."

"Anytime, honey."

Peyton walked down the hall toward Ravensong's room. There was no one else in the hallway today and all of the doors were closed. She found the door labeled *Yard* and pushed it open. She entered a small brick paved patio with potted plants and a few bistro tables and chairs. No one was sitting on the patio, but she could hear voices around the corner of the building. She remembered he had his own private space right outside his room with ferns and redwood trees. He'd told her he liked to sit on a bench beneath the trees during the day.

She hesitated as she neared the end of the building. The receptionist hadn't said anyone was with him, but she could distinctly hear a female voice. Peering around the corner, she could see him sitting on his bench. Elena stood between his legs, her hands resting on his shoulders. Her hair was down, a blanket of brown curls cascading far down her back and as Peyton watched, Joshua reached up and brushed the strands off her shoulder.

"We need you to come home," said Elena. The pleading quality of her voice stopped Peyton from interrupting them.

"I know, but it's not safe, sweetheart."

"How can you say that? You would never hurt anyone."

He placed his hands on her hips. "You don't know that, Elena. You can't be sure. I've tried and tried to remember what happened, but I can't. Would you really risk Tiffany's safety?"

"I love you, I can't stand this anymore." She pressed her forehead to his.

"I know, baby. I'm so sorry. I'm so sorry this happened. This is not what you asked for and I know it."

She curled her hand in his sweatshirt. "I don't care about that. I just want you home."

"I'm sorry. I'm so sorry."

"Stop saying that," she said, then she kissed him.

His fingers tightened on her hips and he angled his head to deepen the kiss, drawing her forward, so that she climbed onto his lap, straddling him. Peyton pulled back and leaned against the building. She felt guilty for spying on them in so intimate a moment.

Closing her eyes, she drew a deep breath. Damn it, she hated this job sometimes. He was completely under her skin and she couldn't stand the thought of what would happen to him if they did convict him of murder. He would be easy prey for the men in prison. And she knew he wouldn't fight back. Elena was right. Peyton was convinced of it. Joshua Ravensong had never hurt anybody in his life, except himself.

CHAPTER 17

Joshua was brought violently awake as the cold water struck him. He sputtered and sat up, rubbing a hand across his face and blinking his eyes. "Why the hell did you do that?"

Terry stood beside the bed, an empty water glass in her hands. "You stopped breathing, dumb ass."

He raked the wet hair away from his forehead, trying to sort his thoughts. Had he really stopped breathing? Lowering his arm, he rubbed the track marks that lined his inner elbow. He couldn't remember how much he'd taken the previous night.

His eyes lighted on her duffle bag, sitting in front of the hotel room door. "What's that?"

She glanced over her shoulder at it. "I'm getting the hell out."

"What?" He pushed back the covers and rose. Looking around, he tried to find his clothes, but he didn't remember where he'd left them.

She walked to the end of the bed and bent over, grabbing something off the floor, then she chucked it at him.

He caught the pants in mid-air, but not before the buckle struck him in the chest. Grimacing, he bent to pull them on. "Why are you leaving?"

She gave him a look that plainly said he was stupid and threw the empty glass on the bed. "Because one of these mornings, I'm gonna wake up next to a corpse." Her eyes lowered to his arm. "The pills were bad, but you're shooting up now."

"The hell I am," he said, pulling the jeans over his hips.

Her brows lifted skeptically. "What the hell are those marks then, dumb ass?"

"Stop calling me that." He clawed his hair back again. "I had some blood tests taken."

"For what?"

290

"To see why I'm so damn tired all the time." He came toward her and put his hands on her hips. "Look, don't leave. I stopped taking the pills weeks ago. You know that."

"You also stopped breathing this morning."

He pulled her against him and bent his head, nuzzling her neck. She had to wrap her arms around him to keep from falling over. "That's why you need to stay."

She pulled his head up and gave him a kiss, a deep, searching kiss, and he knew he had her again, but a moment later she pushed him away. "Listen, baby. You are something, I'll give you that, and if all I wanted was sex, well, we'd be simpatico, but I'm almost twenty-one. I gotta start thinking about the future."

"What the hell does that mean?"

"It means I need something more than a rock star's life. I'm sick of sleazy hotel rooms and jumping from city to city. And I'm sick of wondering what groupie whore you're banging in a dressing room after the show."

He frowned. He hadn't been messing with anyone since she started traveling with the band.

"Look, I need stability and while you've been one fun ride, you are definitely not it."

He sat down on the end of the bed. He couldn't believe she was leaving him. What the hell?

She came forward and kissed him again, forcefully, insatiably. "Take care of yourself, okay? Try not to off yourself when no one's looking." Then she turned away and grabbed her bag, pulling open the door.

A moment later she was gone and she hadn't even once looked back at him.

*   *   *

Jake heard banging in the kitchen and glanced at the clock on his desk. It was going on 6:00PM. He slid his chair back and went to the bed, reaching for Pickles. The little dog was curled in a ball and he yawned as Jake picked him up.

Carrying the dog into the living room, he saw Peyton in the kitchen, searching through the cabinets. An open bottle of beer sat on the counter. She peered over the counter at him and gave him a glare. "Where's the paring knife?" He could hear the edge in her voice.

"Dishwasher."

She turned and threw the dishwasher door open, reaching in for the knife. Turning back to the counter, she grabbed an onion and began chopping it, her movements sharp and jerky. Jake rubbed Pickles' ears as he watched her.

Reaching out with her left hand, she grabbed the beer and swallowed half of what remained in the bottle. "You want one?"

He shook his head. Last night had been enough for him. "You okay?"

"No, I'm not okay."

"All righty."

She finished chopping the onion and reached behind her for a sauce pan that she'd set on the stove. "I'm making chili. You want some?"

He didn't think it would be good to say no. "Sure. You need help?"

"No." She threw the onions into the sauce pan and reached for the beer again, taking another swallow.

He was half afraid to ask his next question, but he wasn't sure if not asking might be worse. "How'd it go with O'Shannahan?"

"How'd it go!"

Asking. *Clearly worse.* He realized he was holding Pickles too tight and he eased his hold. The little dog gave him a lazy blink as if to say, *I could have told you that.*

"How'd it go! It went splendidly. He ordered us from his house and threatened to go Old Testament on me if I pursued him anymore. Then of course, Marco had to assault him."

Jake realized his mouth was hanging open. He cast a pleading look at Pickles, wishing he'd tell him what to say.

"And the worst part is…" She pointed the knife at him. "…he's right. We have nothing. We don't have a motive, we don't have evidence, and we don't have a damn murder weapon. Joshua Ravensong is going to prison and he's going to become everyone's favorite plaything, and there's nothing I can do to stop it!"

Jake closed his mouth and looked down. He didn't know what to tell her. He could appreciate her frustration.

"Just forget it, Jake," she said, shaking her head. "Let me cook and get out my anger, then I'll be all right again."

He nodded. He could handle that. "I'll take Pickles for a walk, okay?"

"Yeah, thanks."

He moved toward the door as fast as he could, reaching for the leash, but just as his fingers closed over it, he heard a crash, followed by the sound of shattering glass.

"Damn it to hell!" she shouted and Jake turned around.

She'd disappeared behind the counter. Jake sidled over, holding Pickles against his chest, and peered down at her. She'd knocked the beer bottle off the edge and it had splintered in to a million pieces, glass going everywhere.

Jake frowned. She'd stopped in mid-motion, reaching for a piece, but instead of picking it up, she just squatted over it, staring at the mess on the floor. "Peyton? You okay? Did you cut yourself?"

Slowly she shook her head, then reached forward and picked up the nearest shard. "I know what he did with the murder weapon."

"What?"

She swiveled and looked up at him. "I know what he did with the murder weapon. How he got rid of it."

Jake's gaze shifted to the shattered bit of glass. "He smashed it."

Peyton pushed herself to her feet and turned toward him, still holding the shard. "And what happens when glass breaks?"

"It becomes a million little pieces."

"And the bastards go everywhere. You never get them all."

Jake's head lifted. "So there has to be some of it left behind."

Peyton touched her finger to her nose. "Exactly."

*　　*　　*

Peyton watched the CSIs comb through Terry Ravensong's apartment. They searched the drains in the bathrooms, they searched the kitchen sink, they vacuumed every carpet and sifted through the vacuum bags, looking for shards of glass. Beyond a few pieces right at the murder site, they found nothing else in the entire apartment.

Jake moved to her side and handed her a piece of paper. "Here's the report on the garbage from the dumpster in the building." He gave her a sympathetic look and she knew she wouldn't like what it said.

Glancing at it, she closed her eyes. "No trace of leaded glass crystal."

"I'm sorry, Mighty Mouse."

She moved toward the big picture window across the room and let the sun spill over her. Russian Hill was elevated enough to get late morning sun and it felt good. She stared out the window, realizing that this was another Saturday that she was working with no break in sight. What the hell sort of life was this? She had no family, she had no boyfriend, and the first man she'd been interested in a long time was facing a murder trial. Oh, and of course, he belonged to someone else. She mustn't forget that, the memory of him and Elena together was still fresh in her mind.

A sense of panic filled her. What was she doing with her life? Maybe her mother was right and this was not the job for her. Even if she met someone, who would put up with these hours, the emotional drain, the danger? Feeling claustrophobic, she reached for the latch on the window and pushed it open. There were no screens to block the air from streaming into the room and she drew a deep breath, letting the ocean breeze calm her. *Breathe in, breathe out,* she told herself, closing her eyes. She really needed to do some yoga or meditation or something. If she didn't find some way besides alcohol to reduce stress, she was going to break or wind up like Frank Smith, waking up some morning with her gun drawn and no memory of what happened.

Opening her eyes, her attention focused on the window. There were no screens. This many floors up and there were no screens, nothing to keep someone from falling out or…or throwing something away. Bracing her hands on the window sill, she looked down. Below her was the ledge to this floor and beyond that the ledges of the other floors all in descending order. Far below was the fabric awning over a back door to the condo complex.

Catching her breath, she squinted into the distance. If you were to haul back your hand, you could aim for the middle of the street, and from eight floors up, whatever you tossed would shatter on impact, the fragments being picked up by the tires of the cars.

But what if you were nervous or your hands were slick with blood and you missed? You might smack the edge of a concrete ledge and the fragments would scatter, some on the ledge and some onto the blue fabric awning.

"Marco?" she shouted.

He came out of the bedroom, gripping the doorjamb with both hands. "Brooks?"

"Marco, come here quick!"

He hurried to her side. She could see everyone else had stopped moving. Pointing out the window, she indicated the ledge about three floors below them. "Look there."

He squinted down, then leaned further out to see better.

"Do you see what I see?"

He brought his head back inside. "If you see glittering bits of concrete, I see what you see."

Peyton smiled, feeling some of the tension slip away. "What's say we get the fire department out here with a cherry picker and explore the ledge just a bit more?"

"I say, which of us is making the call?"

*   *   *

Peyton paced back and forth beside the Charger, glancing up frequently to mark the progress along the ledge and the blue awning. The street had been blocked off, so traffic couldn't get through, and police officers swarmed the area, looking for discarded bits of glass.

Marco leaned against the Charger's door and Jake sat on the hood, his feet dangling over the side. She couldn't stay still like they were. Everything hinged on what they might find on that ledge. Hopefully they'd find a large enough piece that they could get a partial print or something from it.

"Brooks, stop pacing like a wild thing," scolded Marco. "You're making me dizzy."

"I can't help it," she said over her shoulder. "I'm too wound up."

"You need food," remarked Jake. "It's almost 1:00PM and I don't think you've eaten all day."

"I don't need food. I need them to get off that damn ledge." The fire truck had pulled up on the sidewalk, extending the cherry picker, but one of the CSIs had gone up to process whatever they found.

"Do you think pacing's going to make them go faster?"

"If I don't pace, I'll scream."

Marco and Jake exchanged a look.

"This is why men punch things," Jake offered.

She turned and paced back the other way. "If I feel the need, I appreciate you volunteering as a punching bag."

"I didn't..." he started to say, but Marco smacked him in the stomach to get him to shut up.

A car pulled through the barricade and came to a stop in front of the Charger. The door opened and Captain Defino stepped out. Peyton bit her lower lip, certain that Defino was going to scold them.

She surveyed the scene, then walked over to Peyton. "Got a call from the mayor this morning, Brooks."

"I'm sorry, Captain."

Defino shrugged. "I'm beginning to think if I don't hear from him every couple of months that we aren't doing our job." She nodded at the cherry picker. "What's going on here?"

"We may have found the murder weapon."

Defino gave Peyton a surprised look. "Well, let's hope so, 'cause I just got a text that Devan is going before the Grand Jury on Monday."

Peyton couldn't deny she felt betrayed. Her face must have given her away, because Defino clasped her arm in comfort.

"He really had no choice. His boss was pressing for it, especially after he also got a call from the mayor."

Peyton let her breath out, feeling such defeat.

"He was doing me a favor. He didn't have to let me know, but he did."

"I know, Captain." But it didn't make her feel any better about him.

Defino returned to watching the drama play out above them.

Suddenly the CSI climbed down the ladder on the cherry picker. He had a plastic bag in his hands and he passed it to Smith, who was waiting on the ground. Smith looked into the bag, then he turned around, searching the street for Peyton.

Carrying it over to her, he held it behind his back. "What do you want for Christmas, baby girl?"

She clasped her hands together to stop their trembling. "Something heavy and lead and crystal."

He held up the bag and a large piece of crystal winked in the sunlight. "How about with a bloody thumb print on it?"

Peyton felt her eyes fill with tears. She turned to the captain with an expectant look.

"Get that fingerprint processed," said Defino. "Stat." Her eyes tracked back to Peyton. "And while we wait for confirmation, let's get a warrant to search Jedediah O'Shannahan's house."

"On it," said Peyton, reaching for her phone.

*　*　*

Peyton, Defino and Marco sat in the break-room at the table. Peyton's phone lay in the middle of the table between them. They were waiting for a call from Jake. He had taken the shard of glass first to Forensics where they'd lifted the print, then to Abe so he could try to match the blood.

Night had fallen outside the precinct, but no one moved to go home. Defino had ordered in Chinese and the boxes lay discarded on the counter behind them. Marco had boiled a pot of coffee, but Peyton didn't think adding caffeine to her nervousness was a good idea.

When the phone rang, they all jumped. Peyton reached for it, swallowing hard. What if this didn't prove anything or worse yet, what if the fingerprint belonged to Ravensong? She really didn't know how she would react if that proved true. She'd convinced herself he was innocent, but if he was guilty she would be shattered.

Holding it in her hand, she stared at the screen. Jake's number flashed on the display over and over again.

"Oh for the love of God, Brooks, answer it!" hissed Defino.

Peyton thumbed it on and pressed it to her ear. "Jake?"

"Hey, Mighty Mouse."

"Tell her I get to go when she sees the rock star again," came Abe's voice in the background.

"Abe says hi."

"Tell her she owes me some ogling. Is that the word, Jake, ogling?"

Peyton closed her eyes. "Please, Jake. Please. What did you find?"

"Are you sitting down?"

"Jake!"

"Okay. The blood on the shard…"

"Yes?"

"It was mostly Terry Ravensong's."

Peyton felt her shoulders drop. "I see."

"Mostly."

"What does that mean, Jake?" She glanced up to see Marco and Defino eyeing her expectantly.

"The rest of it was not."

"Whose, Jake?" Then her heart began pounding. "Ravensong's?" She knew they drew blood when they drug tested him.

"No, Peyton, not Ravensong's. Someone else."

"Could Abe match it?"

"It's not anyone in the system."

Peyton bit her lower lip, then she drew a deep breath. "Were they able to pull the print in Forensics?"

"Yes."

"And?"

"They got a match through the DMV data base."

Peyton silently began muttering the 23rd Psalm. *The lord is my shepherd, I shall not want.*

"Peyton?" came Jake's voice across the line.

She stopped reciting the psalm. "Yes, Jake?"

"Peyton, it's O'Shannahan."

* * *

"Go home and get some sleep," said Defino, lowering her phone. They were gathered around Maria's desk, while the night pressed in through the precinct windows. "The warrant will be ready tomorrow morning."

Peyton and Marco exchanged a look. "What if he finds out, Captain? Shouldn't we go in tonight?"

"The judge won't grant the warrant until tomorrow. He doesn't want to disturb the neighborhood at this hour."

Peyton gave her a bewildered look. "You're kidding me, right?"

"It's better this way, Brooks."

"How? Someone might leak it to O'Shannahan, then he'll destroy any evidence, skip town, flee the country."

"The judge is aware of that and promised discretion."

"What if the mayor calls him?"

"How would the mayor know what we found?"

"Someone reporting to him. We've had paparazzi swarming this thing since day one."

"Not since Ravensong moved to the psych facility. Besides, Judge Rhinehold is no fan of the mayor, Brooks. Listen, this gives us time to get our ducks in a row. Get some rest. O'Shannahan broadcasts his prayer meeting on Channel 2 at 10:00AM. You'll go into the house while he's at the church."

Peyton nodded.

"I'll be waiting here with Rhinehold on standby. If you find anything, we'll get a warrant for his arrest. If not, Monday morning, we'll present the evidence to Devan and he'll tell us if we have enough. At least it ought to be enough to force O'Shannahan to give us a blood sample."

"What about his wife?"

"She'll probably be at the church with him, right?"

"Right."

"The most important part is getting into the house and searching it. We've either got to link him to the money or find a motive for her death because otherwise, O'Shannahan may just walk."

"We'll find something, Captain. I promise."

"I know. Now go home." She walked toward her office, effectively dismissing them.

Peyton and Marco looked at each other.

"You're not going to sleep, are you?" he said.

"Will you?"

"Like a baby." He slung his arm around her shoulder and walked her to the door of the precinct. "I'm not the one in love with a rock star."

*   *   *

Marco pulled the Charger over to the curb. They were just about a block from O'Shannahan's house. Peyton shifted anxiously in the seat and adjusted her gun in the holster. She wasn't used to wearing it around her waist, but Defino insisted they wear flak jackets. She wasn't sure why. O'Shannahan liked to bash people in the head apparently and that wasn't protected, unless by her hair as Maria would say.

"You're making me crazy, Brooks," snapped Marco.

"I can't stand it. This is the part I hate."

"You hate the dead bodies."

"That and this. Waiting is so hard for me." She reached out and shifted the vent up and down.

Marco stretched all the way over and grabbed her hand, stopping her. He looked up into her eyes. "Stop it."

She bent forward and kissed him on the nose. That earned her a smile and he released her hand, sliding back into his seat. "How'd it go with Billy Miller's family? You never told me."

"They're relieved we caught the guy, but..." He shook his head sadly. "Nothing will ever bring back their son's legs."

"I know. I'm so sorry about that."

Marco shrugged.

"How's Tonio?"

"Still doesn't remember anything and blames himself for them getting into that mess, but I think it helps that he didn't cause the accident. I don't know. He tortures himself trying to remember something that's gone. I can't imagine how frustrating that must be."

Of course, that made her think of Joshua. "When does he get out of the hospital?"

"Another week or so, since he's been in traction. They need to get him up and walking again."

The radio cracked and Marco turned the dial to zero it in. "D'Angelo?" came Smith's voice.

"Here."

"The O'Shannahans just left."

Peyton sucked in her breath and held it.

"On our way," said Marco, starting up the Charger.

He pulled into the driveway. Smith already had a uniform cutting a hole into the frosted glass in the center door panel so they could get in. They were trying to do as little damage as possible. A moment later, the glass was cut, the officer reached in and turned the deadbolt, and they were inside.

"He doesn't have an alarm on the house?" Marco asked Smith.

Smith reached in and flipped a light switch on and off. "We cut the power."

"Nice."

"We try."

They followed Smith into the foyer. Uniforms swarmed the house, searching everywhere, under furniture, in closets. Marco immediately turned right and went into O'Shannahan's study, but Peyton walked down the front hallway to the back rooms. They opened on a great room with a gourmet kitchen and a family room with the largest big screen television she'd ever seen. *All the better to watch himself preach on Sundays,* she thought.

She imagined Kristin O'Shannahan wandering around in the big house and wondered if the woman could be as blind as she appeared. Did she really not know what her husband was doing or did she choose to ignore it so she could have all of this?

Peyton ran her hand across the marble. She had never been moved by luxury or wealth. She liked her little house on 19th and her dog. She wouldn't mind sharing it with a man, but she would never pretend she didn't notice if he was unfaithful…or a murderer.

"Brooks?"

Marco's voice came to her from the front of the house. She walked toward it and then turned toward the study where he and Smith were searching. She paused, lifting her hands to grasp the doorjamb. Marco was bent over in the closet, but he straightened and motioned her to him.

"Take a look at this."

Peyton felt her heart kick against her ribs as she crossed the room and stood beside him. A laptop lay nestled in a black duffle bag shoved deep into the closet. Marco reached in with gloved hands and picked it up, holding it for her and Smith to see.

"You think our reverend is partial to pink?"

Peyton's gaze skimmed over it, then she pointed to a spot on the back cover. "Not unless his real initials are T.A.R."

*   *   *

An hour later, Peyton found herself pacing behind Maria's desk, watching Stan Neumann work on the laptop, trying to find a direct connection between Terry Ravensong and O'Shannahan. They had enough evidence to compel O'Shannahan to give blood and probably enough to free Joshua, but they all wanted a motive, a reason to arrest the bastard right now.

Defino sat in a chair next to Stan; Marco and Smith leaned on the counter; and Jake and Maria sat on a credenza along the wall of Defino's office. Peyton paced. They were running out of time. It was 8:00AM and they had less than two hours before his prayer meeting started. If they were going to get him, it had to be in this window before someone had time to tip him off and he could lawyer up.

"Come on, Stan," Peyton said.

"I'm trying."

Defino gave her a stern look.

Peyton did feel bad. How many times had she called him away from home on the weekend? And he always came, his loyalty to her that strong. He deserved a basket of muffins or something else. Chocolate. She'd like chocolate.

"Hm," said Stan. "She has an encrypted email account."

"And?"

"I just need to trace the root. Give me time."

Time? Peyton ran her hand over her face. They didn't have time. "What's an encrypted email account?"

"An account you don't want anyone to access," offered Jake.

Stan nodded. "It's stupid, really. Anyone with half a brain can hack it."

Maybe, but she hadn't even known there was such a thing. "You can hack it, can't you, Stan? You can hack anything," she purred at him. Perhaps he just needed a little encouragement to get this done.

He stopped working and looked over his shoulder at her. His eyes were huge and round behind his glasses, his lips parted. Peyton hadn't expected that. She glanced up and found everyone frowning at her.

"Stan!" said Marco sternly.

He gave a little start, then went back to work.

Okay, flirting was a bad idea. Marco continued to scowl at her, so she gave him a helpless shrug. She couldn't help it if Stan found her irresistible. Someone had to.

"There you are. I've got you now."

Peyton moved behind Stan's chair. A video sudden burst across the screen of two naked bodies surging together over and over again. "Oh my," breathed Peyton, recognizing Terry Ravensong's long blond hair and the cleft in O'Shannahan's chin. "That's not praying."

Stan quickly covered the screen with his hand, hiding the naked bodies, but the sound of them panting and moaning came through the speakers. He frantically clicked with the mouse, succeeding in closing the window. Then he sank back against the chair as if he'd run a marathon.

No one moved.

Peyton scanned the emails that Stan had brought up and clicked one dated about three days before the deposit went into Terry's account. She scanned it quickly, then looked around Stan at the captain. "She was blackmailing him with that video. She was going to release it the Sunday she died."

Defino's eyes were fixed on the screen. "Go arrest that bastard," she said.

Peyton fought a triumphant smile, then kissed Stan on the cheek. "You are brilliant," she said, whirling away.

Marco and Smith were already in motion behind her.

*   *   *

After Peyton and Marco left the precinct, Jake and the others sat where they were, staring at the computer screen. Slowly Stan lifted a hand and touched his cheek where Peyton had kissed him. Jake swung his legs and lifted his eyes to the clock over the conference room door.

"Uh, Captain."

"Yeah, Jake."

"It's 9:30."

"I know."

"The prayer meeting is televised at 10:00."

"I know."

"It takes about half-an-hour to get there with traffic."

"I know."

"Which means they're gonna get there right in the middle of the sermon."

"I know."

Jake shared a look with Maria, but Defino still seemed intent on the computer screen. Slowly she swiveled in her chair until she was looking at them. "Do we still have that television in the conference room, Maria?"

"Yes."

"Does it work?"

"Last time I checked."

Defino swallowed hard. "We better turn it on."

Stan shifted around as well, then all three of them bolted from their seats and scrambled to be the first into the conference room.

* * *

Peyton stared up at the flashing marquee over the entrance to the massive white building, which was built in the gothic revival style with sharp angles and winged gargoyles on the roof. Narrow multi-storied stained glass windows lined the front of the building, depicting scenes from the *Bible*, most of which Peyton didn't recognize. Probably Old Testament, since O'Shannahan seemed partial to that.

Long stone stairs rose to the entrance, spreading in a semi-circle from the sidewalk to the enormous double doors. The mix of modern with classic, the electronic marquee against the old architecture, was jarring and Peyton couldn't help but focus on the name of his church. *Church of the Blessed.* Just that, the Blessed. It seemed unfinished or profoundly pretentious, either way.

Smith jogged down the stairs to them. "The meeting just started. The pews are filled with people."

Marco's mouth fell open, but Peyton smiled wickedly. "Oh, I'm gonna love this."

Smith chuckled. "I'll bet you are, baby girl. What's the plan?"

306

"Let the uniforms go in first and secure the parishioners, keep them calm. Marco and I will take down O'Shannahan."

"Done."

"Give me a signal when you're in place."

Smith nodded at her and jogged back up the stairs.

"They're filming in there, Brooks," said Marco, his eyes wide.

"Just smile and show them your good side, Marco baby. The camera's gonna love you."

"Which side is my good side?"

Peyton patted his cheek as she moved past him. "All of them," she called over her shoulder.

Smith signaled to her from the door of the church. Two uniforms thrust the massive doors back and officers streamed inside. Peyton and Marco walked up the steps and looked across the vestibule to where the inner doors had been opened. She could see O'Shannahan standing behind his pulpit, a large screen above his head casting his image around the room and through the television airways to thousands of viewers.

He had his hands raised, but as the police swarmed into his service, he lowered them and gripped the pulpit with both hands. Peyton and Marco crossed the vestibule and Peyton removed the warrant from her belt.

"What is the meaning of this, Inspector Brooks?" boomed O'Shannahan through the microphone attached to the lapel on his ornate robes. His hair was perfectly coiffed and rings glistened on his fingers. "You are disrupting a divine meeting of Christian brotherhood."

A murmur rose among the parishioners and they shifted on the pews, but the officers kept them in their seats. Peyton and Marco started walking down the center aisle, headed toward O'Shannahan.

"Why don't you step down and we can talk about this in private, Reverend?" said Peyton, deciding a public arrest might not be good P.R. for the department. It was a circus in here already.

O'Shannahan lifted himself up higher and pointed directly at her. "Woe onto you, sinner. How dare you violate the sanctity of this community, the sanctity of this congregation, when we are in the act of pledging ourselves to God."

Peyton cast a look at the padded pews, the ornate scrollwork on the back of the seats. Video cameras and microphones swung back and forth from the rafters. Even the reverend's pulpit was edged in gold foil.

"That tears it," she murmured to Marco. Lifting the warrant in her hand, she started walking again. "Jedediah O'Shannahan, I have a warrant for your arrest for the…"

"Turn thee away from me, Jezebel, or suffer the wrath of God for your sins." His voice boomed through the speakers above their head.

Peyton stopped walking and looked at Marco. "Jezebel?"

Marco shrugged. "He has a point."

Peyton gave him a snarky smile. "Cute." They moved up the aisle. Kristin O'Shannahan occupied the first seat on the left and her look bordered on panic. Peyton motioned to Smith to get her and he moved in her direction. For a moment, she looked like she might bolt, but he got to her in time and took her arm, helping her to her feet.

"'Put on the whole armor of God, that you may be able to stand against the wiles of the devil'," shouted O'Shannahan.

Peyton and Marco reached the front and angled to the left where stairs led to the pulpit. O'Shannahan turned and pointed at them as they climbed up to him.

"'Blessed is the man that endures temptation; for when he is tried, he shall receive the crown of life, which the Lord has promised to them that love him.'"

Peyton halted in front of him. "Jedediah O'Shannahan, you are under arrest for the murder of Theresa Ravensong."

He continued to point at Peyton, his voice thundering in the now silent church. "'Submit yourselves therefore to God. Resist the devil, and he will flee from you.'"

Marco grabbed his arm and held it out, forcing him to open his palm. Peyton's heart caught. There were no blemishes on his hand. Marco grabbed his other arm and forced him to show both hands. *Nothing on either one of them.*

Peyton whipped around. "Frank?"

He held Kristin by the arm, but he reached for her wrist. She tore out of his grasp, but Frank motioned another uniform over and together they forced her to extend her hands.

A jagged, raised wound ran from her palm outward, held together by surgical tape.

Peyton turned back and stared at O'Shannahan as Smith began reading Kristin her rights.

O'Shannahan gave Peyton a slow grin. "'Be sober. Be vigilant because your adversary the devil, as a roaring lion, walks about, seeking whom he may devour.'"

"Arrest this bastard as an accessory," she told Marco.

Marco twisted his arm behind his back, slamming him into the podium. "You have the right to remain silent." He reached for his handcuffs. "And for the love of God, use it."

O'Shannahan closed his eyes as Marco snapped a cuff on his wrist. "Our father which art in heaven, hallowed be thy name."

"Anything you say can and will be used against you in a court of law," Marco continued.

"Thy kingdom come, thy will be done, on earth as it is in heaven."

"You have the right to speak to an attorney and to have an attorney present during any questioning." Marco began searching under his robes for weapons.

"Give us this day our daily bread and forgive us our debts as we forgive our debtors."

"If you cannot afford a lawyer, one will be provided for you at the government's expense." He yanked him upright and turned him toward the stairs.

"And lead us not into temptation, but deliver us from evil." O'Shannahan opened his eyes and glared at Peyton. "For thine is the kingdom, and the power, and the glory forever. Amen."

"Amen," said Peyton through gritted teeth.

EPILOGUE

Peyton stepped out of the circle surrounding Ravensong and moved back by Marco where he leaned against the front counter of the precinct.

Joshua handed the autograph to Holmes and took the scrap of paper Bartlet held out to him. Smith and Abe were waiting their turn. Maria swiveled back and forth in her chair, smiling at him, and Captain Defino leaned against her office door, watching the exchange.

"I had my first date at an *Avalanche* concert," said Bartlet, shifting nervously as Joshua signed.

Joshua smiled up at him and handed him the paper.

"I lost my virginity to an *Avalanche* song," said Holmes, elbowing Smith in the stomach.

Everyone laughed and Joshua reached for the paper that Smith held. "Make it out to Frank..." He glanced around, then puffed out his chest. "Frankie. My granddaughter."

"Frankie, it is," said Joshua with another smile.

"I came out at a *Blazes* concert," said Abe loudly.

Joshua looked up at him as he held the autograph out to Smith. "Come again."

Peyton and Marco fought a laugh.

"I was in high school and I was dating this girl. I took her to one of your concerts and there you were prancing around the stage in tight pants and belting out a ballad with that sexy voice of yours and my girlfriend said, 'I would so do that man,' and I said, 'So would I, girlfriend.' Then we just looked at each other and we both realized that clearly I was gay."

Joshua glanced over at Peyton, then back at Abe. "Glad...I could...help."

Abe laughed and held out a folded piece of paper. "Can you sign this please? Make it out to Abe. Not Abie." He shot a scathing look at Smith.

Joshua held up the piece of paper. "Is this a bird?"

"No, it's origami."

"Origami?"

"Origami is an ancient Japanese art of paper folding."

Joshua looked confused. "Right, but what is this? Besides origami," he quickly added.

"A bird. A raven to be specific. Get it…raven…Ravensong. I'll have your autograph on an origami raven and it'll say Ravensong."

Joshua hesitated for a moment, then nodded. "Clever."

"Always."

Peyton laughed.

Beside her, Marco made a grunt of discontent.

"What's wrong with you?" she asked, leaning against him.

"I think I'm jealous."

Peyton smiled up at him. "Don't worry, D'Angelo, I still think you're hot…"

"Thanks."

"For an older man."

He gave a sarcastic nod of his head and draped his arm around her shoulders. "Always keeping me humble, eh, Brooks?"

"Always."

Joshua shook hands with each of them, but when he got to Abe, the medical examiner held out his arms. Gamely Joshua let Abe hug him, then he pulled away and walked over to Peyton.

Behind him, Abe held up the autographed raven in one hand and gave her a thumb's up with the other. Peyton nodded at him and he danced a little jig.

Stopping in front of her, Joshua placed his hands in his jeans pockets. "Are you ready, Inspector Brooks?"

"I sure am." She glanced over her shoulder out the precinct door. Paparazzi milled about the parking lot. "But we should go out the back way. Marco can meet us on the street with the Charger."

"Sounds good."

"What is Marco doing?" Marco said at her back.

"Driving us to the hospital to see Antonio."

Marco leaned away from her so he could look her in the face.

"Come on, D'Angelo. We don't have all day."

"All right. I'll meet you out back." He circled around Peyton and headed for the front door.

Joshua wandered over to Captain Defino and held out his hand. She took it with both of hers. "Thank you, Captain, for having faith in your people." He glanced back at Peyton. "Inspector Brooks here saved my life."

Captain Defino gave him one of her rare smiles. "She's a keeper, all right, Mr. Ravensong."

"Joshua, please, ma'am."

"Joshua, then." Reluctantly she released him. "I hope to never see you in my precinct again."

"So do I, ma'am." He leaned over Maria's desk and took her hand, bringing it to his lips. "Thank you as well, especially for the way you treated my Elena."

She gave him a sultry nod, then shot a smug look at Peyton. Peyton let her have her little victory. As they walked to the backdoor, Joshua turned and waved goodbye to everyone.

Peyton shook her head. "Enough already. They're going to faint from all the excitement."

Joshua laughed, a deep, rumbling sound. "At least you're immune."

She looked over at him and caught the simmering look he gave her. She chose not to answer that remark, but oh, was she so not immune.

* * *

The ride to the hospital was quiet after the energy of the precinct. Joshua sat behind Peyton, pensively staring out the car window at the San Francisco fog. Marco was

313

subdued, but then she noticed he usually was whenever they went to see his nephew.

For her part, she was glad the case was over. Once they got Kristin into an interrogation room, she'd confessed to everything. She'd only planned to confront Terry about the affair, but the two of them had gotten into a shouting match. One moment of fury and Terry was dead. Afterward, there was nothing left to do, except call her husband to clean up the mess. Like Antonio's accident, an ill-fated confrontation had ruined three lives. Not that Peyton was sorry to take O'Shannahan down.

Yes, she was glad to put this case behind her, but she couldn't help the ache inside at the thought that soon Joshua Ravensong would only be a memory.

"I love this City," he said in that smoky voice of his.

Peyton looked out at the rising skyscrapers, the people hustling past, a cable car rolling down the hill before them, its iconic red color teasing through the fog. "Yep, I love it too," she said.

Walking through the hospital was a new experience with a famous rock star who had recently been acquitted of a murder charge. People stopped what they were doing. One guy even dropped the bouquet of flowers he was carrying. Joshua picked it up and placed it back in his hands with an understanding smile. In the elevator, people turned and stared at him and once they reached the floor where Antonio was staying, the nurses couldn't stop giggling.

"Do you ever get used to it?" asked Peyton as they headed down the hall toward Antonio's room.

Joshua shook his head grimly. "Never."

Antonio was sitting up in bed when they appeared in the doorway. Rosa sat in a chair next to him, reading aloud from a book, and Vinnie reclined on a couch beneath the widow. He rose to his feet as Joshua entered and the book tumbled from Rosa's hands.

"You must be Antonio," said Joshua, going to the side of the bed and offering his hand.

Antonio's eyes were enormous as he shook it.

Joshua leaned over and offered his hand to Rosa. "Joshua Ravensong."

"Yes you are," said Rosa breathlessly.

Vinnie gave his brother and Peyton a wild eyed stare, motioning toward the rock star with his head.

Marco answered with a short nod.

"I'm Rosa and this is my husband, Vinnie." She reached back and pulled Vinnie to her side.

Joshua shook Vinnie's hand, then turned back to Antonio. "I heard you'd been in an accident."

Antonio nodded. He still didn't seem able to find his voice. Rosa elbowed Vinnie in the stomach and pointed at one of the empty chairs. Vinnie hurried to grab it and set it behind Joshua.

"Please have a seat, Mr. Ravensong."

"Thank you." He sat down and rested his hands on his knees. Peyton noted that the leather armbands were in place hiding his scars. "How's your leg?"

"Better," said Antonio breathlessly. "How are you?"

Joshua gave a laugh. "Better," he answered. "Inspector Brooks told me you have no memory of the accident."

"None. I've tried and tried to remember, but I can't."

"I know. Frustrating, isn't it?"

"You have that too?"

"Unfortunately yes. It's scary, having that gaping hole in your memory."

"Yeah, I keep trying to think of things to make it come back, but there's just nothing there."

Marco put his arm around Peyton's shoulders and pulled her back against him. Bending his head, he kissed her on the temple.

"What's that for?" she said.

"For this. Brilliant idea."

"I know. I'm good like that."

"Yes, you are, Brooks, yes you are."

*   *   *

Jake pulled two beers out of the refrigerator and let the door close. As he straightened, he saw Marco hand Abe a check.

"I don't want this," said Abe.

"Take it. I appreciate what you did, but we're okay now."

Abe folded the check back into Marco's hand. "Then give it to the Miller kid. He'll need it."

Marco hesitated, but he finally gave a nod. "I'll do that."

"Good."

Marco gave him a smile, then walked to the couch and sat down.

Abe smoothed his silk shirt. With his tailored slacks and dance shoes, he looked like he was ready for a night on the town.

Jake frowned. "What are you all decked out for?"

"I'm going out with Peyton."

"I thought you were going to watch the game with us. I ordered a pizza." He carried the beers over to the couch and handed one to Marco.

Marco took it and screwed off the top, then lounged back in the corner of the couch, one foot resting on the coffee table. Pickles lay next to him on his back.

"I can't be swilling beers and burping all the time with you." He cast a sultry look at Marco. "Although I'd do just about anything for you, Angel."

Marco raised his beer and took a sip, then focused his attention on the game.

"Where the hell are you and Peyton going?"

"It's girls' night out," came her voice from the hallway.

Jake turned as she moved into the living room. Her hair was down, curling to the middle of her back in tight spirals; she'd put on make-up and her eyes looked exotic and dark; she even wore a subtle shade of red lipstick and she smelled like jasmine. A little black dress hugged every curve of her petite body and her legs seemed especially long in the ankle strapped black pumps she wore. A silver necklace rested in the low neckline of the dress, showing off a tantalizing hint of cleavage.

Jake stared, his mouth agape.

"Oolala, sexy lady," said Abe, coming forward and taking her hand, forcing her to spin.

She laughed and her hair whipped around her shoulders as she came to a stop.

Jake sat down hard on the couch next to Marco. "Girls' night out? You don't know any girls."

She gave him a saucy look. "Captain Defino and Maria."

"You hate Maria and Captain Defino isn't a girl." He couldn't help but let his eyes trail over her again. "Where are you going?"

"Ravensong's playing a gig at a club in North Beach."

"Wait. Captain Defino's going to a gig?"

"Of course, she loves Ravensong."

"Why's Abe going if it's girls' night out?"

"He loves Ravensong too."

Abe gave a nod, sending the beads in his hair to tinkling, but he gave Marco a wink. "You're still my number one, Angel'D."

Marco lifted the beer in salute. "Awesome."

She shook out the black wrap she carried and swung it around her shoulders. Jake couldn't stop staring at her, even though he knew he should.

Marco kicked him in the leg and he jumped.

"What?"

"Stop it," he hissed.

Peyton caught the exchange and her smile was wicked. She came to the couch and leaned over him to pet

Pickles. Her hair brushed against Jake's chin and he caught his breath, drinking in the floral scent.

"Don't wait up," she said in a sexy voice. Then she walked toward the door beside Abe.

Jake shifted on the couch to watch after her as they walked out, but Marco hit him in the shoulder.

"What?" he said, rubbing it.

"That's my partner you're drooling over."

"Yeah, but did you see her?" He turned back around.

Marco clenched his jaw and briefly closed his eyes. His fingers tightened on the beer bottle. "I saw her and if you keep looking at her like that, I'm gonna have to shoot your ass."

Jake stared at the floor, slowly shaking his head. "But the hair...and the dress...and the legs..."

Marco leaned forward so quickly, he startled both Pickles and Jake. "Shut your mouth, Ryder, or I swear I will shoot you."

"Okay, okay," he said, scrambling off the couch. "Want another beer?"

Marco sank back in his spot, reaching over to pet Pickles. "Bring me two," he growled.

*   *   *

The house lights came up and the applause died away. Peyton sighed and closed her eyes. She could still hear Joshua's voice, see the way his fingers danced over the piano keys.

"He's so very talented," breathed Defino.

"Gifted," said Maria.

"And so damn sexy," said Abe.

They all laughed.

Peyton pushed herself to her feet. "I've gotta go to the lady's room before we go."

They nodded at her and she made her way toward the back of the club. She was glad Abe was driving tonight because she'd had a few too many appletinis. One thing about Captain Defino, she could drink.

She found the bathroom in a narrow, dark hallway and was glad no one else seemed to be around. Once she was finished, she washed her hands in the sink and reached for a towel. Looking up into the mirror, she had to admit it was fun to dress up for a change. She didn't get many opportunities to get out since Devan dumped her. Tossing the towel in the garbage, she pulled open the door and started back toward the clubroom.

"There you are."

She stumbled as she came to a halt and looked over her shoulder. Ravensong reached out and steadied her with a hand on her arm.

"You okay?"

She laughed. "Too many appletinis," she said, glad she wasn't slurring.

He gave her his slow, crooked smile and her eyes were drawn to the beauty mark above his upper lip. "I've been looking for you. I'm glad you came."

His shirt was open at the throat, hanging loose around his hips, and she could see the planes of his chest. Oh, this man was trouble and she was too drunk to think straight.

"You were brilliant tonight."

"I like playing these small clubs. It's a lot more intimate."

Intimate? Interesting word.

"Where's Elena?" *Good, remember Elena.*

"Home with Tiffany. I wanted them both to come, but she thought it was important I get out on my own again, back to performing. Plus it's too late for Tiffany to be out."

Peyton nodded.

He stepped back and gave her a once-over. "If it isn't out of place, you are looking quite amazing tonight, Inspector Brooks."

She felt her cheeks flush with heat. "Do you think…" She caught herself, realizing that the alcohol was making her bold.

"Do I think what?"

Peyton licked her lips and his eyes followed the motion. "Do you think that if you weren't in love with Elena that you and I…"

He moved closer to her and Peyton backed up, bumping into the wall. He braced a hand near her head, trapping her. "That you and I would what?"

She tried to speak, but it was hard with him standing so close to her. She could see flecks of lighter brown in his eyes. "That we would…"

"Have made hot, passionate love to each other."

Peyton swallowed hard. "Yes," she said breathlessly.

He leaned closer, his mouth a breath from hers. "Undoubtedly."

Then he kissed her. Peyton had kissed her fair share of men, but this kiss was dark and sensual, a kiss every woman wants once in her life, especially if it comes from a bad boy, the forbidden fruit. He drew away from her and his eyes searched her face. Peyton realized she couldn't breathe.

"Thank you for saving my life, Inspector Brooks," he said, slowly licking his lower lip, then he was gone.

Peyton closed her eyes and slumped back against the wall.

"What the hell did I just see?" came Abe's voice.

Her eyes flashed open and she straightened, smoothing down her dress. "I have no idea."

"Yes you do. He kissed you."

She made a point out of looking around. "I don't know what you're talking about. We're the only ones back here, Abe."

"Don't play coy with me, missy. You were just kissing Joshua Ravensong. I saw you."

She started walking toward the club. "You must be seeing things. Strange. I didn't think you had that much to drink."

"I know what I saw."

Peyton waved a hand at him and kept going.

"Peyton!" he yelled.

THE END

Now that you've finished, visit **ML Hamilton** at her website: authormlhamilton.com for more information on the Peyton Brooks' mysteries and her other contemporary fiction novel, *Ravensong*.

If you missed the first two novels in the Peyton Brooks' mystery series, *Murder on Potrero Hill* and *Murder in the Tenderloin*, download them now!

Then check out her fantasy series, *The World of Samar*, at worldofsamar.com.

All **ML Hamilton** titles available at Amazon in Kindle and paperback formats.

Made in the USA
Middletown, DE
30 June 2015